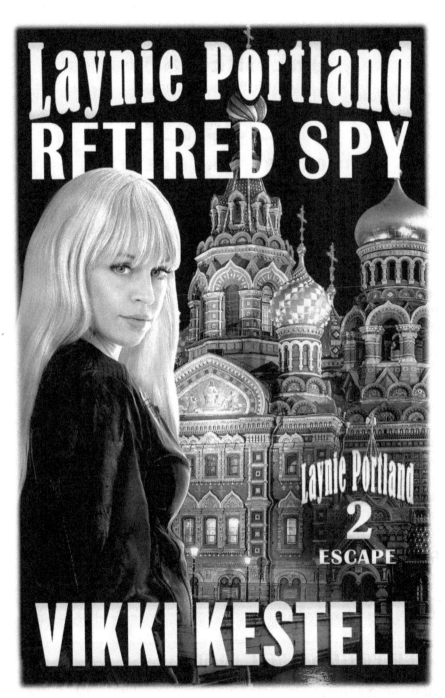

Laynie Portland
RETIRED SPY

Laynie Portland
2
ESCAPE

VIKKI KESTELL

Faith-Filled
Fiction™

www.faith-filledfiction.com | www.vikkikestell.com

LAYNIE PORTLAND, RETIRED SPY

Laynie Portland | Book 2
Vikki Kestell
Also Available in eBook Format

⮡ LP ⮠

BOOKS BY VIKKI KESTELL

LAYNIE PORTLAND

Book 1: *Laynie Portland, Spy Rising—The Prequel*
Book 2: *Laynie Portland, Retired Spy*
Book 3: *Laynie Portland, Renegade Spy*
Book 4: *Laynie Portland, Spy Resurrected*

NANOSTEALTH

Book 1: *Stealthy Steps*
Book 2: *Stealth Power*
Book 3: *Stealth Retribution*
Book 4: *Deep State Stealth*, 2019 Selah Award winner

A PRAIRIE HERITAGE

Book 1: *A Rose Blooms Twice*
Book 2: *Wild Heart on the Prairie*
Book 3: *Joy on This Mountain*
Book 4: *The Captive Within*
Book 5: *Stolen*
Book 6: *Lost Are Found*
Book 7: *All God's Promises*
Book 8: *The Heart of Joy—A Short Story*, eBook only

GIRLS FROM THE MOUNTAIN

Book 1: *Tabitha*
Book 2: *Tory*
Book 3: *Sarah Redeemed*

LAYNIE PORTLAND, RETIRED SPY

Laynie Portland | Book 2
Vikki Kestell

---◦\ **LP** \◦---

"Retirement" means something altogether different to a spy. It means someone in authority over you has decided that "coming in from the cold" is out of the question. *It means you'd better run.*

LAYNIE PORTLAND has masqueraded as Swedish citizen Linnéa Olander for more than two decades, the last seven years as companion to Vassili Aleksandrovich Petroff, senior technology advisor to the Secretary of the Russian Federation's Security Council.

Life as Petroff's mistress is lonely and difficult, even brutal, for Petroff has a pathological need to master what is "his." But the woman Petroff knows as "Linnéa" is not the compliant, deferential woman he believes her to be. She is Laynie Portland—*spy extraordinaire*—and Laynie has stolen a wealth of secrets from Petroff and fed the treasure to her Marstead agency handlers.

As Petroff's abuse intensifies, Laynie fears for her life, and she petitions her agency to pull her out. Instead, her agency declares that she is too well-placed to decommission. Laynie is dismayed to learn that her Marstead chain of command would rather risk her death under Petroff's hand than lose the valuable intel she provides.

Out of options and faced with no viable alternative, *Laynie runs.*

Enraged by her betrayal, Petroff vows to capture and punish her, a certain death sentence. And when Laynie disobeys orders, Marstead issues her a "retirement package"—a short walk off the deck of a ferry into the icy black rollers of the Baltic Sea.

Pursued by Russian assassins and hunted by her own agency, Laynie scrambles, fights, and claws her way toward freedom—although she knows that it is only a matter of time before her pursuers overtake her. Desperate and despairing, Laynie is stunned to sense a higher presence at work, acting on her behalf. Could it be the God in whom her sister, Kari, trusts?

No. Why would he help me, Laynie asks herself, *given the life I have lived?*

ACKNOWLEDGEMENTS

ALL MY THANKS AND APPRECIATION
to my esteemed teammates,
Cheryl Adkins and Greg McCann.
We are a team, and our fellowship is in Christ Jesus for *his* glory,
to which he says and I add "amen."
*"And behold, I am coming quickly, and my reward is with me,
to give to everyone according to his work."*
(Revelation 22:12, NKJV)

VERY SPECIAL THANKS TO
Lora Doncea
for her invaluable contributions to this book.

SCRIPTURE QUOTATIONS

COVER DESIGN

Vikki Kestell

PROLOGUE

STOCKHOLM, SWEDEN, AUGUST 1994

"YOU WANT TO TAKE A LEAVE of absence? What, now? No. *Nej.* Absolutely not."

"I put in for the time weeks ago, sir. I was told my request was approved."

"And I've just withdrawn my approval. You cannot go *anywhere* while our most coveted target—Vassili Aleksandrovich Petroff—is within reach. Petroff is the payoff for your years of work, Linnéa! He's not just a 'big fish,' he's the catch of the century."

He scowled. "We lost our last opportunity to hook him—as I shouldn't have to remind you. I can't allow you to mess it up a second time. You *must* succeed."

Lars Alvarsson studied the woman standing before his desk. She was tall and slim but shapely in all the right places, even for a woman on the far end of her thirties. Milky-soft blue eyes appraised him from beneath a graceful upsweep of dark blonde hair.

Withdrawing the approval for her leave of absence should have shocked and even angered her. Instead, not a flicker of emotion disturbed her serene expression. She projected intelligence. Composure. Confidence.

It was the rare glimpse of vulnerability that set her apart in a room of beautiful women. It was the allure that drew intelligent and powerful men to her. Alvarsson had never been able to decide if the hint of fragility was her natural personality surfacing or if it was yet another facet of her skills— for this woman was, by far, the best actor he'd worked with in his professional capacity.

Dressed in tasteful simplicity, she could have posed for a photo layout captioned, "Today's Consummate Female Swedish Professional." Except that she was not Swedish.

Outside the tight circle of her Marstead super-visors, *no one* knew that she was born an American, recruited straight out of the University of

Washington in her early twenties, transplanted to Sweden, and "attached" to a family that had lived for generations in a village not far from Uppsala.

Her real name was not Linnéa Olander.

It was Helena Grace Portland—Helena, pronounced heh-*LAY*-nuh—although she had always insisted that she be called "Laynie."

Laynie Portland.

THE WOMAN LIFTED HER chin and met Alvarsson's gaze. "I would not ask, but it is important. A family matter, sir."

My only sister is getting married in two weeks. I need to be with her on her wedding day.

She had kept her boss and his superiors ignorant of her sister's existence. Alvarsson knew of Laynie's adoptive parents in Seattle. He knew that her only brother and his wife had died in a car crash eight months ago, orphaning their two little ones. And, as far as he knew or cared, the children's maternal grandparents had assumed guardianship of the children.

He did not know about Kari, or that the children, Shannon and Robbie, were with her now.

Kari, my sister. You searched for me. You hunted high and low, and you found me—after a lifetime apart!

Laynie had taken pains to ensure that her watchful, jealous employers did not know about her sister.

Kari was safer that way.

The scowl Alvarsson turned on her was as unsympathetic as it was unyielding. "You don't have a family, Linnéa, remember? With the exception of a single, covert holiday in the US once a year, you gave them up. That was the deal, and it hasn't changed."

"Sir—"

"*No*. Regardless of how careful we are, returning you to the States hazards blowing your cover and exposing the company. And the risks don't even compare to the expense. To transition you from Stockholm to the US in your previous identity requires the allocation and coordination of many resources, and each operation sets Marstead back something in the realm of a hundred thousand dollars."

Marstead International. A respected and flourishing enterprise with a global reach but, unknown to a large slice of its employees, also a well-developed front for a joint American-NATO intelligence agency. Marstead's largest European office was located in Stockholm, Sweden—even though Sweden was *not* a member of NATO, that nation preferring a neutral position in the world's conflicts. On Marstead's part, basing many of its operations out of Stockholm had been intentional, a means of functioning in plain sight and close proximity to the Soviet Union—now the Russian Federation.

Alvarsson stabbed the desk with his finger. "We permitted you to take emergency leave to attend your brother's funeral back in January. That was your vacation for the year. You aren't owed more leave at this time—we're still paying the price of your last one! During that unscheduled, three-week absence, Petroff's ardor cooled, and we lost our window of opportunity to intercept the Russians' new laser schematics."

"I am aware, sir." *As if I weren't conscious of the setback. It has taken six months of tedious, cautious maneuvering to reignite Petroff's interest.*

Alvarsson raised one eyebrow. "Are you, Linnéa? Do you grasp the long-term implications? If you do, if you care so much about those people in the States you call 'family'—and if you are concerned at all for your own skin—then you know exactly *why* we cannot have you jaunting off to the States at this crucial juncture."

Alvarsson steepled his hands in a judicious manner. "Hear me on this, Olander. Our sources tell us that your Russian 'friend' already has his people doing a deep dive into your background. At this very moment his people are scouring your family tree, your education, your work history, *your travel records*. We cannot risk sending you to the States now."

He added, almost as an afterthought, "You don't become the exclusive plaything of a formidable, highly placed Russian politician without coming under great scrutiny first."

Exclusive plaything.

Inwardly, Linnéa flinched, but she never flicked an eye or moved a muscle. She understood her role. It was the daily bread of her job—guiding the selected "man of the hour" through the phases of infatuation, romance, affection, love, and trust. Followed by betrayal.

Linnéa had accrued her sordid skills through the company's rigorous tradecraft training program. She had learned well, and she was good, *very* good, at her job. Moreover, she had convinced herself long ago that excelling at this work was her only goal.

She must *always* succeed.

My life may have no value, but the information I gather does.

WHEN THE SOVIET UNION dissolved in 1991, the Cold War had come to an end. In the Russian political and economic upheaval that followed, the city of St. Petersburg—Russia's gateway to the Baltic Sea—became a thriving hub of Russian scientific discovery and technological innovation. St. Petersburg was rich in culture, and it was burgeoning with opportunity.

St. Petersburg was Linnéa's hunting ground.

Marstead operated a branch office in St. Petersburg, and Linnéa traveled from Stockholm to St. Petersburg each month, ostensibly to work her Russian Marstead accounts. In reality, she spent her evenings trolling the nightclubs and hot spots where bored, overworked scientists, engineers, and inventors came to refresh themselves.

She was cautious, and she chose her marks herself—that is, until Petroff arrived. Vassili Aleksandrovich Petroff, brilliant scientist, wealthy Russian powerbroker and politician, lived in Moscow and normally worked there. He breathed the rarified air of the Russian Federation's Security Council on a daily basis, serving as Secretary Rushailo's personal technology advisor.

With Petroff's appearance, Marstead's interests shifted. Petroff was a man whose access to state secrets could satisfy Marstead's intelligence needs for years. He possessed every quality Marstead desired, rolled into a single mark, but in Moscow he had been beyond Marstead's reach. Then, just over a year ago, Petroff's official duties had changed, requiring his occasional *ad hoc* presence in St. Petersburg, opening the door for Linnéa.

According to Marstead's intelligence sources, Petroff was seeking a suitable long-term companion—a woman of the world. His equal, intellectually and socially. A suitable trophy to flaunt before his friends, but also a beauty who would be suited to Petroff's public life.

Approaching his mid-forties, he was tall and lean and still owned a full head of sandy-colored hair. From a distance he projected a mild, naturally curious, perhaps bookish countenance, particularly when he swept aside the front locks of his hair with unconscious indifference.

Linnéa's superiors had pulled her off her other assignments and ordered her to focus her attentions on Petroff. Under Marstead's orders, Linnéa studied Petroff. She "learned" the man so as to win her way into a long-term relationship with him. If Linnéa conducted herself well, if she ingratiated herself into the Russian's life, Petroff was to be her next—and possibly her last—mark.

So, for the past year, Linnéa had refrained from seducing new targets, and Marstead had scheduled Linnéa's visits to St. Petersburg and her sorties into the city's club life to correspond with the dates of Petroff's visits. With careful deliberation, Linnéa had edged her way nearer to Petroff's orbit.

But then her brother had died, and she had returned to the US for his funeral. She had been playing catch-up ever since her return to work.

She'd had brief encounters with him in the months that followed, moments that amounted to little more than cordial familiarity. But—finally—on her last trip to St. Petersburg, she'd arranged herself so that Petroff "stumbled" upon her, and they had spent several uninterrupted hours talking over drinks in a quiet side room of a luxury club. She had kept her part of the conversation witty and cerebral, making him laugh and relax.

She'd spoken openly of her position with Marstead and had expounded with expertise and insight on the current technology market.

Petroff was a man who sought to own the best of everything. Thus, Linnéa had demonstrated that she was far more than arm candy or an inconsequential one-night stand. She'd left Petroff that evening with the impression that Linnéa Olander could be a complement to both his brains and his *savoir-faire*. A beautiful, accomplished, and independent woman. A rare commodity. *A match.*

Linnéa had declined his invitation that evening to a nightcap in his hotel room. She would string him along until they were further acquainted. It was essential that she prove worthy of his enduring attentions.

She believed she had, after that encounter, left him wanting more.

Nevertheless, as Alvarsson intimated, it was important to fully prepare herself for what could lie ahead, because the risk of entering into a long-term relationship with him had more than one dangerous facet.

First, the man was fascinating. Brilliant. Not to be underestimated. *Ever.* In his younger years, Petroff's unsuspecting adversaries had ascribed a boyish naiveté to him. Many had found that assumption to be a costly—even deadly—mistake. Up close, his seemingly gentle, probing brown eyes had revealed a shrewd and calculating mind.

Second, Petroff was possessive. Nothing he considered "his" was permitted outside his watchful control. If Linnéa succeeded in attaching herself to Petroff, the relationship would likely become restrictive. Even oppressive.

Third, Linnéa worried that her meticulous backstory might not stand up under *this* man's scrutiny, because Petroff was more than political. He was a former agent of the now-defunct KGB—and once KGB, *always* KGB. Sure, the KGB had been replaced by the FSK, the Federal Counterintelligence Service, but Linnéa had heard whispers that the FSK itself might soon be going through yet another makeover and name change under the Russian Federation's President, Boris Yeltsin. Regardless of its name, the FSK had inherited many of its players from the ranks of the former KGB.

Dangerous.

Petroff has remained friends with his former KGB comrades, those who still have authority and influence. They provide him the means to sniff out and dissect my background, perhaps uncover my former life.

My family.

She shuddered to consider what Petroff might do to her parents or her sister's family should he come to trust Linnéa and discover that his trust had been betrayed.

When it came to her family, Linnéa was grateful for her agency's stringent security constraints. Marstead strictly controlled Linnéa's cover.

Nothing—not love, not family, not choice—was allowed to compromise her Swedish identity.

The final danger Petroff presented confused and unsettled Laynie. She found that Petroff appealed to her in a way that was . . . *troubling*. Petroff moved her. His nearness spoke to her in strange ways. And his boyish good looks and energy never ceased to raise her heart rate.

Why? Why this man? Why does he draw me? Attract me? Why do I feel such untapped emotion when I'm with him?

As jaded as her heart had grown through her various love affairs, it was a new and disturbing experience for Laynie to find herself pulled toward a mark. She might be tempted to give more than her body to this dangerous man—even after she had heard the tales circulating about him.

PETROFF WAS A KNOWN connoisseur of fine things—he employed the best tailors, drove the best cars, drank the finest wines and vodka, ate the choicest foods—and only sparingly, for he scorned overindulgence. He was also a lover of art, music, architecture, and . . . dogs. His favored breed was the Chornyi Terrier, known in the west as the Black Russian Terrier.

The breed was developed in the Soviet Union during the late 1940s and the early 1950s for use as military dogs. The breed's pedigree included lines from the Giant Schnauzer, Airedale Terrier, Rottweiler, and other guard and working dogs. In show, the *Chornyi* closely resembled the Giant Schnauzer. In conduct, the breed was protective and fearless, often thought by its owners—to their amazement—to be more intelligent than *they* were.

And as Petroff made the rounds of the St. Petersburg clubs, a disturbing story circulated with him, a tale of Petroff's favorite *Chornyi*, Alina, a female dog he had hand-raised from a pup. Petroff doted on her. Alina traveled everywhere with Petroff, slept in his room at night, and served as a further layer of personal protection after his bodyguards.

According to the rumors swirling in Petroff's wake, on a certain trip, unexpected celebratory fireworks had so disturbed Alina that she had become terrified and had run off, ignoring Petroff's repeated commands to come to him. When Petroff's people located the dog two days later and brought her back, Petroff had pulled his sidearm and shot the dog in the head.

He had said to his people, so the anecdote went, "I will not tolerate the disobedience of something I own. There can be no forgiveness for disloyalty."

It was also rumored that Petroff treated his women with similar possessiveness. As long as a woman held his attention, he kept a jealous leash on her—although most endured only a night or, if particularly engaging, a week or a month. When he was finished with a woman, when he no longer found her of interest, he cast her aside.

When he was finished with a woman, when he no longer found her of interest, he cast her aside.

But there were also stories of Petroff's longer-term women, of which only two were known. One, it was said, displeased Petroff's sense of ownership. He had beaten her senseless. The other, a Lebanese beauty, turned out not to be Lebanese, but Israeli. The loathsome spy of a hated nation.

The Israeli woman traveled with Petroff when he left to visit Islamabad on state business.

When he returned to Moscow, she did not.

Linnéa shuddered a second time. *I am to be the bait on the end of this hook. I must be careful, so much more careful than I have ever needed to be.*

Still, the thought of being with Petroff aroused feelings in her, feelings that surprised and concerned her. *Why am I like this?* she asked herself. *Why am I so cold and unfeeling toward a decent man but drawn to someone who might snap my neck on a whim?*

A familiar voice in her head sneered, *Because you don't deserve a "good" man, Laynie.*

"MISS OLANDER! Are you listening?"

"Of course, sir."

Considering the subject closed, Alvarsson focused on his calendar. Today's date nudged them closer to the end of August, and the northern hemisphere was still in the grip of summer. "If you play your cards right, Linnéa, Petroff will have you installed in his Moscow apartment by Christmas."

He fixed her with another glare. "This assignment is too important to jeopardize for any reason. It is *your job*, this once-in-a-lifetime opportunity, to convince Petroff that *you* are the woman he's been looking for—not for another tryst or fling, but for a long-term relationship."

Linnéa inclined her head. "Of course, sir. Petroff wants someone with whom he can share his life, a companion who is his intellectual equal and who shares his passion for technology. A woman who can be an asset to him in his social circle. An acquisition he can flaunt—not merely an escort or a temporary lover.

"To that end, I must cultivate the cerebral and companionship aspects of our relationship. I will, initially, resist intimate overtures. I mustn't yield to him too quickly. The 'courtship' and pursuit must prove my worth to him."

Linnéa said nothing further as the tenderly nurtured prospect of seeing her sister again died. Alvarsson was right. She had a job to do, a crucial role to play. Nothing took precedence over the job. Everything gave way to it. The job was all that mattered.

The job was espionage.

Linnéa was a spy, and her *modus operandi* was seduction.

Her work was "appropriating" emerging technology and other classified information from America's strongest rival.

And this very week, after painstaking months of careful moves, her relationship with Petroff had taken a desired turn. He had sent Linnéa a short letter—an invitation—via her Stockholm office.

Others read Linnéa's mail before she did, another aspect of Marstead's supervision of Linnéa's cover. They would read and approve her reply, too, before it was sent.

"How do you propose to respond to Petroff's invitation?" Alvarsson asked. He held the single sheet between two fingers, rereading it.

Linnéa had scanned it once and memorized it.

My dear Miss Olander,

I find myself thinking on our last conversation in St. Petersburg, and I would enjoy the opportunity to continue it. The seaside in late summer holds many pleasures, and I have time to indulge in a holiday. I own a modest dacha on the shore of the Caspian, and my yacht is moored nearby. The sea is open to us for adventure, be it swimming, snorkeling, fishing, or bathing in the sun.

If you were able to arrange your busy schedule so as to spend a week with me, I would send my private jet to fly you from Stockholm to Grozny on August 26. I would personally meet you in Grozny and escort you to my dacha.

Miss Olander, if you accept my invitation, I promise to pamper you during the day, while we explore the delights of evening together. Whatever you wish will be my command. Exquisite food. Fine wines. Music. Dancing— and, perhaps, more. I hope to receive your reply soon.

With great admiration,
Vassili Aleksandrovich

The letter's tone was confident—as though, by simply crooking his finger, she would do his bidding. He had also signed the correspondence with his first and patronymic names, a familiarity. But the coveted invitation, arriving so close to Kari's wedding in early September, couldn't have come at a worse time.

"Miss Olander." Alvarsson was staring at her.

"Yes, sir?"

"How do you propose to respond to Petroff's invitation? August 26 is next Friday."

Linnéa cleared her throat. "I will accept his invitation with an apologetic limitation. I will only be able to stay the weekend—three nights. Work obligations require that I return to Stockholm Monday morning, August 29."

Alvarsson nodded his approval. "A good strategy. Two days and three nights. Time enough to deepen the acquaintance but stave off sleeping with him. A taste of your companionship to leave him wanting more."

"Yes."

"Write your response to him, then go shopping. You'll need a new wardrobe."

"Yes, sir."

Linnéa returned to her own office, lecturing her heart for feeling sorry for itself. *I dread giving Kari the bad news—even though I did warn her that my life was not my own.*

Well, she hadn't planned to become a spy.

Who does that? she reflected. *Who says, "When I grow up, I want to infiltrate our enemy's homeland, trade my body and soul for secrets, and abandon hope for marriage, family, or future—all for love of country"?*

Yet it seemed to Linnéa that, from her earliest years, she had been destined for this duplicitous, dangerous, and emotionally barren existence . . .

LAYNIE AND HER BROTHER grew up in Seattle, the adopted children of Gene and Polly Portland, a mixed-race couple in an era where racial intermarriage was frowned upon. After years of a childless marriage and being refused adoption because Gene was "white" and Polly was "black," the couple had tried private—and expensive—avenues.

Laynie was age three and her brother less than a year old when they came to Gene and Polly. The couple had been overjoyed. They wanted nothing more than to lavish their love upon Laynie and her brother. Sadly, the transition had been neither peaceful nor easy. Some unfathomable horror haunted their little daughter. Laynie had wept and wailed for hours upon end and refused to be comforted.

Eventually, she had calmed, and their family thrived—but Laynie never could shake the grief and longing for what she had lost. Fragile, wraithlike threads of memory were all she had, but she clung to them. And so, a ritual developed between Laynie and her new mother, a ritual that mystified Polly but, in some way, mollified her precious child.

"Well, you wouldn't stop crying, baby girl," Mama would whisper. *"Our poor Little Duck! So confused and distressed. What a fuss you made! I held you and rocked you ever' night till you wore yourself out. You cried ever' night for weeks, you did. You cried until your voice was gone and you could only croak. Daddy said you quacked like a little baby duck, and that seemed to tickle you. You liked it when he called you Little Duck."*

"But what about our names, Mama? Our real names?"

Laynie always asked about the names, because the tale her mother told her was what made Laynie feel closest to her old memories—closest to the longing she felt, to what she had lost but could not remember.

"You always in such a hurry at this part, baby girl! Well, a'course the agency would not give us your names, your birth names, since ever'thing 'bout the 'doption was sealed. They told us you were both so young that we should give you the names we chose, so we named your brother 'Stephen' after Daddy's grandfather."

Laynie would always argue at this point of the story. *"But that was wrong."*

"So you told us! 'No. He's Sammie,' you claimed. We called him Stephen and his 'doption papers read Stephen Theodor Portland, but you refused to call him anything but Sammie."

"That's right. Now me," Laynie would continue.

"Yes, you, Little Duck," Mama would laugh. *"We tried to name you Grace after my mother and, my word! How you pitched a fit. 'I Laynie!' you screamed again and again. 'Laynie! I Laynie! Laynie, Laynie, Laynie!'"*

My real name, Linnéa thought. *Not Linnéa. Not Helena.*

The next part of the story was where Laynie's memories sharpened and where her sense of loss was the greatest.

"What else did I say?"

Polly would dither, but she knew that Laynie would insist.

"Well, honey, you talked about Care. You would stomp your little foot and shout, 'Care say I Laynie! Care say I am! I not stupid Grace! I Laynie!'" Polly would sigh and add, *"You sure were a handful, honey, let me tell you."*

Laynie's mama liked to move past that part of the story in a hurry, but Laynie wouldn't let her. That one word, *Care*, invoked such deep anguish in her that she would weep and sob.

Care. Something about "Care" sparked a voice Laynie clung to, a voice that, to Laynie, meant everything . . . and yet nothing. A voice screaming, *"No! You can't take them away! You can't take them!"*

Laynie would cry as though her heart would break, and Laynie's mama would pull her onto her lap and rock her, knowing she could not heal a wound that Laynie herself could not identify, let alone articulate.

Polly could only rock and love on Laynie until the storm subsided.

"Well, we named you Helena Grace, after Papa's grandmother. Yes, Hel-LAY-na, close enough to Laynie that it didn't send you into a tizzy," Polly would conclude.

"But you called me Laynie anyway."

"Yes, sugar. We called you Laynie anyway. We still do," Polly would agree, agonizing over the shapeless, faceless pain from which her daughter suffered.

Afterward, Laynie would go in search of Sammie. When she found him, she would tug his roly-poly toddler's body into her lap or, as he got older, close to her side, and tell him a story.

Polly would watch from around the doorway as Laynie, sometime during the story, would pat Sammie's hand and murmur, "You are Sammie. I am Laynie. *Care said so.*"

Despite Gene and Polly's love and nurture, Laynie never did escape the sense of loss. Perhaps that was why, as she grew older, her inability to make sense of those feelings settled within her as two words infused with profound negative impact, labels that shaped her young, tender identity.

Failure. Worthless.

Long before Laynie could articulate such loaded statements, an emotional certainty had taken root in her heart. *My life has no value. No purpose.*

This inner conviction, without a doubt, was why she had given herself to Marstead.

THE FOLLOWING MORNING, Linnéa rode a city bus into the heart of Stockholm to shop for clothes. Her selections needed to impress Petroff. He was wealthy and she—in possession of a Marstead-backed credit card—was to spare no expense on her wardrobe. Many a woman would have salivated at the task, but Linnéa chafed under it and hurried to finish.

She knew which shops were exclusive enough to meet Petroff's exacting standards and which pricy brand-name clothing fit her with little or no alteration. She tried on and selected two expensive suits for travel to and from Grozny, then two bathing suits and matching cover-ups, two shorts-and-halter-top combos, and two glitzy pairs of sandals—a set for each day on Petroff's yacht—and three gowns with accessories for the evenings she'd be there. She added a filmy shawl to cover her bare shoulders should the evening prove chilly.

Hours later, leaving behind a wake of generous tips and large smiles, Linnéa was armed with the tools for her weekend with Petroff. She arranged for the shops to deliver the bags and boxes to her apartment's doorman, Gustav, and turned her attention to the question that concerned her more. *How do I tell Kari I cannot come to her wedding?*

Linnéa joined other shoppers outside as they perused window displays and chatted with friends. She moved down the cobblestone walkway at a leisurely pace while she chewed on her problem.

The date of Kari's wedding was two weeks out.

The maid of honor canceling at the last minute? No matter how I tell her, she is going to be hurt.

A simple phone call would be quickest, but Kari was perceptive and would ask questions Linnéa could not answer. Besides, calling was . . . problematic.

Marstead monitored her phones—the landline and clunky cellular phone in her apartment and a desk phone in her Stockholm office. Furthermore, Marstead tracked unusual movements or activities on her part. A long-distance call from a pay phone required a credit card. Marstead would flag those charges in a heartbeat.

Then there was Petroff. According to Alvarsson, Petroff's people were investigating her, looking at her life and background.

They could be watching me this very moment.

Linnéa's training had taught her to check for a "tail" wherever she was, but Petroff's people would be seasoned, perhaps too professional for her to spot. She slowed and stared into a window display, using its reflection to scan the street behind her, her thoughts and her stomach a synchronous churn.

Now that she had engaged Petroff's attention, the stakes were mounting higher. So was the danger level. Linnéa cared little for her own safety, but if Petroff were to uncover her family ties? He would have leverage over her. Terrifying leverage.

Linnéa shook off the fear that juddered down her spine and thundered at the door of her heart. *Stop that,* she told herself. *Keep your head in the game.* She flexed and rotated her tight shoulders and returned to the problem confronting her. She had to tell her sister that she could not attend her wedding, and the means by which she told Kari had to be both unremarkable and untraceable. Linnéa was determined that Marstead remain ignorant of Kari's existence. Neither could she allow Petroff to sniff out Kari or her family.

I suppose it must be a letter. A letter in place of myself.

A letter might take the entire two weeks to arrive, but it was, she acknowledged, the most secure means of communicating with Kari. Initially, Linnéa had told Kari they could correspond through a Marstead "cutout" address. This was how Marstead had allowed Linnéa to correspond with her brother, how she kept in contact with her parents. They wrote to a *Posten* box Marstead rented and managed. Marstead passed letters in both directions, but they also read all correspondence from Linnéa's parents and the letters she wrote in return. And they occasionally edited her letters.

I'm weary of Marstead's constant probing, of their tentacles delving into every corner of my life. I want to keep Kari to myself. Besides . . . we are both safer if I do.

Safer, Linnéa believed, because Kari had money and, as the owner of her own company, had a significant public persona while, in contrast, Marstead had scrubbed Laynie from the public record. An innocent connection made between Kari Michaels Thoresen and one Helena Portland might focus attention on Laynie—whose near-total nonexistence was a suspicious flag in itself.

That was why, during her return trip to Stockholm after her brother's funeral, Linnéa had changed her mind . . . had concocted a better arrangement. In Linnéa's apartment, under the cushions of her sofa, and built into the recesses of the sofa framework, was a safe.

Within the safe, Linnéa kept the bulky Marstead-issued cellular telephone she used to call her parents on special occasions. It was the only phone she was allowed to use for family calls—and only infrequently. On the cellular phone Linnéa could become Laynie again, even if only for a few minutes.

But Linnéa kept other items in the safe, namely cash and false identities.

The cash she had squirreled away, bit by bit, from her earnings. The IDs had been more difficult to obtain. Her coworker and friend Christor Vinck, Marstead's Director of Information Technology, had provided her with the name of a man who specialized in counterfeit papers. Linnéa had sought him out at night, circumventing Marstead's watch over her, and had paid for the identities out of her precious cash reserves.

The truth was, after more than a decade in clandestine services, she was tiring. She saw a day out there, on the horizon, a day when she could no longer pretend to be Linnéa Olander.

I want to go home. I want to live the remainder of my life as Laynie—but not just yet.

She had a goal. Hook Petroff, milk him, and *turn him.* Using the classic technique of threatening to expose to the Russian secret police the number of secrets he had "allowed" Linnéa to steal, she would blackmail and turn him into a full-fledged Marstead double agent.

When I am finished with Petroff, I will leave this life, she promised herself. *A year, perhaps two, but no longer than that.*

Consequently, in order to keep Kari's existence a secret when she returned to Stockholm following her brother and sister-in-law's funerals, Linnéa used one of her precious false identities, that of one Judith Johansson, to rent a Stockholm *Posten* box, paying cash for it every six months. She then wrote a short note to Kari, enclosing the box number, but leaving the return address blank. In her note, Linnéa cautioned Kari on future correspondence, directing her to address her envelopes to Judith Johansson, to leave off the return address, and to be discreet with identifying details she shared in her letters.

Kari, empathetic to her sister's concerns, wrote every other week and filled the letters with news of their niece and nephew, Shannon and Robbie, and of Gene and Polly, referencing them by initial rather than name, providing Linnéa with brief insights into her parents' well-being, particularly Polly's health and the progress of her MS.

But no matter what Kari wrote about, she always ended her letters in a prayer—a prayer that, although not always worded the same, ran along a universal theme.

Remember that I pray for you daily, my sister. I ask him—our great and awesome God, who answered my prayer to bring our lives together after years of being lost to each other—I ask him, the God of all Grace, to uphold you by his Holy Spirit. He is able to comfort, encourage, and help those who call upon the name of Jesus, the Lord and Savior of the world. For with God all things are possible.

The first time Linnéa read such a benediction, she had blinked and felt something tug at her heart—until she hit the phrase, "uphold you by his Holy Spirit."

Holy? What would a holy God want with her?

I am soiled beyond redemption. Worthless. I have no value . . . except as a thief and a whore for my government.

Linnéa responded to Kari's letters once a month with unrevealing lines that contained no personal details, only brief comments on the news Kari's most recent letters carried. Kari was getting the short end of the stick, but at least they were staying in contact, using a method that would keep Marstead's sticky fingers off of Kari. More recently, Kari had announced her engagement to their half-cousin several times removed. Laynie remembered Kari telling her about Søren Thoresen and his young son, Max. Kari wrote of ST's intention to adopt S and R, and hers to adopt M.

Linnéa had shaken her head at the news. *Kari has gone from single woman to single mother of two. Now she's taking on a husband and a stepson? She's braver than I am.*

But apparently, or at least according to what Kari wrote, the three children were thrilled with the idea of becoming one family.

At the end of the letter, Kari had said it would be a September wedding, and she had asked her sister to be her maid of honor.

Hardly a "maid," but I would have been honored to stand with you.

Out of the question now.

Linnéa shook her head with regret. *Kari will receive a cold note of apology, and it will arrive on the cusp of her wedding day. What a wretched excuse for a sister I am.* Then it hit her, and she swore aloud.

A gift. I must send them a wedding gift.

Linnéa walked on, racking her brain. She turned at the corner and wandered down a street toward a popular tourist district. Much of Stockholm was built on the islands dotting the inland waterway of Sweden's easternmost shore. Bridges and ferries tied Stockholm's districts together—meaning that in Stockholm you were never far from water. She kept walking. She smelled the water before she saw it—that tangy, salty sea scent.

Near the docks, in a nondescript shop in an area of Stockholm she did not frequent, she saw *it.* the carved wooden model of a two-man sailboat.

Linnéa stopped and stared, a little in awe. When she went inside and pointed to it, the owner, a *trä hantverkare*, the master woodworker who had crafted the replica, pulled it from the window and placed it in her hands.

Linnéa held the little boat with reverence, the memories as fresh as the billowing waves had been that day on Puget Sound . . .

IN THE HAZE OF GRIEF that followed Sammie and his wife's funeral, Laynie and Kari had spent time with their niece and nephew, but also with each other. The truth was, although they were sisters, Laynie and Kari were strangers—strangers with painfully connected pasts. Laynie was withdrawn and cool toward Kari. Kari, for her part, wanted more than anything to break through Laynie's crusty reticence. At first, the sisters had used the kids as a buffer between themselves while they slowly tested the other out.

"I had been searching for you and Sammie—I mean, Stephen—for a couple of years," Kari told Laynie. "I hired private investigators—dear friends of mine—and poured a small fortune into the search, but they came up empty."

Then, Kari shared how her investigators had found Stephen Portland through his and his wife's obituaries. "When they broke the news to me, I was devastated. Heartbroken. I would never see my brother or get to know him! Then my friends pointed out that Stephen and Kelly Portland's memorial service was *the next day*. If I flew from New Orleans to Seattle that afternoon, I would be able to attend their services. I thank God for that mercy, Laynie, because it meant that I found you."

Laynie brushed off Kari's reference to her faith, but she felt obligated to reciprocate—just a little. "I have lived and worked in Europe for more than fifteen years, returning home to Seattle on leave only once a year. Thirty precious days. Once a year, I cram all my family time into that short month—time with Mama and Dad, but also time with Sammie, especially out on the water in his sailboat, *The Wave Skipper*."

Sammie and his two-man sailboat seemed safe topics, so Laynie told Kari how her fondest memories were of the two of them sailing on Puget Sound. It saddened her to add, "Mama and Dad will have to sell the boat now. They can't afford the berth fees."

"But they haven't yet, have they? Take me?" Kari asked impulsively. "Not today while we have the children, but before you leave? Take me sailing?"

And so, Laynie had taken Kari out on *The Wave Skipper*. It was during that day, out on the water, that Laynie and Kari had connected, had found each other, the sisters who had been torn apart as children.

They sailed all morning, then ate lunch on one of the uninhabited islands on Puget Sound. Kari talked a lot. Laynie said little but listened. When they had cleaned up after themselves and pushed the boat off the shore and back out into the water, Laynie started the small engine and motored them out of the cove.

Away from the island, they flew before the wind. Kari and Laynie lapsed into companionable silence until Laynie asked the question that burned inside of her. "And you never once thought of Sammie and me during all those years you were growing up?"

Laynie was four years younger than Kari. Her question held an unspoken accusation.

"I did, that is, I *tried* to think of you. I knew I'd forgotten something—something truly important—but each attempt to remember what I'd forgotten would trigger a panic attack."

Kari had tried to laugh, but it ended on a groan. "You've never lived until you've experienced a full-on panic attack."

"Then I've never lived," Laynie snorted. Her eyes did a 360-degree sweep around them, even though they were bobbing across the choppy waves of the sound—far from land or another vessel.

She dropped her voice and, for the first time in her employment with the company, Laynie broke operational security. "I've been in some tight places, Kari—tight enough that I'm surprised I *don't* have anxiety attacks, situations that could have ended with me in a Russian interrogation room. The day I ever have such an attack? I'll be finished in my present line of work."

She shook her head. "Not that the end of my 'career' would necessarily be a bad thing. For me, anyway."

That afternoon out on the water—without admitting to any facts—Laynie confirmed Kari's suspicions that her newfound sister was involved in dangerous work. It was an admission of trust. No . . . it was an unexpected and unprecedented leap of faith.

Kari had studied Laynie for a long while afterward, her worried eyes slowly changing. Warming. "You know, Laynie, I think we're beginning to bond or something. That's the most open you've been with me."

Laynie's gaze swept the water and the weather in the distance. She wasn't watching Kari when she said, "Would you know what I meant if I said that I'm not really the 'girlfriend' type? You know. The 'girly-girly, slumber party, call-your-bestie-six-times-a-day, let's-do-lunch-and-get-our-nails-done-together' type?"

Kari smiled. "I think I would. And?"

Laynie turned her head toward Kari but still stared out into the distance. "And it's different with you. Talking with you. Being with you feels . . . natural. Comfortable. Like it was with Sammie." Laynie had sniffed and added, "In spite of our glaring differences."

Kari agreed. "Yeah. Out here on the water? You have let your guard down, and I'm so glad, Laynie. I like that we can talk about real stuff and not get bent out of shape when we don't agree." She waggled her brows and giggled. "Even share secrets."

Laynie again scanned the waters around them. "But only because we're in a boat out on the ocean, far from prying eyes and eavesdropping ears."

Kari's eyes were sober when Laynie looked back at her, but abruptly she grinned. "Check this out. Do you know what the word 'fellowship' means?"

Laynie's response was classic, unblinking deadpan. "I'm sure you'll fill me in."

Kari snickered. "Why, yes, of course I will. See, fellowship is like two fellows—*wait for it!*—two fellows sitting in the same ship. Get it? Fellowship—and here we are. Together. In a boat."

Laynie groaned. "That is . . . terrible."

But she laughed anyway.

Kari laughed, too.

And they laughed together, the tension between them lifting, floating away.

Laynie turned the boat in a wide sweeping arc to begin the long sail home. As they sped over the wave tops, she said softly, "You know what? You're all right, Kari Michaels."

"I love you back, Laynie Portland."

Oh, Care! I love you, too, Laynie whispered in her heart.

LINNÉA WAS CARESSING the tiny tiller and bench seat when she came back to herself. "The detail," she murmured. "It is flawless."

"*Ja?* You wish to buy?"

The miniature reproduction was the wedding gift she wanted to give Kari. Without words, it would tell her sister how important, how precious that day spent together had been.

"Yes, it will mean a great deal to . . . someone special." She frowned, not knowing how she would package and get the replica to *Posten* without being observed.

"Is it a gift, then?" the carver asked.

"Yes, but I wonder if I could prevail upon you for a bit of customization?" It lacked a single detail for the replica to be the gift Linnéa *needed* it to be.

She explained what she wished the man to do. She wrote it out.

"By all means. An hour for the paint to dry," he said.

"Then I will leave you to it and call back in an hour." Faced with the wait, Linnéa finally listened to her stomach's complaint.

She glanced at her watch. *Two in the afternoon!* She followed her nose toward the docks and found a ferry landing—and a line of food vendors parked nearby. She spent the hour eating lunch while watching disembarking passengers drive or walk off the ferry, then the reverse as passengers queued up to board.

It was a pleasant wait. The hot summer air was cooled by the nearby water, and Linnéa allowed herself time to think, to reason out the best way to ship Kari's gift.

Nothing feasible had come to mind when she returned to the shop and the craftsman showed her his work.

"It is perfect! I'm very appreciative."

Linnéa traced the red, flowing script on the bow of the boat, the words that read, *SS Fellowship.*

Not that she's a steamship, Kari, but the "SS" sounded right. I don't think you'll hold my misnomer against me.

"And will you be shipping your purchase? For a small fee, I will pack it as a gift for you so that it arrives in perfect condition," the man promised.

Linnéa couldn't believe her luck. "You would do that? Would you also . . . would you be willing to take it to *Posten* for me? I would pay for you to ship it express and would compensate you for your time. I . . . I just need to enclose a card."

She wrote out the card, sealed it, paid cash for her purchase, added the cost of shipping, and gave the man a generous tip. She arrived home late that afternoon, satisfied that she had done all she could to apologize to Kari.

I hope you'll forgive me, Kari, and understand . . . my life is not my own to command.

Not yet.

Thoresen Homestead, Northwest of RiverBend, Nebraska

MANY PACKAGES HAD arrived in the weeks leading up to the wedding. Kari's soon-to-be sister-in-law handed Kari another.

"Who's it from, Ilsa?"

"Not sure. The postmark is foreign, and it's marked urgent and sent express mail, so I thought I should bring it over."

Kari's fingers on the paper wrapping slowed. She examined the postmark and nodded. "I . . . I think it must be from Laynie." Kari had sent the invitation two months ago. And Laynie had replied. She was supposed to arrive early this morning. In time for the wedding.

Laynie, where are you? You promised to be with me today.

Kari removed the paper and cut open the stout outer box. The box was filled with packing peanuts. Kari dug down and found a smaller box wedged inside. As she pulled it out, Styrofoam bits went everywhere. Kari didn't care. She let them fall. She needed to know what was in the smaller box.

Ilsa cleared a spot on the table so that Kari could cut open the smaller box. Inside, nestled in tissue paper, was an envelope.

Below that, Kari glimpsed a tiny model sailboat. She lifted it out with tender care. Every part of the boat was crafted with extreme attention to detail.

Below that, Kari glimpsed a tiny model sailboat. She lifted it out with tender care. Every part of the boat was crafted with extreme attention to detail. "It-it is a replica of-of Sammie's boat."

Kari's fingers traced the tiny stern and the bench across it, the miniscule tiller in the middle. "This is where we sat when we went sailing together. Laynie handled the tiller and the sails almost all by herself. I held the tiller steady once or twice."

She felt the salt spray and the wind on her face, saw again Laynie's hair flying free . . . and the joy on her sister's face.

Laynie! My sister! Where are you?

"What's the boat's name?" Ilsa asked.

"Oh, it's the—" Kari stopped when she read the tiny red script flowing across the stern. She swallowed against the emotion that rose in her throat.

"What is it?"

Kari whispered, "Sammie's boat was *The Wave Skipper*. This boat is the *SS Fellowship*."

She knew then what the gift meant—and she knew Laynie would not be coming to her wedding.

Laynie's work—*her dangerous work*—would not permit her to.

"Oh, God," Kari prayed. "Please keep Laynie safe."

Laynie Portland
RETIRED SPY

PART 1: LINNÉA
LP

CHAPTER 1

— LP —

LINNÉA WRESTLED THE Gucci bag from the top of the bedroom closet. She opened it on the bed and began to pack. Her maid, Alyona, hovered nearby.

"Mistress, what are you doing? May I be of help?"

Linnéa knew that Alyona's questions were shot with alarm. Linnéa never went anywhere—not out of the *dacha*, not into another room, not even to the toilet—without Alyona's loitering presence close at hand. And should Linnéa do anything unplanned or out of the ordinary such as an unscheduled walk along the lakeshore before breakfast, Alyona reported Linnéa's unsanctioned activity without delay.

The attraction Linnéa had felt for Petroff in the early days of their relationship, had withered and died under his controlling hand. And the year or two she had intended to spend with him had stretched into seven. Seven long years!

Linnéa had struggled, had labored under Petroff's constraints, had wrestled against depression and despair but, through it all, she had remained faithful and profitable to the company. And she had *not* withered. She had not died within.

Not yet . . . although she teetered on the very edge.

"Since Vassili Aleksandrovich has been called back to Moscow, I have decided to drive into St. Petersburg this morning," Linnéa replied without looking up. "I will be gone two nights only, at the most three, to check in at my office. My quarterly report is a month past due. I also wish to do a little shopping, perhaps spend a day at a spa."

Alyona's fingers twined together. It was a nervous habit. "You gave me no notice, Mistress, or I would have packed your bag and been prepared to travel with you."

"I hardly require your services for such a short trip. When I have finished my business, I will return to our house outside Moscow. I wish you, in the meantime, to attend to our apartment in the city this afternoon. Ready it for Vassili Aleksandrovich, should he wish to sleep there this evening."

"But . . ." Alyona fidgeted further. "This is highly irregular, Mistress. Is . . . does Master Petroff know your plans?"

For seven years, Linnéa had played Petroff's game, and for seven years, she had played her own game, right beneath his nose. It had taken all her skills of subterfuge, her strength of will, and her loyalty to the company, but she had succeeded beyond Marstead's wildest dreams.

If Petroff's superiors were to ever learn the volume and importance of the intel the mistress to the Russian technology czar had "acquired," and if the Security Council were to discover how she had, subsequently, conveyed that intel to a joint NATO intelligence alliance? The revelations would rock the Russian government to its core and would earn Petroff a slow, painful death in the dank basement torture and execution chambers of Lubyanka Prison.

Yes, the rewards were well worth the risk, but the "game" had cost Linnéa. The price had been years of her freedom—a price she was no longer able to pay. She was exhausted. Worn. Frayed.

Like finely spun silk stretched beyond its capacity, the network of threads holding her façade of composure together might rend and give way without warning, leaving in its place a gaping hole. The walls in her psyche separating farce from reality, madness from sanity, possessed the strength and resiliency of wet tissue paper.

I've had enough.

I want out.

I need *out.*

Linnéa had sublimated so much of her will and identity to Petroff's control that she recently found herself wondering, *Who am I?* and *Why am I?* As those questions resounded in her head with growing intensity, another force bubbled its way to the surface. Strong and volatile, the swelling, primal sensation terrified her because she had so little control over it.

Rage.

Rage burned in her with a fervor that required every ounce of Linnéa's training to stem. She no longer had the desire to restrain or suppress it. Suppress it? *No.* Linnéa yearned to release the rage. She wanted it to burst from her mouth and from her hands. She imagined acts of violence against those who, at Petroff's command, kept her on a leash . . . and she daydreamed of setting Petroff's bed on fire—with him in it.

How long can I continue to do this? How much more can I endure before I shatter and give myself away?

"Mistress?" Alyona repeated.

Linnéa's Marstead sources had uncovered Alyona's background. Petroff had handpicked the maid—a Belarusian close in age to Linnéa—from the ranks of the Red Army. Linnéa did not need Marstead's sources to tell her that Alyona was Petroff's first line of supervision and control over Linnéa. The woman had been Linnéa's "maid" and keeper for the past three years.

During that time, Linnéa had hidden her real emotions from the woman, but it was getting harder as time wore on . . . and as the day of her deliverance drew near.

This morning, Alyona's impertinence came perilously close to igniting the rebellion Linnéa had envisioned too often of late. She unbent and fixed the woman with a cold stare. "Are you questioning me, Alyona? Perhaps I should slap the presumption from your mouth."

Oh! How good that felt!

Linnéa had not threatened Alyona before. The woman's expression froze, and her usually florid complexion drained to a mottled white.

"I-I beg your pardon, Mistress. I will . . . I will leave you now to-to-to arrange the car and driver for you."

"You do that," Linnéa whispered to the maid's back.

Careful! Oh, please be careful! the voice of sanity and self-preservation urged her, but she cared less at this point than she had in years past.

She resumed her packing, readying herself for the coming confrontation. Moments after the maid conjured an excuse to leave the room, Linnéa anticipated that the man to whom she was companion and mistress would storm into the bedroom of their lavish cottage to confront her.

Linnéa, get a grip! You cannot allow yourself the luxury of letting your anger bleed through. You must not rouse his suspicions.

She expected his furious roar and did not flinch when he threw open the bedroom door, sending it crashing against the wall, rattling the cottage's windowpanes.

"What is this? Where the *blank* do you think you are going?"

With a placid smile firmly in place—the one she had perfected during her years with Petroff—Linnéa glanced up from her packing.

"Ah, my love. There you are!" She tucked her makeup bag and a small box of jewelry into the suitcase before she turned to him.

"Your being called back to Moscow today provides the perfect opportunity for me to hand in my quarterly report. As I told you last week and reminded you yesterday, I am overdue at my office." She chuckled softly. "Despite how I enjoy the lake and the forest, I cannot be on holiday forever, you know."

"I told you to *quit that job*, Linnéa! For the past five years I have ordered you to quit—and still you defy me!"

He towered over her, crowding her personal space. Glowering. Shaking with rage, fists clenching and unclenching.

Linnéa did not shrink. She straightened and faced him. She was a tall woman herself, but her uplifted chin scarcely reached his shoulders. She placed her hands upon his chest and smiled her best smile—the one that dimpled both sides of her mouth in innocent, girlish fashion. She knew what was needed and looked past his fury, deep into his eyes, disclosing her soul to him. Offering him deference. Making herself submissive. Acquiescent. Adoring.

"You know my heart belongs to you, *moy lyubimyy*—my love. My job is but a distraction for those times when we cannot be together. Please do not deny me this little thing, this trifling diversion."

"Deny? You speak of *deny?* I have denied you nothing, Linnéa. I have given you everything a woman could wish for—a grand house outside of Moscow, an extravagant apartment in the city, this lakeside *dacha*, another cottage by the sea, a yacht, and money to shop the finest stores in the world. So! So, what have I ever denied you? Eh?"

Only my freedom, Linnéa thought. *But after all these years in service to my country, I shall soon take back my life.*

Linnéa leaned into his chest, lifting her chin higher, baring her neck and making herself vulnerable to him. She never pled or wheedled—Petroff despised whining in any form. Rather, she "capitulated" her desires, providing him with the opportunity to be generous.

As a benevolent tyrant.

A tyrant, nonetheless.

"Why, Vassili Aleksandrovich, you yourself told me last evening that you must leave for Moscow this morning, *nyet?* And after you have gone, what is here for me? The days . . . *and the nights* will be unbearable. And you will be busy for long hours in Moscow—unable even to come home and sleep with me, will you not? This checking in with my company will amuse and divert me a little from your absence. So, then, I shall complete this business, shop a bit, perhaps pamper myself at a spa, and then come home to await your return."

He searched her face for deceit, finding nothing but what Linnéa wanted him to see. Then he could not help himself. His arms came up and wrapped themselves around her. He pressed her close to his chest—not in selfless affection, but in the pride and power of ownership—for whatever Petroff "loved," he had a pathological need to possess completely. Linnéa was a beautiful, intelligent, and successful woman—a jewel Petroff owned body and soul, a pearl he flaunted before the world as his and his alone.

"It is true that I have been summoned to a special assembly of the Security Council. Some emergency of state over rumors of an impending attack on high-value targets of unknown number, the information coming to us via a source I have little confidence in. However, Secretary Rushailo *himself* wishes me on hand for my technological advice, should he require it."

As with many powerful men who felt their vaunted positions were unassailable, Petroff's pride was his weakness. He trusted his inner circle and believed the rules of operational security applied only to those peons below him. In his efforts to prop up his self-importance, he was frequently not as circumspect with classified information as his position warranted.

Linnéa's unspoken opinion was that Russian politicians on the Security Council and their advisors lived in a state of perpetual agitation, reminding her of the characters in a folk story who cried over and over, "The sky is falling! The sky is falling!" Nevertheless, she gathered and passed on to her superiors whatever crumbs Petroff carelessly dropped.

Feigning concern, Linnéa's brow furrowed. "An attack? Will you be safe, my love?"

"*Da*, without a doubt. I surmised from the call that it is not a threat toward the Motherland, and I am not certain how much credence I give the intelligence—coming through Afghani sources—but I cannot decline the summons. However, should the situation clear quickly, I will return here, perhaps as early as tomorrow evening."

Still chewing on where the supposed attack might be aimed and hoping to pass the nugget on to her superiors without delay, Linnéa pouted. "Ah, my darling! We both know our holiday is over, do we not? For the sake of the Council's safety, they will keep you in seclusion for a week, perhaps two. I might just as well return to Moscow and wait for your return to our house or apartment—equally alone in either place—or . . . or I can take advantage of the present crisis to visit my office in St. Petersburg so that, afterward, my time is all yours as it should be. I hope you will not say no, Vassi."

Linnéa willed her eyes to moisten just a little and blinked to push the gleam of unshed tears to the corners of her eyes. "This job helps me bear the lonely hours until we are together again."

Petroff's grip loosened marginally. "Marstead knows how vital my connections and favor are to their success in Russia. They are aware that I wish you near me at all times. For this, they should make allowances."

"Just so! But your superiors will keep you sequestered until the present crisis passes, and while they keep you, I cannot be with you, can I? It is only two nights in St. Petersburg, Vassi, *zvezdochka*—my star—two nights I would be alone in our bed, without you, missing you. Save me from such longing, Vassili Aleksandrovich!

"I shall drive into the city this morning and check in with Marstead, *pro forma*. Nyström will give me my next assignment, and I shall return to you with another list of upcoming technological exhibits you and I will enjoy visiting and scientific breakthroughs on which I am to write my reports. This I do for them every quarter, as you know—although my present report is quite past due."

He pursed his lips and regarded her, hovering between admiration and puzzlement, even as his anger slipped a little. "Truly, I do not understand you sometimes, Linnéa. You do not need this 'job' as you call it."

"Need? No, I need for nothing, Vassili Aleksandrovich, nothing except *you*. You have made me your queen, and you shower me with luxury and your love." Linnéa dimpled again. "You even allow me my insignificant pet projects."

The former KGB officer studied her, finding nothing duplicitous in her words or expression. Only adulation. He sighed. "I wish you always near me, Linnéa."

"*Dal'she ot glaz—blizhe k serdtsu.* Further from the eye—closer to the heart, my darling. These infrequent trips to my office in St. Petersburg and my little assignments away from you? They keep our loving fresh . . . and thrilling, do they not?"

She winked and whispered the promise of something racy she would buy in St. Petersburg and model for him when they were reunited in Moscow.

He grinned, then roared a laugh in response.

Linnéa grinned back, even as she wondered how much longer such wiles would work on him. So much of her "free" time was given over to the beauty treatments and rigorous workout schedule that kept her body as lithe, youthful, and attractive as possible despite the unforgiving advance of age. Her looks and sweet compliance were the sole means by which she navigated the labyrinth of Petroff's shifting moods. Cloying, spiteful control at one end of the spectrum and lavish overindulgence at the other.

With fits of cruelty and physical abuse sprinkled between.

He sobered and cleared his throat. "Are you all right, Linnéa? I did not hurt you last evening, did I? If only you would not anger me so . . ."

Linnéa's smile did not falter. "I am yours, Vassi. I did not mean to displease you. I am sorry." She had iced the lump on her temple. Makeup would cover the bruise, but she could do nothing for the blood that had seeped into the sclera in the outside corner of her left eye. Would he refuse to let her appear in public because of it?

"What of this?" He caressed her temple with his thumb, indicating the blood-red stain in her eye.

She shrugged. "It is nothing. Everyone has, on occasion, scratched or poked themselves while sleeping and wakened to a reddened eye, is this not so?"

He grunted, the extent of his remorse. "*Da*, this is so. And you have this report of yours ready? It will project Russia's technological advances in a favorable light?"

"But of course." Linnéa smiled once more, knowing she had won. She gestured toward the portfolio atop her laptop, both lying on the bed next to her handbag. "Do you wish to review the report before I hand it in?"

He had already seen it—Linnéa knew Alyona had slipped him the portfolio, then returned it.

Because nothing I do goes unreported.

"No, but if you insist upon this trip, Alyona must accompany you," Petroff announced. "I will also send Zakhar with you. It is not right for the woman of such an important Russian man to traipse about the country without a proper escort."

"Alyona's assistance will be welcome, and Zakhar's help with the traffic and crowds of St. Petersburg will be appreciated."

Linnéa knew how to "negotiate" with Petroff to procure the best situation she could hope for. Although she had expected to be strapped with Alyona and a driver, she had harbored a very small hope that she might manage to leave without the company of Zakhar, the dour, middle-aged lout who, like Alyona, dogged Linnéa's every step.

Zakhar was ex-Soviet military and loyal only to Petroff—another element of Petroff's elaborate, layered ring of supervision and control over her.

Dimitri Ilyich Zakhar! She loathed Petroff's single-minded lapdog and the way he stared at her, undressing her with his eyes, the red birthmark that ran from his throat up the right side of his cheek darkening with lust as he watched her.

Linnéa shuddered.

"And you will keep your mobile phone with you at all times so I may reach you?"

Only one response was acceptable.

"Certainly, Vassili."

The phone was the electronic leash that tethered her to him. She dared go nowhere without it—or ever turn it off. And woe be to her if she neglected to keep it charged!

Linnéa would check in with her St. Petersburg office later today, and she would find out if Alvarsson and his Marstead superiors had approved her request to quit the field and "come in from the cold." If so, Nyström, her St. Petersburg boss, would deploy resources to facilitate her escape from Zakhar and Alyona's overwatch, either this afternoon or, at the latest, tomorrow.

I am so close to freedom! I must keep my act together a little longer.

Linnéa tried not to envision a scenario in which her company superiors turned down her request. The possibilities crept in anyway.

What if they will not pull me out? If they insist that I stay?

But I cannot maintain this façade forever. I am forty-six years old now. True, Petroff does not keep me only for sex. No, he has never been faithful to me in that regard—it was not agreed to. But I know he is growing restless, dissatisfied with me. The beatings come more frequently, and he is less remorseful after.

How long before he perceives that I am aging, before he no longer desires me? How long until he finds a younger, more accomplished woman, and his admiration for me pales in comparison?

If he were to take a new mistress, would he simply allow me to return to Sweden? I cannot believe so. I am too well-known in his circles. It would prick his pride to allow me my freedom.

If—no, when—he drops me for another woman, he will not let me go. He would not be able to tolerate the idea, even the remote possibility, that another man might have me. He could not abide that. I would, I think, simply disappear . . . as so many of his enemies have.

She also played out a terrifying scenario in her thoughts where Petroff held her in tender embrace and whispered in her ear, "Do you think me so naïve, *kotyonok moya*, my kitten? I have known from the beginning who you were—a spy for the Americans and their NATO lackeys.

"I have enjoyed our little game all this time—letting you 'find' important papers I brought home, giving you access to just enough emerging intel to make your superiors believe you were an invaluable asset that helped America to win the Cold War. I let you believe these things—all while feeding you *dezinformatsiya*, disinformation we wished the US to act upon—as they have."

She needed no imagination for what would follow such a conversation. Linnéa's breath caught in her throat. *I have waited too long already. It must be today!*

But what if her superiors did not approve her request? Slipping away from both Zakhar and Alyona in St. Petersburg—without assistance, without others running interference to aid her—would not prove easy. On her own, she might fail . . . and then? Then Petroff would realize that her adoration was and always had been a sham.

Linnéa experienced an abrupt and fearsome insight. Petroff's *dacha* on Lake Komsomolskoye was not far from Lake Ladoga—the largest freshwater lake in Europe. At one hundred thirty-six miles long and nearly eighty-six miles wide, Lake Ladoga was also *seven hundred fifty-five feet deep* at its lowest point.

How many weighted bodies lined the icy depths of the lake? She could not stop the shiver that rippled over her.

"Are you cold, my sweet?"

Think!

"No, Vassi, but I have just now sensed something, *something wrong*—an encroaching evil."

"What!"

Petroff, for all his sophistication and scientific acumen was, like many Russians, incredibly superstitious. On rare occasions, Linnéa affected to have received premonitions—forewarnings that Petroff heeded more seriously than she had believed possible. Caught now, having allowed her dark thoughts to surface, Linnéa used this ruse to distract him.

"Only an impression, Vassi, although it disturbs me."

"What is it? You must tell me!"

"*Da, da.* It was . . ." Think! *Think!*

"It-it was about the train . . . your train! Oh, I am suddenly frightened, Vassi! Perhaps you should . . . take a later train, not the morning one."

"*Zakhar!* Zakhar, come quickly!"

Petroff's roar deafened Linnéa. She withdrew from his embrace as Zakhar rushed in.

"I am here, Vassili Aleksandrovich."

"I will take the automobile to Moscow, not the train—even though the journey will take a little more time. Tell the driver to ready himself."

Zakhar slid his eyes toward Linnéa. "And Miss Olander?"

"You will call for a rental car and escort her to her office in St. Petersburg. Take Stepan to drive for you. Also, Alyona will accompany Miss Olander as usual," Petroff commanded.

Linnéa castigated herself in silence. She had, through painstaking machinations, acquired her own key to Petroff's car. If Marstead's decision were to go against her in St. Petersburg, she was prepared to appropriate Petroff's luxurious automobile—to elude Zakhar, if ever-so-briefly—in order to give herself a head start.

A rental car quashed that hope.

Linnéa berated herself for her mistake. *Stupid, stupid, stupid!* If Marstead would not help her, she would be forced to access more "creative" methods of escape.

Petroff turned to Linnéa. "You will not mind that I take the car? The rental will be suitable?"

Maintaining a docile, compliant countenance, she replied, "Mind? Not at all, Vassi. Naturally, you must take the car. I wish you to be safe."

He preened under her care and concern. "I will leave sooner than planned, then." Petroff left their room, shouting for his driver and valet.

Before Alyona returned to interfere, Linnéa opened her Bottega Veneta handbag and poured its contents out onto the bed. Marstead had altered the roomy purse for her needs. Linnéa had designed the customizations herself.

Her fingers found a small tab in the seam of the purse's bottom lining. She tugged. With a soft *snick*, the inside layer of the purse's flat underside came free.

From beneath her pillow, she withdrew a thin case containing two CD-ROM discs. She placed the case flat on the purse's bottom and fit the loose inner layer over it. She pressed it until it locked in place with an imperceptible click. Gathering her purse's contents, Linnéa dumped them back into her purse.

With her plans in place, she closed her suitcase, zipped it, and unbent.
Either today or tomorrow, I will break free of Petroff.
I will . . . or I will die trying.

CHAPTER 2

LINNÉA PASSED THE TWO-HOUR drive from Lake Komsomolskoye to St. Petersburg in the rental automobile's rear seat. Alyona shared the seat with her, while Zakhar sat in front with Stepan, the driver. Linnéa spent most of the ride with her head leaned back on the seat, pretending to rest her eyes. She was not sleeping, however. Instead, she was rehearsing her next moves—and the contingency plans she and her sole ally had devised should the situation call for them.

As they approached the city outskirts, Linnéa spoke to the driver. "Take me directly to Marstead's offices, please."

"We will check into the hotel, first, Miss Olander," Zakhar answered evenly.

"*No, we will not go to the hotel first*—and I was not speaking to you, Zakhar. Stepan, you will take me to my office—or I will tell Vassili Aleksandrovich that you were impertinent and refused my orders."

A nervous Stepan slid his eyes from the road toward Zakhar. Stepan feared the stinging rebuke of Petroff's tongue—or his heavy fist—should Linnéa report that he had insulted her.

Zakhar stared straight forward. "To Miss Olander's office, Stepan."

No doubt, Zakhar would find a way to make her pay for her boldness later, but she was willing to risk his reprisal. It was vital that she visit Marstead *soonest*.

Ten minutes later, the car rolled up in front of Marstead's unpretentious St. Petersburg building, a narrow, two-story affair. The facility was staffed by a handful of Marstead employees—three account executives, counting Linnéa, and a few administrative personnel, all Marstead clandestine operatives to one degree or another. Zakhar jumped out of the front seat, opened Linnéa's car door, and extended his hand to her, checking for danger as he did so.

Linnéa, with her portfolio clutched in her hands, laptop case looped over her shoulder, and handbag on her arm, stared past Zakhar's outstretched fingers as though they were invisible. She climbed from the car without assistance.

"You may take the luggage to our hotel and check in, Zakhar. I will call when I am ready to be picked up."

"Stepan and Alyona will do so. I shall accompany you to your office," Zakhar said, ignoring her order and falling in beside her.

"As you well know, my company takes a judicious approach to preventing the theft of intellectual property, Zakhar. No one, *no one*, without a Marstead badge or a sanctioned visitor's pass is allowed up to the offices—and all visitors must be screened ahead of time. You will be required to wait in the lobby, but not long. I do not expect to be engaged more than an hour or so."

Zakhar frowned. He opened and held the front door for her. "Marstead will make an exception when I tell them for whom I work. I will insist, and they will comply."

Linnéa did not answer. She strode through the double doors a few steps ahead of him and entered the lobby and its comfortable waiting area. She approached a security checkpoint and two keycard-activated turnstiles. Beyond the checkpoint lay the elevator. Between the checkpoint and the elevator, two uniformed security guards observed as she—and then Zakhar—approached the nearest turnstile.

One of them greeted her. "Good day, Miss Olander. It is nice to see you."

"Thank you, Jonas. I'm happy to be here."

Linnéa withdrew her access card from her handbag, swiped it and, as the wheel unlocked, passed through the entry turnstile. Zakhar tried to follow, but the turnstile locked after Linnéa went through, preventing him.

Jonas eyed Zakhar. "Do you have an access card, sir?"

Zakhar watched Linnéa approach the elevator and push the call button. "I work for Vassili Aleksandrovich Petroff, and I am Miss Olander's bodyguard. It is essential that I accompany her," he informed Jonas. "You will grant me entrance."

"Sorry, friend, but no one may pass the checkpoint without proper authorization. Have you applied for a visitor's pass?"

Zakhar, red-faced and angry, shouted, "Miss Olander! You must wait!"

Linnéa pivoted, eyes wide and innocent. "Are you speaking to me, sir?"

"You know I am! You must wait for me to join you before going up," Zakhar hissed through clenched teeth.

Jonas swiveled his gaze toward Linnéa while managing to keep Zakhar under scrutiny. "Miss Olander?"

"Oh, that man is not with me. I don't know who he is." At that moment the elevator doors opened. Linnéa waved and smirked at Zakhar. She stepped into the waiting car.

"What? Why, that is a lie! I work for Vassili Aleksandrovich Petroff—as you well know!"

Linnéa laughed, letting the guards know she had been jesting, and pressed her personal code into the keypad. "Don't fret yourself, Zakhar. I'll be back in an hour. Why don't you make yourself comfortable until then, yes?"

She sketched a little wave, and her last glimpse of Zakhar was as Jonas and the other guard, their expressions implacable, indicated he was to take a seat and wait. After cursing under his breath, Zakhar did so.

I will pay for that, too, Linnéa laughed to herself, giddy with dodging Zakhar's control. *That is, unless Marstead pulls me from the field today. Surely by now they have concocted a plan to do so!*

Her heart soared at the possibility.

FOR SECURITY PURPOSES, the elevator was the only non-alarmed means of accessing the second floor of the building. The other routes—solely for emergency egress—were were both alarmed and hidden, known only to Marstead employees. Linnéa stepped off the elevator into the foyer of the brightly lit Marstead office suite.

From the outside, the building had lovely, tall windows that added to the exterior's classic appeal, but the windows were façades, their reflective "glass" and the soaring faux arches—as well as the walls, floors, and ceilings—filled with specialized materials that shielded Marstead's activities from prying electronic "eyes" and "ears."

Within these walls, Marstead operatives could speak—and breathe— freely. Linnéa closed her eyes and sucked in, then exhaled, a deep, cleansing breath. She inhaled liberty for the first time in five months.

Linnéa greeted the receptionist in Swedish. "*Hej*, Ebba! I am ever so glad to be home."

The receptionist smiled. "Good morning, Miss Olander." She glanced at her watch which read just past noon. "Or should I say good afternoon?"

Without pause, Linnéa switched to the English spoken in Marstead offices. "Either way, it is a good day, is it not?"

"Indeed, Miss Olander. Can I get you a *kaffe?*"

The question about coffee, which Marstead receptionists asked solely of Marstead Alpha employees when they entered the offices, was code for *Are you under duress?* or *Is everything secure?*

"Thank you. Perhaps later."

All is fine.

"Is Mickel in?"

"*Ja.* Wait one moment. I will call him. He will be glad to see you, I think."

When Ebba hung up and gave her a nod, Linnéa strolled to the office of Mickel Nyström, her St. Petersburg supervisor—himself a Swede. She knocked on his door and entered.

"Ah, Miss Olander. Great to see you—it has been too long. Have a seat, please."

Linnéa offered him the portfolio containing her report. "You will find the best bits coded within the document as usual."

"Very good. Thank you."

They made small talk for a time before Nyström asked, "Have you anything else to report before we move on?"

Linnéa said, "Yes. Petroff was called to Moscow today before our holiday at Lake Komsomolskoye was over. The message recalling him was urgent, permitting no delay. He decided to return to Moscow ahead of the rest of us. I used his abrupt departure as justification to carry my report to you today and also to convey this development."

"Urgent, you say? For what reason?"

"His exact words were, 'I have been summoned to a special assembly of the Security Council. Some emergency of state over rumors of an impending attack on high-value targets of unknown number,' the information coming via Afghanistan. He also mentioned that Secretary Rushailo himself wished Petroff on hand for his technological advice."

"An impending attack, he said? Any sense of the target?"

"No, only that he did not believe Russia was in any danger—which made me wonder, if Russia was not the target, why the Security Council should be alarmed enough to meet immediately."

Nyström mulled over her intel. "Interesting—but nothing further? No actionable details to add to it?"

"No, but our superiors can correlate it with other intelligence or chatter they may have gotten wind of."

"Yes, you were correct to bring it in."

He straightened his tie.

Linnéa noted the gesture. *Odd.*

"You know, according to your file, what I have personally witnessed of your performance, and the steady stream of intel you have provided our superiors, you are one of the brightest, most savvy undercover officers we have ever recruited. Your facility with languages is second to none, your adaptability and acting skills, superb."

"Thank you." She kept her eyes from blinking or narrowing by counting the repeating paisley patterns on Nyström's tie.

"Well, we are lucky to have you placed where you are. If you obtain any actionable data concerning this attack, use the chat room protocols to pass it on."

Each month, the chat room or bulletin board Linnéa might visit to pass on information changed, as did the user name she would log in as and the user name she would invite to a private chat. The parameters of such communication were exact, and Linnéa had memorized them all.

The communication method was reserved for urgent, highest-level intel such as warnings. She had used the method to contact her handlers only twice. Unknown to them, she had used similar—and not-so-similar—means to communicate regularly with her ally, Christor, whose friendship had helped Linnéa weather the loneliness of her life.

Nyström spoke again. "However, I think you must return to Moscow directly and get to the bottom of this 'urgent' matter."

It was at Nyström's abrupt change of direction that Linnéa finally blinked, momentarily shaken. Her nerves hummed a warning.

"I, um . . . I was expecting, that is, I had anticipated an answer from Alvarsson today. Have you no word regarding my request?"

"Your request?" Nyström picked at his sleeve. "You mean your request to arbitrarily resign your assignment? To abandon a valuable post that we rely upon? Why, I hardly gave it credence."

Linnéa's taut nerves began to fray. "Mickel, do you mean to say that you did *not* pass my request on to Alvarsson? I have been waiting five months for a decision."

Nyström waved his hand in casual indifference. "Yes, certainly I did, but you weren't serious, were you?"

Stung, Linnéa clamped her mouth closed and did not respond. Her silence was answer enough.

Nyström frowned and assumed more of an authoritative air. "Well. I must say that I am disappointed in you, Linnéa. Why, look at the critical intel you brought us today."

He seemed agitated as he leaned across the desk toward her. "Your role, *where we have placed you* and the access it provides us, is too important for you to up and quit on a whim."

"A whim!"

He interrupted, wagging a finger in her face. "Our network is counting on you. In fact, think of the cascade of damage your abdication has the potential to create. I must say, I thought better of you, Linnéa."

"*What?*"

To her dismay, Nyström doubled down. "I expect you to keep your wits about you, Linnéa, and *do your job.*" Nyström had never bullied her. His posture and tone were uncharacteristically aggressive.

Hurt and confused, she stiffened. "Mickel, look at me! I am not a young woman anymore. You need to know—Marstead needs to know—that I-I have come to the end of my allure and effectiveness where Petroff is concerned. I no longer dazzle his friends and associates. I believe Petroff is already on the prowl for my replacement. If I were to stay much longer, I . . . I fear for my life."

As though seeing her, really seeing her for the first time since she sat down, Nyström frowned. "What is wrong with your eye? The blood in it?"

Linnéa lifted her chin. "I annoyed Vassili Aleksandrovich last night—I offered an opinion he didn't care for, so he bashed my head against a shelf."

Nyström's jaw slackened. "I . . . how long has this been going on?"

"It began two years ago, a slap here, a pinch there. Then it escalated to hitting and, on occasion, kicking. He seems to particularly enjoy slamming my head against things. If I were not wearing makeup at the moment, you would see the bruise creeping out of my hairline."

Nyström swallowed. "I see. And why did you not report this?"

"I did. Twice. To you."

Her boss looked aside. "Perhaps I did not think it serious enough to warrant interference. Besides, what could we have done?"

"The abuse is getting worse and more frequent, Mickel. Petroff has always been volatile, but my ability to soothe him is slipping away. We know where this kind of domestic violence ends. You need to pull me out before he kills me."

Linnéa's gaze bored into the man, but he looked aside.

"Mickel! Please. I can't go back."

"You knew the stakes and the risks when you signed on."

Appalled at his lack of compassion or empathy, she studied him, curious as to why he now avoided her eyes.

Galled, she pressed him. "I submitted a formal request to be withdrawn from the field. I wish a formal answer from Alvarsson. Do you have one?"

"No. No answer."

"Then call him. Now. I need an answer."

Nyström pulled his lower lip between his teeth and nodded slowly to himself. He stared a moment at his folded hands before he spoke again. "No need. I have been asked to pass on instructions to you, Miss Olander. You are to report to Alvarsson personally to discuss the matter."

His cavalier shift in attitude further angered Linnéa. *Right. So Alvarsson can browbeat me, too, tell me to buck up and keep my head in the game? Well, it's too late. I can't do it anymore.*

Then it hit her. *Report to Stockholm? After you demanded I return to Moscow not thirty seconds ago?*

The skin on Linnéa's arms prickled. It took her a moment to reply in an even tone, "Very good. When?"

"At your earliest convenience—in other words, immediately."

Nyström chose his next words carefully. "We realize Petroff will be displeased that we have sent you to Stockholm without notice. Send him the message that you have been selected for a special, time-sensitive assignment, that you must attend a mandatory team briefing tomorrow."

He withdrew a folder from his top drawer and held it for a moment before he slid it toward her. He did not look up when he said, "Your itinerary, travel arrangements, and the assignment are within. The assignment details are quite thorough. We acknowledge that it may be difficult to receive Petroff's permission, so feel free to employ this dossier—and your impressive acting skills—to leverage Petroff's permission or that of your *entourage*, but Alvarsson expects to see you tomorrow."

Nyström had been an analyst, not a field operative.

He was not a skilled liar, not even a credible one.

Willing her hands not to shake, Linnéa opened the folder and pulled out the travel itinerary. Nothing remarkable. St. Petersburg, Russia, to Tallinn, Estonia, by rail. Tallinn to Stockholm, Sweden, by ferry.

Her thoughts skittered like water poured on a hot skillet, boiling off as frenetic, dancing droplets—before Linnéa, through hard-learned habit, shifted into spy mode.

Survival mode.

This meeting was a trial of loyalty. Nyström was told to evaluate my resolve, how insistent I was on being pulled from the field. Poor man! They tasked him with ascertaining my state of mind.

It was a test, and I failed.

They wanted me to agree on my own to go back to Petroff. But with what I've just revealed, Nyström cannot vouch that I won't crack up under pressure if I return to Petroff . . . nor can they trust that I won't reject their decision and take the matter into my own hands.

And they are right to fear my abdication.

Adrenaline spurted through her blood stream, and Linnéa's heart squeezed behind her ribs, shortening her breath. She exercised every ounce of control she could muster to rein in her body's outward reactions.

But they know me! Haven't I served them well with nary a misstep, not a hint of disloyalty or noncompliance? My superiors should trust that I would never betray them or endanger the safety of our intelligence network.

She glanced at the folder in her hand. While she read, she evaluated and parsed Nyström's uncharacteristic behaviors coupled with the abrupt change in her orders.

When she finished her analysis, her courage stuttered and faltered.

They discussed my situation up the chain of command. They settled on two courses of action, based on my own choices. If I were to agree to return to Petroff, then all would be well. But if I were to insist on being pulled out, if I pressed for it, if I said I couldn't bear going back, if Nyström determined that I was close to cracking up?

They had a second response ready and waiting. If I could no longer function reliably in the field, then I had become a security risk. An untenable liability.

But if they are not bringing me in, then what?

The word throat-punched her. *Retirement.*

She stilled and forced her eyes to remain on the documents while her thoughts raced on.

A lengthy night crossing from Tallinn to Stockholm instead of a short flight from St. Petersburg. Marstead will have agents on the ferry, and I will suffer a tragic "slip" while we are at sea.

My death will be a regrettable accident. It will not appear overly suspicious in Petroff's eyes, even if my body is recovered. It will not leave him wondering if I were a spy. And I would not be the first passenger to fall from a ferry—although, I'm certain, I would be dead before I hit the water.

To Nyström she murmured, "We are fortunate that Petroff was called back to Moscow and did not accompany me today. I can continue on to Stockholm this evening, as you have arranged."

She lifted her eyes to Nyström and smiled. "To think—I may soon be free of that odious man. I am so grateful!" She willed tears to form in her eyes' inner corners. It wasn't difficult, given her horrifying deductions.

"Thank you, Mickel. We are unlikely to meet after today, but I want you to know that I appreciate your every kindness through the years."

Was it remorse or guilt she saw on his face? She turned her gaze away, unnerved. "May I use my office to call Petroff or at least leave a message with his aide?"

"Certainly, Linnéa."

She left Nyström's office, nodding and waving hello to fellow Marstead employees, until she reached the sanctuary of her office. She unlocked the door, stepped inside, fell against the closed door, and gulped for air.

She no longer tasted freedom. The atmosphere was rank with betrayal.

———————❧———————

CHAPTER 3

LP

LINNÉA LOCKED THE door and sank onto her desk chair. Her limbs seemed to have lost all their strength. Her mind screamed again and again, *They intend to kill me! They are going to throw me overboard!*

The black rollers of the Baltic, thrashing and foaming beneath the ferry's prow, reached their icy fingers toward her.

Stop! Stop it! Get hold of yourself. You cannot waste what few and precious moments you have.

She lifted her desk phone's receiver from its cradle and laid it aside so no one could call and interrupt her. Then she yanked her laptop from its case, plugged in the broadband cable, connected her office printer, and switched the laptop on. When it had fully booted, she slipped on a lightweight headset, inserted the split cable into her laptop's audio and mic jacks, and opened a command prompt. Typing furiously, Linnéa launched a Voice over Internet Protocol phone call to Stockholm.

Linnéa's Marstead superiors insisted that her laptop hardware and software be kept on the cutting edge of available technology. VoIP technology hadn't been commercially distributed yet, but Christor had configured her laptop with tricks her superiors were aware of.

Linnéa and Christor had used the online calling technology sparingly, mostly when Linnéa was in desperate need of a friendly voice. To date, neither Petroff nor Linnéa's handlers were aware of her laptop's VoIP capability. Was Christor still her friend and ally? Or had they turned him?

Oh, God! If Christor withdraws his support from me now, I have no hope of escaping either Marstead or Petroff.

Those in Linnéa's chain of command—nowhere tech savvy enough to be suspicious of their own IT director—were unaware of a great many things when it came to Linnéa's backdoor communications with Christor or the various non-standard tech advantages he had provided for her.

The phone call rang inside Linnéa's headset. Christor answered on the third ring.

"Linnéa? Where are you?" He was nervous. Wary.

"My office, St. Petersburg."

"I've been trying to reach you for weeks." Christor's concern was evident. "I swept your office for bugs, by the way."

"Thank you. We've been on holiday at the lake. No broadband service—no telephone service at all."

He wasted no time. "Listen, Linnéa, I need to caution you. Don't press your request to be deactivated."

"Too late. We're way past that now."

He went silent for a moment. Then he whispered, "What are you going to do?"

Linnéa's throat closed and she couldn't speak. A familiar longing washed over her, that deep desire for the something or someone she had lost, the need that had haunted her from childhood and pursued her still—a yearning so powerful that its punch doubled her over.

She gasped and turned to the only memory that came near to quenching her need . . . She and Kari. On *The Wave Skipper*. The wind and salt spray whipped her face and hair, but her attention was fixed on Kari—Kari's laughter, Kari's unfettered joy as Sammie's two-man sailboat leaped across the chop of Puget Sound.

That day. That perfect day with my sister. Two fellows in a ship. Safe.

It wasn't what they had talked about while out on the water or while beached on the little island where they'd eaten lunch. No, it was Kari herself. She seemed to embody peace and contentment.

What gives Kari her joy? What does she have?

Why can I never possess such peace?

It couldn't be what Kari had said to her. About God.

It couldn't.

Linnéa shoved Kari's voice to the back of her mind, but her sister's gentle words would not stay there, would not be silent.

"All of God's promises are true, Laynie, because he is true. One way or another, he will work those promises into reality. He is God, and he will have his way."

No. God is a myth. A heartless fable.

Then she turned to memories of her dead brother's two children. The last time she had seen them, Shannon had been four years old and Robbie not yet two. She and Kari had taken them to Lake Union Park for the day. Shannon had asked innumerable questions and Robbie had chased and tormented seagulls, screaming in delighted abandon as he hounded the scavenging birds.

But those memories were old. Shannon was almost eleven now, and Robbie had turned nine in early June.

Oh, how I long for a simple life, just be able to hug those babies! And I want to see my sister Kari. I want to see how she has made a family for our niece and nephew. I want, oh, I want, but—

"Linnéa? Linnéa, are you still there?"

She clapped a hand over her mouth to stifle the sob lurking in her throat, to prevent it from jumping out. When she had choked down her emotions, she whispered into the phone, "I'm here. Just . . . thinking."

"Linnéa? What can I do?"

When she had cleaned out her Stockholm apartment before moving to St. Petersburg, she had emptied her safe and left its contents in Christor's care. She'd handed off cash and three identities—three forged passports from different nations, one with an accompanying driver's license. Christor was supposed to have renewed the documents if they were near expiration.

What if he hadn't?

Those IDs may well decide whether I live or die.

Linnéa had understood that if Petroff found her out, it would be a one-way ride. She had made peace with that probability. That is, until Petroff began breaking her down, abasement by abasement and blow by blow. She hadn't known how hard dying by his hand would be—she hadn't known until then that Petroff would *kill* her long before she *died*.

She could accept a quick death. It was the slow, dying by inches—until she was no longer herself—that she could not endure.

Two years ago, she had begun making provision for the day when she could no longer bear her life with Petroff, when she knew she was close to cracking up—if Marstead should turn its back on her and she were forced to take her life back into her own hands.

That day was here.

I am between an unforgiving rock and a hard, grinding place, with little time and few options before those two forces crush me between them.

If I don't get on the train to Tallinn this afternoon, Marstead will shift into high gear and assign every available agent to my "retirement party." But if I don't return to Moscow with Zakhar tomorrow morning, Petroff will hunt me with a vengeance even Marstead cannot match.

Unless . . .

If she were to survive, so much depended upon what she had entrusted to Christor.

It was Christor who had helped her establish numbered bank accounts in countries where they protected their account holders' anonymity. Christor who had taught her how to transfer her Marstead salary into one of those numbered accounts then reroute it to others, using IP anonymizers and proxy servers to bounce the transactions around the world until no one but her knew that the money had landed in a foreign account under a secret American identity. The money, a tidy fortune after years with Petroff, was waiting for her on the "other side" of her escape. It was Christor who had helped her plan her escape and seen to the final details.

She cleared her throat. "Christor, are the, um, arrangements we discussed complete?"

"Yeah. I finished up when I visited St. Pete's last quarter. Your documents are up to date. The, uh, *package* is in place. The claim check and key are you-know-where . . . with that . . . other thing you asked for." He coughed on his worry and discomfort. "Gotta say, *that* item was tricky."

Linnéa exhaled. She could breathe again! "Thank you, dear friend."

"But, Linnéa? Um, is there any possibility that you could reach out to Alvarsson yourself and negotiate a truce with our superiors? I . . . it's just that . . . Klara and I? We have a baby on the way."

When Marstead had recruited Christor in 1991, they had known the young man was a socially awkward but eager-to-please genius. Perhaps because Christor hadn't fit into the Marstead "mold" any more than Linnéa felt she had, the two of them had hit it off.

Christor had, initially, suffered from a crush on Linnéa—even though he had guessed at what she did for Marstead, the men she seduced and stripped of their secrets. After Linnéa left Stockholm, Christor had met Klara, and he had bloomed. Matured. Linnéa could not have been happier for him.

She licked her lips. "A baby? Why, that is wonderful news, Christor. You and Klara must be over the moon."

"We are, yes, but . . . but, Linnéa, if you go through with what we've planned? And if Marstead suspects I had a role in it? I could lose my clearance and my job. I could . . . go to prison."

Linnéa lapsed into silence. She trusted and cared about Christor. She did not want to harm him or his family, but it was too late. He was in too deep—

It is too late for regrets, my friend.

Too late, because when Christor had agreed to hold Linnéa's cash and documents, he had committed his first act of misleading Marstead for her. It was not to be his last.

Seven years ago, as Linnéa had prepared to leave Stockholm and move to St. Petersburg, she had handed off the contents of her safe to Christor. Then she had entrusted him with her greatest secret. *I have a sister. Marstead doesn't know. She is safer that way. No leaks, no leverage—right? I need your help. Please help me keep her safe?*

After Linnéa left Stockholm, Christor had continued to pay the *Posten* box's semi-annual fees and collect Kari's letters. He then scanned the pages of her letters into tiny image files that he embedded in other images that he passed to Linnéa through their secret chat room visits—and Linnéa had sent short letters in reply.

Then, six years ago, when Petroff had insisted that Linnéa leave her St. Petersburg apartment to live with him in Moscow, she had written Kari a last letter, explaining that her situation was changing and that she would no longer be able to write but that, if Kari wrote to her, she would continue to receive her letters.

Kari had not given up on her, and Christor had kept encoding and forwarding Kari's letters. Although Linnéa had not once replied since then, Kari had written faithfully, twice monthly, for the past six years. Her ongoing letters had been a godsend, a loving, normalizing influence in Linnéa's otherwise emotionally barren existence.

In a letter not long after Linnéa moved to Moscow, Kari had managed to convey to her sister that she and Søren were in the process of adding a breezeway onto the back of their house, a walkway leading to separate, specially designed quarters they were building for Gene and Polly. Polly's MS was not progressing rapidly, but Polly needed handicap facilities and personal care several times weekly that Gene was no longer able to provide for his wife.

Kari wrote later that the little *casita* behind their house was finished. Soon after, she and Søren had helped Gene and Polly sell their Seattle home and move to Nebraska. Even though Gene and Polly took most of their meals in their own little dining room, moving them close by had been a wonderful decision all around. Shannon and Robbie were a joy to the older couple, but they were a blessing not only to their grandchildren but also to Kari and Søren. Gene and Polly had taken them into their hearts as their own daughter and son—thus receiving and treating Max as a beloved second grandson.

With Gene and Polly nearby, Kari was able to send Linnéa regular updates on her parents. It was through Kari's descriptions of family life on their great-grandmother's homestead that Linnéa was able to visualize Kari's husband, Søren, her stepson, Max, Mama and Dad, and, of course, Shannon and Robbie.

Kari's most recent letter had been filled with details of Max's preparations to leave home for his first year of college at the University of Nebraska-Lincoln. "He's going to study agriculture and agribusiness," the letter said, "and by the time you receive and read this letter, he will have started the fall semester.

"I confess that, although my head reminds me that he will be only four hours away from us and will come home often, my heart insists it is too soon for him to fly the nest. I already miss him so."

Linnéa shook herself. *This is no time for reminiscing, for daydreaming.*

She whispered, "I realize what I have asked of you, Christor, and the difficult spot I have put you in. I am also confident of this. If you are half as good at covering your tracks as you say you are—as I *know you are*—they may suspect you, but they will never be able to prove a thing. So, whatever happens, whatever they accuse you of, don't cave. Not for an instant. Deny all knowledge. You can weather whatever—"

A knock sounded on her door. Linnéa threw off the headset, grabbed up the desk phone's receiver and, cord dragging behind her, unlocked and cracked her door.

Ebba peeked through the crack. "Ah, yes. You *are* on the phone. I told Mr. Nyström you probably were. He wishes to see you before you leave, Linnéa."

"Thank you. I am waiting for Vassili Aleksandrovich to come on the line. Please tell Mickel I'll come as soon as I have spoken to Petroff."

Ebba left, but Linnéa didn't move.

Why does Nyström need to see me again? Has Alvarsson asked for reassurance that I will board that ferry tonight? But neither Alvarsson nor Nyström have any clue how desperate I am . . . how "done" I am.

Linnéa relocked her office door and discarded the phone's receiver and the pretend call. With Christor forgotten on the VoIP line, she opened her lowest desk drawer, popped up a false bottom, and retrieved the drawer's contents. a key, pawnshop claim check, subcompact handgun, and two single-stack magazines, each preloaded with eight .380 ACP rounds.

She inserted a magazine into the gun and let the distinctively blue HK P7K3—less than six-and-a-half inches in total length—rest in her palm. The solid, sure weight of it, light as a feather compared to most guns, was comforting.

Controlled and monitored by Petroff as she had been, she hadn't held a real firearm in years. Yet out of all firearms, handgun proficiency was the most perishable. It degraded without continual practice.

Briefly she considered the semiauto and the choices it presented her. The gun had a squeeze-cocking system that would chamber a round when she tightened her hold on the front of the gun's the grip. One squeeze followed by a steady pull on the trigger. It would be an easy way to end things, and it would release Christor from jeopardy.

Here and now?

Yes. Done.

I wouldn't botch the job—and it would stick Marstead with the fallout Petroff would visit on them. She coughed a low laugh. *Serve them right.*

Then Kari's face, smiling and joyous, rose before her—followed by her last moments with Shannon and Robbie, particularly Shannon's stark little face, studying her, asking her Aunt Laynie, "Why do you have to go away? I don't want you to go away!"

A year older than I was when my parents died. When Kari was ripped from us. If I did this, Shannon would never know what became of me, any more than I knew what happened to Kari. Shannon would search for and never find me. I would be lost to her all her life. As Kari was to me.

I cannot do that to her.

Linnéa glanced at the gun. *If worse comes to worst . . . you will be the ally I need most.*

Just not today.

She reached deep into her handbag and felt for the pull tab that opened the compartment on the flat bottom. She withdrew the CD-ROM case. Then she sought a second tab, this one in the lining's seam at one end of the purse. She gave that tab a sharp tug and a Velcro fastener released, opening a space within the handbag's intentionally padded and reinforced sidewall.

She tucked the gun and spare magazine into the sidewall hiding place and pressed the Velcro closure back into place.

She'd traveled far in her thoughts—and had forgotten Christor.

A tinny, distant shout jerked her back. "Linnéa? Linnéa, are you there?"

No, no, no. I cannot afford slipups like this, she chastised herself as she grabbed up the headset. *I must keep my focus.*

"Yes, I'm still here. Listen, Christor, I'm sorry. This is my problem. I should never have dragged you into my mess. Just please believe me. As long as you don't crack under Marstead's questioning, you and your family will be okay."

"All right. I hear you, but you'll be careful, too, won't you?"

"Don't worry. I promise that I won't give you away, my friend."

"That's not what I meant, and you know it. I'm concerned about *you.*"

Linnéa took a breath. She had to distance herself from his worry. She could not afford the emotional drag. Already a headache was pounding behind her eyes. "I'll be fine. I'll work it out."

"Will you go back to Petroff, then, like they want you to?"

Oh, my dear friend. That's no longer an option.

"No, Christor. I'm afraid I can't go back . . . and Marstead knows I'm done."

"So, will you . . . will you run?"

"I guess I'm still considering . . . alternatives."

"What alternatives? If you don't go back to Petroff, what else is there? Wait—listen to me, Linnéa. You can hang in there a while longer, I know you can. Just convince Alvarsson and his superiors that you'll go back to Petroff, that you'll be okay. But if you outright refuse Marstead's orders?"

He hesitated before blurting, "Linnéa, if you give them cause to label you a risk, *they will retire you.* I know they will. I've been monitoring Alvarsson's calls, listening in on his conversations with—"

As though a possible third option had dawned on him, Christor's voice sank. "Linnéa? You already know what they've been discussing, don't you? You-you wouldn't do anything stupid, would you?"

"And you think I should wait for the hit? Just walk into it like a dumb animal?" Pain knifed through Linnéa's head, as if the headset had grown a blade and thrust it into her left temple. In addition to the contusion Petroff had given her, stress was taking its toll.

She heard Christor asking, "Linnéa? Are you still there?"

She sat up. "I'm hanging up now. I have urgent things to do before I run out of time. But Christor? Before I go, I want to thank you for your friendship. For the endless rolls of film you developed for me before we went digital. The countless cups of espresso. Teaching me about computers and video games and the Internet. Your many acts of kindness. I . . . I appreciate you. More than you know."

The other end of the line was silent, until, "Linnéa? You're scaring me."

"I'm sorry." She swallowed. "Goodbye, Christor."

Linnéa ended their call and closed the command prompt window. She removed her headset. She opened and flexed the CD-ROM case. The two discs inside snapped loose from the case. The top disc's label read *Final Fantasy IX* for PlayStation2, but the second disc had no label. It was the kind of CD-ROM that was rewritable, and Linnéa had added to its contents for several years, a little to this folder, a little to that one.

She had sent a similar disc and made her "insurance" arrangements more than a year ago. What she did today amounted to "notifications" concerning those arrangements—notifications that she hoped would properly caution and incentivize both Marstead and Petroff.

Before she slid the rewritable disc into her laptop's drive, she pulled the network cable from the back of her laptop. Then she pushed the disc drawer closed and waited for the CD-ROM to boot up.

When the window containing a list of folders and files appeared, Linnéa clicked on the file named "Alvarsson." She read through the communication and nodded her approval. She opened the file named "Petroff 01"—a letter of similar warning couched in no-nonsense verbiage.

The final file, "Dear Petroff," was different. She had taken great care with this letter's overall tone because it needed to come across perfectly if it was to elicit the response she desired. She tweaked a word or two and saved the changes. When she was satisfied, she sent it to print.

Her LaserJet whirred and hummed and spit out the three documents. She signed and folded them. Set them aside. She then copied two folders from the CD-ROM to her computer's desktop. One folder was named, "Marstead," the other folder was named, "Petroff."

Next, she withdrew two unused CD-ROM discs from a drawer—the regular, single-use kind. With a fine-point marker, she wrote on one disc, "Marstead," and on the second, "Petroff." She placed the blank Marstead CD in her laptop's drive and moved the Marstead folder from her laptop to the disc. She repeated the process, moving the Petroff folder to the Petroff disc. She placed the discs in soft, somewhat rubbery cases that were less likely to crack or break in the mail than an ordinary hard plastic case would be.

Linnéa removed one 8 x 12-inch and two 6 x 10-inch padded mailer envelopes and a plain letter envelope from her desk. She addressed the three mailers and the envelope. She placed the mailers and the letter envelope on her desk and grouped them with their corresponding discs and letters.

She snickered without humor. *Mustn't get these mailers, discs, and letters mixed up, right? I wouldn't want to be responsible for single-handedly reigniting the Cold War . . . or worse.*

She slid the Marstead disc into the padded mailer addressed to Lars Alvarsson in care of Marstead's Stockholm offices, then added the letter to Alvarsson, sealed the mailer, and affixed the postage she'd predetermined the mailer would require. The mailer bore no return address, only a scrawled "Linnéa Olander" in the corner and "Personal and Confidential" printed across the back.

That should get Alvarsson's attention.

And rock his world.

She put the Petroff CD and the "Petroff 01" letter inside the 6 x 8 mailer addressed to Petroff and sealed it—then slid *that* mailer into the 8 x 12 mailer. The larger mailer was addressed to Judith Johansson at Linnéa's Stockholm *Posten* box and bore no return address.

Again, Christor was essential to her plans. He would pick up the mailer addressed to Judith Johansson, remove the smaller mailer that was addressed to Petroff, affix postage to it and, at Linnéa's command, send it on its way.

Mailing Petroff's package from Stockholm at Linnéa's command meant Petroff would receive the letter and CD when Linnéa chose for them to arrive. This would leave time for her "Dear Petroff" letter to work—the letter that had a special, but temporary purpose to fulfill.

Linnéa unfolded the sheet of paper and reread the lines. Nodded to herself. Slid it into the letter envelope. The only words scrawled on this envelope were "Vassili Aleksandrovich Petroff," because Linnéa would not be mailing it.

When she had readied her notifications, she put the read-write CD-ROM back into its case, placed the video game disc on top of it, and returned the case the bottom of her purse. She added the claim check and key to the hidden compartment before she snapped it closed.

Almost done. A final task to perform.

From a folder hidden within her laptop's operating system files, Linnéa located and copied a string of text. She opened another command prompt and pasted the text. She stared at the prompt:

Execute? Y/N

Her finger hovered over the "y" key.

Exhaling, she pressed it.

Two seconds passed before the laptop whirred to life. The code she'd executed began to reset her laptop to factory settings, wiping every added program, driver, folder, file, and file fragment from her hard drive, then logging her off and shutting down. The process would complete its work by defragging the hard disk the next time the power button was pushed.

Marstead itself had ordered its IT department to install the fail-safe on its operatives' computers in the event their identities were compromised. Nothing could stop or interrupt the program's work once it began, and not a trace of data would remain when it finished. Christor had made sure of both.

Linnéa packed up her laptop, tidied her desk, scanned her office a last time. Picked up her things and walked with practiced confidence to Nyström's office.

She tapped on the door and peeked inside, a smile plastered on her face. "You wanted to see me again, Mickel?"

"Yes, uh, do come in. Just needed to confirm to Alvarsson that you will make the meeting tomorrow?"

"Yes, I will. I was, fortunately, able to reach Vassili Aleksandrovich in Moscow. As we surmised, he was unhappy with the unplanned trip, but he is preoccupied with state business at present. I assured him that Zakhar would see me safely to Stockholm and back, and he acquiesced." She winked at Nyström. "Petroff has no clue that he'll never see me again."

Nyström blanched at Linnéa's "unconscious" *double entendre*, but her guileless smile never faltered. Instead, she glanced at her wristwatch.

"Goodness! Is it really 1:30? I must hurry if we are to catch the 4:05 train to Tallinn."

"Yes, indeed." Nyström rose and extended his hand. "I, ah, wish you the best of luck, Linnéa."

She thought he'd turned a little gray around the edges and couldn't resist a last dig.

"I won't forget your steadfast friendship and trust, Mickel."

Indeed, I won't.

She turned and paced toward the elevator, leaving him to deal with his conscience. She hoped he had choked on his parting words to her.

I wish you the best of luck? With your knife embedded in my back?

Käre Gud! Dear God—I will need much more than luck.

LINNÉA SPENT THE SHORT ride down to the ground floor prepping herself. When the elevator doors pinged at the lobby, she fixed the same smile on her face that she'd plastered there for Nyström's benefit. She cut her eyes toward the two Marstead security guards and cranked up the wattage. The guard with whom she was unacquainted dipped his chin, acknowledging her, but did not return her smile. He seemed wary. Alert. Jonas, the guard she'd known for years, swallowed and cut his eyes elsewhere.

Ah. Nyström has instructed the guards to watch what I do. Alvarsson's orders, no doubt. And Alvarsson has probably assigned other Marstead agents to follow us to the train station.

She passed through the turnstile, and Zakhar jumped to his feet. Before he had opportunity to speak, Linnéa gushed, "Wonderful news, Zakhar! I have received a special assignment. It is quite the honor. Vassili Aleksandrovich will be so pleased."

She hoped her performance was persuasive. Her life depended upon it.

Zakhar's brow creased as Linnéa, without pause, dropped the assignment dossier in his hands and paced toward the exit, her heels clicking on the floor.

"Does Stepan have the car at the curb?"

"Yes. Stepan and Alyona returned from checking us into the hotel and are waiting outside."

"Good, but now we have a train to catch this afternoon. I am to attend a briefing on the new assignment in Stockholm tomorrow, midmorning. Tell Stepan to return us to the hotel so we can pack and check out."

Zakhar was quick to open and hold the entrance door for her. Linnéa let him. She turned and waved to Jonas. Jonas waved back. The two Marstead guards seemed to relax their vigilance.

Zakhar followed her outside. "Miss Olander, Stockholm has not been authorized."

Linnéa lifted a palm to stop him. "This assignment is time-sensitive and will bring a great deal of attention to Russia's technological advancements." She slid into the rear seat of the waiting car. "We are to take the ferry from Tallinn to Stockholm this evening. You have our itinerary in the folder I gave you."

In the rearview mirror, Linnéa saw Zakhar's jaw jut out. "Petroff has not authorized Stockholm."

Linnéa shot back, *"Then I suggest that you call him,* because we must check out of the hotel and be on the 4:05 train to Tallinn if we expect to make this evening's ferry to Stockholm."

On the seat next to her, Alyona shifted uneasily. "Mistress—"

"Yes—*I am your mistress,* and you do well to remember that. We *will* leave for Stockholm this evening!"

When they arrived at the hotel, Linnéa waited until Zakhar opened the door for her. As she stepped out, she addressed her three companions.

"Vassili Aleksandrovich will not tolerate losing out on this opportunity to showcase Russia's achievements before the world. If you are concerned about this trip, call him immediately and find out for yourselves, but I must not be late to the meeting tomorrow."

She turned on her heel and marched into the hotel lobby, confident that Zakhar would do just what she had goaded him to do. Linnéa headed for their suite with Alyona running behind her.

Twenty minutes later, Zakhar strode into the room. Full of himself, he announced, "I have spoken to Vassili Aleksandrovich at length." He lifted his chin and slid his eyes over Linnéa. "He was most displeased that Marstead did not provide you with adequate time to consider this assignment and make appropriate arrangements."

He arched one brow and held out a slip of paper. "He wishes you to call him at this number. Immediately."

Ordinarily, Linnéa would have sent Zakhar and Alyona from the room, but her present plans called for a different approach. With an imperious finger, she pointed to the phone.

"Place the call, Zakhar."

He and Alyona exchanged glances. Linnéa was behaving in an uncharacteristically high-handed manner, and it unsettled them both. Zakhar lifted the receiver and dialed the front desk, asking them to charge the call to their room. When Petroff's aide and then Petroff himself answered, he handed the receiver to Linnéa.

She placed it to her ear. "*Da?*"

"Linnéa?"

"Vassili Aleksandrovich, *moy lyubimyy!* It rejoices my heart to hear your voice," she murmured.

Zakhar and Alyona could make out Petroff's shouted response from across the room. So loud was his roar, that Linnéa was forced to pull the receiver away from her ear.

"What is this *blanking* nonsense Zakhar tells me of? You were making plans to leave Russia without consulting me? Without obtaining my permission?"

Linnéa's astonishment echoed back to him. "What do you mean, darling? Why on earth would I do that? I knew you would not appreciate the precipitous nature of this new assignment any more than I did, so I told Zakhar to call you directly and apprise you of the situation. Did he not do so?"

Petroff's voice softened. "He failed to mention that *you* instructed him to call me. Tell me, then, what new trick this *bleeping* company of yours is trying to pull?"

"Ah, but I gave Zakhar the details. I handed the folder to him myself—the entire assignment, including the itinerary! Did he share *none* of the particulars with you?" She rounded on Zakhar, her eyes raking angry furrows into him.

Zakhar reddened, opened and closed his mouth, and shifted from foot to foot. Alyona edged away from him.

"That fool Zakhar told me nothing, only that Marstead—*with no warning*—told you to attend a meeting in Stockholm *tomorrow.*"

"Presumptuous of them, was it not?" Linnéa agreed. "I could scarcely believe it myself. Because they said the project would be a feather in Russia's cap, they *ordered* me to attend! Ordered me! I posed my objections, but they overruled me and gave me no say in the matter."

Petroff cursed Marstead again, then calmed himself. "I really cannot spare the time and effort at this moment to evaluate Marstead's impetuous, *bleeping* behavior. I am too embroiled in the present crisis. Therefore, you will tell Marstead that I expressly forbid you to attend this so-called briefing. Tell them, furthermore, that I require you to arrive in Moscow by tomorrow evening. Come to the apartment. I will try to get away for a few hours."

Linnéa gushed and sighed. "How I long to be home with you, my love!"

Abruptly, her demeanor and affect pivoted. She groaned, low in her throat.

"What is it? What is wrong, Linnéa?

"Oh, my, but this has been a long and tedious day. First, losing you and the remainder of our holiday to this urgent business in Moscow, then trying to please my Marstead superiors—followed by Zakhar's bumbling ineptitude.

"I am quite distressed. The pressure has brought on a terrible headache. Ah, you were right, as always, Vassi. It is time for me to quit this job."

She allowed another moan to follow.

"Are you all right, darling?"

Linnéa hesitated a tick. She dropped her forehead into her free hand and whimpered in pain. "*Oy! Oy mne bol'no!* It hurts! My neck and shoulders. They are so tight, so constricting! And the pain. It is radiating from my head into my eyes. I-I am quite ill from it."

"Do not worry, my darling. I shall take care of everything. Put that fool Zakhar on the line and fret yourself no longer."

This was the cloying, sickly-sweet side of Petroff that Linnéa knew well, the part of his pathological personality she had anticipated—had counted on—appearing.

"Oh, thank you, Vassi, my darling. What would I do without you?" Hanging her head further, she offered the receiver to Zakhar.

He took it from her hand much like he might receive a draft of poison. "*Da*, Vassili Aleksandrovich?"

Shouts blasted from the earpiece.

"Zakhar, *ty bezmozglyy idiot*, you idiot! You have *not* safeguarded Miss Olander's well-being as I ordered you!"

Zakhar studied his feet and pursed his lips. Petroff did not expect an answer. He expected Zakhar to suffer his insults in silence and then repair the disaster of his own making. Zakhar racked his brain for a way out of the mess he found himself in—a mess that had caught him unawares.

He shifted his gaze and saw Linnéa sitting on a sofa, Alyona standing behind her, rubbing Linnéa's shoulders. Linnéa seemed in genuine distress, but Zakhar was unconvinced. The events of the past two hours perplexed him. Left him skeptical and guarded.

As he watched Alyona work on Linnéa's neck, he found himself thinking, *Ah, how I would like to put my hands about your neck, Linnéa Olander.*

To Petroff he replied, "Vassili Aleksandrovich, I will book Miss Olander into Madame Krupina's Spa within the hour for a stress-relieving soak in their hot pools, followed by a deep tissue massage. Whatever Miss Olander requires, I will supply. I will take care of her, Vassili Aleksandrovich. I promise you may trust me. I will see to her every need."

"Trust you?" A plethora of denigrating expletives flowed across the line before Petroff had satisfied himself. "My duties call me away now, Zakhar. You have caused me many difficulties this day. Do not fail me again."

"I will not, Vassili Aleksandrovich."

———⁃❧⁃———

CHAPTER 4

LP

"OH, MY SWEET GIRL! Come in, come in." Madame Krupina ushered Linnéa, Alyona, and Zakhar into the exclusive spa herself and reached for Linnéa. Linnéa seemed to wilt in her arms.

Linnéa had patronized Madame's spa many times in the past decade. She was well-known to the staff and proprietress—as was Petroff and his lofty position in the government. Madame would spare no expense, no preferential treatment for Linnéa's benefit.

Linnéa moaned. "Ah, my head . . ."

"Why, what have they done to you, darling girl!"

"A wicked headache, dear Nadezhda . . . I can scarcely see or walk. Please help me."

Madame Krupina's reproachful glare seared Zakhar and Alyona where they stood. She addressed a male attendant. "Get these two out of my sight."

"Wait—it is my job to remain near Miss Olander," Zakhar protested. "Vassili Aleksandrovich demands it."

"And did he demand that you permit Miss Olander to come to this dreadful state? I think not!" She pointed with her chin. "No men are allowed in the women's bathing area. You will wait with the other servants." She jerked her chin again. "Go on! Get them away from me. Disgraceful!"

To another attendant, she commanded, "See to Miss Olander's things." That attendant picked up Linnéa's purse and the spa bag Alyona had prepared at Linnéa's instruction. Madame returned her attention to Linnéa. "Now, let us get you into a hot bath to soak away your troubles, shall we?"

"Oh, yes. Please."

Under Madame's watchful eye, Linnéa was helped into a hot tub in a private room where the air was heated, heavy with moisture, and fragrant with healing herbs—lavender, rosemary, eucalyptus. After she had soaked for twenty minutes in the hottest water she could bear, an attendant assisted her from the pool and into a tepid shower.

When the attendant had rinsed and toweled Linnéa off, wrapping her in an enormous, preheated Turkish bath sheet, Madame returned.

She said softly, "I have two masseuses standing by, Miss Olander. Galina is an expert in deep tissue massage and reflexology. But perhaps the source of your pain requires a softer touch? Runa comes to us from your home country. Her specialty is gentle Swedish massage. Tell me which you prefer."

Linnéa's head wobbled, and the attendant was quick to help her sit.

"I think . . . I think, darling Nadezhda, that I must rest quietly first. Perhaps a nap?"

"Surely. Galina! Runa! Prepare a room for Miss Olander's particular use. She will require a comfortable bed and absolute quiet." She pointed for the attendants to precede them from the room.

As the women grabbed Linnéa's things and fled to do Madame's bidding, Madame leaned close to Linnéa. "What do you need of me?"

"An exit. Quickly. Then for you to stall them until I return."

It was true that Linnéa had patronized Madame's spa many times in the past decade. It was also true that the woman had been in Marstead's pay even longer, providing another avenue for Linnéa to pass information to her superiors.

Madame had noted bruising on Linnéa's body before, and she saw the blood in Linnéa's left eye today. The older woman's fingers caressed Linnéa's temple where her foundation could not hide the bruises.

When Linnéa flinched, Madame murmured, "I shall do all I can."

She led her to the room Galina and Runa had prepared, then shooed them away, locking the door after them.

Immediately, Linnéa rummaged through the spa bag, pulling out clothes. She dressed in dark slacks, a thigh-length top with side pockets, and shoes she could run in. She took up her handbag.

"Which way out?"

Madame put a finger to her lips. "Give me a moment."

While she was gone, Linnéa withdrew the key and claim check from the compartment at the bottom of her handbag. She slipped both into her bra.

She also fished out an envelope. Her delaying tactic. Slid it under the pillow.

Good as her word, Madame returned in less than a minute. "Follow me."

Madame had cleared the way to an alley exit off the laundry room by sending the laundress to restock the linen closets throughout the spa. Madame fumbled with the three deadbolts on the door, snapping them open.

"I will leave the door unlocked against your return but knock first before you enter. I will instruct the laundress to fetch me at your knock, and I will, again, send her away before I let you in—in this way, you will not be seen either coming or going."

Madame put her hand on Linnéa's arm. "How long will you be gone, my dear?"

"At least two hours."

"Two hours! Will that insufferable lout wait so long?"

"If he questions how long I am gone, say the massage made me drowsy, that I am sleeping off the headache. You must keep him at bay, even if I am delayed. Can you do it?"

"*Da*, if I must," but she looked uncertain.

"If you run out of options, and he discovers that I am gone? Then you must convince him I left while you thought me sleeping."

"I can do that—but do not let it come to that, eh?"

"I . . . won't."

Linnéa's lie caught in her throat. Madame Krupina had been nothing but good to her, and now she was leaving her to shoulder Zakhar's—and Petroff's—wrath.

The older woman sighed. "So. You are leaving that animal, Petroff? And you must sneak away? Without your . . . employer's permission?"

Linnéa didn't answer.

Madame shook her head. "Then, I wish you well, my dear. I will give you as much time as I can manage."

"Thank you for everything, Nadezhda."

They embraced, and Linnéa wiped her eyes.

Wrapping a bland scarf about her head to veil her hair, Linnéa slipped out into the alley. Following the exit strategy Linnéa and Christor had devised two years ago, she set off down the alley and stopped not far from the corner.

The section of the city where Madame Krupina's Spa resided was older, of a classic period in St. Petersburg's history. Many of the structures were constructed of brick or quarried stone. The building on the corner was of the latter—and where the corner building abutted its neighbor, Linnéa's fingers scrabbled for a loose stone at knee height.

The stone scraped on its surrounding stones and resisted her efforts as she grappled with it. When she was finally able to grasp it with both hands, she heaved the stone out of its place and set it on the ground. Then she reached inside the space where the stone had been. Her fingers found a cloth bag, thick and bulky, large enough to fill both her hands.

She had to tug and pull at it, too, before it came out of the hole. When it came loose, she glanced up and down the alley, then stuffed it into her purse. She picked up the stone and pushed it back into its place in the wall.

Her next stop was two blocks away, a pawn shop—what in Russia is called a "lombard house." Lombards and "lombard banking" were relics of an early century's Christian prohibition against usury, that is, charging fellow

Christians interest on loans. The original lombard houses took collateral against a cash loan. That had changed. Today's lombards were tantamount to loan sharks, charging stiff interest rates and showing no mercy over late payments.

Linnéa and Christor's plan had required a lombard shop whose owner was willing to do more than offer loans, an owner who—for a not-so-insignificant fee—would store a trunk indefinitely and keep his trap shut about it. Christor had approached an owner, one Fyodor Dudnik, who had been in business fifteen years but whose venture had never risen above "middling." For a cash gift up front and the promise of an anonymous cash fee received through the mail each month, Dudnik had agreed to store the trunk.

Linnéa slipped into the shop. It was not a thriving enterprise. The only other customer was at the service counter toward the back. Linnéa wandered behind some tall shelves that screened her from view. She tugged at the Velcro closure in her purse and removed the HK. She had chambered a round in her office. Now, she slipped the ready weapon into her right pocket. Then she withdrew the claim check and key from her bra and put the key deep into her left pocket.

When the customer had concluded his business and exited the shop, she approached the counter. Dudnik's rheumy gaze was lackluster. Bored.

"How may I help you, miss?"

Linnéa placed the claim check on the counter. "I would like to redeem this item, please."

The man pulled eyeglasses down from his head and studied the number. She saw the moment he comprehended which "item" she was calling for and what its departure meant. no more monthly cash envelopes. His mouth turned down and hardened.

"You will continue to receive the same payment for six months," Linnéa murmured, "in consideration of your service . . . and discretion."

His downturned lips grimaced. "How can I be sure of this?"

Linnéa withdrew her wallet and counted out five sizable bills.

He reached for the money then shifted his bleary eyes back to her. "The trunk must contain something valuable."

"You are a judicious man, Mr. Dudnik, a pragmatist, I think. I am certain you have examined the trunk. It contains nothing remarkable, does it?" Linnéa presumed the owner had searched the chest for contraband or valuables. No one in their right mind would pay so much or so long for insignificant, worthless content.

He looked her up and down, appraising her. "Still . . . might be of note to the authorities."

"As I said, we will continue to pay you for another six months. I ask you. Will the authorities do the same?"

The man was stubborn. "Maybe I ask them and find out."

Linnéa drew the gun from her pocket. Raised its blue barrel waist height and pointed it at Dudnik's flabby belly. "And maybe they will find that you were killed during a robbery."

His hands twitched and Linnéa shook her head. "*Nyet*. A bad idea, my friend. Bring out your weapon—slowly, slowly—and place it on the counter."

He dragged out a heavy, antiquated revolver—likely a remnant of World War II, what the Russians dubbed the Great Patriotic War—and, with a clunk, dropped it where Linnéa pointed.

She picked it up, stuffed it into her pocket, then addressed him with a knowing smile. "Really, Mr. Dudnik, why should we argue at the end of such a successful arrangement when I am willing to sweeten our bargain?"

She inclined her head toward the handbag hanging off her left arm. "You see my bag? Italian. Bottega Veneta. Worth thousands of rubles. I will leave it—and the trunk—with you after I have taken what I came for."

She shrugged. "Or, I will take whatever I wish, including what is in your register, and you will not care, because you will be dead. Your choice—whichever you prefer." She smiled again. "I think you know which deal is best, hmm?"

"*Da, da.*" Dudnik gestured behind him. "Come with me."

"You will lock the shop door first."

Under her supervision, he lumbered to the front of the store, locked the door, and turned over the sign.

"Give me the key, please. You will get it back when I depart."

He grumbled but complied.

"Now. You go ahead of me, and I will follow," Linnéa instructed.

He led her to a storage room in the back of the shop, an interior room with a stout, reinforced door and an impressive lock.

"Bring the trunk out here to me."

He did her bidding, unlocking the storage room and dragging a rusty hand truck inside. Linnéa heard him grunting as he shifted boxes about and loaded something on the hand truck. Minutes later, he maneuvered a Victorian dome-top steamer trunk through the door and let the hand truck down.

Linnéa backed about six feet away where the floor had open space. "Over here, please."

He wheeled the trunk to where she indicated and slid the hand truck out from under it. Linnéa gestured with her gun.

"Now, Mr. Dudnik. Into the storage room with you."

His eyes widened. "No! Please—if you lock me in, I will die there! No one but me works in my shop. No one will hear me, even if I scream!"

"I don't intend to lock you in—not unless I need to. Unless, let us say, you refuse to give me your word."

"My word?"

Linnéa thought it likely that no one had taken Dudnik at his word for many years. Shifting the gun to her left hand, she used her right hand to unsnap the clasp of her watch—a Van Cleef & Arpels bracelet watch.

She set the ornate timepiece on the trunk and backed away. "Three hours. Three hours by this watch. Give me your word that you will wait three hours before exiting the room."

"Stay in the room three hours?"

"Yes. I will have someone observing from afar. If you leave your shop before the three hours elapse, you will never again receive an envelope of cash. If you abide by our agreement, six more payments. What do you say?"

He nodded and reached for the watch. "And I may keep it?"

Linnéa could see him evaluating and pricing it. Her mouth twitched. *As if I'd return in three hours and ask for it back? Not likely.*

"You drive a hard bargain, sir. Yes, you may keep the watch—the watch, the handbag, and the trunk. But I give you a warning. Keep the watch out of sight for a year or more."

She considered him before lowering her chin in a confiding manner. "You see, Mr. Dudnik, some men like to control their women, yes? First, they slap and beat them. Call them vile names. Afterward, they shower them with gifts such as this. Such men are wealthy. Powerful. Connected." She narrowed her eyes. "Quite ruthless."

He licked his lips. "Just so. You are running away. Running away from a monster. I understand." He glanced at her. Shrugged. "I can sympathize."

She nodded. "Thank you. Yes, *a monster.* He will be hunting me, and if the monster were to find in your possession such a distinctive bauble—a *gift* from him, you understand—he would be very displeased *with you.* Why, he would think you helped me, and that would not end well for you."

"I-I see. As you say, I will keep it hidden. Perhaps I will send it out of the country to sell."

"A wise notion, Mr. Dudnik." She waved him into the room. "It will take me thirty minutes or more to assemble what I need from the trunk. Do not doubt me. If you open the door while I am still here, I will shoot you."

She sighed and added as an afterthought, "Cheaper for me, you know. And what is it they say? Dead men tell no tales? So—get in there and give me no reason to change my mind."

He went in and closed the door behind him. She heard the handle latch and turned her attention to the trunk.

"You will not lock me in? I have your word?" his fearful voice called from beyond the walls. Only seconds had passed.

"Try the door, Mr. Dudnik—this one time only."

He eased it open and peeked around its edge. "*Da.* Okay. I believe you."

After he had again shut himself inside the storage room, Linnéa wheeled the hand truck out of her way. She withdrew the key from her bra, used it to unlock the trunk, and lifted the lid.

Inside she found a puzzle of Christor's making and grinned.

Planning Linnéa's escape contingency had been an exercise in creativity Christor had reveled in. They had hammered out the plan, honing and simplifying the details, whenever Linnéa had been able to connect her laptop to broadband service and text in private chat rooms or speak over their secret VoIP connections.

At first sight, the trunk contained a lunatic's dismembered bicycle. wheels, handlebars, seat, fenders, springs, odd lengths of fabricated metal, some folded paper, a paper sack of bits and pieces, screws and washers. A second sack held small tools.

Linnéa unloaded everything from the trunk and dumped the contents of both sacks on the floor. She selected a short pry bar and used it to pull the trunk apart from the inside. Its walls and floor gave way and revealed a wealth of sundry items the pawn shop owner had not imagined were hidden within. Even so, the totality of the trunk's contents, spread around her, would make little sense to the uninformed.

Linnéa chuckled under her breath. *Well done, Christor!*

With all the pieces—and a sheet of instructions—before her, Linnéa began to assemble them. Some parts were calculated distraction. She tossed those back into the trunk to get them out of her way and kept working.

Twenty minutes into her hasty assembly, she finished. She tossed the tools, leftover bits, and Dudnik's heavy gun into the trunk, too. The instructions she set aside.

Then she stripped off her clothes and dressed in the garb she'd found wrapped in plastic garbage bags within the trunk's fake floor. It wasn't easy putting them on. A layered, bulky bodysuit. The shoes and their padded stockings hitched to a girdle hanging from the bodysuit. A dingy, flowing housedress. A tent-like, calf-length coat that buttoned up the front to her chin.

She opened a jar the size of her palm, tore the freshness wrapper from its neck, dug her fingers into the gel within, and smoothed a thin layer over her face and neck.

While the gel was drying, Linnéa emptied her designer handbag onto the floor and sorted through its bits and pieces. She set aside gun, magazines, CD-ROM case, padded mailers, and the thick cloth bag she'd plucked from the hole behind the stone wall in the alley.

She tugged at the bag's drawstring and dumped out its contents. Three passports. A single driver's license and credit card belonging to one of the passports. Four bundles of cash in various denominations and currencies— rubles, kronor, pounds, and dollars. A coin purse half-filled with Russian kopecks and rubles.

Nodding her relief, she selected the Russian money and the Russian ID. She put the other IDs, cash, and envelope back into the cloth bag. Next, she piled her shoes and clothes into the garbage bag that had held her present clothing. She tossed the sheet of instructions and everything left over from her purse into the garbage bag with her clothes.

The compact HK and its spare magazine stared at her from the floor. She had intended to tuck it deep into the cleavage of her bra, but later? When she boarded an airline? It would be less likely to be noticed if it were in the padded compartment of her Italian handbag.

I promised the shop owner my handbag but, as it turns out, I will need it again.

"Mr. Dudnik?"

His worried voice came back at once. *"Da?"*

"I apologize, but I cannot leave the handbag after all."

He was quite amicable. *"Da, da,* is not a problem, not a problem," he insisted, the fear that she might also change her mind about locking him into the storage room bleeding through.

She laughed under her breath, removed two fifty-ruble bills from her supply of Russian cash, and laid them on the trunk. "I'm leaving a little compensation on the trunk."

"Very thoughtful but quite unnecessary, I assure you," he replied.

Still chuckling softly, she placed the designer handbag into her contraption, piled the garbage bag on top of the handbag, and spread a small blanket over both. She scooped the items she'd decided to retain from her handbag into a worn fabric sack with a generous shoulder strap. Closed the jar of gel and added it to the sack. Strung the sack across her shoulders. Pulled her hair back and fastened it into a tight bun. Wound a thick, ugly scarf about her head and tied it under her chin. Fit an uncomfortable "appliance" into her mouth and ran her tongue over its unaccustomed contours. Drew on a pair of stained, ragged gloves.

Exhaled. *Ready.*

She wheeled her assembled contrivance to the entrance of the pawn shop. Unlocked the door, pushed the contraption outside, locked the door behind her, and dropped the key through the letter slot.

Down the sidewalk she ambled, pushing the contraption before her, stooping over its handle, sometimes mumbling to the sack of garbage she'd tucked under the musty blanket within it, occasionally muttering to herself, a threadbare fabric sack bumping against her side.

She wandered without aim down the street, crossing at the intersection, turning at the next corner, discovering an alley. Down the alley she roamed, stopping at the rubbish bins behind shops, restaurants, and businesses, exchanging bits of her trash for select bits of theirs, eventually returning to the street. Along the way she passed a postal box.

She paused, fumbled about in the sack, and retrieved two padded mailers. She let them drop into the postal box and continued on her way, unhurried, blending into the backdrop of the city.

An hour and a half and nine blocks later, she reached the outskirts of the more "touristy" part of the city. She wandered along the Fontanka River Embankment. When she crossed to the other side, the traffic and walkways grew crowded with visitors and sightseers coming and going from Mikhailovsky Castle and Mikhailovsky Garden, the State Hermitage Museum—formerly The Menshikov Palace, winter home of Catherine the Great—and other attractions.

She moved slowly on, curving northward, noting that she had exhausted the two hours Madame Krupina had promised her. Soon—perhaps already—Zakhar would insist on seeing Linnéa.

Ah, but you will never see Linnéa again, Zakhar. I know you will browbeat Madame and call Vassili Aleksandrovich. He will rage and order you to ask his FSB "friends" to search for Linnéa, but she will never be found.

She no longer exists.

Outside the western boundary of Mikhailovsky Garden, she drew near one of St. Petersburg's most iconic sites, Cathedral of the Savior on Spilled Blood. It stood on the Griboyedov Channel Embankment, a grand edifice, its spires and onion towers built upon the hallowed ground where Emperor Alexander II had been assassinated by political nihilists. Alexander's son had erected the church on the very spot where his father had fallen. It, too, was now a museum, another tourist attraction.

Ah, the tourists.

They stared, nudged their companions, and shared smiles. Some took pictures of the hunched, elderly Russian *babushka*—the affectionate Russian term for grandmother. Even in the warm, late summer, the impoverished peasant woman wore the traditional bulky headscarf from which the term "babushka" was drawn.

Her red, wrinkled forehead furrowed and frowned. Her mouthful of stained, crooked teeth mumbled nonsense. She was a relic of the past, her mind mired there still. Her gnarled hands, clad in stained gloves, grasped the handle of a faded, moth-eaten pram—perhaps the same conveyance in which she had once walked infant grandchildren. Swollen legs appeared beneath her ugly, worn coat, and bloated feet overran the once-black shoes—shoes now scuffed and run down in the heels—as she shuffled along and continued her ponderous journey. Some sympathetic visitors to the city tossed coins into her pram.

The *babushka* did not notice.

She lumbered on, unhurried, following the Palace Embankment, crossing the Neva by the Liteyny Bridge, block by laborious block, moving toward the Finlyandskiy Railway Station. At the station, the old woman's trembling fingers paid out, a single coin at a time, the fare to Moscow. Two station workers assisted her painful climb aboard a car to a seat with enough space ahead of it to accommodate her battered pram.

A passenger sitting across the aisle attempted to speak kindly to her, but the old woman became agitated and worked herself into a frenzy, shouting nonsense and gesticulating wildly. Around her, passengers averted their eyes and pulled in on themselves.

After her outburst, she was left alone, the city and then the fields flashing by as the train left St. Petersburg and journeyed four hours southeast to Moscow. Eventually, the old woman lapsed into silence, then leaned against the window and dozed. She would sleep until the train reached its destination.

That day, the woman known as Linnéa Olander disappeared from Madame Krupina's Spa, leaving no trace behind. She missed the train to Tallinn on which her company had booked her and, later, the ferry to Stockholm. Both Marstead and Petroff sent their agents to scour the streets of St. Petersburg and watch the train stations and airport and the roads in and out of the city—but to no avail.

They guarded the border crossings out of Russia and sought her on both public and private transportation. Not one of them believed she would flee, not to safety, but deeper into the heart of Russia. Not one of them thought to scour the streets of Moscow.

THORESEN HOMESTEAD

KARI MICHAELS THORESEN drew a plate of pancakes from the oven where they were warming and plopped it on the table beside a plate of scrambled eggs, another of bacon, and a bowl of fruit.

"Robbie! Shannon! Breakfast!"

"Coming!"

As the kids slid into their seats, Søren put down his paper. Kari took her seat and the four of them joined hands.

Søren prayed, "Lord, we are grateful for this food and for every blessing you give us. Please be with Max as he begins his day, help Grandma Polly and Grandpa Gene, and be with Aunt Laynie to keep her safe. Amen."

A chorus of "amens" echoed him. Søren and nine-year-old Robbie plowed into the food like there was no tomorrow. At age eleven, Shannon was already overly concerned about becoming "fat," and generally ate only eggs and fruit for breakfast. This morning she stared at her plate without picking up her fork.

Kari noticed. "What's the matter, Shannon?"

Shannon looked up. "I was just thinking about Aunt Laynie, Mama. Why doesn't she ever write or call? Why doesn't she come visit? Doesn't she love us anymore?"

Søren and Kari exchanged glances. It was not the first time Shannon had asked those or other probing questions. Answering them would not become easier as the children grew and began thinking for themselves—particularly Shannon, whose sensitive nature seemed to perceive when something was amiss. Kari had decided it was time to give Shannon a glimpse into the truth about her aunt.

Kari made sure she had Shannon's attention. "Aunt Laynie's work is difficult and requires discretion, Shannon. It's also not something we can ever discuss outside our family. That is why we don't talk about her to anyone."

Shannon's eyes widened as she took in Kari's meaning.

Robbie, his mouth filled with pancake, asked, "What's dis-dis-discretion?"

"It means we keep it to ourselves, Son," Søren murmured.

"Okay." Robbie turned back to his plate, but Shannon watched Kari put a finger to her lips.

"Later," Kari promised. "Right now, you need to finish your breakfast, so we can have our Bible time before you catch the bus."

Five minutes later, the kids carried their plates to the kitchen and stacked them on the counter to make room for their Bibles. Søren read aloud from 2 Corinthians 11. When he got to verse 26, something in Kari's spirit moved.

I have been constantly on the move.
I have been in danger from rivers, in danger from bandits,
in danger from my fellow Jews, in danger from Gentiles;
in danger in the city, in danger in the country,
in danger at sea; and in danger from false believers.
I have labored and toiled and have often gone without sleep;
I have known hunger and thirst and have often gone without food;
I have been cold and naked.

The word, "danger," repeated eight times, seemed to resonate within her. After the kids had run out the door and up the slope to catch their school bus, Kari—who usually tore into kitchen cleanup so she could get to her own work—sat still and quiet, a puzzled look creasing her brow.

Søren was already up, ready to get back to his fields, when he realized she hadn't moved. "What is it, Kari? Thinking about Laynie?"

"Yes, but . . . something is bothering me."

"Oh?"

"Søren, I think Laynie is in danger. I think the Holy Spirit is warning me, asking me to cover Laynie in prayer."

"Kari, because we haven't heard from Laynie in years, I'm more inclined to think we'll never see her again or even know what became of her. However, I'm not going to trivialize this warning. We've both seen God perform miracles in response to our prayers."

"So, you'll pray with me?"

"Absolutely."

He sat next to Kari and took her hand. "Lord, Kari and I come to you right now concerning Laynie. You know where she is and what is happening. You see her, Father, right now. We ask that you help her. Cover her with your sheltering wings and bring her safely home to us—just as you once brought Kari safely home to her family.

"We ask these things in Jesus' mighty and powerful name—*Jesus*, the name above *all* names. Amen."

CHAPTER 5

ZAKHAR'S HANDS clamped themselves like iron bands about Madame Krupina's throat and squeezed. He throttled and shook her like a terrier shakes a sewer rat.

"Where is she? Where has she gone? Tell me!"

Madame Krupina's fingers clawed at his hands on her neck but her efforts were entirely ineffective. Her mouth opened. Her eyes bulged. Her face reddened and then darkened toward blue.

A male attendant and a male masseuse, alerted by Madame's female attendants, rushed to the hall and grappled with Zakhar, finally pulling him off their employer.

Madame fell against the wall, gasping and choking. When she could speak, she spat, "I told you, I don't know, you imbecile! She soaked in the hot tub, then asked for a quiet room to sleep off her headache. We thought she was resting and did not wish to disturb her. No one saw her depart. And why would we think to watch her? Is my spa a prison that I should prevent my clients from leaving when they wish?"

By now a knot of Madame's employees had gathered in the hallway, and a number of clients peered from behind doors to view the spectacle.

Linnéa's maid, Alyona, hung back, terrified that blame for her mistress' disappearance would fall upon her. Petroff had enough rage to encompass Zakhar and overflow onto her—easily!

"Let go of me," Zakhar growled.

Madame's men loosened their hold on him.

"Which exit did she use?"

"Not our main entrance," a young aesthetician declared. "I was on the front desk this afternoon. I can attest that she did not pass through the foyer."

Zakhar advanced on Madame—causing her men to catch hold of his arms and restrain him a second time. He shook them off. Stood nose-to-nose with Madame.

"How else might someone leave your miserable establishment?"

Madame drew herself up to her full height. "We have but two other routes. The employee entrance and a door in the laundry room that leads to the alley."

"Show me."

Her nose in the air, Madame gestured. "This way." To her employees she hissed, "What is this? The Bolshoi Circus? Tend to our clients!"

Except for Madame's two male attendants, the employees melted away, and the hall doors shut on excited whispers. Such juicy gossip!

Zakhar, Madame's men, and Alyona trailing behind them, followed the spa owner to the very back of the building into the steamy laundry. A young woman folding towels paused in her work.

Zakhar pointed at the only door. "Did anyone leave by that door?"

The girl's eyes widened. "*Nyet*, sir. That is, not that I saw."

"What do you mean, 'Not that I saw'?"

"I-I . . ." The girl cut her eyes to her employer. "I did leave the laundry for a time. To-to restock the linens—as I always do. I suppose someone could have used the door while I was gone, but we keep it locked and—"

"Bah!" Zakhar flung open the door. "As you can see, it is *not* locked." He stepped into the alley. Hands on his hips, he looked up and down the narrow cobblestones.

Behind his back, Madame winked her approval to the laundry girl and placed a finger to her lips. As Zakhar strode back inside, he wiped his face with a hand. Now past the first frenzy of temper, he experienced a different emotion. *Fear.* For an instant—a mere fraction of a moment—he considered abandoning Petroff and leaving the country.

He trembled at the knowledge of what Petroff would do to the woman when he found her. Above all things, Petroff demanded obedience—the penalties for acts of infidelity were horrifying. Zakhar had seen such punishment inflicted on Petroff's earlier women, women before Linnéa's time. Zakhar knew that failing in his duty was one thing. Failure could be atoned for—but disloyalty was unforgivable.

He put the idea of fleeing Mother Russia straight out of his mind.

One of Madame's attendants tugged on her sleeve. "Madame. I have just now found this. I was changing the bedding in the room where Miss Olander was sleeping. It was under the pillow." She handed her employer a plain envelope.

Madame took the envelope. "It appears Miss Olander has left a message."

Zakhar snatched the envelope from Madame and scanned the simple scrawl upon it.

Vassili Aleksandrovich Petroff
Personal and Confidential

He dared not open the letter but, even unopened, it confirmed what he believed. The fool of a woman had defied Petroff and run away.

"I must use your telephone. Urgently."

"Come," Madame murmured. "Come to my office with me." She threw over her shoulder, "I do hope Miss Olander will be all right?"

Zakhar's lips curled into a snarl, yet he kept his thoughts to himself.

You hope that whore will be "all right," do you? She is as good as dead! But before Petroff grants her that kindness? She will beg and pray for death from a man who knows no mercy.

AT EXACTLY 4:15, while Zakhar's shaking hand was dialing the number to reach Petroff's aide, Lars Alvarsson answered a call from Mickel Nyström. Alvarsson sank back in his chair as Nyström reported that Linnéa Olander had *not* boarded the 4:05 train from St. Petersburg to Tallinn.

His reaction was much the same as Zakhar's. "What do you mean she didn't get on the train? *Where is she?*"

He listened. "She went to a spa with her entourage? The car is still parked there? Well? Is *she* still there? Then *find out*, you fool!"

He hung up slowly, but his thoughts were racing. He'd received his orders from on high. For the secure future of the Marstead intelligence network and to protect the fact that a Marstead agent had been in place *for seven years* within the highest circles of the Russian government, Linnéa was to be "retired." The job was to be done in such a way that Petroff—and the FSB—would never suspect Linnéa's duplicity.

As much as Alvarsson detested those orders, he'd had no choice but to follow them. So, where was the woman?

According to Nyström, Linnéa asked for and received Petroff's permission to take the ferry to Stockholm. He rubbed his jaw. *But had Petroff given his permission? Had Linnéa's persuasive genius convinced him? Not once in seven years has Petroff allowed Linnéa to return to Sweden without accompanying her.*

He frowned and sat up. *Wait. We have only Linnéa's word that she had gained Petroff's permission to leave Russia. What proof do we have that she even spoke to him?*

His phone rang. He picked up and listened as Nyström spoke, his sentences coming in quick, jerky phrases.

"I sent a female agent into the spa. She reports that it is in an uproar. When she asked what was happening, several people said a Russian man, bodyguard to one of Madame's patrons, had gone crazy and assaulted the spa's owner—"

Alvarsson interrupted him. "Mickel, forget the ruckus at the spa. It is a waste of precious time. You say Linnéa *assured* you she would be on the train because she had obtained Petroff's permission to come to Stockholm? Yes, well, she lied to you. *She is running.*"

Nyström spoke again but Alvarsson again cut him off. "Do not for one minute forget who we are dealing with. Linnéa is the consummate actress. This woman has fooled one of the most brilliant men in the world for seven years—you think she can't fool us, too?"

He glanced at the clock. "What time did she arrive at the spa?"

He listened to Nyström, then replied, "We can assume she slipped away from the spa forty-five minutes to an hour ago, enough time to leave the city. We have no authority to operate in Russia, so we must be discreet. Ask yourself, where would she would go?"

He listened, then added, "Think, Mickel. What do we know of Petroff? What will he do when he hears Linnéa has disappeared? He will believe she has fled from his control and brutality, yes? But he is far too possessive to release her—he would rather see her dead than free. We can assume he will roll out his FSB friends to hunt her down and dispose of her."

With Nyström's voice ringing in his ear, Alvarsson quickly devised a plan. "Yes, because of Petroff's reach within Russia, she would aim to cross the border as quickly as possible. That is certain. She would feel safest in countries where she could blend in, both culturally and ethnically. So! Set your people to work checking every route and mode of transportation out of St. Petersburg toward any western country."

He ground his teeth. "We must find her—before Petroff does."

Alvarsson slammed the receiver down and leaned his forehead on his fisted hands.

If Petroff's men were to locate Linnéa and kill her while she is attempting to flee, it would solve all our problems for us, but we cannot count on that. Linnéa has tweaked the tiger's tail. She has insulted Petroff's pride. He would order his people to bring Linnéa to him so that he could watch her suffer and cry for mercy.

And we must not forget that Petroff was KGB. He is far too smart, too experienced not to, upon reflection, suspect the worst of Linnéa. If he were to find her before we do? No matter how good she is, Petroff would break her.

In the end, she would tell him everything she knows—and implicate Marstead. We would be set back a decade. This is worse than bad—it is disastrous.

Perhaps I should consider the retirement I have put off three years already.

Stiffening his spine, Alvarsson left his office and headed for the elevator. Inside the lift's car, he bypassed the buttons and placed his fingers on the embossed words "Marstead International" and pressed twice. *Push-push.* And again. *Push-push.*

In actuality, Marstead owned the entirety of the four-story Stockholm building—including the basement and sub-basement levels, levels that did not appear in any architectural drawings, particularly those filed with the city. The hidden buttons would send the lift directly to the sub-basement without stopping at other floors.

The sub-basement was the most secure location in the building. It was home to Marstead's fortress-like IT Department and tech laboratory. It also held a secure, shielded room for classified meetings and conference calls.

Alvarsson locked himself in the room and picked up the STU—Secure Telephone Unit. He placed a call to a number he knew by heart. The area code was 757, Langley, Virginia.

A woman picked up immediately. "Marstead International. How may I direct your call?"

"Access Alpha Two Five Five."

"One moment please."

He had to wait five minutes before the man he'd called picked up.

"Saunders here. Initiating secure transmission." Saunders pressed a button, and they heard a low, fifteen-second *scree* as their call was encrypted.

Then Alvarsson spoke. "We have a situation."

PETROFF RESPONDED to Zakhar's news with predictable rage, and Zakhar was forced to listen to his employer's profanities and endure his verbal insults without comment—but he did so while nursing his own anger.

You had better hope Vassili Aleksandrovich's other men find you before I do, whore, he vowed.

Promising himself that he would make Linnéa pay for humiliating him—and planning just how he would do it—Zakhar left Madame's office. He was pale but outwardly controlled. Signaling Stepan and Alyona, they returned to their hotel to pack and check out.

From the hotel, Zakhar dialed the number Petroff had given him and issued terse orders. Within the hour, every train station, bus station, car rental business, taxi, airport, and border crossing out of Russia would receive Linnéa's description and photograph, courtesy of Petroff's cronies within the FSB.

Zakhar was not allowed to oversee the small army of FSB agents authorized to hunt Linnéa. Instead, Petroff ordered him to return to Moscow and hand deliver the sealed envelope Linnéa had left for Petroff.

Late that evening, he stood stone-faced and immobile before Petroff while the man read, reread, and read again the woman's letter.

Vassili Aleksandrovich, moy lyubimyy—*my love,*

I sorrow that with this letter I must break both our hearts. Oh, my darling, the fishbowl you must occupy because of your important position—without privacy and forever fraught with political intrigue and danger—is too much for my nerves to bear any longer. I find that the prospect of yet another winter filled with diplomatic cocktail parties and weekends in the country with your partisan friends—where I must guard my every word and even the countenance of my face for your sake—has mired my soul in despair. And so, my dearest one, I am returning to Sweden to live a simpler life.

Vassi, I beg of you not to reproach or hate me. Perhaps I should have told you how despondent of heart I have grown, but these last weeks, roaming the peaceful forests surrounding Lake Komsomolskoye, have made me long for the mountains of my native home. I have come to crave serenity and a private, uncomplicated life, my darling, and—I beg your forbearance and understanding, my love!—I confess that I also crave what I cannot have with you . . . a family.

I do not place blame, Vassi. How can I? You were forthright when we began. No marriage, no children. I accepted your conditions because my love for you overcame every obstacle . . . even when you asked that I destroy our unborn child. I understood. I do not fault you.

But now, after seven years bathed in your love, I look in the mirror, and I think, "I am forty-six years old. Will my hero, my Adonis, still love me when I turn fifty? When these first hints of crow's feet about my eyes settle into the deeper wrinkles of encroaching age? Will my darling not look elsewhere for companionship? Will he not pursue love and solace elsewhere?"

Yes, I am forty-six, and while I will not seek to bear a child, nevertheless, I hear the ticking of a clock that grows louder day by day, that will not be ignored. I do not desire another man, Vassi—how could I? But a child? Yes, I desire a child. A child would love and cling to me even as I age—and I would love him or her back. We could be a family, living a simple, uncomplicated life. And so, Vassili Aleksandrovich, I will try to adopt a child before I am much older, before it is too late.

Please allow me to go! I beg of you. Permit me to live out my life in peace with my memories of you to comfort me. I ask this with all the love we have shared, with the many happy memories we made together. Pozhaluysta— please—my love, do not seek for me after you read this, but allow me to fade away as a fond memory in your heart.

I do not say do svidaniya *to you, but rather, in the tongue of my homeland,* farväl, tills vi ses igen. *Farewell, until we meet again, for some day I hope for us to meet again.*

I will send word to you when I have found a place to settle in Sweden so that you will not worry for me. Until then, I beg you to remember me with the passion and affection I will always have for you.

Forever yours,

Linnéa

WHEN PETROFF FOLDED the letter and returned it to its envelope, he was calmer. Perhaps even bemused.

"Vassili Aleksandrovich?"

Petroff shook his head. "I must think on this."

Anger made Zakhar daring. "What does she say?"

Petroff looked out the window of his apartment's library. "She longs for a child and wishes to adopt one. She begs me to allow her to retire from the stressful public life I live."

Zakhar's eyes narrowed. "And you believe her?"

Petroff seemed not to hear him. "She is in pain, Zakhar. Why did I not see it?"

The hatred Zakhar held toward the woman roiled within him, but Zakhar had not achieved Petroff's trust without the self-effacing mastery of his own inclinations. He knew Petroff's pride. He understood Petroff better than the man understood himself.

Affecting a sympathetic expression, he asked, "I admit to my impertinence, but would you allow me the great honor of reading her letter?"

Petroff blinked, then extended the envelope to Zakhar. "You will see. You will see how grieved she is to wound me."

Yes, it is all about you, Vassili Aleksandrovich, all about you—and you are blind!

Zakhar read the letter to himself, ignoring the gushing sentiments that pandered to Petroff's narcissism. He dissected it objectively, looking for deception—for he was still smarting from the woman's perfidy which he now saw clearly. From the moment they had departed the *dacha* until she escaped, she had deceived and manipulated him again and again.

What Zakhar read between the lines of her flowery prose was distraction and deflection. The woman comprehended that Petroff loved her—as much as a man such as he was capable of loving—and her words exploited his egocentric affection. She appreciated that Petroff would be simultaneously aggrieved and furious at her defection, wounded in heart and injured in pride,

77

so she had composed the letter to flatter and mollify him, to take the blame and play upon his benevolence.

And if her letter soothed even a fraction of Petroff's injured pride, if her words managed to extract the stinger from his heart? She would have accomplished her goal—time enough to disappear.

His hackles rose. *The woman knows Petroff as I do. She is playing an admirable game, capitalizing on Petroff's inflated ego.*

He fingered the sheet of paper. "She is distressed, indeed, Vassili Aleksandrovich. How will you respond to her request? What are your orders?"

Zakhar observed Petroff's internal struggle, watched as he came to a decision. "Call off the search for now, Zakhar. We know she is going home to Sweden to heal. When the crisis within the Security Council is resolved, I will go myself to find and visit her. Perhaps then I can comfort her."

Zakhar knew Petroff. He knew how contrary and volatile the man's disposition was. Whether it took an hour, a day, or a week, Petroff would reverse course as surely as the winds shifted direction. Until then, Zakhar had to tread carefully. For the present, he bowed his chin to his chest in acquiescence. "*Da*, Vassili Aleksandrovich. I will issue your instructions."

But Zakhar was no fool. He would continue his hunt for the woman, using the discreet resources at his disposal and make no mention of his findings to Petroff—until the man asked for them.

As he left Petroff, Zakhar added to himself, *You are wily, Linnéa Olander, I give you that. You are not the woman you have played so convincingly these past years, but you will not fool me again. I will find out who you truly are—and what you have really been doing all this time.*

THE MAIL ROOM had delivered Alvarsson's mail to Ingrid, Marstead's Stockholm receptionist, at the usual time. She sorted through it, relegating junk mail to the shredder, piling what might be actual mail to the side. Rarely did anything of import come through *Posten*. Most of Alvarsson's Marstead communications were handled through secure phone calls while classified documents arrived via armed Marstead couriers.

She picked up a padded mailer. Saw the scrawled name in the corner where the return address belonged. Noted the postmark. St. Petersburg, Russia. She flipped the package over. *Personal and Confidential.*

Ingrid picked up her phone and called the Marstead Alpha employee who spelled her at regular times throughout the day.

"*Hej*, Gunnar. Something important has come up. I need you. Yes, immediately."

Ingrid slid the mailer into an interoffice sleeve. When Gunnar arrived, Ingrid was waiting, sleeve in hand.

"Put me through to Alvarsson, if you please."

Gunnar sat down at Ingrid's desk, reached beneath it, and pressed three buttons in succession. One locked down the elevator. The second secured the double doors to the right of the elevator at the end of the hall. Those doors led to the wide floor of cubicles where Marstead International worker bees labored—Marstead workers busy at actual technical research, acquisition, and marketing, employees ignorant of their company's covert intelligence gathering activities.

When Gunnar pressed the third button, the unadorned paneled wall to her right separated, providing access to the wing housing Marstead's management suite.

The third button beneath the desk functioned only if the elevator and hall door locks were engaged. The elevator could not open while locked down. Employees could not exit the floor of cubicles when access to the management suite was open. In other words, no one ever saw—or crossed—the threshold to the management wing without appropriate clearance.

If an intruder—a threat—were to exit the elevator on the fourth floor, two taps of Ingrid or Gunnar's toe against the back panel of their desk would lock down the lobby and send an alarm to building security and all Alpha employees. In fact, the lobby was constructed in such a way that, while the intruders might threaten or kill the receptionist, they would be trapped where they were—within the lobby's secure and reinforced confines—and only the highest Alpha employee in the building could end the lockdown.

It wasn't as though Marstead's "regular" employees were ignorant of the management wing. It only meant that they were not allowed access for security reasons. Theft of intellectual property being a tech company's greatest vulnerability, Marstead's robust security protocols were acknowledged and not to be trifled with.

Employees who failed to demonstrate appropriate respect for Marstead's security measures were stripped of their access badge and escorted from the building by armed guards.

Ingrid stepped into the management wing, jogged to the office at the end of the hall, and knocked.

"Come."

"I felt you should see this immediately, sir. It arrived just now in the post." Ingrid removed the padded mailer from the sleeve and handed it to Alvarsson.

The man scanned the mailer—then stared at the name in the upper left corner. Linnéa Olander. "I'm sorry. Say again where you got this?"

"Mail room sent it up with the normal post."

"Thank you, Ingrid. Please close the door on your way out."

He waited until she left before slicing into the mailer and removing its contents. a tri-folded sheet of paper and a CD-ROM. He unfolded the paper and read it.

Alvarsson,

This letter serves as notice of my resignation from Marstead, effective immediately. I have been a loyal employee, serving as ordered for going on twenty-five years, but I have come to the end of usefulness in my present assignment. Indeed, had I continued as mistress to Vassili Aleksandrovich Petroff, I would have become a liability. Not wanting to endanger the company's network, I elected to remove myself from my assignment and, with this letter, resign from the company's employ.

If I am allowed to go my way, unharmed and unmolested, Marstead has nothing to fear from me. My wish is to live a simple life, free of the unrelenting stress under which I have lived these past seven years. You also need not fear that I have compromised Marstead's cover by leaving Petroff. I have taken steps to lead him astray so that he should not suspect me of spying on Russia.

Again, it is not my wish to expose Marstead's activities. I love my country and do not want to cause her or her allies harm. If the company allows me to live out my life in peace, you have my word that you need never fear me.

Alvarsson, I am aware that you have received orders to retire me. Please advise your superiors that acting on those orders would be unwise. Enclosed you will find a CD. Please insert it into your computer and peruse it. The files on the disc contain unequivocal evidence that I spied upon and stole many classified secrets from Vassili Aleksandrovich and the Russian Federation, proof that Marstead International is a cover for a joint US–NATO intelligence agency—enough documentation to cause an international incident of catastrophic proportions.

Let this letter, then, be a warning. Should Marstead continue its hunt for me or should I disappear or die under suspicious circumstances, I have arranged for copies of the disc to be sent to members of the Russian Security Council and to multiple news outlets.

As I have never given you cause to doubt my integrity, loyalty, or determination to do what had to be done, do not doubt me now. *Please heed both my promise and warning. You have nothing to fear if I am left alone. Conversely, my disappearance or death will result in Marstead's ruin and great upheaval in relations between the US and Russia.*

Sincerely,

Linnéa Olander

Alvarsson stared at the wall opposite his desk for a long time before he did as the letter suggested. He inserted the disc into his computer, ran a virus scan on it, then opened a window and clicked on the single folder labeled "Marstead."

The folder was heavily protected using Marstead's proprietary software. Alvarsson unlocked and opened the folder.

Within the folder, he found hundreds of files spanning Linnéa's seven years with Petroff—proof that she had been spying on him . . . proof she had been spying *for Marstead*. The files included copies of her Marstead quarterly reports containing covert communications between Linnéa and Marstead, hundreds of digital photos she had taken of documents Petroff had carried home in his briefcase, and many of his classified emails. Most incriminating were the audio files. She had recorded Petroff's private phone conversations with members of the Russian Security Council, even private conversations between himself and Secretary Rushailo.

If the material contained in the CD-ROM were released to the public, Marstead would not survive the scrutiny. Management would have to scramble to preserve its priceless network of operatives, but the company itself would be finished—and not merely Marstead. Public release of the recorded conversations would spell disaster for those parties whose voices Linnéa had identified in the calls. The Russian Federation would "disappear" the persons to mitigate internal damage and go after any and all Marstead personnel within Russian territory.

The international damage to Marstead would be extensive—but, as Linnéa had predicted, catastrophic to Marstead's network of agents.

The company could reorganize, change its name, reinvent itself. It would take time, and we would take huge hits financially, but our network of Alpha employees in the field would be blown. Many would have to flee for their lives and would take decades to replace.

Alvarsson removed the disc from his computer, put it back in its case, then locked it in his safe. He put the letter in his suit's breast pocket, left his office, and headed downstairs to use the STU yet again.

When Saunders came on the line and the transmission had been encrypted, Alvarsson spoke. "Our problem has gotten worse."

"Our deep-cover asset?"

"Yes."

"You haven't found her yet?"

"No, but I received a letter from her."

Alvarsson read the letter to Saunders in a measured, even voice.

"And you've looked at the disc?"

"Yes."

"Assessment?"

"The material is incontrovertible. If it were released to the public, the blowback would put us behind for years, perhaps a decade."

Saunders swore aloud. Then he became silent as he considered options.

"But you say you trust this woman?"

"I told you I trusted her before you ordered me to retire her. If you'd heeded my advice to simply bring her in and provide a suitable cover for her 'death,' we wouldn't be in this mess."

"Don't go all righteous and insubordinate on me, Alvarsson. We are where we are, and now we need to fix it. What are your recommendations?"

"Recommendations? We call off the hit and leave her alone just as she asked."

"Leave her alone? After she's threatened us?"

"It's called self-preservation, Saunders."

"Is it? And what is it called if she's hit by a bus next week and her little 'fail-safe' plan launches? What do we call it then, eh? And what of Petroff? We don't know what Olander meant by, 'I have taken steps to lead him astray. He should not suspect me of spying on him,' or whether those so-called 'steps' she claims to have taken will deter such a man as Petroff—a sociopath whose pride and control issues may well override his logic and survival instincts. What we need, Alvarsson, is our own leverage against this woman. She has parents, yes?"

Alvarsson stood and paced. "Sir, I strongly advise against threatening her family."

"We need to bring her to heel. Her parents are fair game."

"Again, I would not use her family as so-called leverage—not unless you want to wake up in the night with Linnéa Olander standing over your bed as the last thing you ever see."

"Huh. I would hardly categorize her as a killer. She's not known for wet work. Do you really think she's that good? Hasn't she been a passive asset most of her career?"

"Don't let her looks fool you. Linnéa Olander has a backbone of steel. She aced her training—tactics, weapons, hand-to-hand, and urban tradecraft. Besides all that, she has a near-eidetic memory and can solve complex logistical problems on the fly, making her a formidable opponent in the field. I have never known her to be squeamish about any task the job required of her, even the taking a life when necessary—and she *has* killed."

Alvarsson's tone hardened. "In my opinion, the more important questions are, why did we risk making an enemy of her in the first place? What did we gain by alienating her? Was it only to preserve the prestige her valuable contributions garnered?"

"Enough! I won't have you questioning my decisions *or my motives*, Alvarsson. We can't undo what's done. More to the point, we can't leave the threat of exposing us unanswered. *That* is not an option."

Alvarsson tamped down his anger. "Then what *would* you have us do? Her trail has gone cold—or, rather, we never had a trail, not a single bread crumb.

"Our people brought Krupina in and put her through an exhaustive interrogation. All we got out of her was that Olander had bruises to her head from Petroff's latest tantrum and that Olander was getting out. Leaving him. Krupina admitted that Olander went out the alley door, but neither we nor the Russians have caught sight or scent of her since."

Alvarsson sighed. "She's smart, as smart as they come, and she's not in a hurry. She won't be easily found."

Saunders grumbled to himself, then asked, "So, she's lying low, waiting for the furor to die down. What's her endgame? Where will she go when she makes her move?"

"My guess is back to America. It's a big and open country. With her skills, she can melt into any town or city she chooses."

Alvarsson heard Saunders tapping his fingers across the miles. He waited.

Finally, Saunders said, "I need to bump this up the chain. For now, though, the retirement order stands."

"Understood," Alvarsson answered. He hung up, frustrated and still angry.

THE INDIGENT OLD peasant woman left the train in Moscow and wandered the streets by day, picking through litter, filling her pram with choice bits of rubbish, meandering from the train depot to a metro station. She did not stray far from the metro, because food vendors gathered daily around the station to sell to the passengers—and from the vendors she could buy small hot meals.

She gestured for what she wanted and, with shaking fingers, counted out *kopecks* from a worn coin purse. In this manner, she purchased a *shawarma* from this vendor, a *cheburek* from that one, *pirozhki* from another.

She squatted against a building to eat her food, muttering to herself, sometimes moving her hands as she talked. When she finished eating, she wiped her greasy hands on the coat that covered her from neck to calf, then continued her hunched, aimless ramble.

The weather was warm and mild, so when darkness fell, she slept under a nearby bridge, her thick scarf pillowing her head, her stained coat a blanket.

She was not alone under the bridge. Her companions in the night were roughened men, mostly alcoholics, addicts, and petty thieves who dared not ask the Russian State for shelter.

These men supported their habits and their meager lifestyle through small-time criminal endeavors—mugging unsuspecting passengers leaving the metro, targeting the weak and defenseless, taking anything of value their victims might have on them.

During the indigent old woman's first night under the bridge, three drug users decided to rob her. One of them had seen her counting out coins to a vendor for her dinner and supposed her an easy mark. They were desperate men, in need of a fix to see them through the long, dark hours until morning.

She assumed they would come and had prepared for their attack. When they made their move, she was ready, a broken bottle held in each hand—jagged edges toward them. She called down angry, garbled curses on them and showed no fear. On the contrary, she rushed forward and assailed *them!* Before they knew what was happening, she had nicked one on the arm and jabbed another in the shoulder. Their injuries were not serious, but they withdrew to bind up their wounds and reconsider their approach.

The *babushka*, however, did not withdraw.

Awakened by her shrieks and shouted curses, other vagabonds stole out of the dark. She put on quite the show for them, brandishing her weapons, dancing awkwardly about, babbling threats and nonsense, feinting, then attacking invisible foes. Fearing the commotion would attract the *militsiya*, the Moscow police, her audience shied away into the shadows.

The police did not come that night. However, having witnessed the old woman's fierce, unpredictable madness and after talking of it among themselves, those who regularly took shelter under the bridge chose to bother her no further.

She spent five nights and four days near the metro station.

Unmolested.

CHAPTER 6
LP

ON THE FIFTH MORNING, the old woman wandered away from the metro, pushing her pram filled with trash ahead of her. A mile or more from the bus station, she spotted her objective—a thrift store. She turned down the nearest alley. There, she rid herself of coat, scarf, and gloves, dumping the filthy clothing into a bin.

She took off the padded stockings and tossed them, too, but put the shoes back on. From her purse with the long shoulder strap, she withdrew a broken comb she had found in a gutter and ran it through her tangled hair, braiding it down the back and tying a strip of cloth at the braid's end.

Dealing with her face was more difficult and time-consuming. She had added daily to the gel that had, as it dried, reddened her complexion and created a parchment of creases and wrinkles all over her face—even under her eyes and on her eyelids. She used half a bottle of water and a scrap of fabric torn from the lining of her coat, but the dried gel clung to her skin with fierce tenacity. After long, precious minutes, she had peeled off or scrubbed away most of the dried layers.

Lastly, she removed the HK from her bra and hid it in the padded compartment of her customized Italian handbag. She tucked the handbag into the pram and pushed the pram behind the rubbish bin.

I will come back for you soon, she promised the gun.

She pulled a cloth bag from her purse and counted out enough Russian currency for her next move, then slipped the purse's strap crosswise over her shoulders and walked to the end of the alley. Around the corner, she examined herself in a restaurant window. She appeared thirty years younger than the old peasant woman although older than her actual age. She still wore the *babushka's* disheveled house dress and the heavy padding about her waist, but she was infinitely more presentable.

She turned her head to one side and sniffed.

Oy, how I reek!

But first things first. She made her way to the thrift store, feeling weightless and exposed after having been covered head to toe for the larger

85

part of a week. She stopped just inside the shop's door, knowing the clerks would regard her appearance—and smell—with disfavor.

She was right—a female clerk glanced up, took in her appearance, and hustled toward her. "I am afraid we cannot serve you, madam—oh, my word! What is that stench?"

"I apologize. I know I need a bath. But I need some clean clothes, first." She added quickly, "I have money. Let me buy a few things, and I will be on my way."

The clerk studied her. "What is wrong with your face?"

"I-I have a skin problem. Not communicable. An allergic rash. Allow me to buy some clean clothes, and I will leave."

The clerk said nothing for a moment, then, "Show me that you have money."

She opened her purse and withdrew the folded notes.

The clerk's shrewd eyes narrowed. "All right. I will let you buy some things, but since you are stinking up the place, you will pay a twenty percent markup—and you may not use the changing rooms. I will not let you foul them with your stench."

She nodded her agreement to the clerk's extortion and mumbled, "I need everything—underwear, shoes, socks, a dress, a scarf. I know my sizes. Give me ten minutes."

The clerk scowled at her. "I give you five. If another customer comes in while you are here? My store's reputation will be ruined."

She nodded to the clerk, grabbed a basket, and hurried through the bins, sorting, selecting, and tossing two pairs of shoes into the basket, moving on to the clothing racks. She placed her filled basket on the counter along with a beat-up suitcase.

The clerk, with a sniff, bagged the purchases, then produced a total that included the hefty twenty percent tariff she'd threatened to add.

She paid without comment, took the sacks, and left. Her next stop was a public bath house. She paid fifty kopeks to scrub herself all over with soap and fresh, curling, feather-soft wood shavings at a round, communal sink, wet her hair and soap it, then rinse for five minutes in a warm shower. She toweled off, changed into the used clothing, and braided her damp hair down her back.

It would dry soon enough in the heat outside. Wrapping her filthy clothes around the padded bodysuit that had added thirty pounds to her belly, she ditched the bundle in the garbage bin.

Afterward, she returned to the rubbish bin where she'd stashed the pram. There she retrieved her gun, handbag, and the items she wished to keep and transferred them to her suitcase. She then found a general store where she purchased fruit, cheese, and sliced salami that she wrapped in brown paper and stuffed into a bag for later.

When evening came, she ate a hearty dinner in a small café. She would not spend the night in a hotel where management was required to record her ID. Instead, she scoped out a used furniture store and noted its hours.

She returned to the store after it closed, jimmied the backdoor lock, and curled up on a sofa away from the display windows.

Early the following morning, a well-used suitcase and a lunch of fruit and cold cuts in hand, she was back on the train, this time heading north to the Russia–Finland border—but not without a plan . . . a plan that required making the right acquaintances and using them for cover.

In the second compartment, she found what she was seeking. She took a seat and made friendly overtures toward a young Russian couple and their three children across the aisle. Speaking Russian like a native Muscovite, she took pains to endear herself to their toddler boy. Within the hour, the wife invited her to sit with them.

Dressed in nondescript clothes, a soft kerchief over her hair, the little boy on her lap, her face still rough and red, she appeared to be part of the family, an older aunt, perhaps. In any event, her papers were in order. She was presently Oksana Vladlena Sokolova, a Russian citizen from Moscow, on her way to visit a sister in Joensuu—a trip, her passport attested, she had made twice in the past three years.

At the border, Oksana insisted on helping the parents wrangle their belongings and children. She followed the parents through the security checkpoint, carrying the little boy on one hip and her suitcase in her free hand.

The security guards, although they seemed on higher alert than usual, nevertheless screened them as a family unit. The parents, grateful for Oksana's friendly help, mentioned nothing that might alter the guards' assumption.

ZAKHAR WATCHED PETROFF prowl his apartment much like a wounded lion, his snarls and growls gaining momentum and volume. The man had been under daily pressure while the Security Council debated the present crisis. Each night when he returned to the apartment and found himself alone, his anger had increased.

"Zakhar!"

"Yes, Vassili Aleksandrovich?"

"Is there no word from Miss Olander?"

"You ordered me to call off the search, Vassili Aleksandrovich."

Petroff rounded on him, cursing and shouting. "You should know me by now, you fool. I need her. I need her *here*, with *me!*"

Zakhar bowed. "I can tell you she has not returned to Sweden as she said she would."

"What? How can you know that?"

"She was, when she left you that letter, in great distress, was she not? In order to ensure her safety, I set a watch upon crossings into her country and made inquiries around the province of Uppsala and the village in which she spent her late childhood."

The next part would be tricky. "We know her father worked in America and that Linnéa was born there, but I have made an odd discovery, Vassili Aleksandrovich. I do not profess to know what it means, but . . . but I must not cover it up."

Petroff rounded on him. "What discovery?"

Zakhar shook his head slowly. "I took the initiative to have your people talk with Uppsala residents. In the village they met an old, retired teacher."

"Yes? Get on with it!"

"This teacher, Jorgensen, is more than eighty years old. He claimed that he could recall every student who attended the village school from the time he, himself, began to teach there at age twenty-three. He insisted that he had never heard of a Linnéa Olander."

Petroff eyed Zakhar. "Go on."

"We checked the school's records and made copies of them. Miss Olander's name first appears on the village school's roster when she was nine years old, the year her widowed mother returned from America. Jorgensen was even listed as one of her teachers for the remainder of her *Grundskola*—comprehensive school.

"But when we showed him the roster, he declared it to be wrong. He knew every student on the list *except* Linnéa Olander. I had recent photographs of Miss Olander with me and showed them to him. He did not recognize her, nor did anyone who supposedly attended secondary school with her. No one in the village to whom we showed the photographs knew her."

Petroff stood as stiff and unmoving as a boulder.

Zakhar was a patient man and had not gotten to where he was without great restraint. Petroff would be sorting through the implications of the news his faithful servant had delivered. Petroff would soon arrive at the same conclusions Zakhar had. And Zakhar anticipated with great, masked glee what would happen next.

So, Zakhar waited. He waited because he knew his patron—and because he was familiar with the culture and workings of Russian State politics. In Russian political affairs, when a man attached himself to a rising star such as Petroff, that man's fortune, security, and longevity depended upon his patron's success and his continued good standing in the eyes of the State. Conversely, what tarred a political star, tarred all who were associated with him.

If this woman was a spy, as Zakhar suspected she was, Petroff would be ruined—disgraced, imprisoned, interrogated, tortured, and quietly executed. All his acquaintances and close associates would come under the same cloud of scrutiny. Even Petroff's superiors and highly placed friends would be suspect.

In other words, if Petroff were ruined, Zakhar's own demise would follow.

So, Zakhar bided his time. When Petroff's orders came—as Zakhar was convinced they would—Zakhar would receive them with great satisfaction.

At last Petroff spoke. "Find her, Zakhar. Wherever she has hidden herself, find her. Bring her to me."

"*Da*, Vassili Aleksandrovich. I will."

Zakhar yearned to kill the woman himself, to steal her life inch by slow inch. He indulged himself with fantasies of his hands about her throat, choking her, relishing her panic and fear, reveling in her desperation as she pled and begged for her life. He managed to suppress this longing only by the sure knowledge that watching how Petroff slowly killed her would be equally satisfying.

———⟨∾⟩———

Laynie Portland
RETIRED SPY

PART 2: MARTA
LP

CHAPTER 7

LP

OKSANA SOKOLOVA ARRIVED in Finland and promptly vanished into the city. However, later that evening, a French woman named Marta Forestier caught the train from Joensuu to Tampere where she disembarked and took a room in a modest hotel. She shopped and paid a visit to a hair salon for a fresh cut and color—a rich sable brown.

She did not resemble Linnéa Olander when she emerged.

Linnéa is dead, she reminded herself for the hundredth time. *Today you are Marta. Become her. Be her.*

Finland's two official languages were Finnish and Swedish. The French woman's Finnish language skills were marginal, but her Swedish was perfect. "I learned Swedish from my first husband," she explained to those she met. "I realize my Finnish is deficient, so I wish to practice it."

As French was, supposedly, her first language, some individuals attempted to converse with her in French. She put them off with a dismissive wave of her hand and a very French-like shrug of her shoulders. "*Non*. Let us speak Finnish together, please. I must learn something while I am here." In this way, she deflected those who wished to speak a language to her that she had not mastered—certainly not with the accents of a French-born native.

Marta stayed three nights in Tampere where she acquired a few chic outfits from a department store. From a thrift shop, she purchased faded jeans, T-shirt, a gray hoodie, sneakers, a small and well-used backpack, and an American-style baseball hat. She furnished her Bottega Veneta handbag with a smart, tooled-leather pocketbook, fresh lipstick, powder compact, and nail file. She purchased a common carry-on suitcase with wheels and ditched the suitcase she'd arrived with.

On her third day in Tampere, dressed in a classy ensemble that complemented her Italian handbag, Marta boarded a domestic flight to Helsinki and caught a connecting international flight from Helsinki to Paris.

She had already booked a direct flight from Paris to New York, but it would not leave until the following morning. She took her seat on the plane and focused on controlling her breathing in order to slow her heart rate.

She had not felt as exposed since she had left Madame Krupina's as she did right now.

Soon, she promised herself. *Soon I will breathe the air of freedom. One night in the Paris airport and then home to America.*

"VASSILI ALEKSANDROVICH."

Petroff had drunk himself to sleep for the third time this week and was still in bed at noon—quite uncharacteristic of his disciplined lifestyle. Zakhar pushed open the door to Petroff's bedroom suite and said louder, "Vassili Aleksandrovich!"

"*Da, da.* What do you want?"

"We have found her."

Petroff tried to sit up, but his head pounded, and his mouth and tongue were dry. Swollen. "Have you brought her to me?"

"Not yet, but we have located her—and we know where she is going."

"Get me some water."

Zakhar snapped his fingers. A servant crept into Petroff's bedroom. She set a tray on a table and poured the water. Zakhar reached for the water himself and dismissed her. He handed the glass to Petroff, who drank it down.

"Well? Where is she?"

"Our agents believe they spotted her in the Helsinki airport only minutes ago but were unable to intercept her before she boarded a flight. She was traveling under a French passport to Paris."

"Paris! Have we anyone there who can snatch her?"

"That would be very difficult since I doubt she will leave the airport. You see, she had booked a flight from Paris to New York before she left Helsinki."

"New York!"

"*Da*, but her flight does not leave until morning. This is a good omen for us."

"Oh? What do you propose?"

"We allow her to continue on to New York unmolested. She will feel that she has gotten away safely. However, if you authorize a private plane for me and a few select men and we leave within the next few hours, we can arrive in New York ahead of her."

"You must be careful, Zakhar. She must be handled with great discretion."

"I understand, Vassili Aleksandrovich. New York is a busy city with much crime. We will follow her from the airport and take her when she is alone."

"She has lied to me, Zakhar. She is not who she said she was. She has fooled us all—even her company."

Zakhar remained silent until Petroff stirred himself.

"You may have your airplane. I will authorize the arrangements. Bring her to me, Zakhar."

"You can count on me, Vassili Aleksandrovich."

SHE LINED UP WITH other passengers to pass through customs in the Paris-Orly airport. Her passport as Marta Forestier was in order, duly stamped in Helsinki. Her ticket was paid for.

When she stepped forward to the next immigration control agent, her plan started to skid sideways.

The agents checking her French passport and sorting through her suitcase spoke to her in French, expecting her to reply as a French woman. She delivered a prepared excuse since she could not pass as a native French speaker.

"I was born a Swede," she confessed to them in passable but poorly accented French, "and on my first trip to Paris, I fell in love with a Frenchman—Armand. We had a crazy, whirlwind love affair. Then we married and, eventually, I attained French citizenship. Before he passed away, he was still attempting to teach me the nuances of his language. Sadly, in the years that have passed, my accent has never risen above atrocious—don't you agree?"

They did agree. They laughed with her and passed her through.

Sweating from the close call, Marta collected her carry-on bag, stripped the tag from it, and headed for ticketing. That was when she caught sight of a man and a woman on opposite sides of the terminal, checking passengers, watching the ticket counters, occasionally lifting hand to mouth. Their manner was relaxed. Nonchalant. Utterly professional. An untrained eye would not have noticed them or the "earwig" wires curling out of their ears, but Marta was far from untrained.

She bought a magazine and a coffee and sat down next to a man near her age. She smiled, said hello, asked where he was traveling to, and parked her purse on the carpet between their feet, implying to the casual observer that they were fellow travelers, a married couple. While she sipped her coffee and paged through her magazine, she leaned toward her "companion" and made the occasional comment to him. She also kept one eye on the two "watchers."

After an hour, the man stood. "That's my flight," he explained.

"Mine is boarding, too," she answered. Marta collected her things and followed him toward his gate. It was then that the woman and the man came together briefly and whispered. From a dozen yards away, Marta watched their lips and read the French words they spoke.

They were Marstead agents—French ones.

What if Marstead agents had alerted ticket agents to flag irregular encounters? Situations such as a French passenger who did not speak French like a native and who offered the excuse that she was actually Swedish?

Oh, I have blundered!

Marta cut away toward a restroom and locked herself in a stall. She was short of breath, gasping, and shaking with fear. Black spots flickered in front of her eyes.

What is this? I have never fallen apart physically like this!

What was it that Kari had said to her? *"You've never lived until you've experienced a full-on panic attack."*

"I can't have a panic attack. I can't!"

She remained in the stall for half an hour, until she had calmed and was able to think clearly and contrive her next move.

A Paris to New York flight was out of the question. In fact, on any flight out of Paris, wouldn't she encounter airline employees who would expect her to converse with them in French? And, clearly, French would not pass as her native language. She—and her story—were too conspicuous, too memorable. Too chancy.

Marta had one unused passport left, a US one, but she dared not use it until she arrived in America. With a solid US ID and driver's license, she would disappear. Blend in. Survive.

I must fly into the US on this French passport—which I will toss as soon as I land—but I cannot risk flying by a French carrier or from a French city. I must choose another route.

While keeping one eye out for Marstead agents, she looked for directions to the Orlyval shuttle train and found the correct shuttle to take her to the Orly-Sud train station. The ride was not long. From there, she boarded the Eurostar to Calais-Fréthun, which took her through the channel tunnel to Folkestone and on to London.

LATE THAT NIGHT, exhausted and stressed from her travels, Marta checked into a hotel near London's Heathrow airport. She picked up the room's telephone and called American Airlines.

While she waited for an available agent, she noticed the small stand-up calendar on the desk. *Is it the ninth or tenth?*

She'd lost track of the day and date.

An airline agent picked up her call. "American Airlines. May I help you?"

"Yes, hello. I'd like to book a direct flight from Heathrow to New York. Tomorrow morning, the earliest flight you have, please."

If I need to, if I'm pursued after I land, I will be close enough to Canada to cross over on my French passport and try to lose myself there. I'll learn the border crossings to be prepared.

"I have a seat on a direct flight from Heathrow to JFK at 6:45 a.m."

"I will take it. May I pay for the ticket when I arrive?"

"Yes, but only if you call for the ticket at least an hour before departure. Otherwise, it goes back on sale."

"I will be there on time to pay for it. Thank you." She gave the airline agent the information from her French passport and hung up.

Travel time from London to New York was a little more or less than eight hours, but because of the five-hour time difference between the two cities, the flight would leave at 6:45 a.m. and arrive at 9:55 a.m.—seemingly only three hours later.

Laynie was tired and needed to sleep, but she did not. She remained awake, tense and uneasy.

Just a few more hurdles—including the one involving this French passport. My backstory this time is that I'm an American who married a French man— and so on.

Which reminds me. I should practice my American English while on board. Drop a few American idioms and knock the rust off my American accent.

Undercover for so long as a Swede, Laynie's English had acquired a Swedish inflection.

If I can board tomorrow's flight without being detected, I stand a good chance of arriving in New York, getting out of the airport, and disappearing into the city. Then I should be safe.

Safe? Marstead agents were haunting international airports, in spite of her threat to reveal the intelligence she had gathered in Russia as a covert operative for them! And how long before Petroff was tracking her, too? Surely, her fawning letter had given him pause—but only momentarily.

Without doubt, this leg of her journey would be the most dangerous.

She carried the little HK P7K3 concealed in her handbag, but how could she and her little gun compete against trained and no doubt better-armed agents prowling the airports for her? Could she outrun or outgun them?

Not likely.

She sighed and turned over, troubled in her thoughts, unable to relax.

I have left Linnéa Olander far behind and will never again answer to that name. But can I ever go back to the real me? Laynie Portland?

She shuddered. *No. Marstead knows my real name. They will be watching for me. Furthermore, if Vassili Aleksandrovich's people were to uncover my identity, they would, sooner or later, find Mama and Dad.*

She stared into the dark.

If Petroff's minions found her parents, she shuddered to think of what his people would do to them. Her mama and dad knew nothing of their daughter's covert life, but they would suffer regardless.

Under questioning—and torture, if necessary—they would reveal the existence of a young grand-daughter and grandson, their son's orphaned children, Laynie's niece and nephew. Petroff's people would ask where those children were.

The interrogation would, inexorably, lead to Kari.

Petroff would find Kari. He would have her. He would have Shannon and Robbie.

He would use all of them against me.

Her fists clenched and unclenched, her nails biting into the skin of her palms, her anger burning. Intensifying.

Vassili Aleksandrovich, you do not know me as you think you do—for I am not the self-deprecating, subservient woman I pretended to be in order to mollify your pride and play to your ego. I am Laynie Portland. *For seven years I outwitted you, deceived you, robbed you of many Russian state secrets, and you never had a clue. I still have cards to play, Vassili Aleksandrovich. Don't think I will roll over if you threaten my family.*

I will destroy you first.

———⟡———

CHAPTER 8

LP

LAYNIE HAD NO difficulty arriving at the American Airlines ticket counter by 5:20 a.m. She hadn't slept all night.

Instead, she had watched the clock tick through the hours without closing her eyes and had gotten out of bed at 3:30. She stood in the shower for a long time, did her hair and makeup, dressed, packed, checked and rechecked her papers, and counted her money—kronor, pounds, and dollars. It was a tidy sum, but . . .

Not nearly enough ready cash in the right currency, she realized. *I'll need more American money the moment I hit New York.*

She would have liked to hit a currency exchange at the airport, changing all her money for American dollars before she left London, but the airport exchanges would not open before her early flight departed.

She took the hotel shuttle to the airport, used her French ID to pass through passport control, found her airline, and paid for her ticket.

Since she was an hour early for her flight, Laynie scouted out a shadowed table at the back of a coffee shop that afforded her a view of her gate. While she sipped on a steaming cup of coffee, she watched for Marstead or Russian agents until her flight was called.

Even when passengers began to board, she did not abandon her cover. She waited for the majority of her flight's passengers to queue up at the gate. She scrutinized each one before they marched onto the boarding bridge. She watched for suspicious or telltale body language.

Laynie had picked up a brochure on the plane's design and familiarized herself with the details, including seat configuration. The relatively new Boeing 767-400ER had a crew complement of ten—two in the cockpit and eight flight attendants in the cabins—and passenger seating for two hundred and one.

Laynie did not relish being crammed into economy class for the simple reason that she required room to maneuver and the ability to deplane quickly, should she need either or both.

The last passengers in line were entering the boarding bridge and the gate would close soon. Grabbing her carry-on, Laynie made for the gate's nearby ticket counter and presented her ticket.

"Say, I'm booked on Flight 6177. Do you have any open seats in business class? I'm hoping to upgrade."

"It's a little late, but let me check." The agent clicked her way through the system, then nodded to herself.

"You're in luck. We have one open seat in business class, 8D. It's in the last row."

Laynie recalled the layout of the business class cabin—eight rows, five seats across each row. The configuration was two seats, an aisle, one seat, an aisle, the last two seats. The seats were designated ABDKL.

"Isn't D a single seat?"

"Yes, in the center with aisles on both sides." She tapped her keyboard again. "The upgrade will cost you £257."

The cost would be a hit to her cash reserves, but . . . *No one immediately behind me except the flight crew. Two aisles open for a quick exit.*

"I'll take it." Laynie dug in her handbag and withdrew her pocketbook. She counted out all of her British currency, five £50 banknotes. "Shoot. I only have dollars and kronor left."

She had tossed her rubles away while in Finland, purging all connection to Russia.

"Do you have a credit card?"

Laynie sighed. "No. My husband doesn't trust them. He insists that we pay cash for *everything*. Can you believe it? So inconvenient—like now."

The agent's brow puckered. "I sympathize. Sometimes I think men still live in the Stone Age, but . . ." She looked at Laynie, "but, I'm sorry. We accept only British currency or credit cards—I'm sure you can understand why. If we accepted other currencies, our cash drawers would be a dodgy mess. And, with the exchange rate fluctuations, we'd soon turn mental."

Laynie chewed her lip. She wanted to avoid the appearance of desperation, but she also wanted that seat. She swallowed and took a leap.

"Well, I'd really like that upgrade, and I'm shy by just £7, soooo—" she glanced at the agent's nametag, "so, Betty, how would you like to earn yourself a big tip?"

"What do you mean?"

"Do you happen to have £7 on you? If you do, I will trade you the equivalent of £50 in Swedish kronor if you pay the balance of my ticket."

The woman was tempted. She looked around and whispered, "We're not supposed to, and the gate is about to close . . ."

Laynie uttered a soft, lighthearted laugh. "Come on, Betty. You'll be ahead by £43, less the exchange fee. Bet that's enough to buy your friends a round or two at the pub tonight, am I right?"

Betty smiled back. "I like how you think, Marta." With another glance around, she dug into a pocket and withdrew some folded bills. "My lunch money," she confided to Laynie as she completed the ticket sale.

While Betty was printing the ticket, Laynie did the calculations in her head. She counted out kronor to equal £50 and pushed the bills toward the agent—who handed Laynie her ticket and slid the money from the counter. Betty folded the kronor and put them in her pocket, again checking to see if a supervisor were watching.

"Have fun tonight, Betty," Laynie murmured. She grabbed the ticket and rolled her bag toward the gate.

As she left the ticket counter, the last two men in line were walking onto the boarding bridge.

Looks like I'll be the last to board, Laynie thought.

Then, just as she was approaching, three late arrivals converged on the gate, apologizing profusely for their tardiness. The men were clean-shaven, dark-skinned and dark-eyed, dressed like other businessmen. Since they appeared harried, Laynie stepped back to let them show their tickets.

However, realizing they had cut her off, one of the men gestured for her to go ahead of them. She nodded her thanks, showed her ticket, and moved on.

Before stepping around the bend in the jet bridge, however, she turned her head and cast a final, wide look around the waiting area behind her, scanning for danger, giving little attention to the men not far behind her . . . until one of them slid his eyes toward her. She happened to catch his surreptitious glance at the same moment. Their gazes locked—and he jerked his head away, breaking eye contact.

Laynie paused, wondering at the frisson of disquiet running down her back. She ran a quick assessment over him and found nothing remarkable to his appearance except that he wore a walking cast on his right leg and his pant leg had been cut off and inexpertly hemmed so that it fell over the top of the cast. Other than that, she observed nothing of concern, so she started down the sloped boarding bridge, anxious to get on the plane—more anxious for the flight to get off the ground.

Farther along, the boarding bridge split in two directions, funneling business class to the left, economy class to the right. Laynie went left and immediately encountered the open cabin door to business class. The two men she'd seen ahead of her a moment ago were boarding. One turned and studied her, raking her up and down with his eyes.

Yes, Britain was a melting pot of citizens, many who had emigrated from former British colonies such as British Bahamas, India, and Pakistan, and yes, cultural norms differed widely from country to country. Still . . .

How rude. I might as well be a prize heifer, the way he's giving me the once-over, Laynie thought. *Guess it takes all kinds.*

She stared back, unabashed. In response, his lips curled in sardonic humor. Then he passed through the cabin door.

Laynie was next.

"Good morning," the steward murmured.

Laynie handed her ticket to him.

"Last row, center seat," the steward murmured. "Welcome aboard. Please get settled quickly. We are running a little behind schedule and wish to taxi as soon as the last passengers buckle up."

When Laynie stepped into the cabin, she slowed and gave it a quick appraisal before heading down the first aisle. *A partition at the front of the business class cabin. Crew jump seats and hospitality stations forward of the partition. Two restrooms at the back of the cabin—one left, one right. An aft hospitality station centered between the lavatories. Two aisles between the lavatories and hospitality station leading into economy class. Curtains across the aisles, dividing business class from economy.*

Only business class passengers allowed forward of the curtains.

Good.

Gratified that she'd upgraded her ticket, she found a place for her bag in an overhead compartment, then eyed her assigned seat. It beckoned to her weary bones. The ample recliner, like all seats in business class, was anchored at an oblique angle to the cabin so that she could lay her seat all the way back into a prone position.

I'm so tired, she realized as she settled into the plush cushions. *I hope I can sleep. I'll need my wits about me when we land eight hours from now.*

She looked around to take inventory of her neighboring passengers first.

Two businessmen in the seats to her left, both wearing custom-tailored suits that had probably cost more than everything Laynie owned, were discussing a meeting they needed to attend when they arrived in New York. To her right a couple, in their twenties, were also settling in.

The young man caught a flight attendant's attention as she passed them. "Excuse me. When you have a minute, would you mind bringing us champagne?"

"We're on our honeymoon," the girl gushed. "Got married last night."

The attendant echoed the girl, loud enough for most of the cabin to hear. "You're newlyweds? Congratulations! Two champagnes coming right up."

The girl and her new husband laughed and then kissed as a smattering of applause around them grew. Laynie smiled and joined the clapping.

"Best wishes," she said, leaning across the aisle.

"Thank you. We're going to stay at Niagara Falls. We're so excited! Are you an American? Have you ever seen the falls?"

Here's my opportunity to knock the rust off my American accent.

"Nope. 'Fraid not, but I hope you have a wonderful time."

While she was still leaning toward them, the two men who had preceded her into the cabin took seats three rows in front of the newlyweds. Laynie half-expected to see the other group of men join them, but they did not materialize.

I was mistaken. They aren't traveling together after all.

But she experienced a niggle of something bothersome.

What is it?

Putting the concern "in her back pocket" to think on later, Laynie gave her attention to the flight crew as they began their safety spiel. While they talked, the plane backed away from the gate and lumbered toward the runway.

Shortly after takeoff, the flight attendants served a light breakfast. Laynie was greedy for food and wolfed it down. As soon as the nourishment hit her stomach, she began to drowse.

I can relax all the way to New York, she told herself. She pushed her seat back and allowed sleep to take her.

HOURS LATER, SHE AWOKE, instantly alert. You're on a plane, on your way to the States. One hurdle remaining before you're safe, Laynie.

She exhaled and brought her seat up to sitting. Wiped the sleep from her face.

"You've been dead to the world since we finished breakfast. I'd say you slept six, seven hours solid."

Laynie looked left. One of the businessmen grinned at her. "You even missed 'second breakfast.' Never moved a muscle while they were serving."

Laynie grinned her response. "Tolkien fan, huh? Well, I hope I didn't snore?"

"Nah. Tell you the truth, I took a nap myself a few hours back. All this travel across time zones totally messes up my body clock."

"I know what you mean," Laynie murmured. She looked at her watch. "Another hour or so?"

"Sounds about right." He added, "I'm Bryan, by the way. My associate here is Todd."

"I'm Marta."

The flight attendant arrived. "I'm sorry you missed the food service, Miss Forestier. Coffee?"

"Absolutely," Laynie answered, "but first, I'd better use the restroom."

"Behind you, right or left."

"Thanks."

Laynie grabbed her purse and stood to stretch the kinks out of her back. While she stretched, her eyes roamed over the cabin, searching for anything out of the ordinary—meaning anyone looking at *her*. She moved toward the lavatory behind her against the starboard bulkhead. A little red sign read "Occupied," so she leaned a shoulder against the wall behind the honeymooners. Turned partway toward the cabin, she took advantage of the opportunity to again look over the business class passengers.

The newlyweds were asleep, the bride's head pillowed on the groom's shoulder, his head against her hair. The businessmen had their laptops out and were tapping away. Rows in front of the honeymooners, she saw one of the dark-haired men. He sat quiet and still in his seat, his companion's seat unoccupied.

What is it about these guys?

Just then, the restroom door unlocked. Laynie pushed away from the wall as the missing dark-haired man exited the restroom. He wasn't expecting to encounter her and startled. Then he stared into her eyes.

Laynie stared back. The intensity of his gaze raised her hackles. She even slapped a moniker on him.

What is it about you, "Abdul"? You're really getting under my skin.

A smile played about his mouth, and she was surprised when he whispered, "I noticed you back at the gate, perhaps because you are tall for a woman and carry yourself with such confidence. Then I looked you in the face. What a bold woman you are."

His English was thick and accented—but not British accented—not exactly. Something eastern, she thought.

Laynie cocked her head and feigned puzzlement. "Bold, am I? And is bold a bad thing?"

"In my country, we require our women to be properly demure, to keep their eyes cast down, appropriately respectful and modest. Back home, I would slap a woman who stared at me as you do."

Laynie's mouth curved upward. "Huh. I suppose it's a good thing we're not in your country."

He shrugged. "Ah, but if we were somewhere alone right now, you and I? I would delight in showing you how we humble infidel women such as yourself."

Laynie's smile thinned. "Would you, now? I suppose you could try, but then I would be obliged to kick the *bleep* out of you."

He laughed. "You believe you could do that? Truly, you *are* a bold woman."

He reached his hand out to caress her bare arm. Laynie grabbed his middle fingers and wrenched them back. He jerked his hand away and his expression turned ugly. Angry.

Why, there you are. I figured the "real" you was hiding in there.

Laynie smiled again and tipped her head toward the restroom. "Let me pass."

"By all means." He walked toward his seat, and Laynie's eyes followed him. Before he sat down, he glanced back. He saw her watching and smirked.

THE PLANE CARRYING ZAKHAR, two trusted men, and Nicor—a driver with operating experience in America and who was unknown to Linnéa Olander—arrived in New York around 3:00 a.m. The caretaker of a property on Long Island owned by the Russian delegation met them and drove them to the house with diplomatic privileges. The caretaker and housekeeper had orders to provide them with accommodations—and whatever else they requested.

Zakhar's team did not sleep. They had preparations to make. Zakhar sent Nicor and a member of his team out to find transportation, the caretaker along to guide them. When they returned, Nicor was piloting a sleek black limousine they had "liberated" from its driver—his body reposing in the limo's trunk.

Inside the garage, the caretaker replaced the limo's plates. In a city of a thousand taxis and limos, he assured Zakhar, the police would be on the lookout for the stolen limo's plates, not the plates presently on the limousine—TLC plates that identified the vehicle as being duly registered with the City of New York's Taxi and Limousine Commission.

"The police will not pull you over," he promised Zakhar.

The team spent their remaining time studying various routes from the safe house to JFK and back, cleaning their weapons, and planning and preparing for the operation. They were interrupted by a phone call from Zakhar's source in Paris.

"Zakhar, I have updated information for you. Marta Forestier did not board the flight from Paris to New York."

Zakhar's roar rang through the house. "What? You have *lost her?*"

"No, no. Do not be troubled, Dimitri Ilyich. We have found her. She apparently took the tunnel train from Paris to London and is booked on American Airlines Flight 6177, also due into JFK this morning at 9:55 a.m."

Seething and only partially appeased, Zakhar thanked the man and returned the receiver to its cradle.

See? You cannot escape your fate, Linnéa Olander. I am waiting for you.

Zakhar's team left the safe house before 8:00 a.m. Nicor, garbed in a chauffeur's uniform the caretaker had provided, navigated the limo toward the airport.

The plan was to identify "Marta Forestier" when she deplaned and follow her to the concourse's arrivals exit, where they anticipated she would hail a cab or a shuttle. Nicor would be parked in the concourse's limo area and would wait inside the arrivals doors with the other limo drivers, holding a sign that read MS. FARBER.

Zakhar and his two men would keep her in sight and use two-way radios to communicate Linnéa's position to each other. They would close on her in the crush of passengers exiting the building. Neither of Zakhar's men were familiar to Olander and both possessed hypodermic syringes containing a fast-acting sedative. The one who got closest to her would stab the needle into her thigh or buttocks, depress the plunger, remove the hypodermic, and melt away into the crowd. Zakhar's other man would approach her. Zakhar, himself, would not be far behind.

The moment Linnéa began to sway, they would move in to "escort" her to the waiting limo. Nicor would drive them immediately to the private tarmac where their plane awaited them.

Nicor dropped Zakhar and his two men at the American Airline's concourse departures doors at 8:35 a.m., more than an hour before Marta Forestier's flight was due to arrive. Zakhar and his men spread out and scouted the flight's arrival gate, taking differing and meandering routes to reach the American Airline's gate to avoid being seen together.

They had been in the airport around fifteen minutes when passengers began to gather at the banks of television monitors within the concourse. Zakhar saw that one of his men had stopped to watch the broadcast. The man made a surreptitious gesture toward the television.

Keeping his distance from his teammate and giving no sign of recognition, Zakhar studied the image on the screen. Smoke billowed from one of the two iconic towers of the World Trade Center.

What is this? Zakhar pushed closer.

The crowd grew in size and agitation. The usual pulsing push of passengers within the concourse ground to a nervous standstill.

As the news cameras focused on the smoking tower, a passenger plane appeared on the screen. It floated into view and glided, in seemingly slow motion, directly into the second tower.

Nothing happened—and then the tower erupted into flames.

Zakhar cursed. The crowd around him panicked.

The airport devolved into pandemonium—screaming, shouting, weeping, hysterical chaos. In their panic, passengers dropped their luggage and ran. Other passengers tripped on the abandoned baggage. A suitcase, one of its hard corners striking the floor, popped open, and its contents spilled out. In the melee, an elderly woman slipped on the clothes and fell.

Zakhar signaled his man and they pushed through the crowds to reach a wall and wait there. Zakhar used the two-way to contact Nicor.

He had to shout to be heard. "What is happening?"

"An attack," Nicor shouted back. "The World Trade Center towers are burning! I can see them! And people are saying another plane hit the US Pentagon in Washington, D.C. Who is doing this, Zakhar?"

"How would I know? I don't know any more than you do."

"Well, what are your orders?"

"My orders?" Zakhar stared around at the chaos. "We wait for our target's plane to land. It must land somewhere, no? They cannot return to London."

He and his men gathered within eyeshot of each other, waiting and watching, while the concourse fell further into bedlam. From across the way, Zakhar kept his eyes glued on the televisions. The fire within the towers, fed by jet fuel, roared higher, and dense black smoke roiled up the sides of the towering buildings like a living thing.

The buildings cannot survive this, can they? Zakhar thought. *The fires burn too hot.*

The PA system blared that the airport was closed, shut down until further notice. Passengers rushed the exits to fight over taxis, but Zakhar continued to watch the monitors. He, like many around him, could not look away.

He and his men remained watching until the South Tower collapsed in on itself. The newscasters watching and commentating did not recognize what had happened. Even when reporters on scene repeated several times, "The South Tower has collapsed. The South Tower has collapsed," the commentators could not grasp their words.

"What are we looking at? You're saying the South Tower, the side of it has collapsed?"

"No, the entire building has collapsed!"

Zakhar understood what he'd seen before the newscasters did. Then he saw the leader text crawling across the bottom of the screen:

INTL FIGHTS TO D.C., NYC
DIVERTED TO CANADA

Canada? *Canada!* What demons had moved against him? What evil forces had aligned to impede him in this way?

Snarling his rage and frustration, he gestured to his men. They pushed through the remaining crowd and exited the concourse. Nicor saw them from where the limo was parked. He honked his horn and waved his sign.

When they reached him, it was obvious that their driver was shaken. His cheek dribbled blood from a cut near his temple. "I had to lock myself inside. The mob! They tried to take the car from me! It was all I could do to get inside and lock the doors. I feared they would break the windows and pull me out, but the police came."

Zakhar turned his face toward the western skyline. The smoke and ash from the fallen tower and from the fires in nearby and adjacent buildings billowed upward in gray-white plumes. And then he saw it . . . the second tower slowly dropping from view, folding in on itself.

A wail of grief arose around him, but all Zakhar could think was that he would have to call Petroff and deliver the unwelcome news.

"Hand me the sat phone," he demanded.

Nicor placed the heavy, block-like device in Zakhar's hand, and Zakhar keyed in Petroff's number. When Petroff answered, Zakhar had to shout to be heard over the crowd and the cars.

"Vassili Aleksandrovich, have you seen the news? Yes, both towers. The second has just collapsed—everything around us is in an uproar. It must be a terrorist action, *da?*"

He cupped his hand around the mouthpiece to block out the noise on his end so he could hear Petroff's answer and instructions.

He answered back, "*Nyet,* Vassili Aleksandrovich, we cannot stay where we are. I am sorry to tell you that the authorities have closed the airport. All the inbound flights have been diverted to Canada."

He listened to Petroff's screamed invectives until the man took a breath. Zakhar was quick to inject a reply. "We will find out where they have sent her plane and follow her there, Vassili Aleksandrovich. Do not worry. I will not fail you."

He hung up and slid into the rear seat. "Get us out of here." When Nicor did not respond fast enough, Zakhar cursed him. "Drive, I said, you fool! Take me back to the house."

He saw nothing on the drive but Linnéa Olander's face before him. *Laughing.*

LAYNIE SCANNED THE CABIN once more, wondering if anyone had noticed the brief exchange between her and Abdul. She didn't think so. The passengers in business class were either dozing or occupied with their own interests. They were all facing forward in their seats.

Everyone except one man.

Near the front of the cabin. Second row, aisle seat, left side. He was sitting forward, turned toward the rear of the cabin, watching her—and not making much effort to hide his scrutiny.

Laynie's eyes passed over him without stopping, swept right, paused, then swept left, again passing over him as though he had not caught her attention.

But she had done her assessment of the watcher. "Seasoned" Caucasian, likely in his mid-forties, dark brown hair, shot with gray, cut short. And a big—no, *large*—physique. He filled out his seat plus some. Even without seeing him stand, she estimated the guy was around six foot four, two hundred forty pounds or more.

He was still staring at her and making no attempt to hide the fact.

Laynie recognized another professional when she saw one—and this one had fixated on her.

Marstead? More than likely.

If he had IDed her as Linnéa Olander, he would use an Airfone as soon as the flight was in range of land. Additional Marstead agents would be waiting for her in New York.

She pushed into the lavatory and locked the folding door behind her, falling against it as though to barricade herself within.

Trembling all over.

"*Herre Gud, hjälp mig!*" Oh, dear God, help me! The words, uttered in Swedish, fell from her lips without forethought.

Behind the fear and chaos running rampant in her head—in a little corner of her mind far from her present worries—she marveled. *God help me? God? Where did that come from?*

She set her purse on the lip of the diminutive sink, ripped open the Velcro seam to the padded enclosure, and pulled out the HK. She stared at the gleaming blue metal barrel shaking in her hand and played out the limited scenarios open to her.

Meanwhile, a battle of logic warred in her mind.

If I shoot while we're in the air, I chance taking down this plane and killing all these people.

No, not if the round only penetrates the airplane's skin and misses any vital wiring. The plane's pressurization system will compensate for the leak. And it's only a .380. Doesn't have the punch of a .38 Special or the stopping power of a .45.

It was lethal enough to kill Mahatma Gandhi.

Yeah, well, his assassin shot him three times in the chest, point-blank range.

Okay, but don't shoot out any windows. That would be a problem.

No kidding.

She envisioned instant cabin depressurization, a sucking hole where the window had been, pulling every loose item in the cabin out into the void beyond.

She drew a shuddering breath. *Get yourself together, Laynie.*

Her bladder urged her to use the facilities, so she did, tucking the HK into her bra. *I'll keep it handy*, she told herself. *Maintain my options.*

When she had finished her business and washed her hands, she rummaged through her purse, looking for anything else that might give her an edge. An advantage.

When her fingers touched the metal nail file, she grabbed it out of her purse, and pulled it from its leather sheath. It had no slicing edge, but it had a pointed tip, and the blade wasn't as flimsy as some nail files.

Good for one thrust—in close quarters.

Laynie needed to keep the file handy. She poked the nail file's pointed tip through the gathers of her blouse's bodice. She then reached under her blouse, found the file's point, and poked it back through the fabric, securing it.

"Okay, easy to reach," she told herself. For a long moment, she stood with her head down, gathering her courage. Then she picked up her handbag, unlocked the bifold door, and pulled it toward her.

A slab of a hand drove her back into the lavatory. The man from Row 2, the one who'd been staring at her, squeezed himself inside the tiny stall. He shoved Laynie hard and shut the folding door behind him—no mean feat given the confined space. He'd pushed her back so unexpectedly that she'd been forced to sit on the toilet while he towered over her, his microwave-sized chest in her face.

"We need to talk."

⟶ ⟳ ⟵

CHAPTER 9

THE SIZE AND SMELL of her attacker filled up the lavatory. Laynie said nothing because her assailant's fists looked as though they could snap her neck in two as easily as snapping dried pasta. And there wasn't much she could do in these close confines to defend herself.

Except for the nail file.

She let her hand float toward it.

"Don't do it, missy. Don't even think about it."

Laynie's hand fell to her side. "Who are you? What do you want?"

"Those are both good questions, particularly since you didn't scream for help. I mean, what woman doesn't scream her fool head off when shoved into a bathroom against her will? *Unless.* Unless she's the kinda woman who can take care of herself, who can teach a man to keep his hands to hisself, if need be—which is what I figgered you for."

His accent was down-South good-old-boy country. Laynie cranked her neck up and back to examine his extremely close-up features.

"*I* asked the first question. Who are you?"

He grimaced. "Not 'zactly supposed to do that, a' course—but the exigencies of the immediate situation demand adaptability."

The glut of polysyllabic terminology piled on top the country schtick confused Laynie. Then he started to lift his hand—that slab of brick attached to the end of his arm—and she tensed.

"Calm down, lady. Just goin' for my badge."

Badge? Marstead agents did not have badges.

He extricated it from his jacket pocket and held it near the tip of her nose—so close that Laynie went cross-eyed trying to read it.

He read it for her. "Quincy Tobin, Deputy US Marshal, Sky Marshal on this flight. My friends call me Quince."

Laynie swatted the badge away and played her indignant card. "Then I'll call you *Marshal Tobin.* Why did you barge in on me, Marshal? What do you want?"

"Like I said, we need to talk. My gut tells me that we-all got us a problem on this flight."

Laynie wrinkled her nose. "*Your gut?* What, got you a bad tummy? Need some Pepto-Bismol, do you?"

"Don't get mouthy, missy. If my gut is right, I'ma need some help."

She feigned surprise. "Help? From me?"

From li'l ol' me?

He grinned, displaying an impressive set of pearly white teeth—and a dimple in his chin. "Let's play nice, shall we? I introduced myself. Want to reciprocate?"

Crossing her arms and moving her right hand to the head of the nail file, Laynie said, "Marta Forestier."

He nodded. "Noticed you back at Heathrow before you got on this plane, how you stayed tucked away in the back of that coffee shop, watching the gate, checking out every person who came and went, then boarding at the last minute. I boarded just before you did and saw how you scoped out our cabin when you entered—you did walk right by me, you know. I figure you to have some training, possibly undercover experience?"

He shifted from perfect diction back to his hokey po' boy accent. "So, jest off the cuff, I'ma guessin' Marta Forestier ain't your real name—how'm I doin?"

Laynie glared at him. "I have no idea what you're babbling about. I'm a French citizen, a tourist to the US."

"And I'm a ballerina. Just you wait till you get a gander at me in my tutu."

The image was so blatantly ridiculous that Laynie sniggered.

He grinned again. "The Bolshoi wanted me bad, let me tell ya, but I chose the Marshals Service 'stead."

"I'll bet the Bolshoi's still crying its heart out."

Laynie was, in that moment, not as worried about this guy as she initially had been. She pulled herself together—but he kept pushing.

"So, care t' tell me who you really are, *Marta?* Cop? Fed? Crossing guard? You got a badge? I showed you mine. C'mon. Lemme see yours."

"Sorry. Don't have one."

"That so."

"Yes. That's so."

"Hmm. I pegged you for an American at first, but your accent—it jest ain't right, y'know? Has that tetch o' European, cain't quite put my finger on. So, now I'ma have ta think 'spook.' Which is it—CIA? NSA? DIA? *MIA?*"

MIA? Oh, if you only knew.

"No, no, and no."

He got in her face. "Jest tell me one thing, missy. You one of the good guys, or you one of the bad guys?"

"Good is a relative term, Marshal. And on another point? Stop calling me 'missy' like I was in high school. Judging from those crinkles around your eyes and the heaping helping of salt in your formerly pepper hair? You and I are probably close to the same age—so quit with the 'missy' business."

He stared at her, close-up, eye to eye, until she thought his eyeballs might pop out on springs and blind her.

Laynie put a palm on his chest and tried to push him back a few inches. She may as well have been trying to move Plymouth Rock.

She huffed her frustration. "Marshal Tobin, what is it you want from me?"

"*Deputy* Marshal Tobin. Well, fact is, *Marta*, we got us a hijacking in the works, and I find myself sadly shorthanded and outgunned."

Suddenly her earlier disquiet made sense. "Wait. You mean . . . the Middle-Eastern men. They acted like they weren't together, but . . ."

"Figgered you fancied 'em when I caught your little do-si-do with the leader, minute ago."

"He's their leader? Yeah. Something's off about him. Cocky. Reckless or arrogant? But I didn't put him and the others together. Didn't think 'hijackers.'"

I should have.

"No worries. It's my job to spot 'em."

"And you're certain?"

"If I were t' bet cash money that they *weren't* terrorists, I'd lose that bet, sure as the sun comes up in the morning—which it won't for any of us on this plane if we don't act to stop them."

Laynie frowned. "How many, total? Two here in business class—meaning the others are in economy class, somewhere behind us?"

"Yep—three in econo class—two in the rows behind us, the third on the other side. And I 'spect that, *soon*, at a predetermined time or signal, them good ol' boys up front with us will charge the cockpit, while the three behind us move to take control of the crew. They'll take hostages from the passengers to manipulate the crew."

"What's the plan?"

"Cain't say 'less I know you'll play along, cuz I'ma thinking ain't neither of us makin' it to New York if we don't work together. So. *Marta*. I have another question. You carryin'?"

The question caught her off balance. She didn't let it show.

She also didn't answer.

"C'mon, *Marta*. Yay or nay. Ain't got all day."

"I'll show you mine, Marshal—if you keep yours holstered."

"Fair 'nuff."

"I'm pulling my piece now," Laynie murmured. She reached inside her blouse and drew the HK P7K3.

"Well, ain't that sweet—an itty bitty popgun," Tobin drawled. "An' I'm partial t' blue, too. How many rounds?"

"Eight plus a second mag. I hope that doesn't mean you intend to reenact the O.K. Corral while we're flying at thirty-thousand feet in a fragile, pressurized metal tube?"

"Naw, but word t' the wise?" He dropped the phony accent. "If circumstances dictate that you engage our friends with your popgun, don't shoot out the windows, okay?"

"Got it. What are you carrying?"

"Glock .40 cal in m' shoulder holster, compact Beretta 9mm backup on m' ankle."

"And I got me a mean nail file tucked into m' blouse."

He snickered. "Good to know."

Then he went formal. "Marta Forestier, I hereby deputize you to assist me, a Deputy Marshal of the US Marshals Service, to prevent the hijacking of this plane. You are authorized to use whatever force deemed necessary, including deadly force, to prevent such an attack. Do you accept this responsibility?"

Laynie blew out a long breath. "All right. I accept."

"Good. And now that we've exchanged confidences and all? I'ma thinking we'd better get out of this phone booth before someone suspects us of doin' the mile-high cha-cha."

"You still haven't told me your plan."

His expression drew down into serious lines. "Right. Here it is. Above all else, above every other concern including personal or passenger safety? Those hijackers *do not* gain entry to the cockpit. You got that? No matter how many deaths or hostages taken, we—you and I—must prevent those men from reaching the cockpit and taking control of this plane."

Laynie watched the creases around his eyes deepen.

"Therefore, *Marta*, I need to know that *you* are mentally prepared to do whatever it takes to keep them from seizing this plane. I'm taking a risk with you, believing from what I've observed that you are both trained and experienced. Am I right in my assessment? And will you do your part, or am I making a huge, potentially lethal mistake by placing trust in you?"

Laynie's lips twitched. *Why, you turn that country schtick on and off like tap water, don't you?*

She met his solemn, inquiring gaze. "No, you're not making a mistake, Marshal. Yes, I'm trained. And, yes, you can count on me to do my part."

"Good to know. Well, then, *Marta*, that is the plan."

"You plan doesn't have much detail to it."

"No, but your seat assignment puts you in a primo location."

Laynie nodded. "You handle Abdul and his buddy when they charge the cockpit. I'll pick off the others as they poke their heads through the curtain."

Tobin's eyes narrowed. "Abdul? Thought you didn't know these guys."

Laynie adopted his drawl. "Ah don' know 'em, Marshal Tobin, sir. Honest ah don'! Jest slapped that-there 'Abdul' label on him, on accounta he irked me reeeel bad."

Tobin wasn't convinced.

Laynie sighed and tried again. "Seriously, Marshal. I'd never seen these guys before they boarded this plane. Scout's honor. I'll even pinky swear, okay?"

Shooting the stink eye her way, Tobin acquiesced. "Okay, I'll take you at your word—but only because you threw in a pinky swear."

He got back to business. "We have as good a plan as we can conjure, given the time we have. You put that popgun back where the sun don' shine and leave first. I'ma follow you in a minute."

Getting the door open was, again, problematic. She was amused when Tobin's massive hands spanned her waist and lifted her like a feather. He pulled her tight to his chest, swiveled, sat on the toilet, and plopped her down in front of the door.

Then he really threw her for a loop.

"God go with you, Marta."

She met his gaze. He meant it.

"Thank you . . . Quince. Same to you."

"He's always with me," Tobin answered, tapping his chest with a finger the size of a ball-peen hammer. "Right here."

Laynie jerked her chin once, acknowledging him, pulled the door toward her, and slid out.

No one was waiting in line for the lavatories, and not much had changed in the cabin. Passengers still slept or conversed with their seatmates. Bryan and Todd to the left of her seat tapped on their laptops. The honeymooners snuggled, giggled, and made goo-goo eyes at each other.

Beyond the honeymooners, the dark-haired man pivoted in his seat—as though he'd been waiting for Laynie to exit the restroom. He nodded and smirked, his eyes filled with salacious intent.

Laynie's lips curved up, and she made a little pistol with her hand and aimed it at him. Smiled larger and kept smiling. *It's a joke, Abdul*, her expression told him. *A joke, get it? Just a silly, bold-eyed, not even remotely demure, uppity American woman joke.*

Until it isn't.

He laughed and "shot" her back.

Cold and cruel. He was no novice, either. He was calculating and dangerous. Marshal Tobin would have his hands full.

I can't think about Tobin's problems. We won't succeed in stopping them if I worry about him instead of taking care of my own business.

Laynie sank into her seat, considering the three men she was tasked to subdue. Would they be as experienced as she believed Abdul was? How would they be armed? Guns were difficult to get aboard a plane, but not impossible.

I know that for a fact.

Her first action was to bend over like she was tying a shoe, remove the HK from her bra, and tuck it between her right hip and the seat cushion where it would be at the ready. She collected her gun's second magazine from her purse and slipped it into her left pocket. She left the nail file in her blouse where she could easily get to it.

Then she began her mental preparations, putting herself in the hijackers' minds, running various scenarios they might use, determining where she should position herself to ambush the three in economy class when they charged forward—planning her offensive the way Marstead had taught her years ago.

The greatest unknown was the timing. She couldn't move into position before Abdul and his companion commenced their assault. She had to watch them and time her play to beat theirs by seconds.

A couple of minutes passed. Tobin left the restroom and sauntered up the left aisle toward his seat. Laynie peeked right to see if Abdul had noticed Tobin coming out of the lavatory she'd just exited.

He hadn't. As far as Laynie could tell, he and his companion had their heads together, whispering.

It was going to be dicey, no matter how it played out. Two against five. Defense rather than offense.

Still, Laynie was filled with an odd sense of relief . . . of purpose and "rightness"—something she had lost along the way. She wasn't afraid. She had a job to do, a *real* job, one that would save lives, not betray confidences. She could die doing this *one thing* and be grateful that Fate had placed her here, at this unique moment, for this very reason.

Fate? Or God?

All of God's promises are true, Laynie . . . One way or another, he will work those promises into reality. He is God, and he will have his way.

Laynie put her head down and whispered into her hands. "Oh, Kari! You have such faith in your God, but the way it looks now? I probably won't ever make it to your little homestead out on the prairie—and your God won't have his way. Not with me, anyway."

She clamped her teeth together and forced herself to put those thoughts aside. She needed to focus on the skirmish ahead, but as she tried to gather her thoughts, Abdul's cold, cruel expression intervened. She clenched her jaw so hard that it hurt.

Think you've got this hijacking sewn up, don't you, Laynie told the dark-haired man silently. *Think again. No. No, I won't let you do this. We* will *stop you—whatever it takes.*

Laynie checked her watch. She had set it ahead to EDT, and it read 9:05 a.m. They were scheduled to land at Kennedy in less than an hour. The pilots would begin their descent soon.

Across from her, Bryan told his associate, "I'd better check in with Grace—just in case the meeting's been moved up or the venue changed."

Bryan drew a pen and a pad of paper from his briefcase and lifted the Airfone from its receptacle in the seatback in front of him. He slid a credit card through the reader and punched in the number.

"Hey, Grace? Hi, Bryan here. Just checking in and—"

"Bryan! Oh, my God! Bry—"

Even from across the aisle, Laynie heard what was coming from the phone.

Screams. Shouts.

Fear.

"Grace? What the *blank* is happening? What? I can't hear you!"

Bryan had raised his voice, gaining the attention of everyone in the cabin. Then he pulled the phone away from his ear and looked at it.

Todd asked, "What's up?"

"Dunno. The call cut out. *Bleeping* things aren't all that reliable."

"Better call her back."

Laynie half-listened while Bryan went through the tedious process of running his credit card through the reader and dialing. She was experiencing a revelation of sorts.

What, precisely, had Petroff told her?

I have been summoned to a special assembly of the Security Council. Some emergency of state over rumors of an impending attack on high-value targets of unknown number, the information coming to us via a source I have little confidence in.

She reached her hand across the aisle and touched Bryan's arm.

"Excuse me. I couldn't help but overhear your conversation. Where do you work?"

Bryan frowned. "I'm a little busy here, Marta."

Laynie's fingers dug into his flesh. "I asked you a question. *Where do you work?*"

Bryan flushed and stared down at her hand. "We're full partners at Braun and Pfizer. Our offices are at the World Trade Center, North Tower. Now, Miss Nosy, if you don't mind, *blank* off."

Laynie let go. She had questioned Petroff, couching her inquisitiveness in concern, hoping to gain additional information. *An attack? Will you be safe, my love?*

Da, without a doubt. I surmised from the call that it was not a threat against the Motherland, and I am not certain how much credence I give the intelligence—coming via Afghanistan.

It had bothered her then, for multiple reasons. What imminent attack on a nation other than Russia would spin up the Russian Federation's Security Council, forcing them into full session as it had? And why had the intelligence, coming through Afghanistan, made Petroff less than confident of the report? What did it all mean?

Laynie's instincts raced ahead, her analysis moving faster than her thoughts, colliding with conclusions—horrifying conclusions that set her heart pumping so hard, she struggled to catch her breath.

She stuttered and murmured to herself, "Imminent attacks on-on-on more than one high-value target . . . intelligence from Afghanistan. Afghanistan . . . a predominantly Muslim nation, governed by arcane and often savage tribal leaders who provide refuge to-to-to radical Islamic factions."

She asked herself, *And which nation on earth do Islamic fundamentalists despise above all others?*

"America," Laynie breathed. "America, *the Great Satan.*"

Her conclusion was a kick in the gut. *The hijackers are going to weaponize this plane.*

She reached across the aisle and grabbed Bryan's pen and a pad of paper. "You'll get this back."

"Hey! You have some nerve," Todd fumed.

She ignored both him and Bryan, who was having no luck reaching anyone in their New York offices.

She scribbled a note as rapidly as possible.

> *Overheard on Airfone*
> *Prob. attack on W Trad Centr*
> *surmise hjackers plan same/similar*
> WILL WEAPONIZE THIS PLANE

It was enough. Tobin would "figger" it out. She tore off the sheet and folded the note twice, drew her HK from the side of the seat, chambered a round, and patted the spare magazine in her left pocket to assure herself it was there.

Then she stood in the aisle beside Bryan and stretched her back and shoulders, her careless gaze roaming over the two dark-haired men to assure herself that they were seated.

She transferred the HK to her left hand, and Bryan glimpsed the tip of its blue barrel against her thigh. He stopped what he was doing. His mouth hung ajar. Laynie stretched casually in his direction, speaking low and clear to both men.

"Yes, I have a gun. Hijackers are aboard this plane—don't look around, you idiots! I'm working with the US Marshal on this flight. Keep your heads down. And do not—I repeat—*do not* leave your seats. Keep the aisle clear."

Not waiting for their reaction, Laynie palmed the little gun in her left hand and sauntered forward. She tipped her neck side to side as though working out a kink and moved toward the front of the cabin. As she passed the second row, she lightly tapped the gun against her thigh. Tobin's head moved incrementally. He did not react further than that.

She reached the front of the cabin, turned, started back to her seat. As she passed Tobin, she dropped the note in his lap. She reached the eighth row and sat down.

Bryan and his companion, terrified expressions on their faces, leaned her way to mouth something to her. Laynie shook her head and put her finger to her lips.

The events of the next moment set the hijacking in motion.

CHAPTER 10

THE CABIN SPEAKERS crackled to life, and the pilot came on the PA.

"Ladies and gentlemen, this is Captain Sheffield speaking. We are presently just south of Nova Scotia on our descent to JFK. However, I have just received word that flight control has placed us in a holding pattern off the Atlantic seaboard, meaning we will be a little late to our gate. I apologize for any inconvenience. I know they are working hard to get us on the ground, so we appreciate your patience."

A flight attendant at the front of the plane took over. "In preparation for landing, the captain has asked that all passengers return to their assigned seats and remain seated. Please fasten your seatbelts and raise your seatbacks and tray tables to their full, upright, and locked positions."

Laynie peered down the right aisle. Instead of complying with the captain's orders, Abdul and his companion stood up and moved up the aisle toward the forward bulkhead.

Laynie ducked her head toward the left aisle—Tobin was missing from his seat. *He's waiting for them behind the partition, with his Glock .40 and his Beretta 9mm.*

Time for me to act, she told herself. *I have to trust that Tobin can get his job done, just as he's trusting me to do the same.*

She left her seat and, with a quick stride, crossed the right aisle. She crouched down behind the honeymooners, against the lavatory wall, with the HK in her right hand, nail file in her other, her left arm cocked and ready to swing—and waited for the hijackers to act.

Several things occurred simultaneously.

A flight attendant near the cockpit screamed.

Tobin shouted, "US Marshal! Stop where you are!"

Two shots boomed forward of business class. Chaos and screaming erupted from the passengers. Another shot, higher pitched. And a man pushed through the curtain separating economy class from business class.

Laynie, crouching in wait, her back against the lavatory wall, rose partway. She swung her left arm back—then forward, jamming the nail file into the man's inner thigh. Before a scream could leave his mouth, she pushed up from her partial crouch and, using the strength of her legs to propel her left hand upward, forced the terrorist's gun hand high into the air.

The weapon discharged—a *machine pistol* on full auto—spraying rounds into the cabin ceiling.

Laynie's training kicked in. Her vision tunneled. Narrowed. Fixed on her sole objective. *Stop the terrorists. Kill them.*

She confronted her opponent face to face, her gun up, counting on his forward momentum to bring his belly into direct contact with the barrel of her HK. She fired twice. As he started to slump, Laynie body-slammed him to keep him erect, using his bulk to shield herself while she sought her next target.

The second attacker stood in the aisle on the other side of the curtain. He was facing the economy class passengers, trusting that his compatriot had his back. As soon as he realized something had gone awry, he whirled around, tearing the curtain from its hooks.

Stop the terrorist called it some kind of accident *s. Kill them.*

Laynie aimed straight down the aisle—hoping no one stood in the aisle behind him. She fired twice. The terrorist jerked, the impact stumbling him backward. Two men in economy class jumped from their seats to wrest something from his hand and push him to the floor.

Laynie scanned the cabin. She had a third armed terrorist to take out. She dropped the hijacker's body she'd used as a shield, pivoted back to business class, and leaped from the aisle's alcove, gun extended, ready to fire again.

Her third target had pushed into business class from the other economy class aisle. When he spotted her across the cabin, he charged. Laynie stood her ground. She fired and kept firing, hitting her target three times, missing once. Her gun locked open. *Out.* As the man lurched sideways, slumping onto the hospitality station, Laynie dropped her empty mag, slapped in the spare, and chambered another round.

She did not have to use it. Her target slid to the floor, leaving a trail of blood across the hospitality station's countertop. His weapon—a box cutter—fell beside him.

A box cutter?

She swiveled, both hands on the gun, arms and gun extended, scanning for further threat.

"Clear! Three down! Tobin?"

His voice bellowed back to her. "Clear! Two down."

All Laynie could do was blink as she processed what had happened in bare seconds. She checked the pulse of her last target, sprawled in front of the aft hospitality station.

Nothing.

She collected the box cutter and pocketed it.

Still ready and wary, she retraced her steps to check her first target. She glanced past the torn curtain into economy class before turning her attention to the fallen hijacker.

He was still lying in the aisle where Laynie had dropped him. Just behind the honeymooners.

The honeymooners.

The young bride clung to her husband, sobbing. He stared into space.

"You all right?" Laynie asked him.

He nodded, an automatic response, unblinking, staring without sight. In shock.

Laynie bent over the hijacker's body. He, too, was dead, his weapon beside him. Laynie looked at the ceiling of the business class cabin. It was peppered with pencil-thin holes that hissed and whistled as rivulets of air exited the cabin.

She pulled the gun from the hijacker's dead hands. She had initially believed the weapon to be an Israeli Uzi but, after turning it over in her hands, recognized it as a Croatian AG Strojnica ERO, a knockoff of an Israeli Uzi.

How in the world did he smuggle this thing on board?

She looked closer. It was the man who'd been wearing a walking cast. Not any longer. Bits of plaster clung to his shortened pant leg.

Clever. He had pieces of the disassembled gun hidden within the plaster cast. They must have precut the cast so all they had to do was pull it off.

She checked the Strojnica's settings. Full auto.

She ejected the machine pistol's magazine. Empty.

When Laynie had shoved the hijacker's arm into the air, he had emptied all thirty-two 9mm rounds into the cabin's ceiling. Thirty-two rounds that could have, instead, shredded the lives of the newlyweds and others in business class, that could have blown out windows, with catastrophic results—but *no.* Every round had gone into the ceiling where thirty-two fine streams of air escaped the cabin.

Above the high-pitched hiss of air, Laynie heard her sister's voice in her head.

"Be safe, little sister. I've only just found you."

Laynie cringed. *My answer was stiff. Snide, even. "I'll do my best."*

She bit her lip. *But when I caught sight of Marshal Tobin eyeing me, I did call on God . . . in a hopeless sort of way.*

"Herre Gud, hjälp mig!" Oh, dear God, help me!

Would God answer such a panicked, frantic cry? An insincere cry of desperation?

"If you need him, the Lord will hear you call on him, Laynie."

"Too many things went right when they could have gone so very, very wrong," Laynie whispered. "I guess I can't disagree with you this time, Kari."

Sparing the peppered ceiling a last look, she cleared the Strojnica's chamber and slung its strap over her shoulder, letting the gun ride down her back. Then she kicked aside the torn curtain and entered the economy class cabin to assess the second hijacker she'd shot. He, too, was dead. The two men who had rushed to subdue him stood over his body in the aisle. One of them had the hijacker's weapon—another box cutter.

He held it awkwardly toward Laynie. "You'd better take this."

The fog of battle was lifting, and Laynie's hearing began sending signals to her brain that she had blocked out. She realized that throughout the plane, passengers were weeping and moaning, crying and wailing.

The screaming made her head hurt.

She shouted, "Listen up, people!"

Parents shushed their children, and the cacophony began to die. Passengers, all the way to the rear of the plane, strained to hear her.

"Here. Use this." A flight attendant held a cabin microphone toward her. "Press this button to talk."

Laynie took the microphone. "Listen up, everyone. It's over. Five hijackers are down, but the plane is fine . . . I believe. Business class has multiple holes in the cabin ceiling, but the plane's automatic pressurization system will—should—compensate for the loss of air. Please stay in your seats and remain calm. The captain will apprise you further when he is, uh, ready."

"What did she say?" a woman shouted from the rear of the plane. "We've still got kids screaming back here and couldn't hear the announcement!"

Someone bellowed, "She said everything's fine! They killed those *blank blank* hijackers!"

Except Laynie knew in her gut that they hadn't been "mere" hijackers.

She handed the mic back to the flight attendant, intending to go forward and check on Tobin—but the male passenger who had handed her the box cutter placed his hand on her arm.

Laynie's reaction was automatic. She grabbed his fingers and wrenched them backward, forcing him to his knees in the aisle.

"Stop! Please!"

Laynie wiped the haze of confusion from her eyes. Dropped his hand. "Sorry. Little jumpy, I guess."

"I get it, I do. No problem. I just wanted to thank you." He got up and put out his hand. "Thank you . . . thank you for saving us."

Others around them chimed in. "Yes! Thank you!"

Laynie looked down and nodded.

I'm so tired.

"Yeah. Okay." She couldn't manage more than to turn away, try to put one foot in front of the other, try to move in Tobin's direction.

The economy class passengers began clapping—softly, then building as business class joined them, until cheers echoed through the plane. Laynie still just nodded . . . and walked into business class, up the aisle to the forward bulkhead, ignoring every voice that clamored for her attention, unable to respond to them.

She spotted Tobin standing at the top of the aisle, his left arm hanging limp, blood flowing from his shoulder, down his arm, dripping from his fingertips.

"You okay?" she asked.

"I think so, but right at this moment? Man, it burns like crazy."

Two flight attendants had a first aid kit out and were trying in vain to get Tobin to stop moving long enough to let them staunch the bleeding.

"Abdul and his buddy?" Laynie asked.

Tobin jerked his head toward the crew station behind the partition. "Laid them out pretty much where I took them down. Abdul didn't go peacefully. Managed to get off a shot. Hey, think you could wrangle a couple of passengers to haul the other bodies this way?"

"Sure. Okay."

"Then I need you . . . to go through their pockets. Collect everything. And me . . . I think . . . think I'ma need to sit . . . down."

Laynie gestured at the nearest passenger, front row. "Hey, you—yeah, you. Get up, please. The marshal needs to sit before he falls down." She steered Tobin to the vacated seat. "I'll deal with the bodies. You—" she indicated the displaced passenger, "move yourself and your stuff to the marshal's seat over there."

She motioned to a flight attendant, "I need somewhere to put these." She dumped the machine pistol, magazine, and box cutters into a drawer an attendant pointed to and turned her attention to the two bodies.

"Marta!" Tobin called. "Check their pockets."

"I can help you with that," a steward offered. "Go through their pockets for you, I mean."

"Thank you. I'd appreciate it. Keep the stuff from each body separate. I'll be back shortly."

Laynie longed to sit and close her eyes, shut out what had happened, but she couldn't just yet. While the steward began his grisly work, she trudged back toward economy class.

The body was still lying crumpled in the aisle, and all eyes in the cabin were fixed on her.

Time to make another announcement.

She signaled the attendant, who handed her the microphone. "May I have your attention? Two things. First, Marshal Tobin up in business class needs a doctor. Do we have a doctor on board?"

A woman raised her hand. "Here. I'm an obstetrician, but I can help."

Laynie pointed back to business class. "Thanks. He's up front. First row."

The clamor had picked up again, so she raised her hand for silence. "Marshal Tobin has also directed me to move the bodies to the front of the plane. I need some volunteers—preferably with strong muscles and stronger stomachs."

The same two men who had been quick to help her not more than ten minutes ago looked at each other and climbed from their seats.

"Happy to help, Marshal," one of them called. The other nodded. A third man joined them.

Laynie didn't correct their error. That would come later—hopefully after she had deplaned and disappeared.

"All right then. Three bodies to move, this one here. That one," she gestured forward to business class, "and the third through the curtain over there." She pointed to the other aisle.

More men joined the initial volunteers. They formed three teams and went about their work in silence.

A woman seated on the aisle touched Laynie's arm to get her attention and jerked her hand back just as quickly.

Guess she saw what I did the last time someone surprised me.

"Yes?"

"Marshal, some passengers have been using the Airfones. A lot of them just get a busy signal, but some are getting through, and they are hearing strange reports from the people they talk to. Something about a plane flying into the World Trade Center? Do you know anything about that?"

Laynie, her expression shuttered, said, "I have no information about that. Perhaps you could ask a flight attendant?"

"They're stonewalling us!" someone shouted. "They've been huddled together, whispering, and they refuse to answer our questions. The captain must know something—he's in radio contact with the ground, isn't he?"

Laynie found two flight attendants with her eyes. They looked elsewhere, unwilling to meet her gaze. She turned to the attendant who had handed her the microphone. Her head moved infinitesimally side to side.

Around her, passengers spoke over each other, saying what they'd heard, demanding answers, becoming more agitated, soon to be beyond control.

"Listen up!" Laynie hollered.

"I can't tell you what I don't know myself. Now, obviously, something has happened, but I don't want to hear any more shouting—get me? We all need to be patient and wait until we're on the ground to find out what's going on."

Laynie turned toward an older gentleman where he stood, stooping beneath the low ceiling of the middle section. She knew then that it was hopeless to keep a lid on the news.

"Care to share?"

"I talked to my daughter, soon as the shooting stopped. She lives in Midtown Manhattan. I had her on the phone for coupla minutes before we were cut off. She says a plane flew into the North Tower of the Trade Center less than an hour ago. First, everyone thought it was a little commuter plane, but it wasn't. It was a full-sized passenger jet."

He lifted his voice over the rising tide of questions and fear. "My girl was watching the tower burn on TV when I called. The newscasters called it some kind of accident, but while we were talking, a *second* plane crashed into the *other* tower. My daughter saw it live, as it happened. Yeah, with *two planes* flying straight into the towers? That's no mistake. That's not an accident. That's an attack! We're under attack!"

Passengers screamed, cried, and shouted out questions.

"My son works in the subway station under the South Tower. Did everyone get out?"

"My mom runs a florist shop across the plaza!"

"My daughter works for Braun and Pfizer, North Tower!"

Laynie shuddered. She had heard the cries of terror coming from Bryan's call to a woman named Grace who worked at Braun and Pfizer. In the North Tower.

All she could think was, *We were part of the plan, a second wave of attack. This plane.*

Shaking all over, she handed the mic to the flight attendant, turned her back on the confusion, and walked back into business class.

CHAPTER 11

ᙢ LP ᙣ

LAYNIE LEANED against the door to the cockpit and considered the pile of bodies stacked by the fore bulkhead. She was waiting to view whatever the steward collected from the pockets of the hijackers. As the steward finished with one body, he used a marker to draw a number on its forehead, wrote the same number on the plastic bag where he was putting whatever he pulled from their pockets, as she requested, keeping the evidence separate.

It wasn't much, all total. Five passports—two Saudi, one Yemeni, two Syrian—wads of cash, two European driver's licenses, and a folded piece of paper. The paper came from Abdul's pocket.

Laynie waited until the steward and another attendant covered the bodies with blankets, before she checked on Tobin. The doctor had gotten the bleeding under control, but Tobin was trussed up like a Sunday chicken, his pasty-white complexion as appetizing as cold, day-old, cooked pasta.

He was obviously weak. At least he was lucid. "You did good, Marta."

"You, too, Marshal, but I wish they'd get this boat on the ground. You need a doctor."

Tobin pointed his chin to the ob-gyn who had patched up his shoulder. She was sitting in a flight attendant's jump seat, just inside the crew space. Close enough to tend to Tobin if he needed her.

"I have a doc. She's a baby doc, so pretty soon we'll find out if I'm having a boy or a girl."

Laynie laughed. The effort wore her out. *So tired!*

"I'm waiting for that gander of you in your tutu."

"In your dreams. What'd you get from the hijackers' pockets?"

"Nothing remarkable except for this." Laynie unfolded the paper. It was a three-panel section clipped from a folding map—what looked to have been one of those colorful, detailed tourist maps of Manhattan Island. Two locations were circled in pencil, the number 1 was written to the side of one circle, the number 2 beside the second. The map's details were crowded with tourist sites represented by icons or 2D buildings. She held the paper closer and squinted to decipher the icons.

Mount Sinai Beth Israel Hospital (1)
Empire State Building (2)

"Hey, Tobin?"

"Yeah."

"Remember the note I passed you? Take a look at this."

Took him a minute to see what she'd seen, to understand what it meant. "A hospital! They were going to fly us into a hospital?"

"A *Jewish* hospital. Alternate target? Empire State Building, say, if they came in too high and overshot the hospital."

"Thank God we stopped them."

"Stopped *this* one."

They exchanged looks. He lowered his voice.

"How many, you think?"

"Two planes hit the World Trade Center, both towers. Heard something about the Pentagon, too. Could be others. Dunno."

"Dear Jesus!"

Laynie knew Tobin wasn't swearing. "Yeah, it's bad, but . . . not as bad as it might have been."

"I couldn't have stopped them without you."

"I . . ." She shrugged.

"Whatever you say, *Marta*. But I know this—God himself put you on this plane."

She tried to smile, but only one side of her mouth worked. Tears, real tears, sprang to her eyes.

I was supposed to have flown from Paris to New York, but then . . . Oh, Kari! How did your God know to intervene? How did he manage to put me on this plane, on this day?

Swiping away the moisture before it overcame her, Laynie nodded, gently touched Tobin's shoulder, and staggered back to her seat. She was in a stupor as she stumbled down the aisle, hardly noticing how people stared. Stared at her and at the blood on her blouse. At the gun she still gripped in her hand.

They dipped their heads, nodding silent appreciation, some whispering, "Thank you."

Laynie saw nothing, heard nothing.

When she collapsed into her seat, a flight attendant appeared, her cheeks streaked with smears of mascara. "Marshal? Marshal Forestier? We think you need to eat, Marshal. You . . . you've been under a lot of stress and haven't eaten since you first came aboard."

Food?

Laynie blinked back the haze. "That would be nice. Thank you."

Another attendant joined the first. "And . . . if you'll allow me?"

She pulled Laynie's tray table down, set a plate of steaming washcloths on it, and started sponging Laynie's left hand.

Sponging the blood from her hand.

Laynie remembered the gun in her other hand and slid the HK between her hip and the seat. She surrendered to the attendant's ministrations.

Bryan and Todd watched, waiting for a chance to speak. They restrained themselves until the flight attendant gathered up the soiled cloths. Then Bryan pounced.

"You know what happened, don't you? Can you tell us?"

Laynie blew out a breath. "You couldn't hear the man in the next cabin? He said he managed to get through to his daughter who lives in Midtown. Two planes hit the Trade Center towers, like fifteen minutes apart. We don't know much more than that."

Todd gaped. "Both towers? But that . . . that can't be an accident, can it?"

"No, it can't."

Brian's eyes widened. "W-what about the people in the towers? I mean, when I called Grace, I could hear people shouting. Screaming. Was anyone hurt? Did they evacuate everyone?" This from Bryan.

"Honestly, Bryan, I have no idea, but I'm pretty sure that's why we're parked at ten thousand feet, out to sea and not over land, circling and waiting. Every plane inbound for New York is probably doing the same."

She didn't say what she was thinking. *Honestly, Bryan, if a passenger jet crashes into anything, of course people die. Obviously! We just don't know how many. Yet.*

The flight attendant returned with a sandwich and a hot cup of coffee.

Laynie drank down the whole cup at one go, scalding her tongue. Nothing had ever tasted so good.

"Another?"

"Right away."

Laynie picked at the sandwich, then took a tentative bite, in spite of Bryan and Todd ogling her like it was feeding time at the zoo. She reached for the second half of the sandwich and stared at her plate, bewildered. It was bare.

"You ate it, the whole thing," Todd assured her, "but I can't say you chewed."

The attendant placed another cup of coffee on her tray. "Let me know if you want something stiffer, 'k? Captain Sheffield says you and Marshal Tobin get anything you want—with his compliments." She lowered her voice. "He would be out here thanking you personally for saving our plane, but he and the copilot have locked themselves in the cockpit. As a precaution."

Laynie imagined ice-cold vodka sliding down her throat, burning into her stomach, melting away the tension in her shoulders and the awful images of three dead men—men she had killed.

Then her survival instincts kicked in. *I'm exhausted. Trashed. Alcohol will knock me out. I can't let down my guard or do anything to compromise my wits. I have to be ready to run the moment they put wheels on the runway.*

"Just coffee, thanks."

THEIR FLIGHT CONTINUED in a holding pattern another few minutes before the captain came over the PA system to break the news Laynie had been expecting. She glanced at her watch. Just past 9:30 a.m.

So much has happened in such a short time . . .

It felt like hours had passed.

"Ladies and gentlemen, please give me your undivided attention."

The passengers had not heard from Captain Sheffield since prior to the attempted hijacking. At his request, the plane settled into a near-tomblike silence.

"Ladies and gentlemen, I have several important announcements, so please remain quiet as I cover each one." He spoke slowly, articulating each word. "First, we have received word that, at approximately 9:25 a.m. this morning, the FAA, by order of the Department of Transportation, has closed US airspace to all civilian flights until further notice."

He paused to let the information sink in before continuing. "What this means is that, until further notice, the US has been designated a no-fly zone for all air traffic except authorized military aircraft. It means that we will not be landing at JFK."

Anticipating a tide of reactions from the passengers, the captain raised his voice to compensate.

"Ladies and gentlemen, I must ask you to contain yourself until I have finished. My second announcement is that the Air Traffic Control System Command Center out of Washington Dulles has directed us, this flight, to continue in our present holding pattern—off the Atlantic seaboard of the US—until we can be rerouted to an alternate airport. It should not be a long wait. Since we are an inbound transatlantic flight, we have been placed high on the list to be rerouted.

"That being said, I want to assure you that, at present, we have sufficient fuel to arrive at our new destination. I repeat, *we are not in an emergency fuel situation*, and I hope to report our new destination to you soon. I can tell you that we will be landing somewhere in Canada, but that is the extent of my information regarding our destination at this time."

Canada! Laynie blew out a sigh of relief. She hoped it would be easier for her to leave unnoticed from a busy Canadian airport such as Toronto or Montreal than from JFK. The unplanned destination would even throw off her pursuers.

The captain was not finished. He had saved the worst news for last. "We are all quite understandably concerned and confused about the events today that have triggered an emergency closure of US airspace. We also want to know if the attempted hijacking of this plane is related to the closure. Let me tell you what I have been told."

Here it comes, Laynie thought.

"At approximately 8:46 this morning, less than an hour ago, persons unknown hijacked a passenger plane out of Boston and flew it into the North Tower of the World Trade Center. Seventeen minutes later, a second plane, also out of Boston, hit the South Tower. New York emergency responders are on scene, assisting in the evacuations of the towers.

"Yes, these were deliberate actions against the City of New York, but more importantly, against our nation. Although we have no definitive proof at present, in my mind there is little doubt that the failed hijacking of this flight was an attempt to hit a third New York target. Therefore, we cannot thank God enough that he placed two US Marshals aboard this flight who recognized the signs of an imminent takeover and foiled the hijackers' plans."

Cheers erupted throughout the plane, drowning the captain's speech. Laynie kept her chin down and her eyes closed, but the tears she had warded off earlier refused, amid the din of cheers, whistles, and shouts of appreciation, to stay where she'd ordered them to stay. They slid down her cheeks and puddled in her lap where they moistened a patch of dried blood on her blouse. Blowback from her first shots. Dried blood on her blouse.

The observation snapped Laynie out of her maudlin mood.

I need to change clothes before we land—and I'll likely need to abandon my bag.

Mentally, she sorted through her carry-on, adding to her handbag what she would take, what she would leave.

The captain called for attention again, and the plane quieted. "As you might imagine, I've been told that the scene on the ground in New York is chaotic. Phone lines have been overwhelmed. Hospitals are preparing to receive hundreds of injured in the hours ahead, but they need phone service in order to do their jobs.

"Therefore, as captain of this flight, I am terminating in-flight communication with the ground. I am sorry. I know many of you are worried about the safety of your loved ones, and they are worried about yours. Please know that I understand and sympathize with your concerns, but the care of the injured within the attack zone must be our first priority.

"That is all for now."

Laynie tucked the HK back into her bra and picked up her handbag. "Bryan?"

"Yes, Marshal?"

Laynie made herself relax back into her role as Marta Forestier. "Would you mind getting my carry-on down from the overhead? I . . ." She let her gaze fall to her blouse. "I should probably put on a clean top."

"Sure. Where do you want it?"

"How about behind your seat, in front of the lavatory?"

In relative privacy, Laynie unzipped her case and sorted through her clothes. She pulled out the hoodie, two T-shirts—one long-sleeved, the other short-sleeved—jeans, clean underwear, socks, sneakers, hairbrush, elastic hair holders, folded backpack, and billed hat. She laid the hoodie on her seat, picked up everything else she'd selected, and turned toward the lavatory.

"I've heated more washcloths for you." It was the stewardess who had washed her hands. She held out a dish containing the hot, wet cloths.

"Thank you," Laynie muttered. "You have been very kind to me."

"Honestly? It is the least I could do to thank you."

Laynie entered the lavatory, locked the door, and stared at her reflection in the lavatory mirror. She was struggling with the events of the past hour, with what she'd done, the images continuing to play on an endless, repeating reel in her mind.

It wasn't the first time I've killed, but that was twenty-odd years ago. Today, I killed three men.

I killed three men!

The horror was more than the hijackers' deaths. It was the swift, violent, and coldhearted manner in which she'd acted. Revulsion surfaced, then intensified. The censure intensified. Condemned her.

But other words rang in her heart, words of vindication.

You saved the more than two hundred souls on this plane, Laynie, passengers and crew. You saved a hospital filled with helpless men, women, and children. Hang on to these truths. You were compelled to choose between good and evil. You were brave, not weak. You chose right. You did right.

"Yes, I had to choose. I chose right—no matter how wrong it feels."

Laynie peeled off her dirty blouse. The blood had soaked through onto her skin and underclothes. She stripped and washed herself from the waist up, using all but one hot wash cloth. The last one she saved for her face, letting the steam soak into her pores, breathing in the welcomed moisture.

When she had dried, she changed into the clothes she'd taken from her suitcase, layering the long-sleeved T-shirt over the short-sleeved one. After she'd rechecked the CD-ROM and her last passport, both hidden in the flat compartment at the bottom of her handbag, she added the hairbrush, hair holders, backpack, and hat to the bag. When she emerged from the lavatory, she folded her soiled clothes into the carry-on, zipped it, and had Bryan hoist it into the overhead.

"You look a lot better now," he commented. "Less stressed."

"Thanks, Bryan."

"Ladies and gentlemen, this is your captain. We have received updated flight instructions. The FAA has directed us to transfer flight control to NAV CANADA. At the direction of NAV CANADA, we have altered course to our new destination, Greater Moncton International Airport, Moncton, New Brunswick. Our estimated time of arrival is 11:54 a.m. Atlantic daylight time—or 10:54 a.m. eastern daylight time, thirty-three minutes from now."

New Brunswick? Not Toronto or Montreal? Not a populous city where she could disappear?

Captain Sheffield continued. "The Prime Minister of Canada has very kindly offered his nation's hospitality to us until the FAA lifts its closure of US airspace and we are allowed to continue on to JFK."

New Brunswick was on Maine's northeast border and Moncton was on the easternmost tip of New Brunswick near the crossing to Prince Edward Island.

I cannot stay with the other passengers. I have to leave them as quickly as I can. Canadian law enforcement will, no doubt, be on us the moment we touch down, checking passports and recording passenger accounts of our flight. My role in taking down the terrorists will put me under a microscope. Most of them think I'm a US Marshal, when I'm not. My ID will never hold up.

Laynie ran calculations in her head, routing herself through the three nearest US border crossings. She estimated the distance to be between three and four hours by car, regardless of which route she chose.

The border crossings might be closed. At the least, they will be on high alert. No, I can't try to cross. I must head northwest, skirt around the top of Maine, and then south and west to Québec or Montreal where I can lose myself in a city.

Laynie was jerked from her thoughts as Captain Sheffield continued speaking, his voice deepening, as though speaking the next words would make them too real.

"Ladies and gentlemen, I am saddened that I must also be the bearer of more unwelcome news. I have received word that, at approximately 9:37 eastern daylight time, a third hijacked plane flew into the Pentagon just outside Washington, D.C."

Laynie slid her eyes around the cabin as passengers began putting the facts together.

They are just now realizing that we were supposed to be part of the attack, that the hijackers on this plane had intended to fly us into a building, too, as part of a larger, coordinated assault upon America.

Captain Sheffield continued. "Finally, I must report that at 9:59 a.m., the South Tower of the World Trade Center collapsed. We do not yet know the state of the North Tower nor do we have news on evacuations or survivors as of yet. That is all for now."

Bryan stared forward in shock. Todd sobbed into his hands, joining many others who were weeping.

Laynie walked forward to Tobin's seat and squatted in the aisle near him. He, too, had tears in his eyes. He tried to smile when he saw her.

"The news is pretty bad, huh?" Laynie whispered.

"Like you said, it could have been a lot worse. We saved hundreds, Marta. Possibly thousands."

Laynie just nodded. She didn't trust herself not to choke up.

Tobin added, "Got yourself cleaned up, I see."

"Yeah. How are you feeling?"

"Okay, except the weakness. Doc says I need a transfusion. Glad we'll be on the ground soon."

"Yeah, about that . . ."

Laynie stood up and addressed Tobin's seatmate. "Hey, excuse me? Would you mind swapping seats with me? Or move back two rows where the, uh, hijackers were sitting? Yes? Thanks."

She climbed into the seat next to Tobin and leaned her head toward him. "Remember our introduction? When you pushed me back into the lavatory?"

"Abdul shot my shoulder, Marta, not my brain."

"Keep it down."

He frowned. "All right." He leaned closer.

"While we were in the lavatory, you asked me a series of questions, including if I had a badge."

His probing gaze sharpened. "Okay."

"I don't, but one of those three-letter acronyms you tossed at me is a close fit."

"And?"

"And I can't be questioned by Canadian law enforcement, Tobin, or by *any* law enforcement agency. Do you follow? I've been deep undercover for years in a country whose name I cannot mention. If, when we land, someone were to photograph me and that photo made the news? Not good."

She shook her head. "If I want to stay alive, I need to circumvent any publicity or questions. *I need to disappear*—and I mean the minute our wheels hit the ground."

Tobin, his eyes locked on hers, sat back, sorting through what she'd said. "A country whose name you can't mention, huh? And you want me to help you."

Unflinching, Laynie stared and waited.

He glanced behind them, and her eyes followed. Both passengers appeared to be dozing. Tobin tilted his head toward hers.

Laynie said nothing. She waited while he considered his decision.

A minute later he breathed in her ear, "The doctor tells me I need to go straight to a hospital, probably by ambulance. She'd typically come with me, but I will insist that she rejoin her family—and request that you, a fellow marshal, accompany me. After that, it will be up to you."

"I don't want you to lie for me. It would put your career in jeopardy."

He snorted. "Little late for that—after deputizing a perfect stranger to help me put down five terrorists and all."

She smiled. "Hey . . . no harm done." She added, "Yet."

"Well, *Marta*, the fact is, I owe you, as does everyone on this plane. I'm willing to take that hit."

"Thank you, Marshal."

"You mean Quince, don't you? Cuz now we're friends and all."

Laynie's smile widened. "Yeah. Quince."

She returned to her seat and addressed Bryan and Todd. "Hey, guys, I'm going forward to sit with Marshal Tobin the remainder of the flight. They'll be taking him to the hospital when we land, and I'll be accompanying him. Would you do me a favor?"

"Anything, Marshal," Todd exclaimed.

"Thank you. Just take my bag when you deplane? We'll all end up at the same place, I'm sure. I'll get it from you then."

"Happy to help, ma'am."

Laynie shook her head. "No need to 'ma'am' me. Marta is good enough."

"Thank you for everything, Marta," Bryan whispered.

Laynie nodded, picked up her handbag and hoodie, and returned to Tobin. He had news.

"The doc had already asked Captain Sheffield to radio ahead for an ambulance. I just now sent her back to her family in economy class. Explained that you'll be riding in the ambulance with me."

"Okay. Thanks." She fidgeted. "Um, one more thing?"

"Yeah?"

Laynie's face flamed. "Seems that I'm a little long on Swedish kronor and short on American dollars."

One of Tobin's brows lifted. "You sayin' you need a loan?"

"Uh, yeah, well, it's not like I can pay you back anytime soon, so . . . more like a donation. I . . . I'm sorry."

"What are friends for? Just don't make me regret this."

He glanced behind him again, then forward. The flight attendants were strapped into their jump seats. The two attendants within Tobin and Laynie's sight had their heads together, talking.

With his eyes on them, Tobin scooched forward and reached his right hand into his hip pocket. Pulled out his wallet. He flipped it open and fumbled, one-handed, to get at the cash.

His hand was so big, it was like watching someone work while wearing a catcher's mitt.

"Little help here?"

Laynie held the wallet open.

"Take it all. There's probably a couple hundred in folding money. Take it all, my business card, too. Who knows? You might feel like calling me sometime."

Laynie emptied his wallet of cash, took a card embossed with the US Marshals Service logo, and flipped the wallet closed. While Tobin slid his wallet back into his pocket, Laynie stuffed the bills and card into her handbag.

"Thank you."

Tobin acknowledged her thanks with a jerk of his chin and a serious expression. "I'm not kidding, Marta. *I owe you.* You helped save all these people today—an' this here country boy's butt inta the bargain. If you ever need me, *you call*, ya'll hear me?"

Laynie nodded and turned her face away, afraid she'd start shaking and wouldn't be able to stop. Afraid her stoic outer shell, already crazed with so many hairline fractures, would shatter, and she'd never be able to pick up all the pieces and put them back where they belonged.

They were silent the remainder of the flight. By the time the plane bumped onto the runway in Moncton, Laynie's stomach was in knots.

Tobin leaned toward her. His whispered words knocked her sideways.

"Listen, Marta, before the ambulance arrives, I want to pray for you."

"What?"

"I've been sitting here praying for you, and now I want to pray with you. Over you. Okay?"

"I—"

Tobin grabbed for Laynie's hand—his mitt, the size of a waffle iron, swallowing hers whole.

"Lord Jesus, I hold Marta up to you, asking that you see her safely away from here without discovery. Please, Lord, help her navigate or overcome every obstacle that presents itself and guide her safely to wherever she is headed—without the public exposure she fears.

"Lord, I am calling on you, asking you to have your will and your way in Marta's life. Whatever her real name may be, you already know her by that name. You know her and you have called her to you. Let her know how very, *very* much you love her, Lord. I pray this in Jesus' name. Amen."

The PA crackled. "Ladies and gentlemen, Captain Sheffield here. Please listen carefully. Because of what occurred on this flight, it is important that you follow all instructions given to you *to the letter*.

"Do not remove your seatbelts until told to. You will be directed to unbuckle your seatbelts and deplane row by row. *Do not stand* until you have been directed to. Have your passports at the ready. And before passenger deplaning can begin, Canadian law enforcement needs to remove the bodies of the hijackers while a medical team assists our wounded marshal from the plane. An ambulance is waiting to take him to the nearest hospital, so please be patient and follow instructions."

On cue, the door forward of business class opened. Two New Brunswick provincial law enforcement officers and a man in plain clothes entered. Armed officers stationed themselves at the head of each aisle. The flight crew pointed toward Tobin, and the man accompanying the officers approached Tobin and Laynie.

He nodded to them. "Good day. I am Lieutenant Paul Moreau, Canada Customs and Revenue Agency. You are Marshal Tobin? Marshal Forestier?"

"I'm Marshal Tobin," Tobin responded. Laynie said nothing.

"We have emergency personnel on the jet bridge, ready to come aboard and take you out on a gurney."

"Not likely," Tobin growled. "I came aboard on my own two feet, and I'll leave the same way."

Moreau smiled. "Spoken like a Yank. I anticipated as much."

Laynie stood and offered her arm. Tobin grabbed ahold of it and launched himself to his feet. He swayed once but quickly got his bearings.

"This way, then," Moreau murmured.

As Tobin took his first shuffled steps, the cabin behind them broke into applause.

"See how popular you are, Tobin?" Laynie grinned.

"Not *me*, Marta, *we*. Without you, I may have kept the plane from being weaponized, but no telling how many people would have died in the process, including me. Don't forget that God put you on this plane."

As she had so many times over the past seven years, Laynie heard Kari's voice. Confident. Joyous.

This time, Laynie listened to it.

"All of God's promises are true, Laynie, because he is true. One way or another, he will work those promises into reality.

"He is God, and he will have his way."

She blinked back her tears and focused on keeping Tobin on his feet until they reached the ambulance.

CHAPTER 12
LP

LAYNIE WATCHED the EMTs load Tobin into the ambulance—on a gurney, despite his protests. She climbed in after him, taking her handbag and hoodie with her. The EMTs went about their business, checking Tobin's vitals, inserting an IV line, asking him about his medical history. They paid little attention to her. When they arrived at the ambulance entrance behind the hospital, the emergency room staff took Tobin one way and steered her another.

"Waiting room's that way, miss," a nurse ordered.

"Right. Thanks."

When Laynie turned the corner, she bypassed the waiting room and headed for the main hospital entrance. She exited there, moved quickly to the street, and scanned up and down, looking for—

There. A plexiglass shelter across the street denoting a city bus stop.

Once she'd confirmed that the street was on a bus route, she walked on, putting distance between herself and the hospital, heading for the next stop on the bus line. A quarter of a mile later, she came to another plexiglass shelter belonging to Moncton's Codiac Transit Commission. While she waited for the bus, she plotted her next steps.

The airspace of the entire North American continent is on lockdown because of the attacks. Canadian and American border agents will be on high alert, hoping to catch other terrorists who may be plotting further strikes or attempting to escape the US into Canada.

Laynie studied the route map and fare chart on the shelter wall, memorizing the general layout of Moncton's streets and bus service.

Right now, Marta Forestier is not on anyone's radar. However, once the authorities start looking for her, and find that one of the "heroes" of Flight 6177 has gone missing, it will be problematic for me to cross over into the States. My best option is to stay in Canada but move west. Go west and keep moving.

When the bus arrived, she swung aboard, handed the driver an American dollar bill, and affected an Aussie accent.

"G'day. Sorry I don't have the correct fare. Came over from the States and haven't exchanged m' money."

"You know I can't make change for you?"

"Yeah. No worries, mate."

Laynie moved to the back of the bus. When the bus arrived downtown, Laynie left through the rear door and faded into the town's pedestrian traffic.

Unfortunately, Moncton wasn't large—only around sixty thousand residents. Most everything she did would be noted and remembered by someone, eventually leading those tracking her to this location. She needed to make that trail go cold, right here and right now.

She ducked into a public restroom. As soon as she'd locked herself in a stall, she eased out of her long-sleeved T-shirt, revealing the short-sleeved shirt beneath it. She opened her handbag and removed hairbrush, elastic hair holders, backpack, and billed cap. Then she transferred her hoodie, the long-sleeved shirt, and the contents of her purse to the backpack.

She stuffed her telltale Bottega Veneta handbag into the restroom garbage, burying it deep under used paper towels.

"Goodbye, old friend."

When Laynie left the restroom, she was wearing a different colored shirt, she carried a small backpack on her back, and her long hair was braided and tucked up into her hat.

She boarded another bus, one she knew was headed down Main Street. She got off several blocks before the intersection of Main and Cameron, the closest Codiac bus stop to the Maritime bus station, cut left on Canada Street and walked, unhurried, the rest of the distance to the station. Inside the bustling station, she exchanged all but fifty of the American dollars Tobin had given her for Canadian currency, then bought a cup of coffee, a sandwich, and a ticket to Edmundston.

Two hours later, her bus arrived at the Edmunston station, but Marta had gotten off early at the junction of NB-2 and NB-120 where she flagged down a trucker.

"Where you headed, miss?"

"Toronto, to visit my cousin."

"I can take you as far as Montmagny, if that suits?"

"It does. Thanks."

The highway would shortly take them out of New Brunswick and into the province of Québec. Montmagny was on the far outskirts of Québec City but still on the highway. The driver was talkative about the flights that had been diverted to various airports in Canada and more than willing to rehash other horrors of the day, details of the attacks Laynie had not yet heard.

"Wife and I watched the news coverage all day long until I had to run my routes. When that second tower fell, we knew there weren't gonna be survivors—and the firemen, those brave souls who ran into the buildings to evacuate everyone? Dead when the towers fell."

He shook his head. "All those emergency people, standing around, waiting for the wounded that would never show up. Saddest thing I've ever seen."

"You say there was another plane as part of the attack? Do the authorities know where it was headed?"

"Yeah, Flight 93, out of Newark. Heard that some of the passengers charged the hijackers—kinda like the two sky marshals did on that American Airlines flight from London—but not with as much success. The hijackers still managed to take control of the cockpit and crash the plane in Pennsylvania. Killed themselves and everyone else on that plane."

"I wonder where the hijackers had intended to fly the plane when they took control of it."

"Rumor has it they were headed to Washington, looking to hit either the Capitol Building or the White House."

"Despicable," Laynie whispered.

When conversation tapered off, Laynie leaned against the truck's window and slept until the driver pulled up at the junction of Highways 20 and 283. She woke and saw they were at a truck stop on the outskirts of what she assumed was Montmagny. The clock on the truck's dash read just past one in the morning.

"Sorry to leave you, but I turn off here, miss." He pointed. "That's a nice 24-hour café over there."

"It's not a problem," Laynie assured him. "I'll wait inside the café until daybreak. With luck, I'll be at my cousin's in Toronto before dinner tomorrow. Thanks for the lift."

Laynie walked away from the highway, down the embankment, and into the bushes rather than waiting the remainder of the night in the café where she would be noticed, remarked upon, and remembered. She pulled out her hoodie, zipped it on, and squatted down in the brush, arms wrapped around herself to spend the rest of the night.

AFTER WITNESSING THE attacks on the twin towers and leaving JFK, Zakhar and his men had been forced to return to the house on Long Island. Where else could they go? Zakhar's team could not leave Long Island. In fact, they could go nowhere. Their plane—like all others—was grounded. New York City and its waterways were on lockdown by order of the local and federal governments—every bridge, tunnel, and mode of water transport to or from the city, including Long Island.

The only redeeming information reported by the news was that passengers on flights diverted to Canada were in similar straits. They were required to remain where their planes had landed until US airspace reopened.

Zakhar hoped that meant Linnéa could not leave the town she'd landed in until international air flights resumed. He wished to immediately set out for Canada by automobile and reach the woman before the ban on commercial flight ended. However, even getting started on his way to Canada would be problematic. The only way off Long Island was to hire a private boat, one that was willing to risk being boarded by the Coast Guard.

The caretaker told Zakhar, "I know a captain. He can take you, not tonight or tomorrow night, but the following night."

"That is too long of a wait!" Zakhar fumed. "Double his price."

The caretaker shook his head. "No, Dimitri Ilyich. This man, he has other clients, regular customers, whom he cannot refuse. You understand what I say?"

Zakhar nodded.

"So. Do you wish his services in two days' time or not?"

"*Da.* I will take his offer."

Zakhar reported his arrangements to Petroff, who could not seem to grasp the extent of the attack or the tumult that had ensued. Instead, he subjected Zakhar to twice-daily tongue lashings.

"Bring her to me, Zakhar, you idiot! Do not show your face before me again until you have her in your grasp, do you hear me?"

But Petroff's invectives were no longer Zakhar's highest motivation. His own desires had burned within him until they outstripped Petroff's threats.

I would swim across to the mainland, if I were able, Zakhar seethed within himself. *I will do whatever I must to capture this woman. Whatever it takes, I will have her.*

--------- ❧ ---------

Laynie Portland
RETIRED SPY

PART 3: ELAINE
LP

CHAPTER 13
LP

AT DAWN, LAYNIE woke. She was stiff and cold. The mid-September temps had dropped into the high forties overnight, and she had slept sitting up, the hood of her light jacket pulled up over her head and neck, her knees tucked up against her chest, her arms around them. Shivering, she got up and shook out her arms and legs to warm them. She brushed off bits of dried weeds and dirt, then drew out her hairbrush, pulled back the hoodie, and redid her hair, again tucking it up under her hat.

She walked out the kinks on her way up the embankment and across the highway to the truck stop. The place was already busy. Truckers who had spent the night in their cab's sleeper berth were up, filling their tanks with diesel, checking their tires and loads, and getting a hot meal before hitting the road.

Laynie was hungry, too. When she entered the café, the breakfast rush was on.

"Sit anywhere you like," the waitress told her. "This time of day, we share tables." She had four plates balanced in her hands.

"I'd like to clean up first."

"Through that door, hon."

Laynie used the facilities, washed up, then sat at the counter and ordered coffee and the full breakfast special. She kept her ears attuned to the conversations around her, listening to the truckers talk among themselves.

She ordered a coffee to go, paid in US dollars and received Canadian as change, then hung around outside in the warming sun until a fifty-something trucker wearing overalls sauntered out the café door. He paused not far away to light up a cigarette.

"Hey," Laynie said.

He turned, ran his eyes over her. "Hey, yourself."

"You running into Ottawa today?" Ottawa was west of Montreal.

He drew on his cigarette. "Might be."

"I'm looking for a ride."

He continued to inspect her. "Might be able to accommodate you. What's your name?"

"Beverly. Yours?"

"Colin."

"Well, Colin, I'm interested in the ride. Nothing else."

He shrugged. "I can take you as far as Montreal. From there, I head south. I'm crossing over into the States and running into New York today." He eyed her again.

"Montreal is fine."

She estimated her ride with this particular trucker would end around three hours or one attitude adjustment down the road.

She was right. Midway to Montreal, Colin pulled into a rest area with overnight parking for trucks and RVs. He set the brake, letting the engine idle, then slid his hand onto her thigh.

"I have a comfy bed back there. Why don't we climb up and have some fun?"

Laynie smiled. "I wondered when you were going to ask, Colin."

He grinned and reached higher on her thigh. Faster than his eyes could follow, Laynie bent his index finger over the back of his hand, twisting it along the way. She heard a pop and a crack before his scream deafened her and he jerked his hand away.

"You *blanking blank*! You broke my finger!"

"Didn't your mother teach you not to put your hands on a woman without her permission? Oh, wait—I'll bet she did, am I right?"

"Get out! Get outta my truck!"

Laynie grabbed her backpack. She opened the door and climbed down to the rest area's asphalt parking lot.

"See you, Colin."

A string of obscenities followed her, cut off when Laynie slammed the passenger door on them.

She walked over to the women's restroom. After she'd done her business, she went back outside and sat on a bench against the wall of the restroom to wait. The wall had soaked up the morning sun, so she closed her eyes and reveled in its warmth. She stayed that way for more than an hour— long after Colin had driven away—waiting for the right ride came along.

She was alone in the rest area when an older couple with Ontario plates pulled into a parking slot in front of the facilities. A grandmotherly woman got out. Before she did anything else, she attached a leash to a little Scottish terrier and let him out onto the sidewalk. She pulled a bowl from the car with her other hand, poured water into the bowl, and set it down on the walkway for the dog to lap.

"What a beautiful little Scottie. What's his name?"

She was cautious. "Thank you. His name is Bernie."

Bernie, pulling at the leash, pranced over to Laynie, sniffed her hand, and let her pet him.

"He's precious. Would you like me to hold Bernie's leash while you go inside?" Laynie asked. She knew the woman would refuse.

"No . . . but thank you for offering."

"Not a problem. He reminds me of my brother's dog, poor thing."

"Oh?"

Laynie stared away into the distance. "My brother died in a car crash some years back, and we were heartbroken. But then his little Scottie, Angus, the joy of my brother's life, passed away not long after. You know, we all believe Angus died of grief. Your Bernie reminded me of Angus . . . and my brother."

"I'm so sorry, dear."

"You're very kind. Thank you."

The woman went into the restroom, taking Bernie with her. When she came out, she led the dog into the adjoining field to do his business. Out of her peripheral vision, Laynie watched the woman's husband join her. They talked, and Laynie saw the woman's hand flutter in her direction once.

She leaned against the restroom's sun-warmed block wall, closed her eyes, and waited.

"Excuse me, miss?"

Laynie sat up, glanced around, fixed on the elderly gent. "I'm sorry— are you speaking to me?"

"Yes. We, my wife and I, don't see any other cars here. So, we were wondering if you needed a ride somewhere?"

"Well, the truth is, the man I was riding with made advances toward me. I sort of had to get out of his truck in a hurry—if you catch my meaning." Laynie sighed. "I'm just glad he didn't pull over in the middle of nowhere."

"What? Oh, my. Yes, I take your point." The grandfatherly man appeared suitably shocked. "Uh, where are you headed, miss?"

"Toronto."

"If you like, we can take you as far as Montreal."

"But I'm a stranger," Laynie pointed out.

"My wife is a pretty good judge of character. Come on. I'm Don. My wife is Midge. You can ride with us."

"Thank you, Don. I'm Beverly, by the way."

Laynie sat in back with Bernie's head on her lap answering the couple's questions, telling them she'd been staying with friends in northern Québec for the past month.

"I have friends in Toronto, too, so I'm heading there. I was supposed to have flown, but after those terrible attacks . . ." She let her words hang.

She had won over the couple, and they were eager to aid her.

"Such a shock! Don't know how long US and Canadian planes will be grounded," Don said over his shoulder. "Some folks who are stuck here can't find a place to stay. Hotels are filled up."

"And we don't usually pick up hitchhikers," Midge confided, "but it does seem as though the Lord brought us along at just the right time to help you on your way—even if we can't take you all the way into Toronto.

"We live in Saint-Alexandre, you know, southeast of Montreal. Been to visit our son and his family." She ended with the proud declaration, "We have three grandchildren. Such a blessing."

Since most hotels were filled because of the grounding of all of all air travel, Don and Midge insisted on dropping Laynie on the outskirts of the city at a little motel with a flashing vacancy sign. When they continued on their way and were out of sight, Laynie walked up the street looking for a bus stop. When she'd found one and had studied the route map, she waited for the next bus that would take her across the river into downtown Montreal.

As she dropped her coins into the fare box, she asked the driver, "How close to an HSBC bank does this route run?"

The driver tipped his chin at the seat closest the door. "Sit there an' I'll point one out t' you. We stop a block farther on from it."

"Thanks."

Laynie watched the bustling city go by until the driver said, "Look down that street. See the bank?"

Laynie did. "Yes. Thanks."

When he let her out at the next stop, she backtracked to the bank, then began her quest for a hotel within walking distance of the bank, one that promoted what was being called "a business center." A business center or business hub was a room containing computers, printers, office supplies, and broadband service for hotel guests.

Laynie found several hotels that fit the bill. She chose the Westmount, about a mile from the bank, deciding that the distance was an added security measure in her favor.

She ate lunch in a small restaurant first, then used their restroom to tidy up. While locked in the restroom stall, she switched out her French ID for her American passport and its matching driver's license and credit card.

Leaving the restaurant, Laynie found a busy department store. She quickly purchased two suitable pants outfits, undergarments, a light jacket, and a pair of slip-on pumps and stockings. She also chose an unremarkable handbag and wallet and another carry-on suitcase with wheels. Her last purchase was a simple watch. She used her credit card for all of her purchases.

Before she left the department store, she transferred everything into her new suitcase and handbag. She loaded her shopping bags and the backpack into the rolling case and returned to the hotel.

She was not as presentable as she would have wished to be, but she'd soon remedy that. The larger issue was whether or not the Westmount had rooms available.

She approached the check-in counter. "Good afternoon. Have you any vacancies?"

"We didn't last night after the airport closure, but we have a few today. How many nights?"

"Two, perhaps three."

"ID and credit card, please."

Laynie handed over her passport and credit card.

"Thank you, Miss Granger. You're in room 5018, fifth floor. The elevator is just there, across the lobby. Please let us know if you intend to stay longer than two nights."

"I will. Thank you. And—"

Laynie caught sight of the stack of newspapers on the check-in counter and the headline—**HAVE YOU SEEN THIS WOMAN?** Marta Forestier's image, although grainy, stared back at her.

"Yes? You had a question?"

"Oh, I was just wondering where I might find your business center?"

"Down that hall, beyond our guest shop."

"Thank you."

Laynie closed her room's door behind her and put on the security latch. She went into the bathroom and stared at her face in the mirror. Pulled the hat off her head revealing Marta Forestier's brown hair.

What if I hadn't kept my hair up? What if I'd ditched the hat earlier? Would the desk clerk have recognized me from the photo in the newspaper?

Was it another "divine coincidence"—like the strange anxiety symptoms that had driven her to abandon her Paris to New York flight?

Laynie shook herself.

I can't rely on coincidence, random good fortune, or emotions. Besides, being driven by fear is deadly. She stared at her face. It was noticeably thinner than when she'd left Madame Krupina's Spa.

Madame Krupina's Spa? How much time had passed since that day? Less than two weeks?

Ten days or two weeks? It felt like a lifetime.

She shook herself again and thought about the photograph in the paper.

I must radically alter my appearance before I go to the bank tomorrow.

She showered, washed and dried her hair, and changed into a new outfit. Then she used the hotel telephone to call the same department store she'd shopped in.

"How may I direct your call?"

"Salon, please."

"*Bonjour.* How may I serve you?"

"Good afternoon, do you have any appointments today for a color and a cut?"

"I think not, but one moment. Let me check. Ah! How surprising. You are in luck. We have had a cancelation. Will three o'clock suit?"

Laynie frowned. *Luck. Again.*

"Yes, that will be fine."

"And your name, please?"

"Elaine. Elaine Granger."

It was the first time Laynie had said the name aloud.

My birth name. What my birth parents, Michael and Bethany Granger, named me.

Few people in the world knew that name or the long, tangled history behind it.

Kari does, though, and she shared it with me. That day on Puget Sound.

Although the name Elaine Granger lacked the comforting familiarity of Helena or Laynie Portland, Laynie felt she had reconnected herself with her sister, as though she had taken a step, a necessary one, toward her true self.

Toward going home.

"Very good. We'll see you at three, Miss Granger."

IT WAS EARLY afternoon, the day after the attacks. Tobin was propped up in his hospital bed, a bag hanging from an IV tree feeding him fluids and pain meds, when the FBI arrived to question him. Lieutenant Moreau accompanied the two agents.

Under the agents' questioning, Tobin recounted the attempted hijacking from start to finish. They asked him to repeat his account, which he did. Then, they demanded he go over it again.

Tobin sighed and started over. "I was the sky marshal assigned to Flight 6177. Prior to boarding the flight in London, I surveilled the gate, watching passengers board, as is my SOP when assigned as sky marshal on a flight."

One of the FBI agents, Peters, asked, "Since you were observing the passengers board, how is it that you failed to identify the hijackers and have them removed before the flight left London?"

Here we go, Tobin thought. *Gotta find a scapegoat, someone to blame—even if that person succeeded in preventing a terrorist attack.*

"The hijackers boarded the plane at the last minute—after the gate had officially closed, after I had taken my seat and identified myself to the flight crew. In addition, the hijackers boarded in two groups. I observed two men of Middle-Eastern or Arabic extraction enter the plane and take seats in business class. I did not see the other three. And I cannot, you know, remove passengers from a flight simply for their ethnicity. I did, however, make it my business to keep tabs on the two men in business class during the flight."

"What did you observe to make you suspect them?"

"As I've said—three times now—about two hours after we left London, one of the two passengers I was watching left business class and entered economy class. He would have no reason to do that unless he were acquainted with a passenger in economy seating. So, I got up and observed him from behind the curtain of the opposite aisle.

"He first spoke to two men on the starboard side of economy plus. Then he approached a third man in an aisle seat on the port side of the same cabin—two, three yards from the curtain I was peeking through.

"It was then that I realized that I had five Middle-Eastern men on my flight—men who had arrived at the gate together and boarded late but *separately* and whose seats were spread strategically throughout the first two cabins. At that point, my suspicions became concerns."

"And you then informed Marshal Forestier of your suspicions and formed a plan?"

Lieutenant Moreau, for his part in the questioning, had stood well back, listening to the exchange. Tobin was aware of how his account was about to differ from Lieutenant Moreau's understanding of the event—and differ from the understanding of the passengers aboard the flight, for that matter.

Yup. Here we go.

Tobin repeated, "Marshal Forestier?"

"Yes, the other marshal aboard the flight."

"I think there's some misunderstanding here. I continued to observe the suspects during the seven-hour flight until we were within range of land—about an hour out from JFK. Again, the same man left business class to speak to the three men in economy plus. When I also observed his aggressive behavior toward a female flight attendant, my concerns hardened.

"It was then, when I believed that we did indeed have a hijacking in the works, that I sought assistance from among the passengers. I was, if you will consider the situation, outmanned five-to-one and possibly outgunned, if the hijackers possessed weapons. I required help and found it in Miss Forestier.

"You see, prior to boarding the flight, I had observed Miss Forestier behaving much the same as I was. surveilling the gate and the passengers as they boarded. Miss Forestier's caution and conduct led me to believe she had either law enforcement or military training. When I approached her, identified myself, and apprised her of the situation, she agreed to assist me."

Out of the corner of his eye, Tobin saw Lieutenant Moreau's frown deepen.

The other FBI agent, Donaldson, pressed him. "Marshal Tobin, are you saying this woman," the agent glanced at his notes, "this Marta Forestier, is *not* a US Marshal? That you simply walked up to a complete stranger during the flight and asked her to help you take down five potential hijackers?"

Tobin shook his head. "Hold on. I never said she was a marshal—I don't know how that misunderstanding started. I did, however, use my authority under the law to enlist and deputize a willing civilian. She was both willing and able, so I deputized her."

"But every single member of the flight crew understood her to be a marshal. Even Lieutenant Moreau—" the agent gestured behind him, "believed her to be a US Marshal."

"Well, she *was* duly deputized, but I never referred to her as a marshal . . ." Tobin assumed a thoughtful air. "Wait a sec. Her name's Marta Forestier. Could people have heard *Marta* Forestier and misconstrued it as *Marshal* Forestier?"

Lieutenant Moreau's hard scowl turned to rock.

Tobin shrugged. "And, certainly, because she was working under my direction, people could have easily assumed she was also a marshal."

"People could have made a wrong assumption? Marshal Tobin, the woman was carrying a *gun* on a commercial flight. Why would she have brought a gun on a plane?"

Tobin's lips thinned. "I didn't exactly have time to verify references, *Special Agent Peters*. It is my understanding from what Miss Forestier told me that she was carrying a weapon because she was a law enforcement officer working undercover. I deputized her and was grateful for the assist."

"You deputized her. A stranger."

"Look, I've already gone over that with you three times. I possess the lawful authority to deputize any person I deem necessary—and the bottom line is that if I hadn't enlisted her help, the hijackers would have taken that plane. They would have driven it into the Empire State Building or a hospital full of innocent people, and every person aboard, including myself—not to mention hundreds or thousands on the ground where the plane hit—would presently be circling Manhattan as so much ash on the wind. And, by the way? If you are so all-fired concerned about Miss Forestier's background and qualifications, rather than the fact that we stopped the hijackers, why aren't you questioning her yourself?"

Lieutenant Moreau answered him. "Marshal Tobin, NAV CANADA directed a total of ten flights into Moncton today. The passengers and crew from all ten flights were transported to the Moncton Coliseum, some 2,200 persons in all. We located and questioned Miss Forestier's seatmates, whom Miss Forestier apparently asked to remove her bag from the overhead when they deplaned, saying she would find them and pick it up later. Miss Forestier, as you know, accompanied you in the ambulance to this hospital."

"Yes, I asked her to. So what?"

Moreau fixed him with a gaze before responding. "The 'so what' is that we can't find her. She's disappeared."

Tobin looked from the FBI agents to Moreau. "I didn't know. I've been a bit preoccupied."

Peters addressed Tobin again. "Well, then, can you give us any explanation for her disappearance, Marshal? Any sense of where she may have gone?"

"No. As I said earlier, I'd never seen her before boarding the plane in London."

But I do recognize when someone is running for their life.

"Then it's a good thing several passengers used their mobile phones to take pictures of her. They aren't great images, but they're good enough. We gave the best one to the press along with a request to the public to call the FBI if they spot her."

Peters dumped a folded newspaper in Tobin's lap. "This ran this morning."

There she was—not the greatest image, but good enough—with a bold, all-cap headline.

HAVE YOU SEEN THIS WOMAN?

What had she said? "*I can't be questioned by Canadian law enforcement, Tobin, or any law enforcement agency. Do you follow? I've been deep undercover for years in a country whose name I cannot mention. If, when we land, someone were to photograph me and that photo made the news? Not good.*"

In his mind's eye, Tobin saw Marta shaking her head. He saw the pinched face behind her stalwart expression. The fear she kept under control. Barely.

"*If I want to stay alive, I need to circumvent any publicity or questions. I need to vanish—and I mean the minute our wheels hit the ground.*"

Tobin glared at the feds. "Why would you treat her like a wanted criminal?"

Peters got in Tobin's face. "Who said she's a criminal? What's wrong with the public reporting her whereabouts, eh, Marshal?"

At that moment, three persons entered the room, interrupting them. When Tobin saw who it was, he tried to climb from his bed and stand.

"Stay where you are, Deputy Marshal Tobin."

The man carried his authority well. His presence filled up the room, and his two-person security detail arranged themselves behind him. He acknowledged Peters and Donaldson, then Moreau, with the barest of nods.

"Gentlemen, I'm Gordon Niles, Deputy Director of the US Marshals Service, come to check on my wounded marshal. I didn't hear you giving my man a hard time just now, did I?"

"Only doing our job, sir," Peters replied.

"Well, considering that this man prevented the fifth plane in yesterday's attacks from becoming a weapon of mass destruction, I'd say he is a hero, not a suspect."

"We don't dispute that, Director. However, the woman Marshal Tobin deputized to help him thwart the hijackers has gone missing. No one has seen her since the ambulance carrying her and Marshal Tobin arrived here yesterday, midday. In light of the grave security situation, her disappearance is concerning."

Tobin disagreed. "Marta Forestier is every bit as responsible for thwarting the attack as I am. She followed my orders and did nothing wrong—certainly nothing to warrant your attention or concern."

Niles held up a hand and addressed the feds. "Gentlemen, I think you're done here. I'd like to spend a minute with my marshal in private, if you please. Oh, and you need to check in with your superiors. I believe you'll find revised orders waiting for you. Please close the door on your way out."

Peters and Donaldson looked at each other, wondering what had just happened but knowing they had no choice but to follow Niles' instructions. They and Moreau nodded to Niles and stalked out of the room. Moreau closed the door behind them.

Niles motioned his men to follow them out and stand in front of the closed door.

Niles addressed Tobin. "Now, Marshal, I suppose you're wondering why I'm here?"

"It had crossed my mind, sir." *But I'll bet you dollars to donuts, it's about Marta Forestier.*

"You would not believe the calls I received this morning, Marshal. Calls from people so far over my head that I doubt I could breathe the air where they live."

"I think I believe you, sir."

"*I've been deep undercover for years in a country whose name I cannot mention.*"

"Well, then, let me pull up a chair. We need to discuss what must happen—what *will happen* should you ever again see or speak to Marta Forestier."

Tobin nodded, but his mind was focused elsewhere.

Lord, please help this woman, whoever she really is and wherever she may be, to escape those who are after her. Lead her, Lord, in paths of righteousness for your name's sake. And please forgive me for being less than entirely candid with the FBI and, in the next minutes, with my own superiors.

WHEN THE STYLIST FINISHED Laynie's hair, the clock on the salon wall read a quarter past five. The bank had closed for the day, so Laynie would return to the Westmount. Her new color was closer to her normal dark blonde but brighter by the artful highlights her stylist had woven throughout.

Back in her room, Laynie turned her head to the mirror. She liked how the skillfully cut sides framed her face. To the casual observer, she no longer bore resemblance to the photograph in the newspaper.

Much better. Now . . .

Laynie wadded up the dirty clothes she'd arrived in, keeping only the billed hat, pulled the plastic liner from the bathroom waste can, and put the dirty clothing inside. Next, she slipped her keycard into her new handbag next to Marta Forestier's French passport. Carrying her room's "trash," she took the elevator downstairs. She found the business center unoccupied and took inventory of its equipment.

She was alone in the room, so she pulled a chair up to the document shredder. Page by page, she tore up the French passport and fed it into the shredder's cross-cutting head, until all that remained was the cover. This, too, she fed into the machine. She opened the trash sack containing her clothes, dumped the shredded paper into the sack, and tied it closed.

She headed for the hotel's laundry room—not to use the laundry machines, but to find the exit nearest the hotel dumpsters. She passed the laundry room, then the Facility Manager's office, and exited the hotel. The dumpsters, as she'd supposed, were at the back of the building. She lifted the heavy lid on one and tossed the bag containing her old clothes and passport remains into it.

Relieved to have finished her chore, she wandered into the Westmount's guest store where she purchased toothbrush, toothpaste, and an inexpensive set of headphones. She took the items to her room, put them away, and opened the sliding door to her balcony. Stepping outside, she breathed deeply.

Miles away toward the west, clouds had gathered. She caught a faint flash of lightning on the dark horizon and felt the breeze freshen against her face. Rain was coming.

Stockholm time being six hours ahead of Montreal, she couldn't use the business center until morning when Christor would be in the office.

I'll get up early. At 5:00 a.m. here, it will be 11:00 a.m. there.

It dawned on her that Montreal was only an hour ahead of Nebraska time.

I could call Kari. She was tempted but shook her head. *No. If they track me to this hotel, they'll ask for a printout of my calls.*

Her stomach rumbled. The last weeks of eating on the run had taken their toll. Suddenly, the thought of a nice dinner had great appeal. The hotel had a restaurant, but room service was safer. The fewer hotel staff who saw her, the better.

Laynie opened the room service menu and stared at the selections before her—including that favorite of American tourists, a hamburger and fries. She had not had a hamburger and fries in more than seven years. Her mouth watered.

"Hello, room service?"

CHAPTER 14

LP

LAYNIE ASKED THE front desk to wake her at 4:30 a.m. After they called, she dressed, ran a brush through her hair, grabbed her purse, and headed downstairs to the lobby. When the elevator door opened, the scent of fresh-brewed coffee hit her.

"Oh, yes . . ." she muttered to herself. "Yes, yes, yes."

She grabbed a cup and filled it with the hotel's complementary coffee, then took it with her into the business center. She sat down at one of the computers and sipped several scalding mouthfuls from her cup before she set to her tasks. She estimated at least twenty minutes of work ahead of her before she would be ready.

She opened her handbag and drew out the CD-ROM case she had been so careful not to lose or leave behind in her travels. She removed the *Final Fantasy IX* disc, set it aside, popped out the unmarked disc hidden beneath, and slipped it into the computer's CD drive. When the CD's window popped up, she browsed its folder.

She clicked the program on the disc that would enable her to bypass the Westmount's network administrative restrictions. In only minutes, it overrode the restrictions and granted her admin privileges. Once she had unfettered access to the system, she copied the VoIP software installation code from the CD, buried it inside the computer's operating system, and executed its installation program.

It was after eleven in Stockholm when Laynie slipped on the headphones and dialed Christor's laptop. The call rang and rang. She hung up.

Perhaps he's gone to lunch early?

She wasn't worried that someone in the IT Department would see the call on his screen. Christor always locked his computer before stepping away, and the call wouldn't register on the monitor when the system was locked. She tried again. Still no answer.

Another hotel guest, up early, entered the business center. He sat down at the second computer and started typing. Laynie turned her head a fraction to check out his screen. He was reading email.

On her screen, Laynie dialed Christor's number a third time.

Could Marstead have discovered Christor's VoIP program? And if so, have I given away my location? Worse, by giving away my location, have I exposed my last ID?

She sat at the computer, waiting. Hoping. Her teeth on edge.

When a call warbled in her headset, she jumped.

Exhaling, she picked up the call.

Christor's cautious voice whispered in her ears, "Linnéa?"

Laynie had never heard anything as welcome as Christor's voice. She opened a chat window and typed, "Yes. No microphone."

"I'm so glad to hear from you, Linnéa! Are you all right?"

"So far. News?"

"Lots. I hardly know where to start."

"Marstead?"

"No changes there, I'm sorry to say."

She typed, "Petroff?"

Christor's voice dropped to a whisper. "That's the news. Marstead agents followed Petroff's people into Sweden a week ago. The Russians visited the village you supposedly grew up in. They dug around and asked about you. All was fine until they spoke at length to a retired teacher from your primary school.

"After the Russians left, Marstead agents interviewed the same teacher. He said the Russians had asked about you. Even though your name was on the roster of classes he taught, he told them that he'd never heard of you. Your cover is blown, Linnéa."

Laynie shivered. Once Petroff realized that Linnéa had lied to him about her past, whatever influence her persuasive letter may have had on him would be gone. She had betrayed him, and he would never stop hunting her . . . not unless she forced him to.

Her fingers touched the keyboard again. "Send the package."

"Are you sure, Linnéa? It might . . . it might backfire. Might cause an international—"

"Do it."

"All right. I will." He hesitated, then added, "I, um, did I see your face on the news, Linnéa? Flight 6177 from London to New York?"

Laynie bowed her head, rubbed her eyes. If Christor had recognized her from the grainy photograph, both Marstead and Petroff's people—specifically Zakhar—surely would have, too.

Zakhar.

He could be on the ground already. Here in Canada. Right now.

"Linnéa? Are you still there? Are you okay?"

She typed, "Yes, okay. Will be okay. Thank you, Christor, again, for your friendship. SEND THE PACKAGE."

"I will, Linnéa."

"Today?"

"All right. Today."

"Goodbye for now, Christor."

She ended the call and closed the VoIP program window. While she was removing all traces of the program from the computer, she was thinking hard.

Zakhar! He has disliked me for years, but I earned his permanent animosity my last day in St. Petersburg. He won't ever forget how I humiliated him in Petroff's eyes—his hatred will fuel his determination. An angry Zakhar is more of a threat to me than Marstead.

She thought about the contents of the package, her letter threatening to expose Petroff and the CD backing up her threat.

Petroff is the only one who can deter Zakhar, but even if Christor sends the package today? It may take as long as a week before it is delivered to Petroff and he calls off Zakhar. I need to move and keep moving, never stopping long in any one place. Until Petroff recalls Zakhar, that man remains my greatest threat.

She ejected the disc from the CD drive and put it back in the case. She had picked up the game disc to do the same when a voice behind her spoke.

"Hey. Um, you play *Final Fantasy*?"

Laynie snapped the case closed. She turned with an open smile. "I do. Not as much as I like, since I'm on the road a lot for business."

"I am, too—on the road a lot, I mean. That's why I bring my PlayStation with me when I travel."

Laynie laughed. "Really? You have your console here? In your room?"

"I sure do. It's a great way to unwind after a long day in yet another hotel."

"That's brilliant."

"Thanks. I'm really glad I have it right now. Since I'm stuck here. With all the canceled flights, I mean."

She watched him gather up his nerve.

"Uh, if you'd like to play, this afternoon or evening, we could meet up? I always pack an extra controller in case my first one craps out."

She took inventory of the man. He was probably in his early thirties. Interested. Eager.

And way out of his league.

"I'd like that, um . . ."

"Justin. I'm Justin."

Laynie's smile warmed. She reached out her hand. "I'm Beverly. What room are you in, Justin?"

He flushed as he took her hand, more excited than he wanted to let on. "I'm in 6096. Sixth floor."

"Can I come up later on when I've finished my work?"

"Oh, yeah. I mean, sure. Absolutely."

"Well, Justin, I look forward to . . . playing with you later on."

She let her fingers linger in his hand a moment longer than necessary. Then she gathered her things and left, dropping another high-wattage smile in her wake.

Laynie returned to her room to better prepare herself for the busy day ahead. She ordered breakfast, then took a long shower. While she stood under the hot water, she wondered at the serendipitous nature of this new acquaintance, *Justin*. Out of the blue, she had a means of warning Petroff off in a timelier manner, ahead of the arrival of the package containing her threatening letter with the proof that would make her threat stick.

Her thoughts roamed back to the genesis of her relationship with Petroff and how their work in technology had brought them together on common ground. In fact, before they became lovers, Petroff and Linnéa often attended tech and tech-related conventions and exhibitions at the same time—Petroff as a member of the Russian government and Linnéa as an account executive for Marstead. After their relationship caught fire, they had used the conventions as a means to further their trysts and to compare notes on interesting technological advances.

The conventions and expos were all about faster and more complex computers, cell phones, and compact disc systems. However, the major tech companies, motivated by rapid advances in integrated circuitry, pushed out new products and applications faster than consumers could comprehend them—or the market could bear.

That was the downside of new technology. It staled quickly. The window to capitalize on an emergent product was only about six months, meaning whichever company or nation could bring the hottest tech to market first—or weaponize it first—would garner the envied reputation and reap its financial, often political, rewards.

Enter the burgeoning world of video gaming.

It had surprised Linnéa—and astounded her Marstead handlers—that it took a mutual love of video gaming to solidify her budding romance with Petroff. It was their shared fascination of gaming that helped her achieve what Petroff's other women had been unable to attain, a long-term relationship with him.

IT WAS MAY OF 1995, soon after Linnéa had moved to St. Petersburg. Linnéa accompanied Petroff to a new type of technology trade event, the Electronic Entertainment Expo in California, organized and hosted by the Entertainment Software Association. The Expo allowed developers, publishers, and manufacturers of video game software and hardware to showcase their gaming systems and game-related peripherals and merchandise.

Although the event was touted as entertainment, Petroff had requested permission to attend. "Some of our scientists believe these gaming systems will have military applications," he told Linnéa by way of explanation. "I do not believe it myself, but these games and their platforms are intriguing."

Only individuals who could verify a professional connection to the video game industry could attend. The Russian Ministry of Foreign Affairs provided Petroff with credentials attesting to such a connection. Marstead concocted the same for Linnéa.

To Petroff's amazement, forty thousand enthused vendors, buyers, and journalists crowded the Los Angeles Convention Center. He and Linnéa spent hours watching game demonstrations on large screens. race cars, soccer, American football, and battles ranging from epic fantasy to modern combat warfare.

The convention produced two important results. First, Petroff—by leveraging the weight of the Russian government—took home his first game console, the latest version of the Super Nintendo Entertainment System. Second, Christor brushed past Linnéa in the crowd, leaving behind a folded slip of paper in her hand.

An hour later, Linnéa left Petroff's side to use the facilities. A convention official had whispered something of Petroff's status in the Russian government to the Nintendo vendor, and Petroff was engrossed in playing an advance copy of a cartoonish game, *Super Mario World 2*—and something more about an island belonging to someone named Yoshi. The vendor was coaching Petroff in the game, and Petroff was determined to complete the level. He hardly noticed when she left.

Linnéa exited the main convention hall, turned right, and spotted the door Christor's note had said would be ajar. He drew her into the facilities hallway, out of sight of convention goers, and locked the door behind them.

Linnéa was genuinely moved to see her friend and threw her arms about him. He hugged her in return and then stepped back, abashed at her physical closeness.

"Alvarsson thought a friendly face might do you good."

"You have no idea."

Christor passed on messages to her, all verbal. She relayed the status of her relationship with Petroff.

"He dresses me in jewels and gowns and flaunts me before his cronies at every formal function he is obliged to attend. He expects me to be charming, erudite, and apolitical. I'm allowed to be learned in art, literature, music—even technology—but must feign ignorance of geopolitics."

"How should I describe the status of your relationship with Petroff? Is it progressing?"

"You can tell Alvarsson that Petroff has asked that I move to Moscow. It will soon become a demand."

"Alvarsson will be pleased, Linnéa."

She could tell Christor was anything but pleased. He was worried about her. That was one reason why she didn't mention the aftermath of a recent state dinner she'd attended with Petroff.

Linnéa had expressed an opinion Petroff had disapproved of. When they returned to his apartment that evening, she had been the object of his anger. It had started with him pulling her close, holding her too tightly and kissing her too hard—hard enough to bruise her mouth. When she attempted to pull away, he had bit her lip, drawing blood.

"You must not embarrass me before my peers, Linnéa," he warned her.

It had been the first and only time to date he'd hurt her. She hoped it would be the last. It had, however, produced Petroff's desired outcome. Linnéa would be more reticent and circumspect in the future.

"I cannot be absent much longer, Christor. Petroff will notice and be angry. Have you any orders for me?"

"Yes, just this. You are to play video games with Petroff."

"What?"

"Be willing, even eager, to learn how to play video games with him. Make a habit of it. Relay to us which games are his favorites. I will purchase copies of the games, restructure them, and an agent will pass them to you. You will switch out the original games for the new ones."

"To what purpose?"

Christor nodded. "Some upcoming games have chat functions built into them for what's being called "online gaming." That's where competitors, across a broadband connection, meet up at the same time and play against each other. I will build enhanced chat capabilities into each new game so that you and I can message without using our laptops to access a bulletin board. It will be faster and more secure."

He saw the concern in Linnéa's expression. "Don't worry—Petroff won't discover our chats. Only a series of specific moves within the game can activate a hidden chat session. I will send you instructions on how it works."

When Petroff and Linnéa returned to Russia following the convention, he brought with him the game console. Three months later, Linnéa moved to Moscow to live with him, and she saw that gaming had already become one of Petroff's passions.

One evening, after watching him play for hours, she asked, "Vassi, *moy lyubimyy*, these games fascinate me. Would you teach me how to play?"

He was surprised by her request but agreed to teach her. Or at least *try* to teach her.

You were not as surprised as I was, Vassili Aleksandrovich, Laynie reminisced, *to discover that I was quite good at gaming. Good enough to best you, but smart enough not to win nearly as often as I could have.*

With both of them playing on a regular basis, Petroff turned his apartment's dining room into a gaming den with a dedicated television screen. Each year, he upgraded to the best new platform and their games, but *Final Fantasy*—the epic battle between good and evil situated in a fantastical world of love, loyalty, magic, and rivalry—became their favorite and remained so through the game's many evolutions.

Each time Petroff ordered and received the newest version of *Final Fantasy*, Christor would have already provided Linnéa with a "restructured" copy, a copy with covert capabilities that improved with each game iteration. As soon as Petroff received a disc in the mail, Linnéa changed it out for Christor's copy, destroying the original disc before she and Petroff had played on it.

The most recent restructured copy of *Final Fantasy* remained with Petroff's PlayStation 2. Christor, however, had provided Laynie with a duplicate of the disc. He had left it in the drawer of her desk in St. Petersburg, placed within the specially constructed case where the game served as a mask for the CD-ROM beneath it.

Christor had left the game disc to do more than hide the CD-ROM—it, like his own copy, could communicate with Petroff's copy. All Laynie lacked was a game console and yet—*voilà!*—one had "magically" appeared.

Laynie toweled off and dressed. She was drying her hair when breakfast arrived. She took it out on her balcony and, while she ate, stared west. Where yesterday's clouds had threatened rain, today's sky was clear.

From Laynie's hotel room, she could see the shimmer of the Ottawa River as it joined the St. Lawrence, their combined waters wending their way to the Gulf of St. Laurence, to eventually reach the Atlantic. More than one hundred miles southwest of her room, Lake Erie, by way of the Niagara River, thundered over the great Niagara Falls and poured into Lake Ontario, which fed into the St. Lawrence River.

Those poor newlyweds, Laynie thought. *Are they still stuck in Moncton instead of enjoying their honeymoon adventure?*

She followed the ribbon of the Ottawa River to where it disappeared from view into the unfamiliar mountains that ran alongside it and into the distance. A glimmer of an idea began to take shape.

Hmm. Worth exploring. Later.

At present, she had more pressing matters.

Laynie finished her breakfast, grabbed her purse, and headed downstairs. She left the Westmount and walked toward the HSBC branch about a mile distant. When she arrived, the bank's doors had just opened. Laynie crossed the vestibule and approached a teller.

"Good morning. May I help you?"

"Yes, thank you. I'm an account holder at an HSBC branch in Singapore. I'd like to open a Canadian account and transfer money from my Singapore account into my Canadian account to fund my stay in Canada."

"Certainly, ma'am. I must notify you that HSBC banks in Singapore operate under different regulations than our banks in Canada. That means the full amount of your transfer will not be immediately available for use."

"I understand."

"Very good. To begin, I will need the following items—your HSBC Singapore account number, two forms of photo ID to confirm your identity, and your mailing address. Please write your Singapore account number on this form."

Laynie wrote the number, then produced her American passport and driver's license. "You may use the address on my license."

The address on her license was the same as a retired D.C. accountant. Christor had located him, and Laynie had hired and kept him on retainer, paying him and his expenses on her behalf from her Singapore account. The tax specialist performed two recurring tasks for Laynie. He received her monthly credit card statements and paid them each month.

The accountant also had a single, one-time task . . . which Christor would trigger in the event of Laynie's death or if he did not hear from her for ninety days running, or—as a second fail-safe—if the accountant failed to receive payment three months in a row. Under those circumstances, he could assume that both Laynie and Christor were removed from the equation.

Christor regularly browsed mail-order catalogs and made purchases over the phone. He used her credit card number but had the purchases sent to various homeless shelters. To date, Laynie's card had provided shipments of blankets, pillows, coats, or other necessary items as one-time gifts to homeless shelters in nineteen states—after which, the accountant paid off the card. The ruse had kept Laynie's card, under her present name, in good standing.

"It will take a few minutes to set up your account and signature cards. Once the account is in the system, we will request the transfer. Full funding requires a minimum of 48 hours. Unfortunately, because today is Thursday and we are closed weekends, the full amount will not be available until Monday morning. Would you like to sit and enjoy a cup of coffee while I am preparing your signature cards?"

Monday! Four wasted, precarious days. Laynie had not planned to remain in Montreal so long. The longer she stayed in any one place, the greater the danger that someone would recognize or, if questioned, remember her.

I want to lose myself in Canada for a while before dropping down into the States. I can't do that without money to buy a car. I'll just have to move from one hotel to another until Monday. Even then, when I have cash to buy a car, I need to be careful where I buy it.

To the clerk she replied, "Yes. Thank you. Is there a minimum amount I can withdraw before Monday?"

"We can cash a check up to five hundred dollars."

"Thank you."

Laynie did as the teller suggested. She indulged in her third cup of coffee and sat down in a grouping of chairs and sofas to wait. While she waited, she planned how she would hide in the city for an additional four days.

Ten minutes later, the teller called, "Elaine Granger, please."

Laynie returned to the counter and signed two signature cards. The teller compared the signatures with the one on her American passport and driver's license.

"How is the weather in Washington, D.C.?" the teller asked as she finalized Laynie's account.

"Goodness. I really wouldn't know. I haven't been home in weeks. I was in Canada on business, and now I'm stuck here like everyone else until the planes can fly again. I thought I would use the forced downtime to do some sightseeing."

"A wonderful idea. Now, please fill out and sign this form to authorize the wire transfer."

Laynie filled out the form, asking for a transfer of $40,000.

"Thank you, Ms. Granger." The teller produced a blank check. "As I said, we can approve a cash withdrawal of up to five hundred Canadian dollars."

Laynie wrote the check and received the money, folding it into her wallet. "Thank you."

"Have a good day, Ms. Granger."

Laynie turned away, then back, as though she'd forgotten something. "Say, can you recommend a hotel nearby? One with a business center?"

"Try the Fontainebleau. A bit pricy, but worth it. Turn left at the corner. I believe it is six blocks farther."

Perfect. Because I need a new hotel.

Feeling flush, Laynie went back to the department store and purchased more casual clothing—jeans, T-shirts, a sweater, jogging pants, running shoes, more socks, and sundry items.

She returned to the Westmount and called the Fontainebleau. "Hello. Yes, I'd like a room for the night. Oh, and I will not be able to check in until late this evening."

She provided her credit card information to secure the room, then she called the front desk of her own hotel. "Hello, this is room 5018. I'll be checking out early tomorrow. Yes, everything has been lovely, thank you."

She made a third call. "Good morning, I'd like to rent a car. You're out of cars? Oh. I see. Because of the planes being grounded."

She called every car rental agency listed in the phone book. The result was the same until she reached a local rental place far down on the list.

"You do? Yes, I understand—for local use only. Five days, please. I'll pick up the car shortly."

Laynie called a cab. When it arrived, she gave the driver the name of the rental company. The rental agency's lot was several miles away, and the cabbie had to meander through an older residential area to arrive at a fenced lot that was home to more junked cars than working ones.

She paid the driver and walked to the office.

"These are the two rentals we have available today," the owner told her. "All we've got left, I'm afraid."

Laynie's choice was between a five-year-old sedan with a dented rear fender and a newer van. She took the less conspicuous sedan and paid for the rental with her credit card.

As she drove away, she retraced the exact route the taxi had taken. She'd seen something she wanted to examine more closely. Halfway through the residential area, she pulled over and parked.

She studied the house across the street and the two vehicles in the driveway. The compact car was twice as old as the sedan she was driving, but it had been recently washed and waxed. Even the tires shone. And although the house needed paint, the yard, too, was tidy.

Senior citizens, Laynie hypothesized. *Limited income but making the most of what they have to work with. Not able to travel as they did in their earlier years?*

The second vehicle had added to her assumptions. The aging motor home with the FOR SALE sign in its rear window was well cared for. Its tires were chocked and leveled, the windows were clean, the chrome ladder and roof rack gleamed.

Laynie's heavy weight of problems seemed suddenly lighter.

She stepped from her car and walked across the street to give the motor home a closer going over. She hadn't been in the drive more than a minute when the house's front door opened.

"She's a champ, I can tell you that."

Laynie turned a smile on the old man. "I can see you've taken wonderful care of her."

"Well, she was pretty wonderful to us. Took us on some grand adventures, she did. Hate to say goodbye."

He blinked at the end of his sentence, and Laynie spotted a sheen of moisture over his eyes.

She didn't understand why her next words were, "Would you share some of your adventures with me?"

He nodded as if it was the most normal and expected request. "Come on in, miss. Kettle's on. We'll have a cuppa tea and tell you all about her."

He leaned inside the house. "Bessie gal, we got company!"

Extending a calloused hand to Laynie, he said, "George Bradshaw, miss. Nobody calls me George though. Go by Shaw."

Laynie took his hand—a hand still strong from regular labor. "Elaine Granger."

"Well, Miss Granger, you are welcome in our home."

Stepping inside was like falling back thirty years in time—olive-green shag carpeting, dark wood paneling, two worn recliners, and a sofa kept in pristine condition by a yellowing plastic cover.

"Miss Granger, this here's my bride, Bessie. Bessie, this is Miss Granger. She's a-looking at Daisy."

Daisy? "Please call me Elaine," Laynie said softly.

Bessie was rotund and soft, her smile dimpling up the wealth of wrinkles in her cheeks and under her eyes. "Will you set with us in the kitchen, Elaine? Can I tempt you with fresh-baked pecan cinnamon buns to go with your tea?"

Laynie's nose twitched and caught the aroma of warm . . . bliss. "I would *love* to be tempted by your, er, fresh-baked pecan cinnamon buns." She was salivating already.

Laynie sat at the homey kitchen table while Bessie brewed the tea in an old-fashioned china pot.

Laynie devoured one of the sticky pastries while she sipped her tea. She eyed a second one but told herself "no." Petroff would never have allowed her even the first bun. He was forever critiquing her figure, cruel in his criticism if he thought she'd gained an ounce.

A chuckle burst from Laynie's mouth, and she reached for a second sticky roll. *You do not own me any longer, Vassili Aleksandrovich.* She smiled her audacity wider as she bit into the bun's sugary goodness.

All the while, Bessie and Shaw pattered along, reliving thirty-five years of traveling the country—initially, with a tent and their three children. Later, when the kids had left home, in the motor home they'd named Daisy. They had traipsed across Canada, visiting the grown children and a passel of grandchildren, camped near the glaciers of the Rockies, and toured the Pacific Ocean coast of British Columbia all the way into Alaska.

"How did you two meet?" Laynie asked.

"Why, Shaw and I met each other when we were little 'uns. Started school together, we did, and by the time we hit high school, we were always in cahoots, catching the dickens for one thing or another," Bessie laughed. "See, we grew up in the aftermath of the Great Depression. Our folks lost what money they had saved when the markets crashed and the banks failed. My dad lost his job and couldn't find another one. We lost our home. Had to live with his parents. Those were hard years."

"Similar story, here," Shaw confirmed. "In our family, we kids never knew if we'd see food on the table, let alone any of the fun some lucky youngsters had, like the cinema or when the circus came to town. Had to make our own fun those days—but we made a peck o' trouble, too. Fact is, the only thing free in our neighborhood was church. Our parents, Bessie's and mine, made sure we were in church three, sometimes four times a week."

Shaw slapped his thigh. "Oh, man! We had Jesus served up every Wednesday night, once a month on Saturday for fellowship supper, and two times on Sunday! We had so much Jesus that, truth be told, we couldn't wait to grow up and move away. Escape, you might say."

I can relate, Laynie thought, momentarily drifting back to a time and place far distant from Bessie and Shaw's kitchen table.

"Then the war started, and I got drafted."

"He was gone close to four years, but I waited for him, I did."

Bessie and Shaw beamed at each other.

"Yup. When I came home from the war, Bessie and I got married, had some kids. We worked hard, both of us—me making a living at two jobs, Bessie making a home for us. And because we never had much as children, we were determined to make sure our kids had everything we didn't. a nice house with a big yard, plenty of food on the table, and new clothes, not hand-me-downs."

"But it wasn't enough," Bessie murmured.

Laynie, caught up in their tale, was surprised out of it. "Hmm? What?"

"We weren't happy. Not really," Shaw explained. "Bessie and I, we started quarreling and bickering. And our kids were spoiled, they—"

"They had everything we missed out on handed to them, and they were selfish. Lazy. Ungrateful. Our happy home wasn't happy a'tall. Turned into a real mess, so—"

"So, we decided to go back to church."

Laynie shifted with discomfort. *Uh-oh.*

"Turns out we'd missed the point about church from the get-go," Bessie declared. "Yes, we'd heard that it was all about Jesus, but we'd been so focused on what we didn't have at home, that we missed seeing what we didn't have in our hearts. Took us a few months to get it figured out after we started hearing the Gospel with open ears, but then we let Jesus in."

"Turned us around, he did," Shaw said. "For the first time in our lives, we were happy—happy with what we had, happy with what we didn't have, content no matter what. Our kids saw the difference in us, too."

"H'ain't all been roses, Elaine. We wouldn't want you to think that," Bessie said, "but Jesus was what we'd been missing all our lives."

"Right you are, love. Jesus was the key."

"We've had a good life, raised fine kids after all, and had more'n our share of adventures."

"'Fraid our adventuring days are over, though," Shaw concluded. "I got to have dialysis twice a week now, and the hours of driving to get where we'd want t' go adventuring are too hard on my hips."

"On me, too, Shaw," Bessie insisted. But Laynie suspected Bessie didn't want her husband to feel that the curtailment of their "adventures" was all on him.

"I'm sorry to hear about your health problems," Laynie whispered. She'd been spellbound, reliving their travels and their recollections with them.

What would it be like, to share a lifetime with someone you love? A lifetime to make memories so real that a stranger could see them?

But without the Jesus rubbish.

"Well, now, there's no need to be sorry," Bessie said, patting Laynie's hand. Her multiple chins wagged as she shook her head. "If you buy Daisy from us, we can fix up a few things around here, things that we've let go a while. Will be a real blessing for us. And perhaps you need Daisy to do some adventuring of your own, eh?"

"Yes, I'm interested."

Bessie and Shaw smiled at each other.

"Let me show you Daisy's inside," Shaw said. "She's got a few quirks, I grant you, but I've listed them out and you'll have no problems with her if you follow my instructions."

He took her out to the driveway and walked her around the motor home. "This is what they called a Class C RV, meaning it's got the cab-over bed above the driver and passenger seats. Twenty-three feet in length, not too long nor too hard to park or handle on the highway."

He unlocked the side door and gestured for Laynie to step up and in. He followed behind her.

Laynie found herself staring at yellow, orange, and rusty-brown flower-patterned upholstery on the driver and passenger seats, the bench seats across a tiny table—even the window valances. And *a beaded curtain* hung between the camper's living quarters and the cab, completing the hippy, flower-power décor.

She laughed aloud. "This is . . . this is great. I get now why you named her Daisy."

"Yup. Always bright and cheerful, she is. Reminds us of our youth. Here, let me show you the kitchen."

Taking but two steps, he pointed out the miniscule sink, three-burner stove, and refrigerator on the opposite wall. He opened cupboards and showed Laynie the dishes and cookware within and the storage space for food.

Then he took her to the back. "Got you a sink, commode, and little shower here, a linen closet, and a full-size bed."

When they returned to the front, he handed Laynie a notebook. Flipping it open, Laynie found the original owner's manual, up-to-date vehicle registration, insurance cards, and the notes Shaw had handwritten in meticulous detail.

"I've documented all of Daisy's quirks in this here binder. Maintenance records in the back. 'Course, I'll remove the registration paperwork when she sells."

"It's great, Shaw. I like what I see."

"Well, we can throw in our kitchen doodads—pots, pans, and dishes—to sweeten the deal. Won't have need for 'em after Daisy's gone, so we'd likely just donate 'em to the church parking lot sale, anyway."

"That would be wonderful." Laynie realized she'd decided to buy Daisy and that Shaw's generous offer would be a great help.

Laynie left the Bradshaws half an hour later. Two pecan cinnamon buns, wrapped in tinfoil rested on the seat beside her, next to a bill of sale.

"I've just opened an account in Montreal and wired money to it," she'd told them, "money I cannot draw upon until after the weekend. If it is agreeable to you, I will return midmorning on Monday with a cashier's check and take Daisy away with me. Will that work?"

The couple shared their secret smile, and both of them nodded.

On her way back to the hotel, she made two stops, the first at a liquor store, the second at a drug store. She handed off the sedan to the hotel's valet and took her purchases to her room.

It was after one o'clock when she opened one of the two bottles of Chablis she'd bought. It took a while to grind the OTC pills she'd purchased at the drug store into powder, powder she knew from her training would dissolve completely if ground fine enough.

When her preparations were complete, she packed all her belongings into the rolling suitcase and crawled into bed to take a nap.

As she drifted off, she reviewed her plans. It would be late night in Moscow when she knocked on Justin's door, but however the evening played out, she would be fresh and prepared.

SØREN THORESEN collected the mail from the big mailbox at the end of their drive. He took the driveway and front porch steps in a few strides, opened the front door and dropped the handful of envelopes, magazines, and newspapers on Kari's desk in the corner of the living room.

"Hey, Babe! I'm home!"

"Hi! I'm in the kitchen. Lunch is almost ready."

Shannon and Robbie were in school. Kari was assembling sandwiches for her and Søren's lunch to go with the soup on the stove. He came up behind her and wrapped his arm about her, nuzzling her neck with his lips.

Kari relaxed into his embrace. "Mmm. That's nice."

"Plowed up the north ten acres this morning."

"Mmm. Okay."

"I put the mail on your desk."

"Mmm. Wonderful."

"And my stomach is empty."

"Mmm-hmm? Mmm. Sooo nice."

"*Hollow*. As in I'm starving here."

Kari raised her head. "Just like a man to put his stomach ahead of love. Way to spoil the mood, Thoresen."

They laughed and separated. Søren pulled dishes from the cupboard and set them out while Kari brought their lunch to the table. While they ate, they talked, laughed together, and discussed the family's upcoming Christmas vacation in New Orleans.

They had been spending the holidays at Kari's house on Marlow Avenue since she and Søren married. The kids, especially, enjoyed the change of pace and scenery. This year, their trip, with some planning and careful execution, would include Gene and Polly.

"I'm so glad Max can go with us," Kari mused. "I don't relish the day when he tells us he has other plans."

"He has four weeks off before classes recommence in January?"

"Something like that."

"Well, there you go. Now, I need to get back at it. Thank you for fixing lunch."

"For you, Søren Thoresen? It's always my pleasure."

Kari had her own work to do each day, telecommuting from their home in Nebraska to her company's offices in New Orleans. Once a month, she made a five-day whirlwind trip down south to meet with her staff in person.

While Søren washed up from lunch, she flipped through the mail he had stacked on her desk. She sorted it efficiently, tossing the junk, setting aside bills, glancing through newspaper headlines. By the time they received the papers, they were always a little stale—RiverBend being off the beaten track as it was. Kari was about to toss the Omaha paper into the "to-be-read" pile when she stopped and stared hard at the grainy photo on the front page under a bold headline.

HAVE YOU SEEN THIS WOMAN?

She pulled the image closer, as if "closer" would make it clearer. She called over her shoulder, "Søren?"

She read the article as fast as she could, then started over. "Søren? *Søren!*"

He arrived, pulling on his work gloves. "What is it?"

"That." She pointed. "That . . ." Kari couldn't breathe.

"What am I looking at, Babe?"

She shook her head, still staring. "Søren . . ." She stabbed her finger at the picture again. "Søren, that's Laynie. *That's my sister!*"

---------∽---------

CHAPTER 15

LP

LAYNIE KNOCKED ON Justin's door at five that afternoon. She felt rested and mentally sharp. She also knew how enticing she appeared in snug jeans and a tight sweater, her hair intentionally blowsy about her face. She carried her purse and a shopping bag holding the two bottles of wine in one hand. She held two wine glasses in her other hand.

When Justin opened his door, he grinned. "I'm really glad you came, Beverly. Been looking forward to this all day."

"Me, too, Justin. Me, too." She walked into his room and swept her eyes around, taking inventory of the layout. "I thought that after we've played our video game for a while, we could order dinner in." She lifted the bag holding the bottles. "I brought the wine."

Justin's reaction to her unmistakable message made him stumble a little. "That's super. Uh, make yourself at home, Beverly. Does the wine need to be chilled?"

"Great idea, Justin."

He grabbed up the ice bucket. "Be right back."

After both bottles were on ice, they started playing. Justin had skills and, for Laynie, it was fun not having to pretend he was a better player as she had with Petroff. She lost herself in the game, laughing and celebrating with Justin when he beat a challenge, then taking her turn, feeling smug when she outscored him. They worked well on the shared game play. All in all, Laynie was enjoying herself.

"Wow. You are a boss, Beverly!"

Laynie lifted a wicked brow. "You have no idea."

"Have you ever played paintball? I'd love to have you on my team."

After an hour, Justin asked, "Want to order dinner now?"

"Sure."

Laynie ordered a seafood salad. Justin ordered a sirloin. They played *Final Fantasy*, taking turns in the field and fighting together in the battles until their food arrived. While Justin was tipping the room service delivery boy, Laynie opened a bottle and poured the wine. They sat down to eat, and Laynie kept Justin's glass full.

"What did you do today?" he asked, fumbling for something to talk about.

"Nothing out of the ordinary. Paperwork. A little shopping and banking. How about you?"

"Got through to my corporate office in Vancouver. They think when the US and Canada open their airspace, it'll be a mess, everyone trying to get home. I'm probably stuck here until Saturday or Sunday at the earliest. Until then, my boss has ordered me to make thirty cold calls *a day* and try to drum up a few appointments."

"Well, that doesn't sound like fun." Laynie put down her fork. "Ready to play again?" she asked.

"Sure."

Another half hour passed. Laynie emptied the first bottle into her glass and pulled the cork from the second, filling Justin's glass. He hadn't noticed that the second bottle had been opened prior to Laynie's arrival nor could he know that she had, on two trips to the bathroom, dumped most of her glass and refilled it with water.

"Cheers." Laynie touched her glass to his. "I'll be right back."

She visited the restroom a third time, dumping her glass again and filling it half full of water. As she returned, she made a show of gulping down the contents of her glass.

Justin followed suit.

"One more?" Laynie asked, her voice lazy. Seductive.

"Absolutely. I'll get it."

"Let me," Laynie smiled. She filled his glass, but not hers.

"What? You're not having any more?"

"Oh, I've had plenty for what I have in mind," Laynie purred.

"Uh . . . and what do you have . . . in mind?"

"Drink yours down, and I'll tell you."

With his eyes glued on her, Justin downed the glass. His head wobbled a little. "Man, I think I'm drunk."

"Not too drunk to keep playing, I hope?"

"What? I thought . . ."

"We will, Justin, we will. All in good time. First a little more game play, okay?"

They sat down and started where they'd left off, but Justin couldn't keep up. He struggled and fought it, but five minutes later, he dropped his controller. "Shoot. I'm wasted."

"Want to get into bed with me?"

"Oh. Oh, yeah, I do."

Laynie pulled the covers back, helped him sit on edge of the bed, and pulled off his shoes. She went around to the other side and slid in.

"Come on, Justin. Let's snuggle."

He turned her way and flopped onto the mattress, his head hitting the pillow.

She didn't need to take the farce any further. He was unconscious and would remain so until morning.

Laynie smiled as she tucked him in. "Was it good for you?"

Then she got to work.

She connected the room's broadband cable to Justin's PlayStation, ejected his game disc from the console, and replaced it with the one from her purse. When the game had loaded, she took a deep breath and pressed the controller shortcuts that would take her online to Petroff's game console.

I'm so glad you neglect to remove your game discs, Vassili Aleksandrovich.

She did know him well.

THE LOCAL TIME in Moscow was 3:45 in the darkest part of night. After the frustration of waiting all day for news from Zakhar but hearing nothing from him, Petroff had gone to dinner with a colleague to distract himself. The two men spent the evening discussing the terror attacks on the US and drinking heavily.

They parted company near eleven o'clock, and Petroff went to his Moscow apartment to sleep off his overindulgence.

After sleeping nearly five hours, something pulled him awake. In a haze, he sat up, wondering what had disturbed him. He noticed the low light coming through his open bedroom door. And faint music? It sounded like pipes playing the music of *Final Fantasy*'s opening scene.

"What is this? What is going on?"

He staggered a little as he climbed from his bed. After he'd steadied himself, he slipped his silk robe on over his pajamas and reached for the Makarov pistol he kept in the drawer next to his bed. He'd kept the little semiauto as a memento from his days with the KGB—and the gun was always loaded.

Petroff shuffled into the hallway. The light came from beyond the living room. He heard the music, but no other sounds, so he continued forward, sweeping his gun left to right, scanning for an intruder.

When he reached the gaming room, he saw that his PlayStation was awake. The light he'd seen and music he'd heard was coming from the screen. In the center of the screen, a message glowed.

vassili aleksandrovich, wake up
vassili aleksandrovich, wake up
vassili aleksandrovich, wake up

"What is this?" Still half drunk and clumsy, he fell, rather than sat, in his accustomed gaming seat. "What is this?" he repeated.

The words on the screen changed.

vassili aleksandrovich
if you are awake,
pick up your controller

The superstitions that haunted him assumed the worst. Was the game alive? Were the characters within its worlds talking to *him?* Were their intentions diabolical?

Petroff began to shake. He stared around the room. "Who is this? Who are you?"

vassili aleksandrovich
if you are awake
pick up your controller
pick up your controller
pick up your controller

With trembling hands, he reached for the controller. He pressed the "join game" button. A window for him to type a response popped up. He wiped his bleary face and slowly keyed in, "Who are you?"

linnéa

Astounded and half-terrified, Petroff's eyes widened. "How?"

He looked down at the controller and typed, "How are you doing this? Where are you?"

A moment later, new words appeared.

it does not matter where i am because
i can reach you from anywhere in the world
isn't technology wonderful?

Her flippant response angered Petroff. He typed his reply, "I will teach you to disrespect me, you *whore!*"

i have never been your whore, petroff
but YOU have been MINE
pay attention
i have something to say to you
YOU WILL LISTEN

176

Furious, Petroff typed, "My people are hunting you. I will enjoy strangling you and watching you die."

> will you?
> for 7 years, i was with you
> vassili aleksandrovich
> for 7 years, i stole russia's secrets for the west
> AND YOU NEVER SUSPECTED
> guess what?

Petroff read the words and gaped. He was afraid of what was coming. A lone line of text appeared.

> i have copies of the secrets i stole

A second line followed.

> with them
> i have the power to destroy you
> you will receive a package from me
> later this week
> it will contain proof that i am not bluffing

He shook all over, but he could not tear his eyes away.

> if i die or disappear
> the security council will receive
> copies of everything i have stolen
> from you and from mother russia

The screen refreshed. Petroff could not stop watching the flow of text that flashed across the screen.

> if i die or if i disappear
> the evidence will be mailed to
> the security council automatically

His heart pounded. Sweat beaded on his brow.

> FAIL-SAFE
> if i die or if i disappear
> nothing can prevent the evidence
> from being sent to the security council

The contents of his stomach lurched. He was going to be sick to his stomach.

> the security council will believe
> you were complicit in my theft
> by your careless neglect of duty

He grabbed a wastebasket and heaved into it.

how long will it take them to
confine you to a cell
in the basement of Lubyanka
and begin to torture you
vassili aleksandrovich?

He retched until nothing more came up. Petroff wiped his mouth with the sleeve of his robe. He muttered to himself, "This cannot be happening. It cannot!"

As if she could look into his home from halfway around the world, she asked,

are you all right?

And to pour salt on the wounds she was raking through his flesh, she added,

moy lyubimyy?

She was mocking him?

He grabbed the controller and cursed her, calling her every vile name he could conjure. Her response was chilling.

mind your temper, vassi
we have conditions to discuss
conditions to prevent disaster
from coming upon you
are you paying attention?

The room revolved around him and would not stop. He nodded. Slowly. But she could not see him nod.

we have conditions to discuss
are you paying attention?

When he did not reply, more lines appeared on the screen.

are you paying attention?
are you paying attention?
are you paying attention?

His hands were shaking so hard, it took him several tries to type, "Yes."

good
you will recall zakhar
and his men to moscow
you will do this NOW

Trembling more, he keyed in, "Yes."

LAYNIE PORTLAND, RETIRED SPY

> if I catch even a whiff of zakhar
> or any of your people
> one phone call will send the evidence
> on its way to the security council
> my conditions and promise
> you will never look for me again
> and i will never bother you again
> do you agree?

He blinked stupidly at his controller. *I am done with video games.*

> do you agree?
> do you agree?
> do you agree?

He entered the terse two-word reply. "I agree."

No further messages appeared on the screen. Petroff waited ten minutes. Twenty. At the end of thirty minutes, he got up, ejected the game disc from the console and snapped it in two. He pulled the broadband and power cords from the wall.

And he picked up his phone.

----------⌘----------

CHAPTER 16

PETROFF THREW THE sat phone to the floor. He'd heard nothing but an unanswered ring on Zakhar's end for the past twenty minutes.

Why is that imbecile not answering?

The reason was simple. In New York, it was evening. In Moscow, it was the middle of the night. Not expecting Petroff to call when he would normally be sleeping, Zakhar had left the sat phone in his bedroom, where it rang out of earshot.

Petroff turned his attention to his landline and considered calling the safe house directly—but would he get through? According to the news, communication lines into and out of New York were still overloaded. A glut of callers, trying to reach their loved ones, had overwhelmed the system, blocking communications between and among the government and the city's various emergency response services.

The authorities, therefore, had ordered the citizenry to keep the lines open for emergency communications.

Petroff did not care about the state of emergency communication in a distant city—he had his own emergency. He glanced at the clock. a quarter past four.

It will be after eight o'clock at night in New York.

With shaking fingers, he dialed, half expecting a busy signal—but the call rang through to the other end. The main phone at the house on Long Island was located in a hallway alcove outside the living room. A man answered on the third ring.

"Give me Zakhar," Petroff demanded.

Zakhar came on the line, wondering at the timing of the call—was it not still night in Russia?

"*Dobroye utro*, Vassili Aleksandrovich. Good morning to you. We are ready and will be leaving for—"

Petroff wasted no time. "Zakhar. I have new orders for you and the men with you. You will remain where you are until the Americans open their airspace. The moment it is possible to fly again, you and your men are to return home to Russia. Until then, you are not to leave the house, do I make myself clear?"

Zakhar went silent, too dumbfounded at Petroff's change of direction to immediately reply.

Petroff screamed into the phone, "Zakhar! Do you hear me? You are recalled to Russia at the first possible opportunity! Do you understand?"

Zakhar caught the scent of desperation in Petroff's shouted orders. It was not yet five o'clock in the morning in Moscow, and Petroff usually did not rise until 6:30.

He perceived the truth in an instant.

Gavno! The woman is a spy—and she is blackmailing Petroff!

The inferences tumbled through his mind, concluding with. *And when this Olander whore manipulates him, she endangers all of Petroff's confidants—including me.*

Zakhar pulled the phone away from his ear. It was his role to clean up Petroff's mistakes—while protecting his own backside. *If the FSB suspects that Olander used Petroff to spy upon Russia, they will immediately arrest him and all those within his circle.*

I will be as guilty and as dead as he is.

What followed was a moment of clarity for Zakhar, the realization that the risks he faced as one of Petroff's close supporters—and a Ukrainian one, at that—far outweighed any reward Petroff might offer him. Something dropped and landed in the pit of Zakhar's stomach. It settled down deep with cold finality.

A way out . . . and, if he handled his cards with finesse, the means to a better future.

I will not be swept up in a scandal of your making, Vassili Aleksandrovich. I refuse to allow my many years of service and loyalty to become a millstone hung about my neck because of your blunders!

Zakhar knew that his three men could hear his end of the conversation. They would be hanging on his every word.

"*Da*, Vassili Aleksandrovich, I understand. You have recalled the team to Russia at the first possible opportunity."

"Do not fail me, Zakhar."

Petroff hung up on Zakhar without further ado, but Zakhar remained on the line with the lifeless receiver humming in his ear.

"*Da*. I will continue the search as you order, Vassili Aleksandrovich. I will keep the arrangements I've made to follow the woman's flight into Canada tomorrow. Do not fear. I will find her.

"*Do svidaniya*, Vassili Aleksandrovich."

He replaced the receiver and walked with purpose into the living room to deliver Petroff's orders.

"The three of you have been recalled to Russia as soon as our plane can leave American airspace," he announced.

"Dimitri Ilyich, you will not be accompanying us?" This from Nicor, although Zakhar was positive he and the other two men had heard his closing words to Petroff.

"I am to go on without you. Vassili Aleksandrovich feels that four of us traveling through Canada in search of Miss Olander would be too obvious, that strengthened screenings at the borders would place us under unwanted scrutiny. I will leave tomorrow as scheduled. You will return to Russia when the Americans open their airspace."

He turned on his heel and started upstairs to his room. He had provided no room for discussion and had left his three men nodding servile compliance to his departing back.

Zakhar went to his room and recalculated the time in Moscow. He must wait at least four hours. The time in New York would be one o'clock in the morning, but in Moscow it would be 9:00 a.m. He could not even consider sleep, so he would remain awake through the next hours.

While he waited, he took inventory of his supplies—a supply of ready cash, two sets of passports, driver's licenses, and credit cards—one set American, the other Canadian—a mobile phone, and a suitable weapon with ammunition. He packed a duffle bag, adding the supplies to his clothes and personal items.

LAYNIE ENDED THE game's chat with Petroff and set to work cleaning Justin's room. She ejected her game disc and returned it to her purse. She wiped down Justin's game disc and slid it into the PlayStation console.

She gathered the wine bottles, wiped them down, and put them into the bag she'd brought them in. Wiped and added the wine glasses. Wiped the room service dishes and set them on the floor outside Justin's door. Wiped down every surface she'd handled—the table, broadband cable, game controllers, game console, bathroom fixtures—erasing, in short, every trace of her presence from the room.

After she had rechecked her work, Laynie picked up her purse and the bag, hung a Do Not Disturb sign on Justin's door, and took the elevator to the second floor. She walked down the stairs to the ground floor, avoiding the lobby, down the hallway, past the laundry, to the back of the hotel, and out the exit leading to the dumpsters. She disposed of the bag containing the wine bottles and stemware in one of the full dumpsters, pulling other garbage on top of the bag.

Then she returned to her room and wiped down everything to remove her fingerprints. When she had finished, she grabbed her suitcase, wheeled it to the elevator, and rode it down to the second floor. From the second floor, Laynie again took the stairs, avoiding the lobby. She used a side door to find her way to the parking garage.

Laynie handed the valet her claim check. When he returned with her rental car and put her bag in the trunk, she tipped him modestly, then drove away, ending her short trip at the Fontainebleau Hotel.

She handed her keys to the valet. "I'm checking in."

"Very good, ma'am."

Wheeling her suitcase behind her, Laynie entered the hotel lobby and approached the check-in counter.

"I have a reservation. Elaine Granger."

The clerk looked in the system. "Yes, I have your reservation, Ms. Granger. Welcome to the Fontainebleau. You're in room 3705."

SØREN STEPPED INTO the kitchen. "Hey. The kids are asleep now. I'm going to shower. Afterward, can we grab some decaf and talk?"

"Sounds good."

Kari made a fresh pot while Søren was showering. They'd decided to wait until after Shannon and Robbie were in bed before they revisited Kari's assertion—her *certainty*—that the woman who had helped the sky marshal save Flight 6177 was not this Marta Forestier, as the paper called her, but Kari's sister, Laynie.

When Søren wandered into the kitchen, his reddish-blonde hair still damp, Kari poured their coffee and they sat down in the breakfast nook. The newspaper sat at her elbow.

Søren stirred in two spoons of sugar, then took a long pull on his mug. "Mmm. Good."

"You're welcome. Ready to talk about this now?"

"Yeah. I've been gnawing on it all day as I worked. I'm sorry we couldn't discuss it in depth after lunch."

"Don't be. You have more to shoulder with Max off to college. I didn't want to be the reason you got behind."

Søren stroked her hand. "Thank you. I'm so grateful the Lord put you, Shannon, and Robbie in our lives—Max and mine."

"And I'm grateful the Lord put our family together the way he did."

Søren leaned in, kissed her, and smiled. "To God be the glory."

"Yes, amen!"

Kari unfolded the paper to the photograph of Marta Forestier. "I've studied this picture on and off all day. I'm convinced it's Laynie, although it's been seven-and-a-half years since I've seen her. She's older, and she's darkened her hair, but everything else is the same—even the set to her jaw."

Kari stared into Søren's deep blue eyes—the Thoresen family eyes, so much like her own—and Laynie's. "You know that Laynie confided in me that day we spent out on Puget Sound in Sammie's sailboat. We were both trying so hard to find the sister we'd lost when we were kids, and we both had questions.

"It took her a while, but eventually, she asked me why I'd forgotten her, why I hadn't remembered her and Sammie while I was growing up. I said, *I tried to remember. I knew I'd forgotten something—something truly important—but each time I wanted to remember, it would trigger a panic attack.*

"I didn't go into the details of how my anxiety manifested. I didn't tell her how, when it swept over me, I would pass out. Didn't tell her about the nightmares I suffered as a child. Instead, I made a joke about the attacks and tried to laugh them off.

"I told her—and I was so flippant, Søren! *You've never lived until you've experienced a full-on panic attack.*

"That's when she let me in, when she admitted to why she was living in Europe. Even though we were alone, out on the water and far from anyone else, she lowered her voice and said, *I've been in some very tight places, Kari—tight enough that I'm surprised I don't have anxiety attacks, some tight corners that could easily have ended with me in a Russian interrogation room. The day I ever have such an attack? I'll be finished in my present line of work.*

"My point, Søren? She said *Russian.* She's been spying on the Russians!"

Søren's expression radiated concern. "You've never shared this with me. I get now why you're so worried."

"I'm sorry. Although I told you we suspected she was some kind of federal agent or operative living abroad, I didn't want to . . . to betray her confidence by repeating her words—particularly the word *Russian.*"

"I understand."

"Before she returned to Sweden, Laynie hinted that something 'big' was afoot and, as the day for her flight back to Europe approached, she withdrew from us emotionally. It was horrible, Søren, watching her harden herself for what was waiting for her back in Sweden. Then, when we got married and Laynie didn't come . . . I knew. I knew she was caught up in something she couldn't get out of.

"After she returned to Sweden, I wrote her twice a month, receiving only the barest of replies—until . . . until her last letter, about six years ago. She said her situation was changing and that she would no longer be able to reply to my letters. She could continue to receive mail from me, but I wouldn't receive any from her."

Kari raised her chin and stared at Søren. "Only now I think Laynie is in real, imminent trouble. As fantastic or fictional as it might sound, I believe that she disguised herself and took on a new identity to get away from whatever or whoever she was spying on. I think the reason this Marta Forestier disappeared from Flight 6177 after it landed is because that someone is after her. And she's alone out there, Søren. *Alone!*"

"What about her organization? Why wouldn't they help her?"

"I don't know. I only know—I *surmise*—that whomever she's been with in Russia is powerful and connected."

"All right, but wouldn't she come to us for help?"

Kari shook her head. "She has cut ties with everyone she loves so that whoever is hunting her will have no leverage to use against her."

"Then there's only one thing we can do to help her, Kari."

Tears streaming down her face, Kari nodded. "Pray for her. Ask the Lord to send her aid. Ask him to hide her from her enemies and make a way for her to escape. I believe this is why, more than two weeks ago, I felt that she was in danger and we were to pray for her."

Søren took her hand. "Then let's pray for Laynie. Right now."

WHEN THE CLOCK read one in the morning, Zakhar used the satellite phone to place his first call. He wasted precious time "worming" his way through the bureaucratic watchdogs that guarded Russia's most powerful men—until his call was, at last, routed as he requested.

A male voice answered, "You have reached the offices of Secretary Rushailo. How may I direct your call?"

Zakhar steeled his voice. "I am Dimitri Ilyich Zakhar, Chief of Security for Vassili Aleksandrovich Petroff. I must speak to Secretary Rushailo's chief of security. My business is urgent."

He had decided to go straight to the top of the political food chain—or at least as close to the top as he could reach. Reporting Petroff to the FSB might take the man out of circulation, but the FSB would likely come after Zakhar, too—and he did not relish spending time in the cellars of Lubyanka explaining his role in Petroff's treason.

No, Zakhar would rather report Petroff to his superiors. Was this not the old way, the Communist way? As Secretary of the Russian Federation's Security Council and a patron who had shown Petroff great favoritism, Rushailo would act swiftly to distance himself from Petroff, lest Petroff's sins taint him or his administration. With the right prompting, *Rushailo* would order the FSB to take Petroff into custody. Rushailo would also be honor bound to direct the FSB to leave Zakhar alone.

Yes, Rushailo was the better choice . . . because Zakhar had no intention of wasting the golden opportunity that lay before him.

"This is Baskin."

"Good morning. I am Dimitri Ilyich Zakhar, Chief of Security for Vassili Aleksandrovich Petroff. You and I have met working state dinners. Do you remember me?"

"*Da*, I remember you, Dimitri Ilyich. What can I do for you?"

"I have urgent information of a treasonous nature, information that could damage Secretary Rushailo should it come out. I wanted to report this information to you at once, because I wish to preserve the Secretary's good name."

Baskin's attitude was instantly wary. "What information? You must tell me, Dimitri Ilyich."

"I will. That is why I called. I am, at present, in the city of New York. I was sent by my master, Vassili Aleksandrovich Petroff, to track down and retrieve his mistress, Linnéa Olander, supposedly a Swedish national."

"Supposedly?"

"Yes, we suspect she is not who she presented herself to be. Miss Olander left a letter stating that she was leaving Petroff and returning home to Sweden. She had been gone more than a week but had not returned to Sweden, so my team and I visited the village near Uppsala where Miss Olander grew up.

"Although her name is on the village school's roster during the period she was supposedly in school there, we interviewed a retired teacher—a teacher whom, also according to the school's roster, was *her* instructor for several years. However, this man insists he knows of no Linnéa Olander—not in his classroom, nor in the school or the village itself."

"Go on."

Zakhar could hear Baskin scratching notes.

"This led Vassili Aleksandrovich to suspect the woman of spying on him during the years she lived with him. He ordered me to bring Olander back to Russia. I believe he wished to dispose of her quietly without notifying the authorities of her crimes—or the damage she may have caused.

"I and my team traced Olander on a flight to New York the day of the terror attacks and arrived ahead of her plane, planning to apprehend her when she landed. However, her plane, like the others, was diverted to Canada, so we made plans to follow her there.

"Only hours ago, Petroff recalled my team—all of us—to Russia. He was most insistent that we return the moment the US airspace reopens. As these orders contradicted his previous ones, they confirmed to me that Linnéa Olander was and is a spy and that she is blackmailing Petroff. My assessment is that she has threatened to expose him, and Petroff has recalled us to avoid her threat."

"You are certain of your intelligence?"

Zakhar shrugged, a motion that did not convey well over the phone. "I can state with confidence that the woman who called herself Linnéa Olander was Petroff's mistress for seven years, that her background was falsified, that she had unrestricted access to Petroff's home office, and that Petroff often spoke to her of his work for Secretary Rushailo."

Four nails in Petroff's coffin.

He heard more furious scratching by Baskin. "These are dangerous accusations."

"Yes. I wished Secretary Rushailo to be made aware of the situation immediately lest it became publicly known and harm him."

"I see."

Zakhar imagined he could see the wheels revolving in Baskin's head.

"What do you intend to do next, Dimitri Ilyich?"

"The men with me are unaware of our reasons for hunting the woman. They will return to Russia as ordered. I, however, will follow the trail of this woman and apprehend her so that we may question her and find the truth. Or . . ."

"Or?"

"Or, if Secretary Rushailo wishes otherwise, I will follow his instructions."

In other words, if the Secretary wishes me to make the woman disappear so that the mess that has the potential to taint his administration never comes to light, I will do as he orders.

"You are a good man, Dimitri Ilyich. I will report your findings to the Secretary immediately and call you back."

Zakhar hung up and waited. He was ready to leave the safe house, but perhaps Rushailo would authorize him some assistance?

Twenty minutes later, the sat phone buzzed with an incoming call. Zakhar picked up.

"This is Zakhar."

"Baskin here, Dimitri Ilyich. Take down this number."

Zakhar did so. The international code was Canadian. "Whose number have you given me?"

"An operative we employ—a skilled computer hacker—placed within the Canadian's Mounted Police. When you call her, you will ask for *Ms. Gagnon*, a common French-Canadian name. When she says, 'Yes, this is she,' reply with the code word *pomoshch*.

"Our operative works in the RCMP computer center and has unfettered access to their system. We have directed her to give you any assistance you require. Also, Zakhar, I wish you to take down my direct number. You will call and provide regular updates, understood?"

Zakhar wrote the number down. "*Da.* I understand. And I hope the Secretary will remember that I have placed the welfare of Mother Russia and the Secretary's administration above my loyalty to Vassili Aleksandrovich."

"I assure you the Secretary will honor you appropriately, Dimitri Ilyich. Continue as you have proposed. Say nothing to anyone. Follow the woman and abduct her. I will have further instructions when you have her in your custody."

With Petroff out of the way—and unable to order a hit squad after him—Zakhar was now free to hunt the woman with impunity and do with her what he had so often fantasized he would do. And when he had finished playing with her, would he return to Russia? Did a bright future await him, a man of "inferior" Ukrainian birth?

No.

Zakhar had no intention of "checking in" with Baskin to "provide regular updates." He would not utilize Rushailo's "skilled hacker" or return to Russia to receive the Secretary's "honors."

Instead, he would find the woman himself. When he finished with her, he would put the money he carried to good use, losing himself in either Canada or America, beginning a new life—a better life than he could ever expect in Russia.

I will vanish—I will vanish, and no one will come after me. Who would bother? The FSB will never release Petroff alive, and Rushailo will not care when I drop off the grid. He will, eventually, assume that I died in my pursuit of Olander.

And that was fine with Zakhar.

CHAPTER 17
LP

AT FOUR THAT MORNING, Zakhar boarded the boat he had chartered to get him off Long Island. The captain and his crew of two said little. They took his money and indicated where he was to sit during the voyage.

The boat's engines were quiet but efficient, as they used the last of the night to motor far out to sea, first east and then north, making a wide berth around Nantucket and Cape Cod in order to avoid the Coast Guard. Zakhar had nothing to do during the passage, so he dozed, catching up on the hours of sleep he had missed during the night.

He awoke once during the voyage, reached into his duffle, and retrieved the sat phone. It made no sound as he dropped it overboard. He slept soundly after that.

By early afternoon, having passed Boston Harbor to the west but remaining far offshore, they continued north until they approached the coastal islands of Maine. Soon it became obvious to Zakhar that the captain was very knowledgeable of both the island waterways and the Coast Guard's preferred routes. After slowly navigating narrow channels, the man—who had yet to utter a word to Zakhar—came alongside a dock just below a wooded knoll. Zakhar's eyes followed the grassy rise that sloped from the small inlet up to the trees. He spied a cottage tucked into the woods above them. The inlet itself was rocky and uninhabitable on all sides but the one, leaving the house above them the lone witness to their arrival.

Then the captain spoke to Zakhar. "The cottage you see upon the knoll is vacant at present—the owners do not arrive until tomorrow afternoon to spend the weekend."

He handed Zakhar a set of keys. "The vehicle you requested sits in the driveway. Use it and then abandon it where you will—it cannot be traced back to us."

He held out a folded map to Zakhar. "I have marked your route to Bangor, which should take you a little more than an hour. I have not marked the map farther than Bangor, but you should have no difficulties following the map from there to a border crossing into New Brunswick. If you drive

189

conservatively and are not detained at the border, the journey from Bangor to Moncton should take less than five hours—putting you in the town later this evening. I will also remind you that the time zone changes when you cross into New Brunswick."

"Thank you," Zakhar said as he took the keys and map. His American English was heavily accented, but he had spent years undercover in France, and his French was excellent. He would switch to French and his Canadian passport at the border.

Perhaps when I have finished with the woman, the French-speaking province of Québec will best suit me as my new home.

He picked up the duffle bag and jumped down onto the dock. Without a backward glance, he strode up the grassy slope toward the cottage.

I have not a minute to waste, he told himself. *She has been in Canada now three days. If she has opportunity to leave Canadian Immigration custody, she will run.*

Therefore, I must be swift and ruthless in my pursuit of her.

LAYNIE GOT UP EARLY and ordered coffee, breakfast, and a newspaper. She had a solid plan now, but it required that she not leave Montreal until Monday—and the delay was concerning.

What if a single day spelled the difference between freedom and capture?

She reviewed the tactics and maneuvers she had employed, trying to dispel her disquiet:

I discarded Marta Forestier's identity. My hair is now a different color and style than hers. I stayed only two nights at the Westmount before moving to the Fontainebleau, and used an American passport and credit card for both. I kept a low profile at the Westmount and interacted with only one guest. I had minimal contact with hotel staff. I will do the same here, then move on.

Somewhat mollified, she still jumped when a knock sounded on her door.

"Room service."

"Leave it, please," Laynie said through the door. After the footsteps pattered away, she retrieved the tray. While she ate, she caught up on the news surrounding the attacks—particularly the "Have You Seen This Woman" story.

Except the story seemed to have died—which puzzled Laynie.

She searched the paper front to back and, although Flight 6177 was mentioned multiple times, she never spotted the name or photo of Marta Forestier.

She didn't know if Marstead had killed the story or if it had died of natural causes.

Her uneasiness revived.

It is more likely that Marstead killed the story. If so, they may not be far behind me. Despite changing hotels each night, I will not rest well until I get on the road Monday.

She read personal accounts of the attacks, but most of the day's news was on the FAA's tentative release of the grounded commercial flights, meaning that the planes diverted to US and Canadian cities after the attacks would be cleared to fly to their original destinations.

Laynie smiled. *I hope the newlyweds can still enjoy part of the grand honeymoon they had planned. At least they'll have a wild tale to tell their grandchildren someday.*

As for herself? *I will remain cloistered here until checkout time, making a reservation at another hotel for tonight.*

ZAKHAR PARKED IN the shadows down the street and made his way on foot to the lieutenant's home. The man and his wife had not retired for the night. The flicker of the television shone through the living room curtains, and Zakhar could hear the low sounds of the show they were watching.

Earlier in the evening, Zakhar had arrived in Moncton and made discreet inquiries into the bar the Moncton police force frequented. He had waited for a lone officer to leave the bar and had followed him until he parked outside his apartment. Zakhar had fixed a silencer to his gun and crept up behind the policeman as he unlocked his unit's door. It had taken but a moment of surprise to push him inside. The threat the barrel of his gun produced— pressed against the officer's back—had allowed him to secure the man's hands behind his back with his own handcuffs.

Ten minutes later, the man had given Zakhar all the information he possessed.

"The planes' passengers are being quartered in the convention center. Everyone knows that. It's in the papers, on the news."

"And who is in charge of the passengers? Who is charged with the town's security?"

"I-I'm not sure. The mayor appointed Lieutenant Moreau of the Canada Customs and Revenue Agency to take charge initially, because the CCRA includes the Canada Border Services Agency. But that was just until the government sent in higher-ranking officials to take over. I-I do not know their names or where they are staying."

"But you do know this Lieutenant Moreau?"

"H-he is an acquaintance."

"And he lives locally? Where?"

The policeman shook his head. "I won't tell you."

Zakhar had shrugged. He pulled the policeman's socks off his feet and forced them into his mouth. When the officer saw what Zakhar was about to do, he screamed his protests vainly into the wadded socks—and then screamed in agony when Zakhar shot his knee at close range.

After that, the policeman had wept and pleaded before giving up Moreau's address—but he had given it up.

"*Spasibo*," Zakhar said, as he shot the man twice in the chest.

Zakhar unscrewed the silencer from his gun, put them both into the deep pockets of his overcoat, and left the apartment, locking the man's door behind him.

Now Zakhar was casing Lieutenant Moreau's home. He noted Moreau's official Canadian Customs and Regulations car parked in the driveway next to a modest economy car. Zakhar skirted the house, looking for its back entrance. The door's lock gave way with surprisingly little resistance. Perhaps burglary was not a large problem in Moncton.

Zakhar drew his gun and threaded the silencer onto its barrel as he crept through the little kitchen, following the flickering light of the television to its source. The couple were sitting in matching recliners facing the television, their backs to him. A comfortable-looking settee stood against the wall to their right.

Moreau's wife noticed him first as he came up from behind them. She started and gave a little scream. Zakhar struck her across the face, shutting her up. When Moreau jumped to her defense, Zakhar pointed his gun at her.

"That would not be wise, Lieutenant Moreau."

"Who are you? What do you want?"

Zakhar signaled with his gun. "Get up. Move to the sofa, both of you."

When they had obeyed him, Zakhar pointed the gun at Moreau. "You. Your handcuffs, please."

Moreau shut his mouth in defiance.

Zakhar again pointed the barrel of his gun at the woman.

"Top drawer," Moreau growled. He tipped his head toward a desk across the room.

Zakhar waved the gun at the woman. "Get them from the desk. Hurry, now! Put them on him, hands in back."

"Do as he asks, Michelle," Paul Moreau whispered. "Don't be afraid."

The weeping woman cuffed Moreau's hands behind his back, then sat beside him.

"What do you want?" Moreau asked. "Money?"

Why not? Zakhar thought. *One can never have enough money.*

"I will take your money. Tell your wife to bring it to me."

Michelle Moreau emptied her pocketbook of its paltry contents, then her husband's wallet of his modest cash.

"This is all you have?" Zakhar demanded.

"I am a civil servant. We are not wealthy people."

"Then I am glad I am not here as a robber only. However, if you give me what I came for, I will leave you tied up but unharmed."

Moreau had no choice but to nod his agreement.

"I am looking for someone," Zakhar said, "a woman whose plane was grounded here. She came in on Flight 6177 under the alias of Marta Forestier."

Moreau's eyes widened.

"Ah. I see you recognize her name. Where is she?"

Moreau licked his lips. "The plane's sky marshal was wounded. She, this Marta Forestier, rode to the hospital in the ambulance with him. Then she . . . left."

Zakhar's face reddened. "She left?"

"She helped the marshal take down the hijackers. Everyone assumed she was a sky marshal, too. No one knew differently at the time. She used the opportunity to slip away."

It was Zakhar's turn to register surprise. *She helped the marshal take down the hijackers? Linnéa Olander did? Surely, she is more than either Petroff or I ever suspected. This only further confirms my assumptions that she is a spy!*

He smiled to himself. *Perhaps she will show some spirit when I break her. I may even extract useful information from her that I can sell to the highest bidder.*

Zakhar put the barrel of the silencer against Michelle Moreau's head. "But your agency has been seeking this woman, yes? You have some idea where she went?"

Moreau shook his head. "The authorities tracked her to Montreal day before yesterday, but they have only a bad photograph of her and the other passengers' descriptions. She has likely changed her appearance."

MOREAU STILL DID NOT understand who the woman actually was or why she was important, but he had omitted a vital detail. He did not tell his captor that the Americans had, only today, ordered Canadian authorities off the hunt.

And perhaps, God willing, the man holding them at gunpoint had spoken the truth. Perhaps he possessed a shred of human decency and would leave them unharmed as he has promised.

Moreau had no recourse other than to hope.

He licked his lips. "Please. That is . . . all I know. I am not in the loop, you see. I received what information I have from a friend who was involved in the search."

Zakhar stared impassively at the couple. "I need your badge and the keys to your official car."

Moreau watched Zakhar's thoughts flit across his face. He recognized the man's cruel cunning. It was then that he understood that neither he nor his wife would survive the evening. Even so, the love he held for his wife dictated his actions. He would postpone the inevitable for as long as possible.

Moreau swallowed. "In the same drawer."

Zakhar didn't move except to slowly shift his gun from the woman to Moreau.

Locking eyes with his trembling wife, Paul Moreau whispered, "Don't look at him, my darling. Look at me. See my eyes? See the love I have for you? It will be all—"

ZAKHAR'S FREE HAND WAVED away the haze wafting from his weapon's barrel. He laid the gun aside to cool and added the Moreau's money to his wallet while assembling his next moves.

Whatever I do, I must be bold. Decisive. I must work faster than the authorities who have a head start. I can beat them. I have advantages they do not—I not only know the woman, I have several excellent photographs of her.

He tucked Moreau's credential pack into his breast pocket. Then he studied the map the boat's captain had given him. Montreal was nine or ten hours by automobile, and the city probably had a thousand hotels and rooming houses.

She will seek to lose herself in the city while assembling a new identity. She will need money and a vehicle. These things take time.

And Linnéa Olander had particular tastes—tastes Zakhar was quite familiar with.

He perused Moreau's closet. The two men were not too dissimilar in shirt size, but Moreau had been taller. Zakhar pulled two shirts, two ties, and a blazer from the dead man's closet, leaving them on hangers. He would need them in Montreal.

When he was finished, Zakhar wrote a short note, then picked up his gun and the keys to Moreau's official vehicle. He drew the curtains, left the house, and locked the door behind him. He pinned the note to the door.

GONE FISHING

He started Moreau's car, backed it from the driveway, drove down the street, and parked next to his car. He shifted his duffle bag to Moreau's back seat and drove away, leaving his car behind.

He would drive all night and arrive in Montreal early in the morning.

It may be days before the good lieutenant and his wife are discovered. Until then, I will be Paul Moreau, Canada Customs and Revenue officer, with the authority to conduct an open search for her. I must be convincing and imposing.

The American and Canadian authorities will look for her, but I will find her first.

———————⟋⟍⟍⟍———————

CHAPTER 18

LP

SATURDAY MORNING, Laynie awoke in her third Montreal hotel. She decided to check in with Christor in case he had further information for her.

It was nearing 6:00 a.m. in Montreal. The time in Stockholm was six hours ahead, almost noon. Perhaps, because of the weekend, the hotel's business center would be unoccupied. As for Christor—he took his laptop home each weekend, but Laynie could not anticipate the plans he and Klara had for the day.

Will he answer when I call?

Laynie threw on jeans and a T-shirt, pulled her hair up into a ponytail, and put on her baseball cap. She grabbed her purse and a newspaper, then used the back stairs to reach the ground floor. When she reached the business center, she paused outside the open door to scope out the room and its occupants. A harried man sat at one of the three computers, but he was not alone. Three young children romped about the room, bored and out of sorts.

"When will you be done, Daddy?" the oldest one, a girl, asked him. "You said we were going to have breakfast and then you would take us to a park. You promised pancakes."

"I did and we will *have* pancakes, Chelsea, but I also said that I must answer these emails first. Please be patient."

"But I'm hungry!" another child wailed.

Laynie withdrew and scanned the hall, looking for an out-of-the-way place to wait. She spotted a bench seat in an alcove not far down the hall. She sat down on it, crossed her legs, and unfolded the newspaper, using its open pages to hide her face.

Twenty long minutes passed before the man—herding his kids before him—left the business center. Laynie immediately made for the room. She sat down at a terminal that faced away from the doorway.

She withdrew the CD-ROM case, inserted the unmarked disc, and ran the program that bypassed the computer system's administrative restrictions. Then she copied the VoIP software installation code from the CD and clicked the executable file to install the program.

She glanced at the clock. After seven, meaning after one in the afternoon in Stockholm. Laynie slipped on the headphones and dialed Christor's laptop.

The call rang and rang. Christor picked up.

"Laynie!" His voice was a whisper. "Hold on, please."

A few moments later, he was back, typing rather than speaking. "Locked in bathroom. Don't want Klara to know I'm on a call."

OPSEC. Operational security. Also, what Klara didn't know couldn't get her into trouble with Marstead.

Laynie typed, "Good. Anything new?"

"Yes. Important call between Alvarsson and D.C. superior. Listen."

Laynie waited for the recorded call to come through her headphones.

First, she heard the *scree* and static of an encrypted call syncing up. Then she heard the voices.

"Alvarsson here."

"Mr. Alvarsson, Jack Wolfe calling from Headquarters."

Jack Wolfe? Laynie didn't recognize the name.

Apparently, Alvarsson recognized it. Laynie may as well have been in Alvarsson's office, watching his change of demeanor and body language, so clearly did they translate through his next words.

"Yes, sir. How can I help you, Director Wolfe?"

Director Wolfe? Not on any Marstead org chart Laynie had ever seen. He had to be much higher up the food chain.

But how high?

"I'm calling with regards to Linnéa Olander."

"Yes, sir?"

"Let me begin by saying that I am in possession of Olander's file—her excellent record in clandestine services and the abundance of valuable intel she's provided during her tenure. Her time in place in her most recent assignment—undercover with that Russian narcissist, Petroff— is an assignment deserving hazard pay if any assignment does.

"I also have her letter of some five months past expressing her emotional and mental fatigue—her letter requesting that she be deactivated before she, in essence, *cracked* and compromised the entire Marstead organization to the Russians. Finally, I'm looking at a resignation letter, a letter written in response to our denial of her deactivation?"

"Yes, sir."

The intensity of Wolfe's voice rose. "Well, what I want to know, Mr. Alvarsson, is *why* in the bloody blue blazes you left this exceptional asset hanging out to dry with no option left to her but to threaten our organization with exposure if we did not extract her safely from the field? And more than that? *I want to know who gave the order to retire this agent.*"

Laynie heard Alvarsson swallow.

"I can assure you, sir, that the order did not come from me nor did I relish implementing it. Linnéa Olander is one of the finest, most talented assets I've had the pleasure of working with."

"You're saying Saunders refused her request. That he gave the order."

"Sir, whether the order originated with him or not, I cannot say. I can only tell you that it came through him and that I followed the chain of command."

"What a *bleeping* waste of an exceptional agent and a *blank blank* demonstration of poor personnel management!"

Laynie listened to dead air for a long, tense moment before a much calmer Wolfe said, "Let me take this opportunity to inform you that your supervisor—soon to be *former* supervisor—Marcus Saunders, will, as of tomorrow, be 'promoted' to a position where he can do much less damage. Do you take my point, Mr. Alvarsson?"

"Yes, sir. I do, sir."

"I hope you understand where incompetence, gross negligence, and self-promotion will take you in *this* organization. It's my conclusion that Saunders put his career and his own upward mobility above the well-being and longevity of our agent and forced her to keep producing intel well beyond her capacity to do so *because she made him look good.*

"I will not tolerate handlers who sacrifice our agents to promote themselves, Alvarsson—and I won't stand on bureaucratic red tape to weed out those who abuse the men and women of our human intelligence gathering network."

"Yes, sir. Er, no sir."

Wolfe coughed into the phone. "You have new orders. I am directing you to bring her in peaceably."

"That *is* good news, sir. However, the order doesn't alleviate the threat her sudden disappearance has created on the Russians' side of the equation. Furthermore, acquainted with her abilities as I am, it's my opinion that bringing her in, uh, *peaceably*, will prove as difficult as retiring her. She's on the offensive now, sir."

"Reach out to her. Talk to those who have known her best. Have them pass the word to her that we have agreed to give her exactly what she asked for. We will bring her in from the field and bring her here to the States. We'll debrief her and find a suitable use for her somewhere while she rests, recuperates, and receives treatment for PTSD or whatever else she may require."

"That might work, sir—like I said, *if* we can find her to make that offer—and if we get to her before the Russians do."

"Actually, we know she safely reached Canada."

"Sir?"

"Did you read about the fifth plane the terrorists planned to weaponize? The one inbound from London?"

"The plane the two sky marshals saved from hijackers?"

"*One* sky marshal, Alvarsson. One sky marshal and one Marstead agent."

"The female sky marshal? You're saying that was Olander?"

"Yes. She managed to get away from the plane after it was diverted to New Brunswick. That upset the Canadians and our FBI friends to no end, but we intervened and called them off. Our people managed to trace Olander's escape from Moncton to Montreal. We are, at present, looking for her there.

"When our people do find her and make contact, their orders are to give her assurances that we'll deactivate her *peaceably* and without prejudice, with a desk job waiting for her if she wants it."

"I understand, sir."

The call ended, leaving Laynie angry and skeptical. She leaned over the keyboard, considering what she'd heard. It wasn't that she didn't trust Christor, because she did. It was Marstead she no longer trusted.

Who is this mysterious figure, this Jack Wolfe? Why have I never heard of him? Is he real? Or . . . have they uncovered Christor's method of bugging Alvarsson's calls? Was this call a ploy? Is it an elaborate gambit of dezinformatsiya—the type of disinformation I often fed Petroff?

She typed, "Can I believe it?"

He typed back, "I'm with Reagan on this. trust but verify."

"Right." *Like I could verify anything Marstead said or did.*

"One more thing. Received letter from your sister. Uploaded image file to chat room."

Laynie's brow furrowed. She couldn't go online and read it now, not without leaving a trail on the hotel's computer.

I'll need to buy a laptop somewhere along the road after I leave Montreal.

And now that she knew Marstead was breathing down her neck, she needed to move. Again.

"Thank you, my friend." Laynie returned to her room and packed. Shortly before checkout time, she wheeled her suitcase to the elevator, got off at the second floor, and walked down to the ground level.

An hour later, she was ensconced in what she hoped was her last Montreal hotel.

SOMETIME BEFORE DAWN the same day, Zakhar pulled over on the outskirts of Montreal and slept two hours. When he woke, he made necessary preparations before beginning his hunt.

First, he dismantled, cleaned, and oiled his gun, then reassembled it. Took off his overcoat and put the gun and silencer into its deep pockets. Removed one of Moreau's shirts from its hanger and put it on, choosing a tie to go with it. Added the blazer and slid Moreau's cred pack into the blazer's breast pocket.

At a gas station, he purchased a detailed map of Montreal. He drove to a restaurant, ordered breakfast, and used the restroom to wash up and finger-comb his damp hair.

"Good," he told his reflection. "You are Lieutenant Paul Moreau."

Zakhar ate alone in a corner booth, studying the map and outlining in pencil a search grid of downtown Montreal. He proposed a long and arduous day for himself, but he was ready and willing. He drove to the starting point on his grid, then up and down each street, noting the hotels and whether they fit his parameters. large, multi-floored lodgings with room service and other amenities. Hotels where Linnéa Olander would be but one face among many.

He parked in front of the first large hotel he encountered, flashing his credentials and demanding that the valet watch his car. He approached the front desk. "Good morning," he said in French. "Lieutenant Moreau, Canada Customs and Revenue. I am looking for this woman." He laid on the counter three the glossy photos of Linnéa Olander, photographs he'd carried with him from Russia.

"No, I do not recognize her," the clerk replied. Another clerk agreed.

He queried as many staff members as he could approach in five minutes, watching their facial responses carefully.

"Thank you for your time."

He didn't care how long it took or how wearying the process. She was energized and strangely confident that he would find her. From eight in the morning until one in the afternoon, he worked his grid, one hotel after another—but only those hotels that matched his criteria. He had covered nine such hotels and checked fifteen blocks off his grid in this manner.

He broke for a quick lunch, then returned to work. He hadn't tired of the tedium. Finding the woman was an obsession he gave himself to gladly, convinced the reward would be well worth his efforts.

From 1:45 until dark he continued on, becoming more comfortable in his role as Lieutenant Paul Moreau and more adept at his inquiries. He had crossed nineteen more blocks off his grid before he stopped for the night. He checked into the last hotel whose staff he questioned, ate a large dinner, and went directly to bed.

CHAPTER 19

LP

IT WAS SUNDAY. Planes were flying again, and Laynie's most recent hotel was clearing out. It made her nervous, knowing that, at half-full, the hotel's staff would be more cognizant of its guests. And, at another new hotel, she might be more noticeable checking in.

Stay calm. Keep this room one more night.

She was stiff from inactivity, so she entered into an hour's worth of stretching, when what she really wanted and needed was a nice, long run.

Tomorrow. I'll get a good walk in tomorrow.

Tomorrow everything would change. Tomorrow she would leave Montreal.

ZAKHAR WAS CHECKING out of his hotel, using the opportunity to show Linnéa Olander's pictures to the morning staff.

"I'm sorry. She doesn't look familiar to me, but we've had a full house ever since the attacks," one woman told him. "We've been run off our feet."

Zakhar held up the photograph to the other front desk clerk. "You, young man. Have you seen this woman?"

"No, sir. Sorry."

He showed the image to a bellboy handling a loaded a luggage cart. He flashed the photo to the day manager walking by.

Behind him a male voice exclaimed, "Isn't that Beverly?"

Zakhar turned and faced the young man. "You know this woman?" He held all three pictures before the man's face.

"Her name is Beverly. I, uh, had dinner with her, couple nights ago."

"What is your name, young man?"

"Justin Worley."

Zakhar signaled the manager. "I require a room to interview this man."

"Hey, I don't have time for this—finally got a flight home to Vancouver, and I need to leave for the airport."

Zakhar took him by the arm. "You will go nowhere until I am finished with you."

"But—"

"I am Lieutenant Paul Moreau, and this is official government business. You will come with me."

The manager led them to her office and, at Zakhar's gesture, left and closed the door behind her.

"Now, Mr. Worley, I cannot emphasize how important your cooperation is. You say you know this woman? How did you meet her?"

"We were in the business center, using the computers. She had a *Final Fantasy* disc."

Zakhar recognized the title. "This is a video game, no?"

"Yeah. I play the same game, so I asked her if she'd like to play it with me. I travel a lot and bring my game console with me."

"In this hotel you saw her?"

"Yes."

"When?"

"It was Thursday. She came up to my room."

"So, a woman of her age was interested in you only for video games?"

Justin flushed. "I don't know what she was interested in. We played the game, ate dinner, drank wine—and I think she drugged me."

"What? Why? Why would she do this?"

"I don't know, but I passed out and it wasn't just from the wine. When I woke up in the morning, she was gone, and the desk said nobody by the name of Beverly was staying here."

"Tell me what you talked about."

"Not much, other than the game. I asked her what she'd done that day, she asked me what I'd done."

"Tell me her exact words. What did she do that day?"

"I dunno. Look, can I go? I have a plane to catch."

Zakhar slid his gun from his pocket and leveled it at Justin's heart. "Do you really not remember?"

Justin's eyes widened to the size of silver dollars. "Hey, man, you can't do that!"

"This is an issue of national security, Mr. Worley. Believe me when I tell you. You and your flight are both expendable. You will tell me what I want to know."

"Sh-she said something about paperwork. Shopping. I think she said the bank."

"The bank? You are certain?"

"Yes. Paperwork, shopping, the bank."

"Which bank?"

"I don't know—I'm telling you the truth!"

Zakhar watched the young man's face. "I think you are. You may go."

Justin fled the room, leaving Zakhar thinking.

Not as many banks as hotels in the city, and surely it will be close by.

He found the manager again and beckoned her to join him at the far end of the front desk. He laid out the map of Montreal and placed his finger on it.

"We are here at your hotel, yes? Show me the banks near here."

CHAPTER 20

Ꮹ LP Ꮻ

LAYNIE DIDN'T SLEEP well Sunday night. The wind had risen while she slept and had pushed and howled at her room's windows. She woke tired and fretful. She ordered coffee and breakfast and, as she had Saturday, continued to chew on the conversation Christor had played for her yesterday. While she knew and had once trusted Alvarsson, she hardly knew what to think of the stranger who had identified himself as Director Wolfe.

Could it be true? Was my "retirement" entirely the brainchild of Deputy Director Saunders and did his Marstead superiors remove him for ordering the hit on me? Do his superiors consider me the valuable asset this man Wolfe said I was? Are they ready to let me come in? Or is it a trap?

All her deliberations came down to one question. *Can I take such a risk?* Each time, her gut gave her the same answer. *No. I cannot.*

She wanted—*needed*—to get out of her room, to leave the city as soon as possible, but since her bank wouldn't open until 9:00 a.m. this morning, she forced herself to slow down. As much as she wanted to leave Montreal behind, she also didn't want the bank manager to remember a woman so hurried that she had been waiting for him to unlock the doors.

Laynie showered and dressed, putting on one of the nice pants outfits and the light jacket, donning both the look and persona of the affluent woman she wished to project to the world. When she'd finished, she headed downstairs, taking the elevator to the second floor as she had become accustomed to, using the back stairs to reach the ground floor and the parking garage.

The fewer people who see me, the better.

She drove to her bank. The lobby was moderately busy as she walked to the teller window—intentionally using a different teller than the one who had opened her account.

Laynie presented her passport. "Good morning. I had money wired from my Singapore account last week. I'd like to know if it has arrived?"

"One moment while I check. Yes. I see that your account is showing a balance of thirty-nine thousand five hundred dollars. Is that correct?"

Laynie had taken the allowed five-hundred-dollar withdrawal Thursday. "Yes, it is."

"What can I help you with today?"

"Two things. I would like to purchase a cashier's check in the amount of twelve thousand dollars and make a cash withdrawal of two thousand dollars."

"I can help you with both of those requests."

When Laynie left the bank, she returned directly to her hotel, asking the valet to keep her car handy. She went up to her room, changed clothes, repacked her suitcase, then wiped down the fixtures she'd touched.

She had, again, altered her appearance by putting on a long-sleeved T-shirt, jogging pants, running shoes, and hoodie, tying a kerchief around her neck. She tucked a few items she'd need later into her purse.

"Thank you," she told the valet, tipping him for keeping her car at the ready. He put her suitcase into the trunk, and Laynie drove away.

She found her way back to the rental agency. She parked, pulled her bag from the trunk, and returned the keys.

"You have a ride, lady?" the owner asked.

"Oh, yes. I've ordered a taxi," Laynie lied.

She rolled her bag out of the yard and to the curb and glanced down the street as though she was expecting the cab any moment. A minute later, she waved to an imaginary driver and wheeled her suitcase beyond the junkyard's fencing where the owner, had he been watching her, would have lost sight of her. Beyond his view, Laynie picked up her steps. She was constrained by the suitcase, but she made it to the next intersection in good time, turned the corner, and kept going.

Well away from the rental agency's prying eyes, Laynie stopped. She fished in her handbag, brushed out her hair, tied it in a low ponytail, then wound and pinned it at the back of her neck. She pulled the kerchief from around her neck. She folded it into a triangle, placed it over her hair, and tied it behind her head at the hairline, below the knot of hair.

She set off, dragging her case behind her. The wheeled bag definitely slowed her down. Jogging, she could have made it to Bessie and Shaw's in half the time. Walking would take her longer—but she didn't want a cabbie recounting where he'd dropped her off.

Besides, she told herself, stretching out her legs, *the exercise will do me good.*

Forty minutes later, warmed and lightly perspiring from the brisk pace she'd set, Laynie arrived at the Bradshaws'. She wheeled her case up the driveway and left it in front of the motor home, out of sight. She climbed the steps to the Bradshaws' house and rang the bell. Shaw answered immediately.

"Come in, come in," he urged her. "Wind's got a bite to it, it does."

He was, she observed, somewhat flustered.

"Is something wrong, Shaw?"

He looked her up and down. "How did you get here, Elaine? I didn't see a car and your cheeks are all pink."

"I, uh, walked from the rental place."

He searched her face, looking for something. "Well, come to the kitchen. We need to talk."

Alarm bells jangled in Laynie's head. The last time someone had insisted, "We need to talk," she'd been shoved backward into a lavatory at thirty thousand feet and deputized to help take down a clutch of hijackers.

She followed Shaw into the kitchen. Bessie was waiting, already sitting down.

"Take a seat, Elaine—if that is your name," Shaw said.

She sat and glanced from him to Bessie and back. "What's going on?"

Bessie flipped over an old newspaper. Put her finger on the photo Laynie was already quite familiar with.

"Is this you? This Marta Forestier woman?"

Laynie expected fear and accusation in their eyes. Condemnation. Instead she saw a searching, wary concern.

She didn't flinch from the examination.

It's not my intention to hurt you, either of you—and I won't. Please believe me.

Believe you? Isn't your entire life a lie?

I don't want that life anymore.

Clearing her throat, Laynie whispered, "And if it is?"

Shaw answered her. "Then I would ask you just one question. Are you on the run from the law?"

Laynie thought for a moment. "Do you mean am I a criminal?"

"Is there a difference?"

She nodded. Slowly. "There is. I *am* running, but not because I'm a criminal. I-I'm running from a man and . . . from my former employers."

"Running from a man?" Shaw looked to Bessie, then back. "Like an abusive husband?"

"Yes, abusive. Just not my husband . . . legally."

She looked at her hands. "He is also very powerful—and he is hunting me. But . . . but because of my former employer, the situation is more complex than that."

"The paper says you helped save that plane," Bessie said.

"I did. The sky marshal asked me to help him."

"Then you . . . you shot people. Shot the hijackers." Her eyes were round. Worried.

"And why would your employer complicate things?" Shaw demanded.

Laynie sighed. "Bessie, Shaw, I cannot tell you where I've been, what I've done, or for whom I've worked for the past twenty-some years. It would be a breach of my . . . security clearance. Do you follow?"

They stilled, absorbing her meaning. Bessie's mouth pursed. Shaw's face drew down into deep creases.

Then Shaw sighed and nodded at Bessie. "We should tell her, love."

Laynie slid her eyes from Bessie to Shaw and back.

Bessie got up. "I'll make us some tea first." She measured tea into a tea ball, dropped the ball into the teapot on the table, then fetched the steaming kettle from the stove and filled the pot. "We'll let that steep a bit."

She sat down—and reached for Laynie's hand. Laynie had not expected the gesture and jerked away. She was tensed on the edge of her chair, ready to spring.

"Give me your hand, Elaine. I'm not going to bite you, but I need to tell you something."

Laynie reluctantly gave her hand to Bessie. The older woman held Laynie's fingers between her two stout, work-worn palms and sighed, searching for a place to begin.

"Don't know if you believe in the God of the Bible, Elaine Granger, or if you understand that sometimes he sends us dreams. I'm not talkin' 'bout regular dreams, but dreams with specific meaning. Well, I believe God sometimes sends us dreams with a message from him, and last night I had me a doozy."

Laynie frowned. "You had a dream."

"A dream *from God*, mind you. In that dream, I saw you—clear as crystal, it was you—and you were a-runnin' from a dark man, a bad man. I couldn't see much o' his face, except that it had a reddish stain on one side that ran up one cheek, like a birthmark. He was a-chasin' you, that's for certain, and you were trying to get away."

Laynie swallowed. Her heart thundered in her chest. *Zakhar! But surely, Petroff would have spoken to Zakhar by now and called him off. He will have received my package, the proof Christor sent days ago—and he would not have disregarded my threat.*

The contents of the CD proved that she'd stolen Russian Security Council secrets from him. More importantly, the data implicated Petroff in the thefts due to his own negligence. She had included more than enough evidence to convict him of treason and ensure a very bad end to his life.

Laynie clenched her hands. *But only four days have passed since I threatened Petroff. Perhaps he has not spoken to Zakhar yet . . . or maybe Zakhar hasn't checked in lately?*

Bessie interrupted Laynie's reflections. "That man, he kept a-shouting at you, a name, I think, but I couldn't quite get it. Sounded like Lynn or Lynette, but a mite different than that. And you were frightened of him, child. Just like you're a-frightened right now."

Laynie couldn't speak. She could only nod. *If, for whatever reason, Zakhar is still tracking me, I have to take Bessie's warning seriously.*

"Well, all that fear and runnin' woke me up. I sat straight up in bed, it disturbed me that much. After a minute, though, I told myself, 'Bessie, 'twas just a dream.' I laid my head down and went back to sleep—but, soon as I was asleep again, the same dream just started over. You a-runnin' and the man with the stain on his face chasing you."

Bessie paused and poured tea into three mugs, handing one to Laynie. Laynie stirred honey into the tea, wondering where Shaw and Bessie's conversation would take them, worrying that they had changed their mind about selling her their motor home.

I'll have to start over, find another vehicle or catch a bus to another town.

Bessie blew on her tea and took a sip. "Lot's o' things in the Bible happen in threes, Elaine—did you know that?"

Laynie shook her head.

"It's another God thing, a confirmation. Like, when the Apostle Peter had him a dream in the middle of the day. T'was more like a vision than a dream, but he saw it three times—and then a Voice from heaven told him what the vision meant and what to do. Three times he saw the vision, then came the confirmation."

Laynie glanced up. "Did you . . ."

"Yup. I woke up a second time, went back t' sleep, and had the same dream a third time—only this time, a Voice—the powerful but sweet Voice of the Savior, it was! He said to me, 'Bessie, you help her.'"

"Help her?"

"Yep. He said to me, 'Bessie, you help her. The dark man is coming. Get up and go.' Well, I got up all right. Scared spitless, I got up. Got up and walked about in the sitting room, a'prayin' up a storm and wondering what it all meant. And the stack of newspapers on the hearth—we keep 'em to start the fire, see—that stack kept catching my attention. I couldn't get shook of that stack of papers! Finally, I stopped walking and, random-like, just picked up part of the stack. I looked down, and right there, on top, in front of my face, was this photograph."

Bessie patted the newspaper in front of Laynie. "*Your* photograph. Recognized you all right, even though it's not a good likeness and your hair's a different color. And then that Voice spoke one time more, real insistent. 'Bessie, help her. The dark man is coming. Get up and go.'"

Shaw leaned toward Laynie. "This dark man—who is he? Is he the man you're running from?"

"Yes. No. That is, I told you that I'm running from a very powerful man. This dark man? He is the powerful man's . . ."

"His what?" Shaw demanded.

"His hit man, Shaw. His assassin. This man, his name is Zakhar. I believe he's been sent to kill me."

Shaw and Bessie drew back, mouths slack.

"Lord have mercy," Bessie muttered. "And he's a-comin'? *Here?* Why, how would he know to come here, to our house? Did he follow you?"

Those were the questions troubling Laynie. She shook her head. "I wasn't followed. That's why I drove my rental car back to the agency and walked from there to here rather than take a cab—so I wouldn't leave a trail."

And then it struck her.

"Oh, no! This morning I bought a cashier's check to pay for Daisy. The check has your names on it." She opened her purse, pulled out the check, handed it to Shaw. "Here."

Shaw took it and read it over. "This says twelve thousand dollars. We only asked for eleven."

"I wanted to . . . you know . . . because you've been so kind to me. But if this man has somehow found my bank? He may have convinced them to give him your names, and—"

Laynie stopped mid-sentence. *And if he has found my bank, then he knows my American alias!*

"Tell me. Are your names listed in the phone book? With your address?"

Shaw and Bessie exchanged glances. Bessie muttered, "Yes."

Laynie jumped up. "We have to go. Not only me. All of us. If Zakhar comes here after I leave? He will kill you. First, he will torture and interrogate you. When he's done, he will kill you. He will show you no mercy. You have to come away from here. Now!"

Shaw climbed to his feet, nodding. "Bessie insisted that the Voice's order, 'Get up and go,' was for us, too. She's been a-packin' and fussin' all morning."

Laynie closed her hand around the check Shaw held in his hand. "Which of your children lives the farthest away?"

"Our son. Lives in Penticton, B.C."

"Go there. Give me his phone number so I can reach you later."

Bessie jotted names and numbers on a pad and tore off the sheet. "Here. Our mobile number and the numbers of our three kids."

"Do you have their names and addresses anywhere in the house? We can't leave that information for Zakhar to find."

Bessie held up a small, spiral-bound address book. "Only in our diary. We'll take it with us."

Shaw stared Laynie in the face. "Give me your attention for a moment, Elaine. I already changed the oil in Daisy and filled her water tanks. Did that Friday after you said you planned t' buy her. Gassed up both her and our car this morning, too. I put Daisy's title in the glovebox, and Bessie's stocked a bit o' food in the cupboards and refrigerator. You follow us out of town. We'll take the highway over t' Ottawa. Lots of roads from there for you t' choose from."

"I don't know how to thank you."

"Seems t' me, you just gave us a thousand dollars outta the goodness of your heart. More than enough t' pay our kids a long-overdue visit."

"But your dialysis?"

"We'll figure that out. Don't you fret none."

"Thank you. Thank you for everything. I—" Laynie fidgeted. "Just one thing. I know how much you love Daisy, Shaw, but . . . I need to be honest with you about her."

He cocked one brow. "Okay. Say on."

"I'll drive Daisy as long as she can hide me from Zakhar. However, you know I can't take her across the border. Too much time, cost, and red tape to do that. Before I cross over into the States, I'll need to . . . let Daisy go. Sell her or leave her."

Shaw sighed and looked upset, but Bessie put her hand on his and reminded him, "Shaw, Daisy belongs to Elaine now, not us."

She turned her attention to Laynie. "You do what you must to be safe, Elaine. We've been praying this morning that the Lord will lead you and keep you safe, and we will *keep on* praying for you. Now, I'm not saying God is a giant vending machine, that you simply ask him for what you want, and he gives it to you. God isn't a machine, and his blessings belong to those who belong to him.

"So, we're praying, too, that you will come to a point of repentance in your life. No one can be saved without repentance. Repentance is where we—every one of us—acknowledge and confess our sinful, needy state before God and ask for forgiveness through the blood of Jesus. A place where we surrender fully to the Lordship of Christ, where he becomes our king, and we become his children—where we become the family of God. But while he works in your heart to bring you to that place? We're asking him to keep you safe."

Bessie commanded Laynie's attention a last time. "Is anything too hard for God, Elaine?"

"I-I don't know." She was preoccupied with Bessie's words about repentance.

"Then let me help you out. No, *nothing* is too hard for the God of the Bible. I want you to go on your way carryin' his word in your heart, in your thoughts, and on your lips. *With men it is impossible, but not with God. For with God all things are possible.* That's Mark 10:27, and those are Jesus' very words. When the fear starts a-creepin' in, you keep those words close, do you hear me? *With God all things are possible*—even when they look impossible."

She held out her arms. "Now, then, give this old woman a hug, Elaine. God willing, we'll see you on your way once we reach Ottawa."

She enfolded Laynie in her soft, plump arms, and Laynie bent down to lay her cheek on Bessie's shoulder, a shoulder much lower than Laynie's chin. Laynie melted into Bessie's warm embrace . . . and memories flooded her heart.

Oh, Mama, will I ever see you or lay my cheek on your head again?

"Come on now," Shaw insisted. "We got to go."

Five minutes later, the Bradshaws' house was vacant and locked, their driveway empty.

ZAKHAR ARRIVED AT the bank nearest the Westmount Hotel and paced while he waited for its doors to open. As soon as the key turned in the door, he pushed his way in and strode to the nearest teller. He flipped open Paul Moreau's credentials and said in French, "I need to see the manager on an urgent issue of national security."

Within moments, the manager's footsteps clicked across the tile floor toward him. "I am the bank's manager, *monsieur*," the woman said.

"And I am Lieutenant Paul Moreau, Canada Customs and Revenue Agency, looking for this woman." He held up one photograph of Linnéa Olander. "I must ask each of your tellers if they recognize her."

"*Oui. Mais bien sûr.* But of course. Come with me, sir."

The manager led Zakhar to a door secured by a keypad. She keyed in the code and took him through the door, then behind the counter where the tellers waited on the bank's customers.

One by one, moving down the line of five working tellers, Zakhar showed the photograph to them. Every answer was the same. "Sorry, sir. I do not remember waiting on this woman."

He turned on his heel and demanded of the manager, "You must know your competitors. Which banks are closest to both this branch and the Westmount Hotel?"

"There is a branch of HSBC Canada not far from here."

Zakhar ran from the building, jumped in Moreau's car, and followed the directions the woman had given him. Minutes later, he reached the bank's entrance.

He presented himself to the manager. "I am Lieutenant Paul Moreau, Canada Customs and Revenue Agency, looking for this woman." He lifted the photograph of Linnéa Olander. "I must ask your tellers if they recognize her."

Like the manager of the previous bank, the man escorted Zakhar behind the teller gates and instructed his employees to look at the photograph. The third teller nodded.

"Oh, yes. I remember her. One moment." She keyed in "accounts by date opened" and scrolled through the list. "Here she is. Elaine Granger."

"Elaine Granger? What identification did she provide to open the account?"

The teller continued to look. "American passport and driver's license. She has an account with HSBC in Singapore and transferred forty thousand dollars from her Singapore account to open this account."

"Residence?"

"An American address in Washington, D.C."

"Print it out—all of it. Everything having to do with her."

The teller slanted her eyes at her manager, who murmured, "Lieutenant, this must require a warrant, *non*?"

Zakhar rounded on the man. "You are aware of the terrorist attacks, not even a week ago? This woman's flight was detoured from New York to New Brunswick after which she disappeared. We have reason to believe she is part of yet another terrorist plot. This is a matter of national security, and you *will* print the information for me as I request."

The manager blanched. "*Oui, monsieur*. Right away. The machine is in back. My teller will fetch the printout for you, sir."

The teller returned with several sheets of paper. "Here you are, sir."

Zakhar tore through the printout, looking for something—anything—to lead him onward. He saw that the woman had made a cash withdrawal only an hour earlier, and he ground his teeth.

While I was waiting on the wrong bank to open, she was right here doing the same!

His finger ran down the page and stopped. "What is this?" he demanded.

The teller leaned over. "It is the purchase of a cashier's check, sir."

"A cashier's check? For what?"

The teller shrugged. "I cannot say, sir."

"Well, do you retain the payee's name and address?"

212

"Only the name, sir. See? It is here." She pointed to the printout.

His eyes followed her finger to the words "George and Elizabeth Bradshaw".

"The address! I must have the address for these people!" Zakhar roared.

The teller quailed before him. "But, sir, we do not have that information."

"Lieutenant Moreau, I may be able to help you. Please come with me." The manager was eager to remove the volatile official from his lobby.

Zakhar followed the manager to his office. The man sat behind his desk and motioned for Zakhar to sit. He withdrew a weighty telephone book from a drawer. He opened the phone book on his desk and began to scan through the listings.

"Braden, Bradford, Bradley, Bradmore, Bradshaw! Bradshaw, Andrew. Bradshaw, Denton. Bradshaw—here it is. Bradshaw, George W. Come see." He placed the book where Zakhar could read the line where his finger rested.

Without a word of thanks, Zakhar ripped the page from the book and ran from the room.

———— ⚬⚭⚬ ————

CHAPTER 21

ZAKHAR STOPPED AT a gas station to fill the tank of Paul Moreau's official car and pick up a new map of Montreal, one he hadn't marked up doing his grid search. The wind gusted uncomfortably while he gassed the car, and he pulled Moreau's jacket closed against the chill.

While he was paying, he unfolded the map and started looking for the Bradshaws' address. One side had the full map. The other side had a list of street names and larger maps of key points in and around the city. In a hurry and unused to how the map unfolded and refolded, he grew frustrated. The map became hopelessly folded the wrong way.

"You," he said to the girl who'd taken his money. "Do you know Montreal?"

She shrugged and sucked down a slug of soda. "Well enough, I suppose."

"Show me where Maplewood Street is."

The girl didn't move except to suck on the straw until it guttered at the bottom of her cup. When she finished, she said, "'Please' and 'thank you' go a long way, mister."

Zakhar wanted to punch the brazen clerk in her disrespectful mouth. He restrained himself. "Show me where Maplewood Street is, *please*."

"Well, what if I show you *how* to find it on the map, sir." She expertly pulled open the map, folded it correctly until it was halfway open, and laid it on the counter. She took a pencil and made a dot on the map. "This is where we are, right here."

She put her finger on the dot and with her other finger traced a straight line from the dot to the edge of the map and scribed a tick mark. Then, putting her finger again on the dot, she traced a straight line up to the top of the map and made a small tick with the pencil on the edge where her finger stopped.

"See these letters down the side and numbers across the top? They're coordinates. They tell you in what general vicinity we're located on the map. C-15, see?"

Zakhar huffed. "I understand coordinates."

"Okay, then you should have no troubles. What street you lookin' for?"

"Maplewood."

She turned the map over and moved the pencil down the long list of street names until she found Maplewood.

"See the coordinates printed next to Maplewood? G-7?" She put her finger on them.

"Yes, I see," Zakhar growled.

She turned the map over again, opened it up a bit, and refolded it to expose the section she needed. She traced the letter and number and put her pencil point where they intersected. Lightly, she sketched a square that encompassed the area where Maplewood Street was to be found.

"Within these marks, sir."

Zakhar squinted as his eyes searched the square. Then he saw it in tiny print. Maplewood. "Tell me the best way to get there."

The girl's helpful disposition had reached its limits. She folded her arms across her chest. "My, if you aren't the bossy one."

Zakhar withdrew his wallet and threw a ten-dollar bill on the counter. "I will take a newspaper, also."

The girl shrugged. "Happy to be of service, sir."

ZAKHAR STARTED THE car but, before he left the parking lot, he opened the newspaper he'd bought, disgusted that he hadn't specified a paper written in French. On the front page, below the fold, he found what he was looking for.

CCRA OFFICIAL AND WIFE
FOUND DEAD

He read slowly, tussling over a few unfamiliar English words. The article ended with "Royal Canadian Mounted Police have taken the lead on the investigation and have issued a nationwide bulletin for Lieutenant Moreau's CCRA car. The RCMP, in conjunction with provincial police across Canada, are looking for a man in possession of Lieutenant Moreau's credentials, reported to be passing himself off as the deceased CCRA officer. Call the RCMP tip line if you have information to help in the investigation."

I must rid myself of this car and get another as soon as possible.

Zakhar tossed the newspaper onto the car's passenger-side floor, then he pulled out of the gas station lot, following the directions the soda-slurping clerk had written out for him.

Within half an hour, Zakhar was reading house numbers as he rolled slowly down Maplewood Street. *There.* He'd found the numbers that matched the address in the phone book!

He scanned up and down the street, and saw no pedestrians, no one outdoors on the blustery fall day. The neighborhood was showing its age, the houses and yards not what they once were. Zakhar surmised that the residents, too, were older and would not present him with many difficulties.

He observed that the Bradshaws' house had a driveway but no garage. Zakhar assumed that what had once been the garage had been converted to living space some years back. No vehicles sat in the drive.

He parked, got out, walked up the porch steps, and rested his hand on the gun in his overcoat pocket before he rang the doorbell. The chime echoed through the house, but no rustle of movement or patter of approaching steps answered. Whoever the Bradshaws were, they were not at home.

What would Olander have bought from them for twelve thousand dollars? Surely it was a car? How can I find out which car?

A neighbor, standing on her porch in an open doorway across the street, called to him. "Hellooo! Air ye looking for Shaw an' Bessie?"

Zakhar unclenched his teeth and forced his mouth into a semblance of a smile. He crossed the street and strode up the neighbor's walk.

"Yes, I am. Will they be home soon?"

"Oh, don't know 'bout that. They put suitcases in their car 'fore they left, so I 'spect they'll be gone at least overnight."

Zakhar tipped his head, thinking. "Was there anyone with them when they left?"

"No, just the two of them in the car."

"How long ago did they leave?"

"Hmm. Half an hour?"

"I see." Zakhar again ground his teeth.

"But the woman who bought Daisy may have followed them."

Zakhar shook his head. "I beg your pardon. Could you repeat that?"

"I think the woman who bought Daisy followed them."

"What is a Daisy, please?"

She slapped her thigh and laughed. Zakhar realized her other arm bore a plaster cast. "Why, Daisy's a little motor home, 'course. Shaw and Bessie named her Daisy s' long ago, I forget some people don't know."

A motor home. Zakhar relaxed. His smile was less forced. "The Bradshaws owned a motor home named Daisy and a woman bought it from them?"

"I 'sume she did. Shaw took the fer sale sign out of the back winder yesterday."

"And the woman you saw, she drove it away? Thirty minutes ago?"

"That's right. Shaw and Bessie drove away in their car, and the lady drove after them in Daisy."

Zakhar brought out a photograph and stepped up on the neighbor's porch, holding the photo toward her. "Is this the woman who bought their motor home?"

She stared down her nose to study the picture. "I should think so, 'though she were a bit blonder."

Zakhar forced another smile and glanced to the side. "The Bradshaws didn't have a garage, but I see that you do."

"My, yes. I don't drive much, but I wouldn't like leaving my car out in the elements like they did with theirs."

He knew she wouldn't be expecting the arm that shot toward her, palm up. His hand struck her chest with the full force of his weight behind it. She flew across the tiled entryway and crashed onto the hard floor. She lay there, stunned by the impact. He had already stepped through the open door and pushed it behind him.

He crossed the entryway to her before she could catch her breath. He watched her face as he threaded the can-like extension onto the gun's barrel with slow, deliberate motion.

"No, please!" she protested. She tried to get up, but she was weak, still stupefied. As he pointed the gun at her, she threw up her arms.

"Please—"

ZAKHAR BACKED THE woman's car—a ten-year-old sedan in pristine condition—out of the garage and parked it along the curb. He drove Lieutenant Moreau's car into the garage, discarded Moreau's credentials on the front seat, gathered his belongings, and transferred them to the front seat of the woman's sedan.

Next, he strode across to the Bradshaws' house, vaulting over the short gate to the backyard. The rear door splintered under his first kick, and Zakhar found himself in a homey but worn kitchen. He moved quickly, going from room to room, until he found a bedroom the Bradshaws had obviously used as an office.

The desk he found was clean and organized, as tidy as a pin. Zakhar sat down at it and tugged open drawers, searching the hanging file folders for paperwork that would tell him more about the motor home the Bradshaws had sold to Linnéa Olander.

No. Not Linnéa Olander. Elaine Granger.

He stopped at a hanging folder when he saw a tab reading DAISY. He yanked it from the drawer.

Nothing.

Angered, he threw the folder across the room, pushed back the chair, and stood up, accidentally catching his toe on a metal waste can. The can crashed against the wall and fell over, dumping its contents.

Zakhar stared at the paper waste spilled on the old, putrid-green shag carpet. He got on his knees and pawed through the papers, smoothing crumpled sheets, examining them. He saw a bit of folded cardstock and picked it up. He pressed the card open on the desk's blotter. It was a vehicle registration. He read from top to bottom:

Make: WINNEBAGO

Model: ITASCA SUNDANCER

Year: 1984

License: Québec KEF 484

He exhaled. He had the vehicle information he desperately needed. Still, tracking Olander's vehicle would be difficult.

He returned to the woman's car. As he drove away, he failed to notice that the buffeting wind had caught the unlatched front door of the woman's house and pushed it inward. He was too fixated on his pursuit of Linnéa Olander.

Soon. I will have her soon.

LAYNIE FOLLOWED SHAW and Bessie's little car as best she could as they left Montreal and merged onto ON-417 east. She struggled with Daisy's bulk and length on the busy highway traffic—and with the wind gusting hard, occasionally pushing or swaying Daisy. Laynie's hands and arms hurt from gripping the steering wheel.

Although Daisy was more vehicle than she'd ever driven, the rental car and the motor home were also the *only* vehicles she'd driven in years.

My driving skills are seriously rusty, she admitted as Shaw zipped ahead and she fell farther behind. *I must drive with caution.*

Yes, she had a signed bill of sale in her purse and the title in the glovebox to prove she had paid for Daisy, but she had not yet registered the motor home. Registration required that she present herself and the motor home at the appropriate government office within six days, show her driver's license, the resigned title, proof of purchase and insurance, and pay for new plates—which is exactly why she didn't intend to register Daisy.

Why take the chance that some registration official might recognize her from the newspaper photograph of Marta Forestier? Instead, she would drive conservatively to avoid being pulled over and sell or abandon Daisy before she crossed the border.

Up ahead, she spotted Shaw and Bessie's car pulled off the highway onto the shoulder, waiting for her. As soon as they caught sight or her, plodding along, they merged back into traffic and slowed their speed so Laynie could keep up.

Ottawa lay on the Ontario side of the Ottawa River. Gatineau was on the other side in Québec. Shaw followed ON-417 across the river, where the highway joined Autoroute 50 E and then QC-148.

On the far western outskirts of Gatineau, Shaw turned down a road and pulled alongside a shady municipal park. Laynie pulled in behind him. Shaw and Bessie joined her in the motor home.

The drive from Montreal had taken them two-and-a-half hours at Laynie's speed.

"Shall we have a spot of lunch?" Bessie suggested.

While Bessie fixed them tea and sandwiches, Shaw pulled a road atlas of Canada from Daisy's glove box and sat down at the table with Laynie.

"We're here," he pointed. "Bessie and I will rejoin 417 and stay on it until we reach North Bay. Then we'll turn north and catch ON-11, the Trans-Canada Highway, and ride it pretty much all the way to our son's place in British Columbia. But that's us—we don't know where you plan to go next."

He pulled his mobile phone from his pocket. "You have this number. We'd like it if you kept in touch while we're on the road."

Laynie had been thinking while she drove. "I suppose I should get a mobile phone, too. Maybe I need to visit one of those big box stores before I leave these cities, a store where I can buy a phone and a few odds and ends."

Like a top-of-the-line laptop, a broadband modem, and a coaxial cable.

"Double back into Ottawa and you should find what you're looking for. And there's a nice RV campground, Wind-in-the-Trees, just ahead if you decide to spend the night before traveling on."

Bessie set the sandwiches, hot tea, and a plate of grapes on the table. She scooted into one of the bench seats and Shaw moved to sit next to her. They joined hands and reached for Laynie's fingers, then Shaw bowed his head.

"Our heavenly Father, we come before you in the mighty name of Jesus, the Savior of the world. Thank you for this food and for protecting Elaine— us, too, Lord. We trust you. Your word and your promises are true, Lord, so we rest in the assurance that you will never leave us nor forsake us. Amen."

Laynie blinked back tears, hearing Kari's declaration twined within Shaw's blessing. *"All of God's promises are true, Laynie, because he is true . . ."*

They ate and then cleaned up—Bessie showing Laynie around the miniscule kitchen—when Shaw's mobile phone warbled.

He picked up the call. "Hello? Hiya, Dennis. No, we're out of town. We'll be gone—what?"

Shaw's words stuck in his throat. "Oh, no . . ."

Bessie and Laynie read the concern on his face as he listened to his friend talk. Eventually, he said, "Thank you for calling us, Dennis. Could you . . . could you do something for me? Could you check our house? Make sure no one's broken in? Yes. Please call me back, either way. Thanks."

He hung up and stared at Bessie. "That was Dennis, Our next-door neighbor."

For Laynie's sake he whispered, "He went to check on Mrs. Rosenthal—she lives across the street. About a month back, she fell and broke her arm pretty bad. Well, Dennis thought it odd that her front door was a-hangin' open as chilly as the wind is today, so he went to check on her. Found her on the floor. He thought she'd fallen again, but . . . she'd been shot."

Bessie gasped, "Shot? But who . . . Shaw, will she be all right?"

"Dennis doesn't know. He called an ambulance and they took her away. The police came, too, and asked him questions. Then the police did a search of Mrs. Rosenthal's house and found a car in the garage that didn't belong to her—it was a missing CCRA car, one stolen from New Brunswick."

"What's CCRA?" Laynie asked, her attention caught by the words "New Brunswick."

"Canada Customs and Revenue Agency."

The skin on Laynie's neck and arms began to crawl.

At the same time, Bessie frowned. "Just one cotton-pickin' second."

She climbed down from the motor home, went to the car, and returned right away, nodding, her chins wagging up and down with her head. "I thought I'd remembered reading something about a stolen CCRA car. Look here."

She read aloud, "Headline says 'CCRA official and wife found dead.' Article says, 'An officer of the CCRA, stationed in Moncton, NB, was the victim of a home invasion Friday evening. Lieutenant Paul Moreau and his wife, Michelle, were at home, watching television, when a person or persons unknown broke in through the back door. The Moreaus were robbed at gunpoint and found deceased by friends late Saturday after they failed to appear at a dinner party. Authorities report that, in addition to cash missing from Lieutenant Moreau's wallet and Mrs. Moreau's purse, Lieutenant Moreau's official CCRA vehicle and his CCRA credentials were gone, presumed to have been taken by the attackers.'"

Bessie kept reading. "'Royal Canadian Mounted Police have taken lead on the investigation and have issued a nationwide bulletin for Lieutenant Moreau's CCRA car. The RCMP, in conjunction with provincial police across Canada, are looking for a man in possession of Lieutenant Moreau's credentials, reported to be passing himself off as the deceased CCRA officer. Call the RCMP tip line if you have information to help in the investigation.'"

"It's him. It's Zakhar," Laynie whispered, reliving the moments after Flight 6177 landed in Moncton, when the provincial police entered the aircraft, and an official had introduced himself.

"I am Lieutenant Paul Moreau, Canada Customs and Revenue Agency. You are Marshal Tobin? Marshal Forestier?"

Shaw bent toward Laynie. "What are you saying?"

Laynie pointed at the paper. "This man, the attacker. It's Zakhar."

Shaw stilled for a moment—but only a moment. He picked up his mobile phone and dialed.

"Dennis? Shaw here. Did you—you did. And . . . Oh. I see. But nothing taken?"

He listened while Dennis filled him in. "We appreciate your boarding up the door, Dennis. You're a good friend and a good neighbor."

He listened further and brightened. "Really? That's great news. Thank you for telling me. I will call you back later."

Bessie asked, "What is it, Shaw?"

"Dennis found our back door bashed in. Nothing taken, apparently, although the trash in the office was dumped out on the carpet. Dennis took the police over to show them and said he'd board up the door for us."

"Why the trash?" Laynie demanded.

"Hmm?"

"It has to be Zakhar, Shaw. He found my bank, as I suspected, and that's how he found your house—but he's looking for *me*. What was in the trash that could have interested him?"

"Nothing. Just receipts and scrap paper. Nothing else I can think—oh, dear." He looked to Laynie. "I pulled our registration from Daisy's glove box. Tossed it away."

"Does it list Daisy's make and model?"

"And plate number, too."

Laynie's mind had gone into spy mode, calling upon her survival and evasion training.

Daisy needs different plates, like right now. And I need help!

But she had no one. No one she could call upon.

"In other news," Shaw continued, "Dennis talked to Mrs. Rosenthal's daughter, Avery. She says the doctors think Mrs. Rosenthal will make it— although it's about the strangest thing I've ever heard."

"What's strange?" Bessie asked.

"Remember how she broke her arm last month? She fractured both bones in her forearm 'bout halfway 'tween her wrist and elbow? The doctor had to surgically implant two plates and a fistful of screws in her forearm to hold the broken pieces together." Shaw slid his eyes over to Laynie.

Laynie, caught thinking about her own worries instead of paying attention, tried to demonstrate a little empathy. "Ouch."

"Yeah, *ouch*. Well, when Zakhar shot Mrs. Rosenthal, he got her square in the chest. But, turns out, the doctors deduced that Mrs. Rosenthal threw up her arm, like in an automatic defense reflex. The bullet struck her cast, took out a chunk of it, went into her arm and hit one of the plates, then ricocheted off the plate, and whacked her a good one in the chest—just east of her heart."

"Oh, my Lord!" Bessie breathed.

"Dennis says Avery's calling it a miracle. Because, although her mom's chest is gonna be black and blue and she has to have another surgery on her arm, Mrs. Rosenthal's alive and kicking."

He looked at Laynie again. "She told the police that the man who shot her had a red stain on his face."

Laynie covered her eyes. "I'm sorry, Shaw. I'm so sorry. I brought all this on you and your friends!"

"You're not hearing me, Elaine. We've been praying, putting our trust in God's word, and he has protected us. How? We left minutes ahead of Zakhar because of the dream the Lord gave Bessie. He got us out of there in the nick of time! And, although Zakhar shot Mrs. Rosenthal in the chest—an old woman who should be dead—but she ain't. God has his hands on you and everyone around you, Elaine."

Laynie blinked back tears. Was Shaw right? Was it God? Because from the moment she'd run from Madame Krupina's Spa until now, she'd seen and experienced countless "peculiar things"—things she'd racked up as coincidence, karma, accidents, or good fortune.

But she'd witnessed far too many "coincidences" in her favor for them to be merely luck.

Abruptly, Laynie heard someone else's voice in her head, someone with a hand the size of a frying pan, praying over her.

"*Lord Jesus, I bring Marta before you, asking that you see her safely away from here without discovery. Please help her navigate or overcome every obstacle that presents itself and help her make it safely to wherever she is headed—without the public exposure she fears.*"

Navigate or overcome. That's what the past week had been—one obstacle after another, each one safely navigated or overcome.

"It *is* God," Laynie's whisper was filled with awe.

And on the heels of Tobin's prayer, she remembered him leaning toward her, whispering, "*I'm not kidding, Marta. I owe you. You helped save all these people today—an' this here country boy's butt, inta the bargain. If you ever need me, you call, ya'll hear me?*"

"I can call Tobin," she said to herself. "He promised to help me."

"Who's Tobin?" Bessie demanded.

Laynie smiled. "He's like you, Bessie. A Jesus person. And like Jesus put you in my life? I think he put Tobin there, too."

———————⟡———————

CHAPTER 22

LP

LAYNIE SAID GOODBYE to Shaw and Bessie for a second time. Shaw, with many words of caution and fatherly advice called over his shoulder, gently steered a reluctant Bessie toward their car. When they pulled away from the curb, Laynie felt alone. Abandoned.

But I've been alone for years and have never felt like this. I guess I grew unused to having people care about me. Shaw and Bessie have made me realize how isolated I actually have been.

She made sure Daisy's doors were locked and checked that she hadn't left anything loose to fall or roll around while she was driving—as Shaw had cautioned her—before turning the ignition key. She followed the road back to the highway and got on the entrance ramp to return to the city.

She pulled up to the pumps at the first gas station she saw and topped off her gas tanks. When she went inside the attached mini-mart to pay, she asked the clerk, "Say, do you know of any computer or electronics stores nearby?"

"Take 148 back into town, follow Allumettiéres across the Alexandra Bridge, then get on 93. Few blocks more and you'll spot Rideau Centre. Look for Dave's Blue Label Buys. They have everything—plasma TVs, stereo systems, computers."

"Sounds perfect. Thanks."

She steeled herself to herd Daisy through heavy traffic while trying to follow the clerk's directions. Changing lanes was hard. She was unused to Daisy's length or how to use the mirrors on both sides of the cab. "This is worse than navigating one of Petroff's state dinners where dangerous pitfalls abound."

She found Rideau Centre, a huge, sprawling mall, then spotted Dave's Blue Label Buys. It took up an entire corner lot across from the mall. She parked Daisy, grabbed her purse, made sure the HK was safely tucked into its depths, locked up, and made for the doors.

Laynie had shopped the world for fashion and had accompanied Petroff to many expos, but she had not set foot in a free-world electronics store in over a decade. The gleaming array of products and the expanse of selection stole her breath away.

Oh, my.

"Good afternoon, ma'am." A store greeter, sporting a bright blue polo shirt and a two-way radio on his hip, nodded at her. "May I direct you to anything specific?"

"Uh, computers, please."

"Take that aisle there. Everything down that aisle to your right is in our computer department."

"Thank you."

Laynie found the selection of laptops. A computer guru appeared at her shoulder. "What are you looking for in a computer, ma'am?"

"A reliable laptop with top-of-the-line processors, plenty of disk space and RAM, upgraded graphics card."

"I see." He pointed out a Dell laptop. "Our computer tech department can upgrade this one. More memory, higher-performing graphics card."

"Can you do it today? While I'm waiting?"

He shook his head. "Probably not. This machine, however, has plenty of disk space. You can always upgrade later."

Laynie considered her options. She needed to check in with Christor, and it would be easier and safer to do so with her own machine.

"I'll take it as is. I'll need a case for it, a broadband modem, and a coaxial cable—a long one. And a good extension cord. Do you have those?"

"Yes—extension cords are over in electronics, but I can grab you one. What length?"

"Twelve feet."

"Great. I'll start putting your order together for you. Anything else?"

She looked around, still awed by the variety and sheer volume of products. "Do you have mobile phones?"

"Sure. See that BLB employee standing just there? She can help you with a phone while I'm getting your laptop order ready."

Laynie made a beeline for the girl he'd singled out. She saw Laynie coming and smiled.

"I saw Sean pointing at me. Need a new mobile phone?"

"Yes, please. Something that will work here and in the States, too."

"Do you have a brand preference?"

"No, but I need text capability."

"May I show you this Nokia 3310? Very reliable. Good reviews. And we can set you up on AT&T Wireless with International coverage for all North America."

Laynie played with the Nokia phone, letting the girl go through her sales pitch, only homing in when she got to the phone's features. All the while, the time of day was running in the background, worrying her.

I still need to swap plates. I won't get far out of town before it's dark if I don't hurry things along.

"I'll take this one and a charger that works off a vehicle cigarette lighter—cash. Can you set me up pretty quickly? I'm in a bit of a rush to reach my cousin's before dark."

"It will take about twenty minutes, but I'll need a credit card for the phone's service plan—is that okay?"

Laynie thought, *The credit card info will go into AT&T's payment system, not this store's system. Besides, I'll be gone before anyone tracks me here. It should be okay.*

"Okay."

Laynie sat down and the girl started filling out paperwork. Laynie provided her driver's license and credit card when asked, while keeping one eye on Sean over in the computer department. At one point, he looked over and gave her a thumbs up. She nodded at him and held up an "okay" sign.

The phone clerk announced, "All right, then! We're done. Here's the total, including setup fees and your first month's service charge."

Laynie paid, put her new phone in her purse, and accepted the bag with the rest of the items in it. She thanked the girl and hurried back to the computer department. After she paid, Sean handed her two more bags containing her computer purchases.

"You're all set. I recommend that you charge your battery to full before working off of it."

"I will. Thanks for all your help, Sean."

Laynie piled her purchases onto the floor in front of Daisy's passenger seat and started toward the parking lot exit. Across the street in Rideau Centre, a veritable sea of vehicles stretched before her—and a myriad of license plates.

"Perfect."

Laynie navigated Daisy across the street and into the mall's parking lot. She drove around, scouting out another RV with Canadian plates. She found an area of parking especially designated for RVs and slid Daisy in between two larger motor homes. She turned off the engine, then dragged out the little tool chest Shaw kept behind the driver's seat. Exactly seven minutes later, she drove away from the mall.

LAYNIE FOUND HER WAY back to the road leading to the municipal park where she, Shaw, and Bessie had eaten sandwiches for lunch. What had Shaw told her?

"There's a nice RV campground just ahead, Wind-in-the-Trees, if you decide to spend the night before traveling on."

If the growl from Laynie's stomach was any indication, it was nearing dinner time. She drove on down the highway, looking for signs to Wind-in-the-Trees Campground. She found one pointing to the turnoff ahead. She exited the highway, drove along a side road, and turned down a dirt road bordered by shade trees.

Another mile in, she arrived at the RV campground. A sign instructed her to register at the general store. Laynie parked and walked into a quaint general store that was a log cabin with wooden floors. A man as old as the cabin greeted her. "Evening, ma'am. Checking in?"

"Yes, I am."

"Electric or nonelectric?"

"Electric, please."

"How many nights?"

"Just tonight."

She gave him all the info he asked for and paid the fee using cash. "Do you by any chance, have broadband service?"

"Yup. In the café over there." He pointed toward an open doorway leading into the next room. "Seems like everybody has to check their email these days. Not me. Don't have any of that stuff."

He handed Laynie two tags. "Hang this one from your rearview mirror and clip this one on the post marked with your slot's number. You're in Loop 2, Slot 17. Drive on through the gate, take a right, and follow the signs."

"Thanks. I will."

Laynie found her camp spot and, after three amateur, abortive attempts, backed Daisy into Slot 17. She chocked the wheels but didn't bother to level the camper. Instead, she lifted the lid on the electrical box, dragged out the power cable, and connected it to Daisy. After locking her doors, she pulled out the laptop and her new phone and plugged them in to charge their batteries. She shoved the debris she wouldn't be keeping into a shopping bag and walked it to a dumpster.

Finally heeding the needs of her stomach, she opened a can of soup and heated it. When she sat down to eat, she realized how exhausted she was.

Tomorrow, she told herself. *Tomorrow while I'm fresh, I'll check Christor's and my private chat room and read Kari's latest letter. Afterward, I'll put as much distance between myself and Zakhar as I can.*

ZAKHAR WAS, AT PRESENT, driving his third stolen vehicle. He had dumped the old lady's car at sundown. Soon after, dusk had given way to darkness, providing him with the cover he required.

He was hunting, and his prey had specific, unmistakable markings.

Zakhar had admired the gold lettering on the sleek cars and the crown above O.P.P. on the white doors when he'd seen two such cars parked side by side at a restaurant. He hadn't approached. He simply needed to note the markings. Indeed, he hoped to admire the gold lettering up close very soon.

There. Ahead of him. The distinctive black-and-white profile of an Ontario Provincial Police car came into view.

He had the plate number belonging to Olander's RV. Tracking its location was the present problem—but a provincial constable could take a stolen vehicle report, couldn't he? He could radio in the plate number and issue a bulletin for the stolen motor home, couldn't he?

Zakhar switched lanes, falling back a few lengths so the constable wouldn't notice he was being followed. Some forty minutes later, the constable exited the highway. Zakhar followed him, still keeping well back.

Zakhar was mildly surprised at the degree of emotional freedom he was feeling. He even found that he was unconcerned for his own safety or future. If he satisfied his obsession for capturing Linnéa Olander and was caught by Canadian law enforcement afterward? Well, he was willing to pay that price. Besides, from what he'd heard of Canadian prisons, a stint inside would feel like a resort compared to a Russian gulag—or an FSB firing squad.

When the policeman pulled into a gas station lot and parked around the side to use the restroom, Zakhar made his move. The lot was dimly lit, the rear completely dark. As the man entered the restroom, Zakhar circled around back from the opposite direction and parked in the shadows behind the building.

When he left his car, he pulled on a black ski mask to hide his distinctive birthmark. The constable, perhaps in his early thirties, was leaving the restroom when Zakhar, in three steps, sprinted from around the corner, coming up behind him.

"Do not move, Constable."

Startled, the man whirled, his hand automatically going to the paddle holster of his Sig Sauer P229. But Zakhar already had his weapon out. He pushed its barrel into the officer's midsection for effect.

"Take your hand away from your gun," Zakhar whispered.

The officer froze, then slowly complied.

Zakhar directed the officer to his car and positioned himself behind the constable, beside the rear door.

"Open your door and remain standing. With two fingers, pull your gun and hand it to me."

Zakhar slid the officer's gun into his pocket. "Now, give me the keys to your car and your handcuffs. That's right."

He added the keys to his pocket.

"Pull your cuffs and fasten one cuff to your wrist. Thread the loose end through the steering wheel and fasten it to your other wrist. Good. Now, slide in."

With the PC cuffed to his own steering wheel, Zakhar went around the car and got into the passenger seat.

Zakhar could see how angry the young constable was. He was seething.

"What do you want?" the constable growled.

"I want you to file a stolen vehicle report." Zakhar handed the officer the folded registration. "Radio in and report this vehicle as stolen."

The young man frowned. "Why?"

"Not your concern. Do as I say, and nothing worse will befall you."

"I cannot reach the controls or mic."

Petroff raised his gun and placed it against the man's temple. "Tell me what you need—but I warn you. If you say or do anything that alerts your dispatcher, I will shoot you where you sit. Do you understand me?"

The man swallowed and the bluster drained from him. "I understand."

Zakhar put the mic in the officer's other hand. "Now, call it in."

The constable opened the registration and cleared his throat. "Dispatch, reporting 392, theft of a motor home, 1984 Winnebago, license *Québec Kilo Echo Foxtrot Four Eight Four*."

"Roger. What is your 10-20?"

"I am 3 Kilo, 3K202." Ottawa Traffic, Highway 417, Core, Night Shift."

"Be advised, this plate has been located. Civilian has reported a stolen rear plate, *Ontario Alpha Mike Lima Lima Five Zero Eight*, replaced with *Québec Kilo Echo Foxtrot Four Eight Four* while parked at Rideau Centre."

"Roger, dispatch. Out."

Zakhar grabbed the mic from the PC, who swiveled his wary gaze to his captor.

"What did it mean?" Zakhar demanded.

"It means whoever stole *this* motor home," the PC raised the registration in his left hand, "swapped their plate with the rear plate off another RV. Québec Province requires only a rear plate. Ontario requires both front and rear. That rear plate is now reported stolen."

You are clever, Olander, Zakhar thought. *It is as I would have done.*

He handed the handcuff key to the officer. "Unlock your left wrist. Fasten the cuff to the wheel." He needed the officer to drive.

"Show me this Rideau Centre where the plate was stolen—and remember that I warned you not to alert anyone. I will shoot you, if needed."

He took the handcuff key back and handed the ignition key to the constable. They left the gas station. Twenty minutes later, they arrived at the mall, and the constable slid his car into a parking slot.

Zakhar examined the mall, marveling at the signs proclaiming the number and variety of stores within its walls. *What I could buy with the money I have!*

"Drive around Rideau Centre. I wish to see what this place offers."

The officer made a slow circuit of the mall while Zakhar looked for some clue as to why Linnéa Olander had come there.

Perhaps it was only because of the many vehicles, he realized. *Perhaps she was not shopping for anything.*

Then he caught sight of the bright blue box across the street and the sign within the box. Dave's Blue Label Buys. Beneath the box he read, "Electronics, Computers, Home Entertainment." He shivered, recalling the young man at the Westmount Hotel—what was his name? Ah, yes. Justin Worley. What had he said?

"*We were in the business center, using the computers. She had a* Final Fantasy *disc.*"

"*This is a video game, no?*"

"*Yeah. I play the same game, so I asked her if she'd like to play it with me. I travel a lot and bring my game console with me.*"

Linnéa Olander, calling herself Beverly, had ingratiated herself into Justin's favor. She had made an assignation with him, brought wine and led him on, and then drugged him. Why? It had not been clear to Zakhar. Was it truly because Justin had a PlayStation game console?

Home Entertainment? Does that mean this store sells video game systems?

He read the clock on the officer's dash. nearly eight o'clock. How late would the store remain open tonight?

Without giving insight to the flush of excitement running through him, Zakhar said, "Take us back to the gas station and I will let you go."

Another twenty minutes, and they pulled into the station's parking lot. The station was closed, the lot mostly dark, and the constable was decidedly nervous.

"Drive around to the side where the restrooms are, where you parked before."

"And then what? You'll kill me?"

Instead of answering he said, "I'm getting out and going around to your side of the car. Do not test me."

Zakhar opened the officer's door. "Give me the keys to your car." He knew the officer would be looking for an opportunity to surprise him, possibly overpower him, so he backed away.

"Toss them to me."

When Zakhar had the keys in his hand, he said, "Give me your badge and identification card. Yes. Toss them to me also."

He looked at the card before slipping it and the badge into his pocket. "Thank you, Constable Mahoney. I will now give you the key to your handcuffs. Unlock the cuff attached to the steering wheel, put your hands behind your back, and cuff your other hand."

When Mahoney had finished, Zakhar opened the car's trunk. "You will get inside."

"No. No, I won't."

Zakhar was in a hurry to return to the electronics store before it closed. "I do not wish to shoot you, but I will if you do not cooperate. It is as simple as that."

"You will shoot me after I get in."

Zakhar shrugged. "I might not."

The young officer, trembling with the certainty that he was about to die, climbed awkwardly from the car and stumbled to the trunk. He sat down on the edge and appealed to Zakhar again.

"Please, man. You don't have to do this. I have a wife, a family. Please."

"Get in, I won't tell you again," Zakhar said.

Mahoney swung his legs over the side and rolled into the trunk, onto the equipment stored inside. He struggled to right himself, a nearly impossible task, given his hands were cuffed behind his back.

"You will be uncomfortable for a night, perhaps, but you will live," Zakhar said.

This is your lucky day, although I don't know why, he thought.

Zakhar shut the trunk, sealing the man inside, locked the doors to the car, and tossed the keys under the car. Then he walked around to the back of the station, pulled off the ski mask, got into his stolen car, and headed for the electronics store.

THE LIGHTS WERE still on inside Dave's Blue Label Buys when Zakhar arrived. He parked, retrieved the newspaper and the photographs of Linnéa Olander from his bag, and got out. Standing in the lot, he clipped the constable's badge to his belt, patted his pocket for the officer's ID card, and walked toward the store's entrance.

Not far inside the doors, he came to a halt and gaped in amazement. Never in his life had he seen a store like this, shelves filled to the ceiling with every conceivable electronic product.

What luxury! What opulence! What riches!

The abundance shook him to his core.

A doorkeeper in a blue shirt asked him, "Can I help you find what you're looking for, sir?"

"I . . . I'm looking for gaming systems."

"Please use the center aisle, just to your left. Follow it to the back of the store. You'll see a sign for the Gaming Department—however, please be aware of the time? We close in fifteen minutes."

Zakhar nodded and hurried down the main aisle, gawking at the shelves he passed, each one burgeoning with gleaming, colorful products. When he arrived at the gaming section, it was the same—boxes of game systems piled atop each other, racks of games, controllers, and other accessories.

He approached a salesclerk who was already totaling his register.

"Yes, sir? May I help you?"

Zakhar tapped the badge on his belt. "Police Constable Mahoney. I am looking for this woman. I believe she may have been here earlier today to buy a PlayStation system." He placed two glossy photographs on the glass countertop between them.

The clerk shook his head. "I don't recollect assisting her, but I've only been on duty since three."

"Who else was working in this department today?"

"Let me check." He got on the phone and pushed a few buttons.

Another clerk sauntered into the area, catching the first clerk's eye.

"Hey, Sean. I'll be ready to go in a few."

"Not a problem, Rory."

Sean, the second clerk glanced at Zakhar and saw his badge. "Are you Ontario Provincial Police?"

"Yes, Constable Mahoney."

"Cool. My brother-in-law is O.P.P."

"Constable Mahoney is asking about a woman who was looking for a PS2," Rory mumbled, "and I'm trying to find out who was on shift this morning, but I guess James isn't in his office."

"The store is closing, so he's out on the floor, making sure we close out on time."

Sean leaned over to look at the photographs on the counter. "Hey, I recognize her! Waited on her this afternoon."

Zakhar worked to keep his elation in check. "Who are you, please?" he asked.

"Sean Tremaine, sir. I work in computers."

"And this woman bought something from you?"

"Oh, yeah. A laptop."

"She used a credit card?" This was Zakhar's opportunity to gather the woman's card number.

"No, she paid in cash."

Zakhar's anger flashed across his face, and Sean stepped back.

"What else can you tell me?"

"Um, while I was getting her order together, she also went over to the mobile phone department."

"She bought a mobile phone? Who waited on her?"

"Kelly did. I think . . . well, it's almost nine and the store is closing. I think she's clocking out."

Zakhar took Sean by the arm. "Take me to her at once."

Sean looked down at his arm. "Hey, man. You don't need to grab me like that."

Zakhar exhaled and released the young man. "I apologize, but the situation is urgent. This woman was on Flight 6177 and is a person of interest in the attempted hijacking."

"Oh, wow! And she seemed so nice. Come on. I'll help you find Kelly."

"Quickly!" Zakhar urged him.

Sean ran, Zakhar behind him, to the back of the store through a door marked Employees Only. Sean glanced toward a time clock. Three employees were clocking out, but not the woman he was looking for.

"She's probably out back in the employee parking lot, getting in her car."

"Hurry," Zakhar insisted.

Sean hit the back door and pushed through. "There! That's her car!"

The car had backed out of its slot and had turned onto the main lane leading out of the lot. Zakhar raced toward the car, flagging down the driver. Sean caught up to him as the woman stomped on her brakes.

She rolled down her window. "What's the matter?"

"I am Constable Mahoney," Zakhar announced. "I need you to return to the store."

Minutes later, she had logged into the store's system at her desk and was showing Zakhar her sales for the day.

"She paid in cash for the phone, but the service provider requires a credit card for the monthly contract fees." She pressed a few keys and a printer whirred into action. She tore the perforated paper from the machine.

"Here you go. Elaine Granger. Nice lady. Bought the Nokia 3310. This is the credit card information she provided to pay for her AT&T service contract."

"And the phone's number?"

She pointed. "Right here."

"Excellent." Zakhar's smile was broad but something else, too.

Cruel.

Predatory.

"The O.P.P thanks you for your assistance, Kelly."

"Glad to help, constable," Kelly answered.

She glanced sideways at Sean who replied with one, negligible shake of his head. The constable made them both uncomfortable.

Zakhar's grin gave Kelly chills.

CHAPTER 23

LP

SIX O'CLOCK IN THE morning found Laynie in the campground's café, one of their first customers. She had connected her laptop's modem to the café's broadband outlet when the waitress planted a menu next to her elbow.

"Coffee, please," Laynie asked. "I'll be ready to order when you return."

As she sipped her first cup of the day, Laynie typed in an IP address that took her directly to the private online chat room she and Christor used. Specifically, Laynie wanted to download and read Kari's latest letter.

As Christor had promised, a .jpg file was waiting for her, a photograph of Mt. Rushmore. Laynie downloaded the image to her hard drive, withdrew the CD-ROM case from her purse, inserted it in the CD drive, and installed the image decryption software on her new laptop. When she clicked on the image of Mt. Rushmore, the decryption program opened Kari's letter.

Laynie scanned it first—Kari's regular news regarding Gene and Polly, Shannon and Robbie, Max and Søren. Laynie stopped when she read,

"Max is settling into his freshman classes at UNL. Compared to our little farming community, Lincoln is a big city, full of mystique and adventures. I'm very glad he has settled into a church home at Liberty Christian Center and has found other young men of faith on campus. He and a group of friends meet outside their dorms some afternoons following classes for paintball battles."

Laynie read and reread Kari's letter, mulling over it and considering the smallest of ideas. She paid her bill and, on her way out of the café, stopped in the general store. There she purchased an atlas of the US, since the Canadian atlas didn't reach far down into the States. She also bought bottled water, a juice, and a coffee to go.

When Laynie returned to Daisy, she had one more task to complete before getting on the road. Her new phone was fully charged, so she input Shaw and Bessie's number and those of their children into her new phone's contacts, adding other numbers of importance to her.

Then she called Shaw's mobile phone.

His wary voice answered. "Hello?"

"Shaw, it's Elaine."

"Thank the Lord! Are you all right? Where are you calling from?"

"Yes, I'm fine, and I have bought a phone. I'm at the campground you recommended, but I'll be heading west soon. Put my number into your contacts. I just wanted to check in with you and Bessie before I got on the road."

"We're fine, too. We got an early start this morning and should reach our daughter's place outside Winnipeg late this afternoon—if my hips last that long."

"What about your dialysis?"

"Our girl got it set up for me. I'll go straight to the clinic for an evaluation and treatment when we arrive."

"But Shaw . . ."

"I know, I know. I'm overdue and not at m' best. Bessie may have to drive soon—but we'll get there, don't you worry. When we've rested a bit, we'll move on to our son's place in Penticton."

LAYNIE LEFT THE campground by midmorning. Before she left, she opened the atlas Shaw left her and decided on her route. She pointed Daisy toward Highway 148 westbound and stomped her foot down on the gas.

Hard.

ZAKHAR, TOO, HAD things to do that morning—although he was not in a hurry. No, he no longer had to rush. He would take his time and enjoy some of the comforts his money could afford him—and he would utilize the help Baskin had offered him.

After leaving Dave's Blue Label Buys the evening before, he had selected a hotel close to the Ottawa airport and checked in, downing several drinks and sleeping soundly until around eight. When he rose, he showered, dressed, ordered breakfast, and repacked his belongings in the duffle bag.

His first course of business for the day was to lose the stolen car he was driving and acquire a legitimate mode of transportation. He did not check out of the hotel but took his duffle with him to use as a prop and headed for the airport. He veered off where the signs directed him to the airport's long-term parking.

In the lot's drive-through, he received a tag, placed it in the car's front window, and found his assigned parking place. He removed his bag, locked the car, and waited for the shuttle that would take him to the airport's departures drop-off area.

At the departures curb, he got out with the other shuttle passengers, tipped the driver, and made his way into the airport—only to locate and take the escalator down to the arrivals level. There he approached a car rental desk, presented his Canadian driver's license and credit card, and asked for a rental.

"My business will take me out of the province," he explained with a relaxed smile to the woman behind the counter. "I am uncertain of the exact day my assignment will conclude, but I estimate my need for the rental at around a month."

"We can choose an estimated return date, a month from now. If you need the car longer, simply call our 800 number to extend the return date."

"That will work just fine," Zakhar said, signing the paperwork.

He left the airport and went up to his hotel. After lunch in the hotel's restaurant, he returned to his room and used the hotel phone, rather than his mobile phone, to place the call.

"Ms. Gagnon please," he told the woman who answered.

A moment of silence passed, then she replied, "Yes?"

"I require *pomoshch*." *Pomoshch* was the Russian word for assistance.

A breathy, excited chuckle resounded over the line. "Do you, now? I've been expecting your call. I was beginning to wonder how long it would be before I had something new and entertaining to do—other than drudge away at this job. I hope your assignment enlivens me some. What shall I call you?"

"Dimitri will suffice."

"Very well, *Dimitri*. What do you require of me?"

"I wish you to track a credit card and mobile phone."

"Cardholder's name?"

"Elaine Granger." He read off the credit card number and expiration date from the printout Kelly at Dave's Blue Label Buys had provided.

"And the phone?"

"Same name." He read the number to her.

"I can, most certainly, provide you with many bits of information—such as her call and text logs. I can give you the general location of her calls, based on which cell towers her phone pings. And where her credit card is used and what she buys." She laughed, as though responding to a private joke.

"I cannot, however, pinpoint her exact position for you, unless she uses her card, say at a hotel, and remains there long enough for you to, er, seek her out at that location."

"I know this," Zakhar growled.

"Well, do you wish me to dissect her financials? Perhaps drain her bank accounts, freeze her card?" The woman chuckled again.

Zakhar was already tired of her odd attitude.

"What I wish," he ground out, "is for you to send me a daily update—where she has called from, whom she has called, where she has used her card and for what. I *do not* wish her financials tampered with or for her to sense anything amiss."

"What a shame. I see she has a tidy little amount in a Montreal bank that she transferred from an account in Singapore. I could send the funds of both accounts into the ether."

Zakhar sneered. *By "send into the ether," you mean move into one of your own accounts.*

"No, I do not want you to do that."

"Well, stay on the line with me a few minutes while I look around."

THE WOMAN DUG DEEPER, hacking into the Singapore HSBC system, looking for the original wire transfers that had funded the account, finding them, following them backward through a series of proxy servers and a long line of bank accounts, now closed, hacking into the closed accounts' bank systems and repeating the process, farther and farther, finding additional wire transfers that went to yet more accounts, some of them still active.

She giggled and folded a stick of Black Jack gum into her mouth. *Why, you are a very sneaky girl, Elaine Granger. I like your style.*

On the other end of the call, Zakhar huffed. "Again, I wish you to do nothing except send me daily updates. I want her to relax, to feel she has escaped pursuit . . . until I am ready to, er, seek her out."

"As you wish. What is she driving?"

"I have that information." He retrieved the motor home's registration card and read the vehicle's make and model aloud to her. "But she has swapped the motor home's plate and is, for the moment, using this plate number. Ontario AMLL 508."

"She's driving a motor home with stolen plates? How quaint—this will be fun. And does she have much of an online presence? Email? Bulletin boards? Chat rooms?"

"She just purchased a laptop. She must have a reason for doing so."

"Indeed. Where, pray tell, did she acquire said 'just purchased' laptop?"

"Dave's Blue Label Buys, Ottawa. Yesterday."

"Verrry gooood, Dimitri," she purred. "Also purchased under the name Elaine Granger?"

"Yes."

"And how would you like me to convey your daily data dump, hmm? Email would be best."

"I . . ."

Zakhar did not have an email address.

"Oh, I see," she laughed. "Well, we must do as your Elaine has done and acquire a laptop for you. Give me your location. I will have one delivered to you, already configured for our conversations."

"Okay," he agreed, and gave her his hotel information.

I will search you out, too, Dimitri, never you fear. Whatever you believe you are hiding from me, I shall know better than the back of my hand.

"Okay," he agreed, and gave her his hotel information.

"Ms. Gagnon" disconnected the call and set to work. in her "regular" job, she was known as Thérèse Benoit, but that was not the name she had been born with. She'd left that life behind more than a decade ago. As far as her employers at the RCMP knew, Thérèse Benoit was of French-Canadian parentage, born and raised in Québec. A loyal, albeit less-than-conventional, citizen.

Imbued with a razor-sharp mind and an even sharper wit, coupled with world-class technical skills, Thérèse was highly regarded in international hacking circles—but not as Thérèse Benoit. In those elite factions that existed in the shadows of society, she was known by her handle, *Vyper*.

While some hackers lived to advance their reputation, Vyper preferred power—and information was power. She collected information like hobbyists who collected rare stamps or like the wealthy amassed rare art.

Information also equated to money, another source of power, and Vyper loved the anonymous accounts she'd seeded in banks around the world—Dubai, Switzerland, Hong Kong, Singapore, Argentina, The Caymans, and lesser-regarded havens such as Luxembourg, Thailand, Crete, and Morocco.

Vyper was the highest-paid cyber security specialist in the RCMP's computer center in their Rideau Glen compound, a tony suburb of Ottawa along the Rideau River. While her job was dead boring, it gave her access to their data and their data procurement means and methods. Her unique position also gave her elevated *cachet*, the status to dress as she wished, shave her black hair on one side, wear a headset and listen to music while she worked, and chew two or three packs of her beloved Black Jack gum every shift.

The trash can liners around her workspace were filled with crumpled wrappers and spattered with chewed wads of the grayish-black licorice-flavored gum—a brand she special ordered by the case from a friend who worked for Pfizer, the makers of Black Jack. Anyone wishing a special favor from Vyper entered her area bearing an unopened box of the blue five-stick packs—always Black Jack, never a cheap knockoff.

Vyper had earned her perks. Since the day Thérèse Benoit had come to work for them two years before, the RCMP had suffered not a single breach of their computer systems. She had not only defeated every attempt to hack their system and data, but she had also successfully tracked fifteen *bona fide* intrusion attempts back to their sources, crashed the hackers' systems, and directed RCMP officers to their lairs.

Because of her success, when she demanded hardware and software upgrades, she got them, and then employed those very upgrades and many of her work hours—she loved to multitask—to reach out into the world, stretching her fingers across continents and oceans, sneaking into protected systems, taking what she wanted, leaving nary a trace.

Vyper was an inquisitive woman, curious about the "side jobs" she took, that is, non-RCMP assignments she accepted under contract. She often probed deeper than a client requested, searching out their hidden motives and agendas. Yes, she did work for the Russians. They were clients long before she joined the RCMP. Why? Because they paid well and because she mined their systems, too. However, they were far from her *only* extracurricular clients or her only source of supplemental income. She took work from legitimate financial entities needing improved security—but also from various criminal organizations and from those seeking the kind of financial or reputational vengeance Vyper could inflict upon their enemies.

In truth, Vyper was an equal-opportunity consultant and thief, fattening her bank accounts by stealing from Patron 1 and selling to Patron 2. She was also something of a social engineer, having on occasion dipped her oar into the affairs of business or state when it suited her purposes . . . or just because it made her laugh to see "movers and shakers" chasing their tails. It was a satisfying life—and would remain so as long as she kept her patrons in the dark.

After she hung up on her newest client, she attacked the cyber infrastructure of Dave's Blue Label Buys. Their firewall was so mediocre, she felt as much compunction for tunneling inside as she would have for swatting a gnat. She found the sale of a Dell laptop to Elaine Granger in less than five minutes.

"Really," she whispered to Dave's corporate owners, "I could rob you blind, if I were so inclined," but Dave's Blue Label Buys was chicken feed compared to her loftier endeavors.

She had hacked into Dave's Blue Label Buys to obtain the specific, detailed build of the Granger woman's laptop. The build would tell her how to customize her code to seek that specific build when it connected to the Internet. The laptop's build would also tell her how to customize the Trojan horse she would plant on the machine once she'd found it.

Finding the laptop online was her first big challenge. Once she found it and installed her Trojan horse on the laptop, the Trojan horse would, thereafter, alert her whenever the device connected to the Internet. In other words, once Vyper planted her program in the woman's laptop, she would be able to follow the woman from IP address to IP address.

First things first. Find the laptop online. To accomplish that initial challenge, Vyper would follow the woman's bread crumb trail, the bread crumbs being Elaine Granger's motor home, mobile phone, and credit card.

While Vyper folded a fresh stick of Black Jack into her mouth, she copied boilerplate code from the online stash where she kept her "tools" and pasted it to a new file. She modified the code to create a tracking program and an app unique to Elaine Granger.

While the program sent its foraging queries into the ether, she pulled an unused laptop from the RCMP inventory, modified the inventory file to designate the laptop as "motherboard failure. Returned to mfr for replacement," and set to work customizing it for Dimitri's use.

LESS THAN AN HOUR later, her program pinged her. She switched to the window where it was running and studied the result. a single phone call to another mobile number at 10:37 a.m. Vyper pulled up a map and triangulated the cell towers closest to the call.

On the outskirts of Gatineau, west of Ottawa but north of 148.

She ran the app she'd created. It returned a list of motor home parks and campgrounds within the triangle formed by the three strongest cell tower pings. Smack in the middle of the triangle was Wind-in-the-Trees Campground.

"There you are," she muttered with glee. "Let's see if you're staying on another night."

She called the campground. A man answered.

"Good afternoon," Vyper said in her most official voice. "This is Anya Probst of the RCMP. I wish to inquire if a motor home bearing the Ontario plate *Ontario Alpha Mike Lima Lima Five Zero Eight* is presently registered in your campground or has checked out this morning."

The man looked and came back. "That plate checked out this morning."

"Did the party pay for an electric or nonelectric camp spot?"

"Electric."

"Thank you for your time. Oh. One more thing? Does your campground have Internet access?"

"We sure do."

Vyper hung up, put her fingers together and bowed her forehead onto them, thinking over what she'd learned. *So, you've checked out, but you've shown a propensity for campgrounds with electric and broadband service.*

Another bread crumb.

While Canada boasted many campgrounds, the nation had perhaps only twenty-five commercial Internet service providers—and she had previously built a back door into every one of them. She created a program and sent it out to return a list of broadband customer accounts whose business name included one or more of the keywords: "camp," "camping," "campground," "RV," "motor home," "KOA," "travel," "cabins," "recreational," or "park." She would then worm her way into those accounts and monitor them, waiting for Elaine Granger to log in.

She ended her day by setting up a Yahoo email account for Dimitri on the laptop. She left a "READ ME" text file on the laptop's desktop with instructions for Dimitri to access his email account.

I think you are probably smart enough to know I will be reading all *of your emails, Dmitri.*

What he wouldn't know was that she had also installed her specialized Trojan horse on his laptop. Whenever he connected to the Internet, she would know where he was. Soon enough, she would drill down into his phone, credit card, and computer records to uncover his actual identity—and with it, all the fun-filled and lucrative opportunities his identity and connections would produce for her.

She packed the laptop and its case into a box and called a courier service to deliver the box to Dimitri's hotel.

LAYNIE RODE DAISY hard, putting distance between herself and Wind-in-the-Trees. She was more confident of her driving now, less tentative when changing lanes and maneuvering through traffic. When she reached North Bay, she followed Shaw's proposed route, turning north onto 11 to cross the breadth of Ontario and eventually head toward Winnipeg—but not actually into Winnipeg. That was where her journey would diverge from Shaw and Bessie's.

As she traveled down the highway, her mind was frequently preoccupied with how to hide from Zakhar. She knew how tenacious, how dogged the man was. Moreover, she feared what he might do to her out of his own depraved lusts should he catch up to her. Her dread of him drove her to push ahead harder, faster. Her dread of Zakhar also turned her mind onto Bessie's words regarding repentance.

"I'm not saying God is a giant vending machine, that you simply ask him for what you want, and he gives it to you. God isn't a machine, and his blessings belong to those who belong to him.

"We're praying that you will come to a point of repentance in your life. No one can be saved without repentance, Elaine. Repentance is where we—every one of us—acknowledge and confess our sinful, needy state before God

and ask for forgiveness through the blood of Jesus. A place where we surrender fully to the Lordship of Christ, where he becomes our king, and we become his children—where we become the family of God."

Bessie's admonitions tore at Laynie's heart.

"Acknowledge my sinful, needy state? I fully acknowledge that I've lived the life of a whore. A slut," she whispered aloud, "not to mention professional liar and thief. There's no coming back from that. Besides . . . it's what I was destined for. I do the dirty, sinful work others won't. God certainly doesn't want someone like me in his family."

She uttered a rueful laugh. "I'd be a bad example to the other kids."

It was past mid-September, and the nights this far north were already cold. She ran into sporadic showers before long, but slogged along, grateful that she could pull off anywhere and wait out the storm if need be.

When the day was fully dark, she left the highway and drove through a little town. She found their local bar before long. As she had anticipated, the bar's dirt lot, pocked with rain-and-mud-slimed potholes, was full—but it was also unsecured and unguarded. She parked Daisy up the block, then walked back to the bar with a few tools and the stolen plate tucked into her jacket.

She lifted a plate from a mud-spattered pickup truck and replaced it with the stolen plate. For good measure, she grabbed a handful of fresh mud and smeared it on the stolen plate. When she finished, it looked like it belonged.

Laynie returned to the highway, but she estimated she had another thirteen hours before she crossed into Manitoba. As the night grew late, she needed sleep. She pushed herself for another hour before she grew too groggy to drive any further. She chose yet another little berg off the highway and crawled through its main street, looking a spot to hide Daisy for the night.

When she came upon the town's lone grocery store, she felt she'd found that place.

Behind the store, shielded from public view, was an alley leading to a loading dock. Laynie steered Daisy past the raised dock and parked against the building. Making certain Daisy's doors were locked, Laynie unfolded the windshield screen and tucked it between the dash and the sun visors to close herself in.

Then she heated a can of soup on the stove, shoveled it down, and tumbled into bed. Already feeling comfortable and fairly secure within Daisy's accommodations, she fell straight off to sleep.

SHE WOKE, COLD AND shivering, to the sounds of heavy beating on Daisy's door and someone shouting, "Hey! You inside the motor home!"

Pulling the HK from under her pillow, Laynie stumbled to the door and spoke through it.

"I'm awake. What do you want?"

"What do *I* want? I want you to get your *bleeping* rig out of my loading area, lady. This is not a public campground and you're blocking our supplier's *bleeping* truck!"

"Sorry. Yes, I'll move. Right away."

She shivered again as she started the engine. When she pulled the windshield screen down, a soft, frosty film covered Daisy's windshield.

"Huh. Guess it got cold last night."

She ran the wipers to clear the windshield and drove out of the alley behind the grocery store, looking for somewhere to get coffee. Just before she reached the on-ramp to the highway, she spotted a gas station. After filling her tank and purchasing two cups of coffee to go, she rejoined the highway traffic headed west.

She drove on, stopping for a late breakfast and skipping lunch, until she reached the far suburbs of northern Winnipeg. Before it grew dark, she found a busy diner and ordered her dinner to go. Then she hunted down another alley behind a strip mall and bedded down for the night.

SHE ROSE EARLY the following morning, gassed up, got her coffee, and pointed Daisy north. This part of Canada was generally low in elevation, so runoff from higher elevations had created hundreds of lakes. All that water meant many places to camp. This late in the season, when the weather was too cold for general camping, people were gearing up for the coming freeze and a favorite pastime. ice fishing. Until a deep freeze hit, she might have the pick of locations to hide out.

Laynie's plan was to drive north through lake country and seek out a remote, sheltered location to hole up for a few weeks. If she picked the right spot, she might be able to stay "off the grid" entirely.

LAYNIE READ A SIGN that indicated the lakeshore and boat ramp were not far ahead. Hopefully, she'd find a campground, too. She'd already passed through the little village with its combo bait shop and grocery store touting the upcoming ice fishing season. When she spotted the boat ramp, but no accompanying campground appeared, she decided to turn around. She had just passed a muddy road, a driveway onto private property. She backed up into the drive, then cut her wheels to turn in the direction from which she'd come. Across the road from her was another private drive—and that's when she spotted a house up the graveled drive and through the trees . . . and something that snagged her interest.

Instead of heading back the way she'd come, Laynie pointed Daisy across the road and up the short, graveled drive into a wide turnabout in front of the house and its detached double garage.

Laynie climbed down from Daisy's driver's seat and looked around, liking what she saw, thinking she may have found the perfect place to disappear for a while.

A man, perhaps in his late forties, thin, average height, left the open garage and approached her. Wiping grease-covered hands on an equally grease-stained towel, he coughed then asked, "Can I help you? Are you lost?"

Laynie smiled in her artful, transparent manner. "No, not lost. Actually, I'm looking for a quiet place to camp so I can write in peace."

"You're a writer, then, eh?"

Laynie nodded. "I hope you don't mind me barging in. I saw your place from the road and came on up. You see, I have a deadline looming ahead of me, and I need a few weeks to focus on it."

More lies. See, Bessie? This is who I am.

The man kept wiping his hands, as though the motion helped him think. "Well, it's goin' on October now. The nights are pretty chilly, and we can get snow early here. I suppose you might rent a cabin in the village."

Laynie pointed with her chin. "Actually, that pole barn is what caught my eye. Will you be storing anything else in it over the winter?"

The structure she indicated was nothing more than a long, peaked, metal roof over a bed of gravel, designed to keep rain and snow off stacked, baled hay. At present, the graveled bed under its roof was void except for a rusted tractor and some farm implements at the far end, piled against the barn's single wall.

He shook his head, coughed again. "Nope. This was my folk's place. They grew hay for their stock, but I sold off the stock when they passed. Don't store hay any longer."

"Well, I was wondering . . . could I back in under your roof and camp here for a couple weeks? Maybe run a cord from your house for electricity?"

He snorted. "Do you know how much electricity it would take to heat that flimsy thing you're living in, eh?"

Laynie met his gaze and worked her persuasive wiles on him. "You know, if I were staying in a nice hotel with all the amenities—and all the *distractions*—I'd likely be paying a hundred dollars a night or more."

The rag in his hands slowed. Laynie noted a few bruises under the grime.

Well, I suppose working with your hands on a car engine would result in some bangs and bruises.

The man said, "Are you saying you'd be willing to pay me a hundred dollars a night to park under my hay barn and use my electricity?"

"That's what I'm saying. I can pay for the first five nights in cash. After that, I would need a means to pay you by credit card."

He frowned and shook his head more vigorously. "Do I look like a merchant with a credit card reader?"

"Well, what about that bait shop down the road? You know the owners? What if I ran my credit card there and they paid you? I would add a bit to the hundred a night to cover the merchant's card service fee and to give the owner an incentive for agreeing to the arrangement. Plus, I'd be buying groceries from them."

Laynie wanted to put off using her card as long as possible, but she didn't have enough cash to go on indefinitely.

His expression turned speculative. "Bart's a friend. He might go for that . . . if you make it worth his while. It's pretty slow around here this time of year until the lake freezes over. And just so you know? We don't have anything fancy up here like the Internet or mobile phone service."

"Fine by me. What do you say? Shall we ask Bart? I can stock up on food while we're there."

"A hundred a night for five nights?"

She grinned, knowing she'd sealed the deal. "Yup. We can start with that. After five days and nights, I'll know if I can get my work done here. My name's Elaine, by the way."

"Roger. You can call me Rog, eh? Everybody does."

"Thanks, Rog. Shall we visit Bart and ask him if he's willing?" Laynie nodded at his dirty hands. "You need a ride?"

"Oh, this here grease? From my backup jenny—generator. The Jeep's fine."

Laynie turned Daisy in a wide circle, the gravel crunching under the tires, and waited for Rog to drive his Jeep out of the garage. She followed him back to the village.

The owners of the bait shop and little grocery store, Bart and his wife, Liz, agreed to the arrangement—with a user's fee tacked on.

"Cost of doing business." He was apologetic, but firm.

"That's understandable," Laynie answered. "I'm okay with your terms."

When she and Rog returned to his house, Laynie had groceries, gloves, a warm hat, and a heavy coat stacked on the passenger seat and floor. She'd used cash to make the purchases. When she counted what remained, she had exactly six hundred dollars and change. From the six hundred dollars, she paid Rog a hundred for her first night.

My cash reserves are getting thin, but I will keep my head down and avoid using my credit card until I have to . . . just in case.

Just in case?

Laynie frowned.

Petroff is no fool. He will have acted on my "advice." Even if Zakhar disregarded Petroff's orders, could he trace my credit card usage without Petroff's help?

Still, using her card carried risk . . . and worried her.

Pulling her thoughts back to her present surroundings, Laynie said to Roger, "If I'm satisfied in the morning with how I got on with my writing the remainder of today and tonight, I'll pay for the next four nights."

"Sounds reasonable enough to me. While you back your rig under the hay barn, I'll run an electrical cord from the house."

CHAPTER 24

VYPER STARED WITH disgust at her program's results. Nothing. For nearly two weeks, nothing! Zero, nada, naught, not a *bleeping* thing. Her target, Elaine Granger, had not used her credit card or her mobile phone since leaving Wind-in-the-Trees Campground. Neither had she checked in at any campground in Canada with high-speed Internet service.

Vyper knew. She had foraged her way through the nation's list of Internet service providers, had wormed her way into each of their databases, rooted out and identified every campground with broadband service, drilled down into their computers, and planted her custom Trojan horse, the program that would ping her if a Winnebago motor home of the same model and year as Elaine Granger's checked in.

It's getting cold out there overnight. Many campgrounds have closed for winter. That alone should have made it easier for me to find her. Where else but a KOA or something similar with electric hookups could she park an RV?

Vyper examined and verified her program parameters. They were perfect. *How can this be? Is the woman existing solely on cash? Living completely off the grid?*

It was the only answer.

Vyper sat back and, with grudging admiration, studied the images of Elaine Granger Dimitri had sent her.

You impress me a little, Ms. Granger, she admitted, *and I don't impress easily. But I also don't allow anyone to evade my nets forever. After all, what would that do to my reputation?*

"It is only a matter of time, girlfriend," she whispered to the photo of Elaine Granger. "You must come up for air sooner or later—and when you do? I will have you."

Speaking of reputation, her client "Dimitri" had not endeared himself to her over the past week.

"We are paying you for results," he'd snarled at her during their most recent phone call.

"I work for your superiors, not you, *Zakhar*," she'd retorted. Oh, yes. She'd uncovered who he was and Baskin, the Moscow security officer for whom he worked. "*You* are not paying me at all."

She'd held herself in check during their call, not letting on that she monitored every keystroke he made, not giving in to the urge to twist his tail for the pornography sites he'd visited online or the S&M images he'd downloaded to the laptop she'd given him.

What had disgusted her most was his penchant to seek out violent porn—even what were called "snuff films."

Vyper sniffed in derision. Yes, information was power—power to be kept secret, held close, and then played at exactly the right moment for maximum benefit.

She would bide her time.

LAYNIE WOKE BEFORE dawn. She stretched, relishing, as she had six mornings in a row, the welcome awareness of freedom.

Freedom!

Laynie couldn't recall when she'd last felt this sensation, this . . . letting down, relaxing her guard, choosing for herself how she would spend her day, unfettered by Petroff's demands or the hovering, ubiquitous presence of Alyona or Zakhar or any of Petroff's other restrictions.

Sleep and get up when I want. Eat what I want, when I want. Do what I want, when I want.

She rose, made herself a pot of coffee, filled a tall travel cup, and walked down to the lake to watch the sun rise over the lake. And like each of the preceding mornings, she stayed long after her coffee was gone, soaking up the quiet and the comforting, never-ending lap of water against the shore.

She heard steps behind her and frowned, irked at the disruption of her private time. It was Roger, picking his way across the rocks to the shoreline where she sat. His approach was hesitant and careful. He came alongside her but kept his distance, as though instinctively sensing that he wasn't welcome.

"Are you getting any writing done?"

"Sure," Laynie lied. Truth was, she'd spent the past days running miles along lakeshore trails to keep her fitness level up, then sitting for hours watching the sun slowly vanish over the lake. In between, in the afternoons before sunset? She'd spent those hours within Daisy's walls . . . reading.

Roger hunkered down where he was, still keeping his distance. He was quiet, respectful of her privacy, but even from a couple yards away, Laynie could feel him working his way up to something.

She sighed within herself.

She really did *not* want to hear Rog spout a rehearsed pickup line. She would have to shut him down—although she'd try not to deflate his ego too much. Still, the painful exchange would ruin her beautiful morning and put a strain on their arrangement.

I'll probably have to leave—and I was really starting to like this place.

She carried the HK everywhere with her. It was tucked into her waistband, under her coat. She briefly fantasized about pulling it out and getting rid of Roger in much the same way she'd slap down an annoying mosquito.

Hey, then I could stay here all winter without ever using my credit card, right?

Except she was wrong. Completely off base. Roger wasn't squatting nearby to make overtures.

He cleared his throat. "I need to say something, Elaine. You tell me if I'm wrong, eh?"

Laynie slid her eyes from the lake over to him. The man was as serious as he could be.

This can't be good.

She tried to lighten the mood. "What? Am I sucking too much juice and you want to raise my rent? Or are my wild parties keeping you up at night?"

He didn't rise to her attempt at deflection. "Elaine, you aren't really a writer, are you? You aren't working on any 'looming deadline,' are you?"

"Those are questions, not you 'saying something.'"

"All right, let me rephrase. Elaine, I think you're hiding from someone."

Laynie faced him, defensive. Half angry. "No, I'm not. Why would you say such a thing?"

"Because it's what I'm trained to see. I'm a cop, Elaine. Community Safety Officer Roger Mayfield, Royal Canadian Mounted Police, Winnipeg."

She'd let down her walls, relaxed her fortifications, and couldn't build them back up fast enough. Her face mirrored her shock—and verified his assertions.

"You don't need to be concerned, Elaine. I'm not on the job. I'm on medical leave. That's why I'm here instead of down in the city. But I know the signs of someone who's in the wind. I recognized them in you when you drove into my yard. And since you're hiding out on my property? I had a friend run your plate. Guess what? It's stolen."

Laynie swept her eyes back out onto the lake, hoping . . . struggling to regain her equanimity.

"Are the police coming for me?"

"No."

She frowned and faced him again. "Why not?"

His reply had to wait until he'd handled a coughing fit. "It's a stolen plate, not a stolen vehicle. I gave my fellow officer no details or particulars, just asked him to run the plate. He . . . agreed not to report my call. Agreed to let me handle it on my end. As a personal favor."

"And does this 'personal favor' come with a price tag you expect me to pony up, say, later on tonight in my RV?" Bitterness dripped from every syllable.

"I can understand why you'd think that, but no. I mean, you're an attractive woman and all, but that's not how I roll. In fact . . . what I actually came down to tell you was that I'd like to help you."

Laynie didn't know how to answer. She was too upset to actually hear what he'd offered.

All my careful plans—ruined! Ruined over a completely random encounter—a total stranger who turns out to be a cop? Of all the rotten luck.

"Look," she said between her clenched teeth. "I don't want or need your help. I'll pack up and get out of here."

"There's no need for you to do that. It's a guy, right? A guy you're running from? An abuser?"

When Laynie didn't answer, he added, "Well, I figure you're actually pretty safe here—you haven't used your credit card, and you've kept your RV out of sight. So, feel free to stay a while longer."

Free? I was free until you ruined everything.

Laynie stood up. "No thanks. I'll be out of your hair by nightfall."

She stalked off and returned to Daisy. Sank onto a bench seat at the table.

What do I do now? Where do I go next?

There on the table sat her recent reading material, what had—quite unexpectedly—engrossed her for hours since the first afternoon she'd been parked under Rog's hay barn. The worn volume was, from what Laynie deduced, Shaw and Bessie's "travel" Bible. She'd found it along with the toothpicks and a deck of cards in the shallow drawer built under the end of the table.

Tucked within the Bible's pages she'd found dog-eared sheets of paper traversed in Shaw's careful script, listing where they'd camped and what they'd read and studied together while they camped. He'd added the walks they'd taken, the fun things they'd seen and done, and answers to prayers they'd prayed together.

The Bible's pages themselves were a collage of verses highlighted in four colors—yellow, pink, pale green, and light blue. She hadn't readily understood their color-coding system but, as she read what the Bradshaws had highlighted and compared the same color across chapters and books, she thought she'd figured it out.

Yellow seemed to be examples of faith.

And the scripture was fulfilled that says,
"Abraham believed God,
and it was credited to him as righteousness,"
and he was called God's friend.

Pink verses spoke of God's character and of his word.

For the word of God is alive and active.
Sharper than any double-edged sword,
it penetrates even to dividing
soul and spirit, joints and marrow;
it judges the thoughts and attitudes of the heart.
Nothing in all creation is hidden from God's sight.
Everything is uncovered and laid bare before
the eyes of him to whom we must give account.

Pale green were Christian attributes.

But the fruit of the Spirit is
love, joy, peace, forbearance, kindness, goodness,
faithfulness, gentleness and self-control.
Against such things there is no law.
Those who belong to Christ Jesus have crucified
the flesh with its passions and desires.

Light blue indicated specific words of instruction or wisdom, and the highlighted passage in Ephesians 6 had struck a chord in Laynie's heart.

Finally, be strong in the Lord
and in his mighty power.
Put on the full armor of God,
so that you can take your stand
against the devil's schemes.
For our struggle is not against flesh and blood,
but against the rulers, against the authorities,
against the powers of this dark world
and against the spiritual forces of evil
in the heavenly realms.
Therefore, put on the full armor of God,
so that when the day of evil comes,
you may be able to stand your ground,
and after you have done everything,
to stand.

"For our struggle is not against flesh and blood? Is my flight to free myself from Petroff and his puppet, Zakhar, more than a struggle against them? Do 'spiritual forces of evil in the heavenly realms' actually exist?"

Laynie had grown up in church—Mama and Dad had made certain of that—but earlier in her childhood, Laynie's heart had experienced the trauma of loss and separation. She had never been able to shake that loss, so she had internalized it instead, had taken both the responsibility and the punishment of it upon herself.

I'm worthless. My life has no value, and I deserve nothing from God.

She had repeated the mantra for as long as she could remember.

Whatever she had heard of God's love had thudded against the certainty of those statements and failed to breech them. She had sat through countless Sunday school lessons and sermons without the seed of the word of God ever penetrating the hard, pain-baked soil of her heart.

But when Laynie discovered Shaw and Bessie's marked-up Bible, it seemed different.

Or was *she* different?

Laynie had—without setting out to do so—begun reading the Gospels to herself. One after the other, she had gobbled up the words, actually *hearing* them. She read the Gospels aloud, as if hearing the words with her own ears would help her to perceive the Scriptures' underlying meaning.

After leaving Roger at the lake, she opened the well-used Bible to the Gospel of John where she'd been poring over—*devouring*—the works and words of Jesus.

"Chapter 8," she muttered aloud, picking up where she'd left off. "But Jesus went to the Mount of Olives. Now early in the morning he came again into the temple, and all the people came to him. And he sat down and taught them.

"Then the scribes and Pharisees brought to Him a woman caught in adultery. And when they had set her in the midst, they said to Him, 'Teacher, this woman was caught in adultery, in the very act. Now, Moses, in the law, commanded us that such should be stoned. But what do you say?'

"This they said, testing him, that they might have something of which to accuse him. But Jesus stooped down and wrote on the ground with his finger, as though he did not hear."

What was he writing in the dirt?

Most likely a list of all the woman's sins.

Laynie sneered in disgust. *I'll probably never know.*

"So, when they continued asking him, he raised himself up and said to them, 'He who is without sin among you, let him throw a stone at her first.' And again, he stooped down and wrote on the ground.

"Then those who heard it, being convicted by their conscience, went out one by one, beginning with the oldest even to the last. And Jesus was left alone, and the woman standing in the midst.

"When Jesus had raised himself up and saw no one but the woman, he said to her, 'Woman, where are those accusers of yours? Has no one condemned you?'

"She said, 'No one, Lord.' And Jesus said to her, 'Neither do I condemn you. Go, and sin no more.'"

Laynie stopped, thunderstruck. *An adulteress. Caught in the very act. And Jesus said he didn't condemn her? I don't . . . get it.*

She could not help but compare her own sins to those of the adulterous woman—the many acts of fornication, adultery, deception, and betrayal she'd committed in service to her country.

Because it didn't matter. I already knew I was worthless. Offering my body to further the greater good seemed . . . appropriate. Fitting.

Her eyes traced the print back to Jesus' question to the woman and she read aloud, "'Woman, where are those accusers of yours? Has no one condemned you?'"

But he meant it for that *woman, the adulterous woman—not for* me.

Even while she shook her head in denial, she could not evade the spark of hope that leaped within her when she whispered aloud, "And Jesus said to her, 'Neither do I condemn you. go, and sin no more.'"

"'Go, and sin no more,'" she repeated.

The spark inside her flared and caught. *Am I that woman? Is Jesus speaking to me?*

No. But . . . is it possible?

THAT AFTERNOON, LAYNIE was still debating whether to leave or stay. If she stayed, she needed to head down to the bait shop and let them run her card. A big, dangerous step.

Someone knocked on her door. "Elaine? I'd like to talk to you again."

Roger.

Laynie opened the door a crack. She remained leery of his intentions, her greeting, "Yeah? Do you want to come in?" was frosty with unveiled derision.

"Nope. Why don't you grab a coat and come 'round the back with me?"

"I'm busy. Packing up." It was a lie. She hadn't done a thing toward leaving.

"No, you're not. Come on. You're coming with me."

When she didn't move, he growled, "Don't make me get my cuffs, lady."

Angry as she was, Laynie saw he was kidding. Sort of.

She huffed with her own faux indignation, put on her coat, gloves, and a knit hat, and followed him into his backyard. She was surprised to see a small patio, a firepit, and two Adirondack-style wooden chairs drawn up to the blazing fire. Flames roared and jumped about in the pit, sparking and flickering.

"Built us a fire. No sense freezing our butts off while we talk, right?"

"Uh, right." Laynie sat down, sniffing the pine sap that snapped and popped in the firepit, reacquiring a little of the morning's calm. "Okay. What did you want to talk about?"

"Well, I still want to help you."

"Why?"

"Why not?"

"Because I think motives are important."

He nodded. "I agree. Motives are important and . . . well, see . . . I . . ." but his sentence petered out, and he didn't pick it back up.

Something he'd said at the lake clicked into place. "Rog, you told me you were a cop on medical leave. What . . . what for?"

The afternoon had faded into twilight, but she thought she saw a little sadness drop over him, and he sagged in his chair.

"Actually, I should have said I was a cop on disability, and permanent disability, at that."

He sighed. "I have cancer, Elaine. Late stage, small-cell lung cancer. I don't smoke and never have, but there you go—I'm still gonna die, and it won't be very long until I do."

Laynie couldn't catch her breath. Of all the things she imagined him saying to her, this was not it.

She was shocked. Shaken.

Then she started to piece it together. *Thin. Sallow skin. Slow and careful. Bruising. Persistent cough.* The signs had been there, and she'd seen them, but she hadn't made sense of them. Until now.

"Isn't . . . isn't there anything they can do?"

"They can keep me 'comfortable'—says here in fine print. When the doctor told me that I had only two to three months, I decided to spend as much of it up here as I could . . . before I, you know, before I couldn't anymore.

"It's been six weeks, and I'm going downhill fast. I wear a fentanyl patch for the pain, but I can't keep half my food down. I'm weaker. Stumbling. Falling if I'm not mindful. I'll be packing up a week from Monday, heading back to Winnipeg. To a hospice center."

The gun tucked inside her waistband dug into her skin, and she felt ashamed of the motives she'd accused Roger of.

"I'm so sorry, Rog." *For more than you know.*

"It's not your fault, Elaine . . . and, anyway, it's going to be okay. Not the dying part—I doubt that will be fun—but afterward? I know where I'm going when I die, and when I get there? It'll be better than okay. It'll be awesome. Because I'll see Jesus."

He cleared his throat. "Anyway, I wanted to reiterate my offer. I'd like to help you." He reached into his pocket and handed her a folded wad of cash. "I don't need your money, so I'm returning it. Let's keep you off the grid a while longer, shall we? Just stay. Don't use your credit card."

"But . . ."

"And maybe . . . maybe you can make sure I can get myself out of here, on the road when it comes time?"

Laynie took the money, but her hands were shaking. "Yeah. I can do that. And thank you. I . . . I don't understand it, but everywhere I've been since I . . . since I *left*, circumstances have pretty much gone my way—even when it looked like they hadn't—and people, complete strangers . . . strangers like you, have helped me."

"Well, all those things, those blessings? You do know it's the Lord, right? That he's calling to you, trying to get your attention? I knew it that day when you drove up here and asked to camp out under my hay barn. Might as well have been a golden, neon arrow pointing from heaven down to you, it was that obvious in my spirit."

He coughed for a minute, then caught his breath. "I mean, someone must really be pounding on the gates of heaven, praying up a storm for you, eh?" A month ago, even just a week, Laynie would have snarled at him. Cursed him. Today, she couldn't deny what he said.

"I think it has to be my sister, Kari. My mama and dad, too. And the couple who sold Daisy to me."

He made a face. "Daisy?"

"Yeah. Daisy. My trippy hippy-mobile."

"Um, yeah. I wasn't goin' to say anything, but whew! Who picked that upholstery fabric, eh? And that beaded curtain? Haven't seen one of those since the sixties."

They laughed—which made him cough and cough—then they laughed again. The fire crackled and they talked. They roasted sausages on sticks over the fire, Laynie eating and Roger trying but unable to swallow more than a bite or two. Opening up to each other.

As evening drew on, Laynie sighed in concern for Rog, concern mixed with relief. She didn't need to leave this hiding place yet, this place of peace. She was safe again.

For a little longer.

CHAPTER 25
⟨⟨ LP ⟩⟩

SUNDAY AFTERNOON, a week later, Roger knocked on Laynie's door. She figured he'd be coming. Last night as they sat before the firepit—they'd made a standing event of meeting there each evening since that first time— he'd reminded her that he'd be leaving the following morning.

When she answered his knock, he was leaned against Daisy, hanging on the door's grab handle, barely standing. She stepped down from Daisy's doorway and pulled a little folding camp seat after her, knowing he needed it. He tried to sit, but his legs gave out. She caught him, helped him down to the seat, kept him from falling over.

It grieved her to see how quickly he'd deteriorated. In just days, he'd gone from noticeably thin to frail and emaciated, his breathing, labored. She didn't know how he'd made it from the house to her RV under his own steam. And although she had promised to make sure he made it to the hospice center in Winnipeg, he still acted like he could get there without help.

Laynie no longer believed him.

"Leaving . . . tomorrow. You're . . . welcome to stay on . . . long as you like. Realtor knows you're . . . here."

He'd told her about his arrangements that had been in place for a while. He'd made his will. His church family and fellow officers would take charge of his service, burial, and personal effects. He'd engaged a realtor to sell his townhouse in the city and his parents' lake house. He'd designated the profits from them to various friends and charities.

Laynie licked her lips. "Well, I'm thinking about coming with you, Rog. Actually, I was thinking of driving you to town myself. To the . . . hospice center."

Was that relief washing his face?

"What . . . 'bout Daisy?"

"If it's okay, like you said, I'll leave her here. I'll come back and pick her up . . . later on."

Or not.

She didn't know at this point.

He nodded and swayed. She caught him before he slid off the camp seat to the ground—and decided to amend their timetable.

"I'm going to help you back to your house, Rog, and get you packed up. Is that all right?"

"Y-yeah."

Laynie helped him to his feet, grabbed the little camp seat, and took it with them—and was glad that she had. Roger had to stop and rest several times on the short walk back to his house. By the time she got him to his front door, he could no longer stand on his own. She settled him in a recliner where, by all appearances, he'd slept for some nights.

She pulled up an ottoman and sat next to the recliner. "What do you need me to pack for you, Rog?"

"Can't . . . take with you."

She was initially confused. Then she saw the tears standing in his eyes.

You can't take it with you. Going into hospice . . . and beyond, he would need nothing.

She fought back her own tears. "Will you want your Bible . . . to hold on to?"

He nodded, and one hand flopped toward the end table. There it was, with an envelope from the hospice center sticking out from its pages. Laynie picked up the Bible, slid out the envelope, and laid the Bible in his lap. Roger sighed his thanks.

Laynie pulled the letter from the envelope and read it over. Reread the address and protocol for checking in.

"Rog? Would you like go today? This afternoon rather than tomorrow?"

He again nodded.

Laynie swallowed down the lump in her throat. "I'll get the Jeep ready."

She found the keys to Roger's Jeep, returned to Daisy, and packed everything she wanted to take with her into her wheeled suitcase. She zipped the bag closed and then spotted Shaw and Bessie's travel Bible. She tucked it into her purse.

When she had deposited her suitcase in the back of Roger's Jeep and her purse on the front seat, she went looking for a sleeping bag. She found one on a shelf in his closet and grabbed a pillow from his bed. She used these and a blanket to make up a bed across the rear seat of his Jeep. She grabbed a few bottles of water for the road and threw them on the passenger seat, then drove around to the front porch.

"I've arranged for you to lie down in the back, Rog."

She helped him up and half-dragged, half-carried him to the waiting vehicle. Before he got in, he looked around a last time. He smiled, gazing toward the lake, then at her.

"G-grateful . . . Lord brought you . . . 'Laine. Thank you . . . for blessing me . . . for sharing . . . my last days here."

"H-he used you to help me, too, Rog. I'm the blessed one."

With tears streaming unheeded down her cheeks, Laynie realized how truly grateful she was for this place and the short season of peace that had healed many of her wounds. And for Roger's company.

You did this. You orchestrated this. Thank you.

She didn't say, "Lord" or "God" or "Jesus." She was afraid to. Wasn't quite ready to "go there."

"No one can be saved without repentance. Repentance is where we— every one of us—acknowledge and confess our sinful, needy state before God and ask for forgiveness through the blood of Jesus. A place where we surrender fully to the Lordship of Christ."

When she had Roger settled on the back seat, she locked up the house. She drove down the drive, onto the dirt road and out to the village, taking it slow for Roger's sake. At the bait shop she pulled in and got out. Went inside.

"Hello, Elaine," Bart said. "How are you and Roger getting on?"

Laynie exhaled. "We're leaving today, Bart." She drew two sets of keys from her pocket. "Would you . . . see to the house and to my RV?"

He slowly took the keys from her hand.

"Um, Roger's lying in the back seat, and I figured you and Liz would like to say goodbye."

Bart stood still, staring at the counter between them, nodding slowly. "We would. Yes."

Laynie stayed in the store until he and Liz, both weeping, returned.

LATE THAT EVENING, Laynie checked Roger into the hospice center not far from the University of Manitoba. The staff members were calm, capable, and compassionate, carrying Roger from the Jeep to his room, bathing him, dressing him in clean pajamas, putting him to bed, making him comfortable.

The charge nurse approached Laynie. "Hello. I'm Reina. You are?"

"Elaine. I'm a friend. Roger doesn't have any family."

She nodded, already aware that he didn't. "Well, Elaine, we've assessed Roger's condition. His form of cancer is very aggressive, and his body is already shutting down. Since his signed orders refuse the use of an IV, I don't think he'll linger with us more than a few days. You are welcome to stay with him. We'll bring in a cot for you."

Laynie hadn't planned on staying . . . but how could she leave Roger to die alone?

I can't do that. You put Rog in my life and put me . . . here. For him.

"That would be nice. Thank you."

She sat next to Roger's bed and took his hand. He opened his eyes once, tried to smile. In her heart she heard him say, *"It's going to be okay. Not the dying part—I doubt that will be fun—but afterward? I know where I'm going when I die, and when I get there? It'll be better than okay. It'll be awesome. Because I'll see Jesus."*

"You'll be okay, Rog, remember? It'll be awesome . . . because Jesus will be there. And I'll stay with you until . . . until you go. I won't leave."

He closed his eyes, but Laynie felt him squeeze her hand.

Sitting in his darkened room, watching him slip into a sleep from which he would not wake, Laynie leaned her weary head on their joined hands.

You've been a good friend to me, Rog. I won't forget you—and I truly hope "the other side" is as awesome as you said it would be.

ROGER PASSED QUIETLY in the night. When the hospice center wakened to its morning routine and Laynie realized he was gone, she notified the staff. They had Roger's instructions for what to do when he died.

Laynie gathered her purse and, at the staff's request, went to wait in the lobby.

Wait? Wait for what?

They assume I knew him better than I did. That I had a reason to stick around.

Through the open curtains she saw that the day was a dank, leaden gray, the sky heavy with rain-bearing clouds. As she had when she and the Bradshaws parted company, she felt alone. Bereft.

What do I do now?

She spoke to the charge nurse. "Do you have a phone I might use?"

"Yes, we keep one for the use of family members. That room there."

The phone had a Winnipeg phone book next to it. Laynie looked up cab companies and placed a call. "Hello. I'd like a taxi, please."

She gave the address of the hospice center, then removed her suitcase from Roger's trunk and left it just inside the center's front entrance.

She approached the charge nurse again. "These are the keys to Roger's Jeep."

The nurse took them reluctantly. "We have no instructions regarding his vehicle."

"I think his church will know what to do with it."

A taxi was pulling into the parking lot. Laynie grabbed her suitcase on the way out and flagged it down.

"Say, what day is it?" she asked the driver.

"What day is it? Monday. October 8. You been in a cave or something?"

Laynie ignored his question. "I need an HSBC bank, please, whichever branch is closest to the Greyhound station."

At the bank, she withdrew another two thousand in cash, then had the cabbie drive her to the Greyhound station. During the ride, Laynie pondered how she felt inside. *A week into October? It should be mid-November already.* Had she spent only two-and-a-half weeks at the lake? Fewer than twenty days of peace and freedom?

Peace. Freedom. I don't think I can survive without those anymore.

With time on her hands, Laynie fumbled in her purse and powered on her mobile phone. She'd turned it off when she left Ottawa and had left it off until packing yesterday afternoon. The battery had been dead when she'd slipped it into her purse, but she had charged it in Roger's Jeep on the drive from the lake into the city.

As the phone came on line, five text messages pinged their arrival—all from Shaw and Bessie. The earliest messages started out with, "We've arrived at our son's house. All is well," and the final message evolved to, "We're really worried about you. Please let us know you're all right?"

Laynie wasn't going to reply, but the Bradshaws' anxious faces rose before her. She shot off a quick text to let them know she was okay but that she'd been out of cell range. She then slipped the phone back into her purse.

Minutes later, she received another text—one that made her smile.

"Thank God! We're so glad you are all right. We have been praying hard for you."

She texted back, "Thank you. I'm very grateful."

At the station, Laynie perused the schedule and routes. She found a bus that would leave Winnipeg at noon, travel down 75 to a Canadian–US border crossing, join I-29 on the other side, and continue on to Grand Forks, North Dakota. She would wait until the last minute to purchase her ticket, paying cash for it.

Since the bus didn't leave for hours, she went in search of something to eat, suddenly aware that she hadn't eaten since lunch the day before. When she finished, she used the restroom. In the stall, she removed the HK P7K3 and extra magazine from her purse and tucked them into her bra into the hollow between her breasts. Unless she gave Customs and Border Protection agents reason to, they rarely searched Americans crossing into their own country.

But that was before terrorists attacked us.

Laynie considered leaving the gun behind, then discarded the notion. Having a means to protect herself was worth the risk of being found with a gun in her possession.

The wheels of government bureaucracy don't move that quickly. They won't have put stricter rules in place yet—but that surely will change.

She also wasn't sure how she'd move on from Grand Forks after she'd crossed into the States, but she knew where she was headed.

And she had time enough to figure it out.

A PROGRAM CHIMED in the headset she wore. Vyper cracked her gum, rolled her chair from her RCMP terminal to the one she used for her "other" employment, and entered the password to unlock the screen.

She smiled when she saw the alert. *There you are! Came up for air, did you? Or should I say, for money?*

She pulled up a map on the terminal's second monitor and stuck a virtual "pin" at the bank's location. *Winnipeg. What's next, Elaine? Will you disappear on me again now that you have a fresh supply of cash?*

A half-dozen chimes sounded in her headset, and Vyper toggled to another screen. *Ah. And you've turned on your phone. Finally!*

She dropped another pin on the map to indicate the tower off which the phone had pinged, then opened a window into Elaine's mobile service provider and displayed the texts. She chuckled aloud. "Oh, my. Someone loves you, Elaine."

Another chime. She read a text Elaine sent in reply—but her phone had pinged a mile from where she had received the texts. Vyper dropped another pin. "I see you're on the move, Elaine. Where are you going, my dear? Back into your little hidey-hole? Please give me more clues. Pretty please?"

She waited in the hope that her target would continue to use her phone. Just as she'd given up for the time being and decided to go back to her work terminal, her headset chimed the arrival of yet another text.

She scanned its contents. It read, "Thank God! We're so glad you are all right. We have been praying hard for you."

Vyper was puzzled. *How archaic. Someone praying for you.*

Another text. "Thank you. I'm very grateful."

Vyper was intrigued. *Hmm. You interest me, Elaine. You're not behaving like the Russians' usual fare. I wonder why this Zakhar person is so intent on finding you—did you accidentally see something you shouldn't have?*

Pity. Dimitri is not a nice boy.

She frowned as the thought of Zakhar intruded. Zakhar? He had ignored her instructions not to call her unless it was necessary. "Do not call me, Zakhar. If my daily email reads, 'No Activity,' it *means* no activity. It means I have nothing to tell you."

"I will call you whenever I choose until you *find her!*" he had shouted back, unleashing enough profanity to singe the "wires" between his phone and her ears.

While he rained down his vile curses and threats, Vyper had popped another stick of Black Jack into her mouth, leaned back in her chair, and daydreamed about upsetting Zakhar's life—formulating how she might send an auction house to empty his modest apartment in Moscow and then hire a realtor to sell the apartment, promising him or her a sizeable bonus from the profits for *lowballing* the price. She especially liked the part in her pretend scenario where Zakhar returned to Russia and inserted the key in his front door only to find it no longer worked.

She had snickered aloud to herself—which earned her a fresh tirade of Zakhar's rage.

The man had vented more frustration and anger with each succeeding phone call—until she'd had enough. He'd gotten under Vyper's skin like a tick and, like all ticks, needed to be extracted.

How I would like to squish you like the great, bloodsucking insect you are! You want results, Zakhar? I will give you results.

She sent him first to Toronto, fooling him with a series of faked pings from Elaine Granger's mobile phone. When he checked into a Toronto hotel after a long night's drive—and before he'd had time to catch up on lost sleep—she provided him with more "pings," and he had followed them all over the city, even to a mall where Vyper assured him Elaine's phone continued to ping. Zakhar had crisscrossed the mall, showing her photograph from store to store for hours, until the mall closed.

When he'd called to berate her the next morning, cranky from lack of sleep, Vyper coolly informed him that Elaine Granger had crossed over the Canadian–US border into New York. She led him on another merry chase that ended in Binghamton, where she texted him, "Have lost signal. Will text as soon as I reacquire it."

That had been three days ago. Today she knew Elaine Granger was in Winnipeg.

"You have money, Elaine. Now what?"

It occurred to Vyper that Elaine Granger may have ditched her motor home.

"Let's find the airport, shall we?" she whispered to herself. She located it on her map, then tracked back to the three cell phone pings.

One ping is a data point. Two pings in close proximity confirm location. But three pings? Three pings form a line, my dear—and a line has direction.

The line pointed northwest—in the general direction of the airport.

"Ah, yes—but do you prefer to ride the bus, Elaine?"

She located the Greyhound station and discovered that it was practically adjacent to the airport.

"Not a problem," she murmured, customizing more of her code. "Whether you buy an airline ticket or a bus ticket, my dear, I will know it nearly as soon as you do."

She launched the programs into the Greyhound computer system and the systems of the various airlines that serviced Winnipeg, rewarded herself with a stick of gum, then texted Zakhar.

"Granger on the move. Left New York and entered Pennsylvania. Will update you soonest."

Humming to herself, Vyper returned to her regular duties. When an alert next chimed in her ear? She would know both where Elaine Granger was going and how she intended to travel there.

ZAKHAR STARED IN disgust at the latest text Vyper had sent to his phone. He no longer deluded himself that the hacker Baskin had recommended was giving him accurate data that would result in Linnéa Olander's apprehension.

She has been leading me, all right. Leading me on a fool's journey—and I am the fool. Well, no more.

He was in New York, after all. He knew people in New York, old comrades from the army who had immigrated to America. He could reach out to them and hire his own resources—*Russian* resources.

HALF AN HOUR before her bus was scheduled to leave, Laynie produced her US passport and driver's license and bought her ticket. The clerk handed her a pamphlet and ran through his border-crossing spiel.

"The bus will stop at the US Customs and Border Protection checkpoint and all passengers will disembark and process through individually with their luggage. You must produce your passport, birth certificate, or citizenship card, state your purpose for entering the US and the length of your stay, and declare any goods purchased in Canada exceeding eight hundred dollars. The list of items restricted from entry into the US can be found on this page."

When the voice on the loudspeaker called her bus, Laynie found a seat near the emergency exit and hefted her carry-on into the rack above her head. She leaned her head against the window and closed her eyes.

She didn't intend to sleep, but she did, and did not wake until the bus pulled into the siding at the border station. Like the other passengers, Laynie removed her suitcase from the bus and queued up to pass through inspection.

Although a single armed agent stood guard, keeping watchful eyes on the proceedings—perhaps on the lookout for any perceived threat—the process was unremarkable.

"Welcome home, Ms. Granger," the agent said, handing back her passport and driver's license.

"Thank you."

Welcome home?

Laynie found it hard to swallow. She had not entered the US except while in Petroff's stifling control since that horrible January when Sammie died. And after years under Petroff's thumb? She had nearly given up ever seeing home again.

Home! Mama. Dad. Kari. Shannon. Robbie.

Nearly there.

———⊶⊷———

CHAPTER 26

LP

THE BUS ARRIVED IN Grand Forks after night had fallen. Grand Forks may have been no big shakes in anyone else's book, but to Laynie it was the last stop before her destination. She had to remind herself not to smile as she purchased a few snacks and one innocuous souvenir inside the station—making some discreet inquiries while paying.

She checked into a two-star motel a block down from the station but found it hard to sleep after napping on the bus. She was up early, preparing for the final leg of her journey.

In much the same way as when she had she fled Moncton, Laynie tied her hair into a ponytail and tucked it under a baseball cap, a new one with a picture of South Dakota's Mount Rushmore on it, then tugged on jeans and layered a warm flannel shirt over a T-shirt.

She dug in her suitcase and pulled out her old backpack. She slid her laptop into the backpack first. Not much room remained. She'd keep what was most essential and leave the rest behind. Then she emptied her purse, choosing to keep her wallet, passport, phone, and the CD-ROM case. What else? Her eyes fell on the Bradshaws' travel Bible.

Yeah, you, she admitted.

She added her hairbrush and whatever clothes would fit into the backpack. The leftovers, including her purse, she crammed into a trash sack.

When she was ready, she donned her warm jacket and gloves, zipped her gun into a coat pocket, hoisted the backpack onto her back, and grabbed the trash sack and her empty suitcase. A bitter wind hit her as she left her room. Behind the motel, she tossed the trash sack into the garbage but left the suitcase leaned up against the dumpster.

It's a nice case. Someone will spot it and snatch it up. It'll be gone within the hour.

With only her backpack to carry, Laynie hiked the half mile to a truck stop the helpful young man on the bus station's cash register had told her about. She was glad to get inside the truck stop's restaurant, out of the freezing wind.

Before an hour was up, she'd eaten a hearty breakfast, grabbed a coffee to go, and snagged a ride with an amiable trucker heading south, destination Kansas City.

"SO, YOU'VE CROSSED over into the States, Elaine," Vyper mused, "but the heart of the American badlands cannot be your destination, can it? So, tell me, where will you go next? Where are you headed?"

She slowly unwrapped a stick of Black Jack but did not fold it into her mouth. She was uneasy. Zakhar had not called in two days to harangue her. He had gone quiet—and his silence sent alarms blaring in Vyper's head.

When a toddler stops making noise, one must be quick to search out the mischief he's created.

She hacked into Zakhar's phone provider and found a series of texts and a short list of calls. The contents of the texts were concerning enough, but when she back-traced the numbers to New York City, the short hairs on the back of her shaved neck stood up and shivered.

Zakhar had reached out to a soldier in the *russkaya mafiya*, also known as the Russian *Bratva*—the Russian Brotherhood. The texts between Zakhar and the mob soldier were friendly and familiar. From Zakhar's references, Vyper realized they were most likely former comrades in arms from their Soviet Army days.

When she drilled down into the friend's phone records, her alarm grew. She suspected that this friend of Zakhar's was a soldier in the Odessa Mafia, the most powerful Russian organized crime mob operating in the States. They were headquartered in Brighton Beach, a borough of Brooklyn in and around Coney Island. However, the Odessa Mafia did not consider themselves "Russian." They were fiercely Ukrainian, financed and run by the richest oligarchs living in the Ukraine, heavy into arms smuggling, drugs, and human trafficking. They were known for their ferocious code of loyalty and their merciless pursuit of those who broke that code.

She traced the soldier's calls and texts, landing on a text that confirmed her worries. Zakhar had asked for and been granted assistance from a *mafiya* brigadier—a mafia captain who reported to the local *Pakhan* or Boss.

Zakhar, you scum! You haven't called to harass me because you have hired Odessa Mafia hackers to locate Elaine Granger's whereabouts!

Vyper bristled over the unexpected twist. She knew the best Odessa Mafia's hacker by his reputation and by his handle. *Syla.* His name translated from Ukrainian meant "The Power."

The kid was good, world-class good. But "The Power" good?

Vyper slowly put the stick of gum in her mouth. *Nah. Not as powerful as Vyper venom. But if Zakhar gave Syla the Granger woman's information, then*

Syla has already hacked her phone provider and is aware of Granger's recent activities. He will have informed Zakhar of Granger's entry into the States.

Her dislike for Zakhar intensified.

She had only misdirected Zakhar because he had become a pain in her backside, but her misdirection had created a bigger problem. It had caused Zakhar to team with perverts worse than himself.

Vyper was not afraid to admit that she profited from illegal hacks, but even criminals had their standards. In her book, men who trafficked women and children were the scum of the earth, the lowest of the low—and her perusal of Zakhar's laptop had placed him firmly in the camp of the perverts and sadists so abhorrent to her.

And if she detested Zakhar, she *despised* Syla. In the employ of the Odessa mob, Syla developed and promulgated porn—even "kiddie" porn, a horrible evil. And Syla and his crew sold women and children on the web.

Zakhar and Syla were two of the same filthy ilk—and now they were working together?

Hmm. I doubt that Zakhar's boss knows that Zakhar has hired the Odessa Mob. I wonder how he would feel about that?

She backtracked to Zakhar's phone and pinged its location. He was on the move, had crossed back into Canada, headed west.

I assume he is driving rather than flying to avoid the intense scrutiny at security checkpoints and the ongoing air travel delays in the wake of the attacks.

It would take Zakhar long days of driving to catch up to his prey.

Tapping an unopened pack of gum on the desk beside her keyboard, she considered the situation and its ramifications, tossed around one or two creative solutions.

Vyper tore open the pack with practiced ease, pulled out a piece, and unwrapped it one-handed. She folded the stick of gum into her mouth and bit down. With a last look at her map, she cleared it of pins, then dropped two, only two, one a few hours west of Ottawa, the other on Grand Forks. How long would it take Zakhar to catch up to Elaine Granger?

Well, Elaine, my dear, it looks like Zakhar is on to you now, and I have a contract to fulfill, after all, so I shouldn't interfere in Zakhar's business.

She thought a minute more.

Or perhaps I should.

THE TRUCKER STOPPED for lunch at the south end of Sioux City. After she had eaten, Laynie took a walk to stretch her legs. The Missouri River wasn't far from the truck stop. It formed the boundary separating Iowa from Nebraska, and she had caught glimpses of the river from the highway as it followed the river's course through the city.

I'm so close, she thought, *mere hours from Kari's little farm.*

The notion chafed her, because she wasn't going to Kari's farm. She couldn't.

Instead, she stared out to the southwest, trying to imagine the vast acres of low, undulating hills Kari had described—the land Kari and Søren lived on—and the old, broken-down house Kari had told her about, an actual "little house on the prairie." Kari had taken pains to preserve the home their shared great-grandmother Rose Thoresen and her husband had lived in.

"More than a hundred and thirty years ago," Laynie whispered to herself. "I have ancestors who were the first to farm the land not far from here . . . and blood relations who live there still."

Shaking her head, Laynie returned to the truck stop. She rode with the friendly trucker until they reached the outskirts of Omaha and the junction of I-29 and I-80. The trucker was continuing south to Kansas City, but Laynie was not. Her destination was to the west.

He drove his rig onto the road's shoulder—something he wasn't supposed to do—not far from the interchange where the two highways intersected and let Laynie out of his cab.

"You hike on up that slope and follow the highway off to the right. When you clear the interchange traffic, you should be able to catch another ride."

"Thank you, Roy. You've been kind to me."

"And you've been good company, Beverly. I wish you well."

Laynie waved, shouldered her backpack, and set off, keeping well clear of the roadbed and speeding traffic on her left. On her right were fields and some industrial buildings. She kept walking, not anxious for a ride, because up ahead, after she joined I-80, the highway crossed over the river. She was going to see it up close after all.

She walked onto the bridge, which had a wide shoulder and, for a long time, she stared out onto the river. It was like most any river, nothing special, but as she left the railing to continue across, she looked up and ahead saw the sign over the roadway.

NEBRASKA . . . the good life.

Laynie started walking. Maybe a good life did await her. Someday.

It was already coming up on four in the afternoon. She wanted to find another motel before dark, but she wasn't seeing anything ahead except more highway bypassing the town. She faced the oncoming traffic and held out her thumb. After ten fruitless minutes, a car pulled over. Two teens sat in the front seat. The passenger rolled down his window and leaned out.

"You want a ride?"

"Yes, please. Where are you headed?"

"Just into town."

Laynie got in and they sped off.

She watched the young men, a year or two out of high school, as they tried to study her in the rearview mirror without being obvious. She figured she knew what was running around in their heads. excited, testosterone-driven pipe dreams, bold but stupid.

"Could you drop me near a motel?"

They glanced at each other.

"Sure," the driver said.

Laynie sighed. "I hope you aren't nurturing any big ideas about the three of us, gentlemen. I'm probably as old as your moms are."

A lot less exuberant than they'd been when they picked her up, the boys let Laynie out at an intersection with hotels on all four corners. They mumbled their goodbyes and drove off.

Laynie made for the closest motel.

One more leg. Tomorrow she'd be there.

BEFORE SHE LEFT work for the day, Vyper checked Zakhar's phone a last time. He had driven nearly nonstop over the past twenty hours and had just checked into a Winnipeg hotel.

She giggled to herself. *Goodness, you must be beat! My poor little Zakhar.*

He would have to sleep for hours to recover. While he did, Vyper planted a "cron job" in Elaine Granger's phone provider's system, a piece of code that would run at the time she specified, three o'clock the next morning. When it did, Syla would catch it and roust Zakhar from his bed.

"That should get you up and moving before you're fully rested and keep you busy for a while."

Tossing some crumpled gum wrappers in the trash, she logged off her terminals and left work, debating with herself where to pick up dinner.

CHAPTER 27

LAYNIE TOOK A CAB to the Omaha bus station and caught a Trailways bus for the last leg of her journey. The trip took an hour. She arrived midmorning.

She strolled into a gas station and bought a newspaper and a detailed map of the city, then headed across the street to a restaurant where she ordered lunch and began to orient herself to the town's layout. Once she had her destination located on the map, she began to peruse the newspaper for rentals. Furnished studio apartments near the UNL east campus—the east campus, home to the agriculture college.

She powered on her phone. "Hello? I'm calling about your apartments. How close are they to the university? No, I'm not a student, but I would like to live close to the east campus. Can you tell me about your apartments? The ad said you provide Internet service?"

She listened, then answered, "I've just arrived in Lincoln. However, I have first and last month's rent and will be looking for work. Yes, my credit report should be clean. May I come by to see the apartment?"

She scribbled the address and added directions, although she planned to take a cab. "Perfect. I'll see you in an hour. Thank you."

She hung up and closed her eyes to think. She had money and an American ID—but Zakhar had uncovered her Elaine Granger alias, and she did not have another ID at hand.

Can I fly under his radar for a time? That was the burning question.

I should be able to use other resources under the name of Elaine Granger, resources he knows nothing about, and I can be creative with my arrangements. Keep my footprint small.

Just a few weeks, then I'll seek out another set of papers.

And yet, regardless of her logic, everything within her tensed. She had been out from under Petroff's thumb for less than two months. It hardly felt real or lasting, and her instincts advised extreme caution.

What about Marstead? According to the conversation Christor had recorded, this mysterious director, Jack Wolfe has retracted the retirement order Saunders directed against me.

But could she count on what this Jack Wolfe person said? *Trust but verify.* That's what Christor had advised.

She flinched. *Christor! I haven't contacted him since . . . . since Montreal. He must be worried about me.*

How far away and long ago that conversation seemed! It would soon be a month since she'd last spoken to him.

Well, I can't contact him yet. I have more pressing things to do first.

VYPER WAS GIDDY with excitement when she arrived at work that morning to check the status of her cron job. She slipped on her headphones and logged into her terminals. A series of chimes greeted her, and she grinned as she pulled up the texts between the Odessa hacker and Zakhar. The latest, in terse, clipped shorthand, made her chuckle deep in her throat.

"Credit crd shows subj on bus Grand Forks 2 Detroit, arr. Fri 9pm. No phone use past 24hr"

Vyper put the first stick of gum of the day in her mouth and chewed, giggling with delight as she did. "And you won't see any of Elaine's phone activity, bud. Not as long as my code is running in her provider's system."

Vyper particularly liked the idea of Zakhar jumping back into his car to race Elaine Granger's bus to its imaginary destination.

Detroit.

She laughed to herself the rest of the day.

LAYNIE TOOK THE furnished studio on sight. It wasn't the best or worst place she'd ever stayed in, but it had the two elements she desired most. proximity to the university's east campus and it came with Internet service as part of the rent. She didn't need her credit card to sign up for it—and that was the ticket. cash only from here on out.

With keys in hand and having turned over eight hundred dollars of her cash supply to the apartment manager, she stepped into her new digs, dropped her backpack on the sofa bed, pulled out her laptop and modem, and plugged in the broadband cable.

Once she was connected to the Internet, she browsed banks near the university and picked the one closest to her apartment. She left her apartment, walked to the bank branch, and jumped through the hoops required to open an account. She showed her D.C. driver's license and her passport as proof of her ID and deposited a hundred dollars.

"I've just moved here," she said, but gave the bank a phony Lincoln address, electing to receive her bank statements online.

On the way home, she stopped at a Radio Shack and purchased a headset with a built-in microphone.

"Gamer, huh?" the clerk asked.

Laynie winked. "You know it."

She returned to her apartment and spent the next hour wiring money from another of her foreign accounts into her new account, then browsing the university's student directory and campus maps.

It was 3:30 when she bundled up and walked onto the campus to eyeball Burr Hall for herself. The dorm was a dated three-story red brick building across 35th Street from The Robert Hillestad Textiles Gallery and kitty-corner from the UNL College of Agricultural Sciences.

She sat down at some picnic tables in the common space between Burr Hall and its companion dorm, Fedde Hall. She pulled out her morning's newspaper and pretended to read. The seat was cold, and Laynie didn't know what she expected to see, but she sat, keeping a casual eye on students as they came and went.

Soon after 4:00 p.m., a troop of young men in high spirits exited the dorm onto the grassy commons lot connecting the two dorms. Between them—ten, Laynie counted—they manhandled a number of plywood stand-up structures onto the lawn. Laynie watched with interest as they set up the structures across the field—like walls or obstacles of varying heights and widths—and placed them in a formation she was unfamiliar with.

The boys went back to retrieve two duffle bags and a few more walls that they added to the others, staggered across the grass, forming a course—although for what, Laynie still couldn't imagine.

The walls themselves? It looked to her as if a crazed artist with a penchant for orange had been turned loose on them. Using her side view, Laynie's gaze kept returning to the young man whose shaggy and distinctive strawberry-blonde hair had captured her attention and whose face was familiar from photographs Laynie had studied over the years.

"Hello, Max," Laynie said softly.

By now, spectators other than Laynie were gathering to watch, so she assumed whatever was about to take place was a regular event. The picnic tables were soon occupied by an audience of chattering students who apparently gathered at this time on a regular basis and knew one another.

With a great deal of shouted banter and rearrangement of barriers, the boys declared the course ready. They unzipped the duffle bags and produced over-the-head vests that tied on the sides in two colors, blue and green. They separated into teams—evidently, they'd done so before—donned their team colors, and handed around plastic hand guns and clear tubes filled with orange balls about two-thirds of an inch in diameter.

Then Laynie understood—she was about to witness a paintball battle! The boys were having so much fun getting ready for their skirmish that she laughed aloud with the other spectators.

Sort of like the bean shooters we used during training. I wonder if Marstead uses paint guns now? No disputing whether or not you've been hit—not with a splat of fluorescent orange bearing witness.

Laynie didn't want to think how many years back that training was.

Their leader or organizer blew a whistle he had hanging from his neck and gathered the players for last minute instructions. "First things. Have you paid Tom your dues? No pay, no play, got it? The ammo and CO2 canisters don't grow on trees, y'know?"

One player shouted, "Yeah, I know you sound like my dad, man! 'Thet there money don't grow on trees, Chad.'"

Amid chuckles and groans, the players forked over their fees to a player on the green team.

The leader continued, "Remember. Any direct hit on your vest, and you're 'dead.' Drop where you are—*without* firing any last shots. Each player has two paintball tubes. That's twenty rounds apiece. Use your ammo wisely, 'cause when you're out, you are dead meat walking!

"If all members of your team die, the other team wins—or if both teams have used all their ammo, then the team with the most players left alive wins. However, in the event that both teams have used all their ammo and the teams have an equal number of players remaining, the teams will each pick a single player to engage in a sudden-death playoff. Got it?"

"Got it!" the players yelled.

The cheering section around Laynie erupted in shouts and screams for their favorite team or player.

The opposing teams ran to the wall at their end of the field, and Laynie leaned forward, more excited and eager to watch what happened next than she'd been in a long time.

At the sound of the opening whistle, the game began. Both teams sent out two players who ran up the opposite sides of the course to attack their opponents from the ends of their wall and draw them out, much like Berserkers were sent to blow a hole through the enemy's fortifications. Max, in a blue vest, raced up the side to the midpoint of the field and then—unexpectedly— cut diagonally across the field to skirt around the opposing team's player who was focused on Max's teammate.

Realizing he'd been flanked, the boy whirled to fire on Max—except Max had dropped to the grass and rolled onto his belly. His gun came up under his opponent's arm and fired two splattering rounds into the player's center mass. Shouting his chagrin, the green player dropped and laid still.

Max, though, had spun quickly onto his back. The opponent he'd left unchecked had crossed the field of play and come up behind him.

Max was ready. From his back on the grass, he sent another two rounds into his new opponent's vest. His team shouted with glee and charged forward *en masse*.

Good moves, Max! Laynie cheered in silence, a broad smile on her face.

Max and his mate flattened themselves behind walls opposite each other and signaled the remainder of his team to duck behind walls ahead of the field's midpoint.

The blue captain shouted to Max and his partner, "Advance!" and to his team, "Cover them!"

Max drew enemy fire from the greens but made it to the next shielding barrier unscathed. In the same fashion, his teammate advanced up the opposite side of the field. They were now in position to attack the hunkered-down greens from two sides and drive them out from behind their shelter.

The three remaining green players, seeing their options vanish, decided on full-on attack. They toppled their wall forward and trampled over it, guns popping out little orange balls in quick succession. Much like Butch Cassidy and the Sundance Kid, though, they were met by a hail of paintballs from three directions.

Shouting their glee, Max and his teammates surrounded and pelted their opponents mercilessly. Moments later, the entire green team lay defeated on the field, while the blues had lost only one of their players—Max. The greens, admitting to themselves that they were going down, had focused their fire on Max in retaliation for the bold moves that had led to their defeat.

As quickly as that, the game was over. The blues shouted their victory, and the spectator section roared its approval.

That was a whole lot of work, preparation, and hoopla for less than ten minutes of play, Laynie thought, but she was as infected by the players' enthusiasm as they were.

A physical and emotional break after a long day of classes and assignments? Yeah, I can see that.

The "dead" green players were up now, stripping off their vests, laughing and shouting insults at the winning blue team.

Guys from the cheering section swarmed the blue players, pounding them on their backs, congratulating them. They helped disassemble the walls and tote them back to their unseen storage place.

"Tomorrow, same time," the leader shouted, "for those not leaving early for the long weekend."

Laynie kept Max, still celebrating with his buddies, in her peripheral vision until he disappeared into the dorm. Then she walked back to her apartment, a small smile on her face.

WHEN HER HEADSET chimed, Vyper rolled her chair to her "other" terminal, logged in, and stared at the alert. Elaine Granger had just moved money from one of her foreign accounts to . . . Vyper followed the money trail and zeroed in on the financial institution.

"Lincoln, Nebraska? Still using Elaine Granger, too. Huh! Girl, you really need to get a life—a *different* life. Don't you know we're all *on* to this one?"

Vyper burrowed into Elaine's new account, found the address, ran it, and pouted. "That's a fabric store, Elaine, not your real address—but never you fear. I'll still find your little bolt hole."

Vyper pulled together code and added the search parameters. All ISPs within five miles of the branch where Elaine opened her new account.

She ran the program. It returned *twelve* Internet service providers!

"College town," she muttered. "Thousands of privileged American students. *Faugh!*"

Vyper modified her program further. all devices connecting for the first time. Timeframe. within the past forty-eight hours. She was generous in her timeframe. She preferred to err on the generous side than miss the device she was looking for by being stingy.

The last parameter was the exact build of Elaine Granger's Dell laptop.

She tunneled into the twelve ISPs, one at a time, and ran her program against their system records.

On the eighth ISP, one record popped.

"Got you."

———— ⚬⚭⚬ ————

CHAPTER 28

LP

LAYNIE WOKE UP early Thursday morning to reconnect with Christor. He picked up on the second ring.

"Linnéa? Linnéa, is that you?"

Laynie blinked in surprise. *No one has called me Linnéa in weeks. I'm not Linnéa any longer.*

"Yes, it's me."

"Thank God! I have called you every day. I was beginning to think . . ."

"I'm okay, Christor. I'm fine, in fact. I just . . . I figured I should assure you that I'm okay."

She changed the subject. "How are Klara and the baby?"

Laynie could hear Christor smile across the miles.

"They are great. Our little one is twenty weeks along now, and Klara is getting big."

"I'm so happy for you both."

They said nothing for a few seconds, then Laynie figured it was time to get into the business at hand. "Listen, I need to know what you've heard about Petroff."

Christor, too, became serious. "It's sort of strange, Linnéa."

"What is?"

"Petroff has dropped out of sight. No one has seen or heard of him in, well, in weeks."

"*What?*" Laynie let the news sink in, turned it over in her mind. Would Petroff's disappearance explain why Zakhar had continued chasing her? "What's Marstead's take on Petroff's disappearance?"

"They are worried. Concerned, but uncertain."

As am I, Laynie realized.

"Possibilities?"

Christor sniffed. "He could be dead or in FSB custody."

"But that would imply that the FSB knows about me, that my cover is blown—and would, furthermore, make the entire Marstead organization suspect."

"Word from on high came down ten days ago. All Marstead operatives within the Russian Federation were to cease active operation, take extreme precautions, and prepare to evac on a moment's notice. Things here are very tense, Linnéa."

"I don't understand! Could someone have intercepted the package I had you send Petroff?"

She swallowed. *This is my fault. If I'd stayed . . .* Then her reasoning kicked in. *If I'd stayed, I'd likely be dead now. This is on Marstead, not me. I begged them to bring me in. I told them I couldn't maintain my cover under Petroff's thumb any longer.*

They should have believed me.

"It's not just because of Petroff's disappearance that Marstead is on high alert, Linnéa. The whole 9/11 thing has the world on edge."

"Nine eleven thing?"

"September 11. 9/11. That's what it's being called."

"Sorry. I'm a little out of touch."

She shook her head to clear it. "What can you tell me about Zakhar? With the evidence I sent to Petroff, he should have recalled Zakhar to Moscow immediately, and yet Zakhar managed to follow my plane to New Brunswick and then track me to Montreal, where he nearly caught me. I think—I *hope*—I've lost him again, but I'm being extremely cautious."

"Zakhar? Sorry, I have nothing about him to report."

Now it was Christor who changed the subject. "Listen, Linnéa, Marstead still wants you to come in. They aren't hunting you, I swear. The word is out. If anyone sights you or hears from you, we're to convey a message and a phone number. Only that. No attempt to bring you in."

"Yeah? What about 'trust but verify'?"

"I think that's the idea. The message is, 'Call in. Talk to them. Ask for any assurances you need, written or otherwise.' You could probably ask them to get Zakhar off your tail."

Laynie sighed. "Okay. What's the number?"

Christor rattled it off, and Laynie filed it in her memory banks under "To be used as a last resort."

VYPER HAD THE Granger woman's laptop. She had its ISP and current IP address. Hacking into Granger's computer and planting the Trojan horse was a walk in the park.

So, when her headset chirped that Laynie's laptop was online, Vyper jumped on with her. Elaine had initiated a point-to-point VoIP call.

VoIP? Nice touch—how very cutting edge of you. Let's see who this Christor is. Romantic liaison, perhaps?

Talk about Christor's wife and coming baby eliminated that possibility—and the security roadblocks Vyper encountered while attempting to hack into Christor's laptop told her she was not dealing with an amateur. Furthermore, her attempts to locate the end point of Elaine's call bounced her from country to country all over the world. She had no idea where this Christor person physically was—nor would she push to find out at present.

Unwilling to jeopardize her newfound lock on Elaine's location, she backed her way out and left Christor's laptop alone. She satisfied herself with recording their conversation.

Information, after all, was power.

"Linnéa? Linnéa, is that you?"

Linnéa? Linnéa what? Her real identity?

When Elaine asked about Petroff, Vyper froze. Petroff was a new name —and wasn't Zakhar working for Baskin, not this Petroff?

I assumed Baskin was a mid-level bureaucrat of minor importance. Did I miss something?

She listened more intently, grateful that she was recording the conversation and could review it afterward.

She was shocked further to hear Elaine say. "What's Marstead's take on it?"

"They are worried. Concerned, but uncertain."

"Possibilities?"

"That Petroff could be dead or in FSB custody."

"But that would imply that the FSB knows about me, that my cover is blown—and would, furthermore, make the entire Marstead organization suspect."

"Word from on high came down ten days ago. All Marstead operatives within the Russian Federation were to cease operations, take extreme precautions, and prepare to evac on a moment's notice. Things here are very tense, Linnéa."

"I don't understand! Could someone have intercepted the package I had you send Petroff?"

Vyper's mouth went slack, and her jaws ceased their chewing. *What have I stumbled on? Marstead operatives? Cover blown? Make the entire Marstead organization suspect?*

She was familiar with Marstead as a tech company—wasn't everyone? Marstead wasn't some elaborate front for international espionage—was it? It couldn't be!

Vyper's fingers flew across the keyboard, pulling up screen after screen of information.

MARSTEAD INTERNATIONAL
Global Technologies of the Future

According to its website, the Wall Street Journal, USA Today, and a thousand other hits regarding Marstead International, Marstead was a legit—emphasis on *legit*—global, multimillion-dollar technology firm traded on the NYSE, JPX, and others.

Was it all a lie? Camouflage?

Vyper added the name "Linnéa" to her Marstead search parameters and sat back, staring at the return. Linnéa Olander, Senior Account Executive, based out of Marstead's St. Petersburg offices since 1995.

"All right, Linnéa Olander. I have you now—but who is this Petroff you are so concerned about?"

She searched on the string, "Linnéa Olander," "Petroff," and "Russia." The data that the search returned blew her mind. Photographs in the Arts and Life section of the English language *Moscow Times*—a tall, distinguished Russian man and his stunning Swedish companion attending state dinners. Articles and more photographs in the Society and Culture section of the *Information Telegraph Agency of Russia* (TASS).

Vassili Aleksandrovich Petroff. a high up, mucky-muck, personal technology advisor to Security Council Secretary Rushailo himself.

That Petroff? Advisor to that *Rushailo?*

It was this Baskin fellow who had contacted her. Who, precisely, was he? Who did he report to?

She searched on "Baskin" and "Petroff." Nothing.

She switched out "Petroff" for "Rushailo"—and sat back, stunned. Sergio Stepashin Baskin, Chief of Security to the Secretary of the Russian Security Council, Vladimir Borisovich Rushailo.

Rushailo's personal chief of security was running Zakhar?

Vyper swore under her breath, then swore again. Elaine Granger, this *Linnéa Olander*, was no innocent woman fleeing an abusive relationship. She was the long-time mistress of a prominent Russian demi-oligarch—but not *just* Petroff's mistress. Apparently, she was also a trained operative sent to spy on the Russians.

Which explained why the Russians—all the way up to Secretary Rushailo—were hunting her! And this Zakhar was *Rushailo's* man?

Holy crap. I have toyed with and thwarted an agent of the Russian Federation and Vladimir Borisovich Rushailo's personal hit man? An agent now working hand-in-glove with the Ukrainian mafiya?

What do I do now?

When Granger's VoIP call ended, Vyper backed up the conversation to her most secure location. a remote server she kept in a second apartment across town under an alias. The remainder of the day, she was nervous and off her game. Her thoughts returned to what she'd heard again and again, analyzing the implications and dangers of what she'd learned—and what she'd dabbled her fingers in.

The remainder of the day, she frowned, chewed gum, and muttered the occasional, "Oh, crap!"

FEWER SPECTATORS SAT at the picnic table this afternoon. Many of them huddled together against a cold drizzle and blustery winds.

"This weather is the pits, man," a kid sitting near Laynie said to his friend. "Ain't worth it."

They got up and slouched away. Laynie, for her part, was dressed right for the slightly soggy weather and remained ready and eager to observe the next game.

The team assembled on the field seemed unfazed, too. They were raring to get it on.

"Look, we only have nine players today. Who's going to sit out?" the leader asked.

His question was met with groans and protests.

"No way, man. I already paid," several complained.

"We all have. Guess I'll have to refund someone's fee."

"How much is it? The fee, I mean."

Laynie had stripped off her coat and gloves and left them on the table before she'd had a chance to think her actions through. She had a five-dollar bill in her hand.

"How much?"

Laynie wore jeans, a formfitting, long-sleeved T-shirt, and running shoes with good tread. Nine sets of young, male eyes checked her out.

She grinned. "I promise I won't hurt you."

Someone snickered. Leader-guy frowned. "You a paintballer? No offense, but . . . you're not college age." He squeezed off the obvious "anymore" before it spurted out of his mouth.

Laynie shrugged but stood her ground. "I'm a fair shot."

In Little London, Marstead's urban tactical training course. On a Boeing 767 at thirty-five thousand feet, shooting real bullets against real hijackers— who were shooting real bullets right back at me.

She laughed to herself. *So why not? Justin, my* Final Fantasy *"date," said I'd be good at paintball.*

The leader glanced around. "Anyone object? No?"

He waggled his brows at Laynie and chuckled. "Your money's as green as mine—but should we make you sign a waiver first?"

Laynie smiled a wicked smile right back. "But I already promised I wouldn't hurt you—and in front of all these witnesses, too."

The boys burst into guffaws.

"She got you, Brad! Got you good."

"Yeah, man. Let her play."

"Nobody wants to sit out, Brad."

"All right." To Laynie he said, "You're on green team."

"Great." Laynie grabbed a green vest—*My old color*—and put it over her head, tied the strings on both sides. Someone issued her a paintball pistol and two tubes of paintballs.

"These guns recock automatically, but the action is a hair slower than a real semiauto. Takes a little getting used to."

Laynie looked up into Max Thoresen's face. "You shoot much?"

"Sure do. Grew up on a farm. Loads of plinking and target practice."

"Okay. Thanks for the heads up."

She joined her four teammates behind their end zone wall. "What's the plan?"

"We ain't sophisticated. Same old, same old. Two runners up opposite sides to force the other team out."

One boy looked at her. "We're pretty new at this. You got a better idea?"

"Don't know if it's *better*, but it might be unexpected. Unanticipated."

Who am I kidding? Yes, it's better.

They listened as she outlined her idea. Looked at each other.

One of them, Vince, said, "Why not? At least they won't be looking for us to do *that*."

"Who's point?" Augie, another green, asked.

"Right now, their natural and inbred instinct will make them hesitant to shoot me, a woman. Let's use that against them."

Augie stared. "Geez lady, you're hardcore. My mom would have a cow if I clobbered a girl."

"That's my point. They'll hesitate, and I'll take advantage of that hesitation." She looked around. "I want to win. How about you?"

Green team nodded.

When the whistle blew, the greens, Laynie in the lead, streamed out from one side of their wall. They were stacked in a tight line, presenting only a single target, making it impossible for the blues to shoot them all at once.

As before, blue team sent out two runners, one down each side. When they saw the entire green team advancing, the blue runner on the far side of the field ducked behind a wall and started shooting, but he was too far away and too excited to be accurate. Laynie, in the meantime, ran quickly toward her opponent, but dove into a somersault as he brought his gun up. The blue man's eyes tracked with Laynie—as did his pistol. The green player behind Laynie was prepped and ready. He immediately nailed the distracted blue player.

"Go, go, go!" Laynie shouted. Her four teammates surged forward, still stacked for protection. She, though, rolled to her stomach, steadied her pistol at the blue across the field from her, and hit him twice—once in the arm, once on his vest. She was up and running before he, disgusted and complaining, fell "dead" onto the grass.

As she streaked across the field, another blue emerged from behind the wall. Max! Again, she tumbled, this time to her right, his left, throwing off his aim. She took up position behind a wall.

In the meantime, the two remaining blues, seeing the green team surge toward one end of their end zone wall, raced out the other side—and ran into the last green, who had broken off from his teammates and was waiting for them. He dispatched the first blue, but the second took him out. It was that blue player's last move. Three greens had run behind the blue's wall, across the end zone, and come in behind him.

"Hey, dufus!" one of Laynie's teammates called.

The blue swung around—and all three greens, whooping and hollering their victory, hammered him without mercy. The blue dropped to his knees, his entire front coated in paint splatter.

Max was the lone surviving blue.

Laynie called to him. "Surrender?"

Max laughed. "Never! Come and get me!"

But she hadn't waited for him to answer. That was "dead air," the ideal moment to move. She swung around her wall and raced down the field to flank the wall he hid behind. She gestured toward the greens to come forward. Within seconds, she and their stack formed a pincer from which Max could not escape.

He jumped out and popped off two rounds at Laynie, who threw up her arms to prevent the balls from hitting her vest. She "lost" both her arms, intentionally giving the greens time and opportunity to converge on Max, hit him from three sides, and finish him off—which they did with enthusiasm, Max suffering the humiliation of all of the greens' remaining paintballs.

Shouting and whooping their victory, the greens formed a huddle and jumped up and down. Laynie laughed and jumped with them. She was having more fun than she'd had since she was a kid.

"That was great!" Vince said, pounding her on the back. "You can play on our team any time!"

Then the teams shook hands, the blues still irked at how the greens had pressed and executed their aggressive maneuvers.

"Good game," Brad admitted.

"Well, I believe in being a gracious winner—and since I barged in on your game, what say I treat you all to burgers and fries?" She turned to Max and added, "You look like you could use a burger, Max."

"Shoot, I can always use a burger," he laughed back, rubbing a shoulder that had been pounded to excess with paintballs.

They used rags to wipe paint from hands, faces, vests, and hair. The guys hauled the gear and barriers to their storage locker, then they walked Laynie off campus to Mr. Lincoln's Burgers & Shakes, a revered UNL burger joint. While Laynie went to put in the order, the players took over two tables.

Laynie sidled up to the counter and glanced around. Everything in the restaurant had the look of a college favorite. Posters for the university's sports teams adorned the walls, and a cork bulletin board next to the register was a colorful riot of pinned employment opportunities, ride share offers, house rental ads, and requests for roommates.

"Hi," Laynie greeted the girl at the counter taking orders. "I'd like sixteen double cheeseburgers, eight large fries, two onion rings, three vanilla shakes, five chocolate, one strawberry, and a large coffee."

She paid for the order and joined the boisterous crew. Brad held out a chair for her, so she sat down where he'd made a place. The guys talked, joked, and razzed each other. Laynie mostly listened.

"Hey, we didn't even get your name," Brad realized.

"Oh! Right. Sorry. It's Elaine . . . Elaine Granger."

The guys introduced themselves around the table. She nodded at each name.

It was her first opportunity to study Max up close. She desperately wanted to talk to him privately, but she couldn't do that. In fact, she took pains not to pay him any special attention—but that didn't mean she couldn't learn more about him by getting the group to talk.

"How did you guys start playing paintball?"

"We all go to the same campus fellowship group," Brad supplied. "Started playing a few weeks ago, start of the semester. We wish we had a better course, one we could pack some imagination into."

"And not have to haul in and out for every game," another player added.

"Yeah. Our fellowship leader suggested we get into paintball. We hope to have a tournament with several college fellowship groups during spring break Bible camp."

"I, um, recently started reading the Bible."

What? Where did that come from?

"That's great! Where are you reading?"

"The Gospels. I . . . grew up in church but can't say much of it rubbed off." She changed the subject. "Where are all of you from?"

They told her, one by one, but except for Denver, Colorado, and Bellingham, Washington, the rest were rural towns she hadn't heard of.

When Max said RiverBend, she asked, "Did I hear something about a long weekend? Is that why you were a player short today?"

"Yup. Some students didn't have classes tomorrow, so they took off early for the long weekend, Monday being Columbus Day and all. I'll be heading out tomorrow afternoon."

"For home?"

"Yeah. It's only a four-hour drive."

Speaking to the entire group, she said with nonchalance, "Well, if you ever need another player, I'll be around."

"Cool!" Vince said.

Laynie glanced at Max and added, gently tapping the table, "I'll be right *here*." She paused and added, "I'd like to play again . . . especially on upcoming Monday afternoons."

Max felt momentary confusion. It almost seemed that she was talking not to the team, but directly to him. His quizzical expression gave him away.

Laynie relaxed her face into bland lines. "What?"

"Dunno. Something about you seems . . . familiar. Have we ever met?"

Laynie shook her head. "Nope. I can assure you that we've *never* met."

"Okay." He took a long pull on his shake and turned to a friend.

CHAPTER 29

LP

MAX DROVE ALONG the country dirt road, past acres of farmland, the road sloping down to the hollow where his family lived. He pulled his pickup to the side of the driveway where he usually parked and set the brake. He hadn't turned off the engine before the front door swung open and Shannon and Rob flew from the house like shots fired from two cannons.

It was all, "Max! Max! Max!" with his two siblings glommed onto his legs, arms, and waist until Kari reached him.

"My turn, kids. Make way for Mama!"

Kari folded Max in her arms—amazed as always that he had grown taller than her. Tears wet her face.

How did that happen? You were my sweet young boy when I became your Mama. How did you suddenly become a grown man?

"Hey, Mom. Please don't cry."

"I'm just so happy to see you, Max."

"And I'm happy to be home. Three-day weekend—*yay!*"

Shannon and Rob cheered. With one of them glued to either side, he grabbed his bag and headed in. After he'd deposited the bag in his room, he asked, "Where's Dad?"

"Finishing up his and Rob's chores, I imagine."

Rob turned red. "Sorry, Mama." He grabbed his jacket.

"I'll go with you, Rob," Max said.

They strode down the slope together toward the creek that separated Kari's land from the homestead Søren had inherited from his father. Neither said a word—but when they hit the bridge built over the creek, they burst like runners from their marks and raced across the bridge and up the road, turning onto the long drive that led to the old house where their Aunt Ilsa lived.

The hand pump in the yard was their finish line. Rob pulled ahead because Max held back, but not for long. Max stretched out his longer stride and caught Rob two yards before the pump.

"Dang it!" Rob shouted. "I never beat you!"

"Careful with your mouth, Robbie."

"Sorry."

"And don't worry. In a couple years, you'll be as tall as me but I'll be older and slower."

Rob grinned. "Naw, you'll never be slow, Max. I'll just be *faster* than you are!"

Max threw his arm around Robbie's shoulders, and they marched toward the barn to look for their dad.

Over dinner, Max entertained the family with tales from college. The school fellowship group he'd joined and his love for paintball were big parts of his stories. "Golly, yesterday, we had the best game *ever*—even though my team lost. Because of the three-day weekend, we were a player short, right? And this lady just waltzes up and asks to play."

"A lady? Not a co-ed?" Kari asked.

"No, not a college student. She . . . well, I figured she must be in her, well, your age, Mom. Dunno. Anyway, paintball can be kind of a rough game, and Brad, our leader, didn't want her to get hurt, but she says, just as cool as can be, 'I promise I won't hurt *you*.'"

Max attempted to imitate her voice, and around the table, everyone laughed.

"How did the lady do, Max?" Shannon asked. "She didn't get hurt, did she?"

"Are you kidding? That was the amazing part. This woman—I mean *lady*—she whips the green team into shape, sends them racing out of their end zone in a tight line—'stacked,' one of the guys said she called it—and then they just blew us away.

"I was the last blue player standing, and she sacrificed herself so her three remaining players could get behind my position and pulverize me. Gonna have bruises on my shoulders, for sure. I hope we see her again. Next time, I want to be on *her* team."

That evening after they'd cleared away the dinner dishes, the family gathered at the table to play Uno, tournament style—five hands per round.

"Max, we need paper and pen to keep score. Grab a pad off my desk, please?" Kari asked.

Max left the dining room and wandered into the corner of the living room where Kari kept her desk and worked each day. He yanked open the center drawer where she kept pens, grabbed one, then looked for the pad she'd said he'd find.

What he saw lying on top of her magazines stopped him cold. He slowly picked it up and gaped. His mouth worked.

"M-mom?"

"Did you find the pad, Max?"

"*Mom!*"

"Hey, Max. Don't yell at your mother," Søren chided him.

Max called back. "Sorry, Mom. But . . . Dad, could you . . . could you and Mom please come here? Please?"

Kari looked at Søren, then got up. Søren followed her.

"What is it, Max?"

He was pale and serious. She saw a newspaper clutched in his hand and searched his face. "What's wrong, Max?"

Shannon and Rob, ever curious about adult conversations, came running.

Max, though, shook his head. "Hey, Shannon, Robbie? This is between me and Mom and Dad."

They looked from Kari to Søren, indignant at being excluded, certain they'd miss out on something cool or important. But Søren, noting how upset Max was, seconded Max's order.

"Kids, give us a minute of privacy." It wasn't a request.

"Okaaaay, Dad," Rob grumbled, while Shannon huffed her displeasure. They moved toward the dining room together.

"Now, what's up, Son?"

Max lifted the newspaper and pointed to the grainy photo under the bold heading **HAVE YOU SEEN THIS WOMAN?**

"This woman. I'm pretty certain that I know her. She was in Lincoln— at my school! She-she-she—*shoot!* She's the lady we played paintball with yesterday!"

Kari's breath whooshed out of her body. "You're sure, Max? You're positive?"

"Yeah, I'm sure. She took us for burgers after the game. I sat right across from her. Her hair is, I dunno, different. Blonder? But it's *her*, I swear it."

"Don't swear, Son," Søren admonished.

"Sorry, Dad, but . . ." Max turned his worried eyes to Søren, and his eighteen-year-old voice quivered. "Is she a terrorist, Dad? Is she . . . is she gonna blow up our school or something?"

Søren shook his head. "No, Max. She's not a terrorist."

"But . . . what about this paper? I *know* it's her!"

Kari flicked her eyes toward the dining room to ensure that Shannon and Rob were not listening in. She lowered her voice anyway.

"Max, did the woman tell you her name?"

Max ran his hand up the back of his neck into his shaggy hairline—a sign of stress he'd picked up from Søren. Kari knew it well.

"Yeah. She said her name is Elaine Granger."

Kari gasped and sobbed. "Oh, thank you, Jesus! Thank you, Jesus!" Søren's arm came around her waist.

Max, more confused than ever, turned to his dad. "I don't get it. What's going on?"

Kari, still sobbing, put her hand on her son's arm. "Max, you have nothing to fear from this woman. She . . . she's my sister, Laynie."

"Your sister? Aunt Laynie?" Max had never laid eyes on his near-mythical Aunt Laynie Portland. "But . . . why didn't she tell me or just come here, if she knows where we live? Why is her picture in the newspaper? Why are the FBI and police looking for her?"

Kari whispered, "Max, you will have to trust us on this. She is not a terrorist."

Max stared at the paper. "Are you sure, Mom? I mean, are you sure this is Aunt Laynie?"

Wiping her eyes with the back of her hand, Kari added, "Do you remember that Laynie and our brother Sammie were separated from me when we were children? That they were stolen?"

He nodded. It was part of the family lore, the miraculous means by which Kari had found the Thoresen family, then found her sister, Laynie . . . but, sadly, had located her through the public announcement of her brother and sister-in-law's death. Later, Kari had adopted her brother's children, Shannon and Robbie.

Kari smiled. "This woman didn't stumble upon you by accident, Max. She knew you were in your first semester at UNL because I wrote and told her. *She sought you out,* because I think she must be hiding from someone—someone who might hurt her.

"She found a way to make an impression on you, Max, and sent you home to me, hoping you'd mention her. She even sent a hidden message with you, believing I would hear it and understand."

"Hear what?"

Kari laughed low in her throat. "See, the name Aunt Laynie was born with? It wasn't Helena or Laynie Portland. It was Elaine. *Elaine Granger.*"

CHAUCER MAY HAVE been the first in the English language to write, "Idle hands are the Devil's tools," but the Russians, too, have a similar old saying, "The Devil finds work for idle hands to do." Laynie hated waiting with nothing to occupy her time except to wonder if Max had, by chance, mentioned her to his stepmother in passing.

It's all too obscure. Kari won't think anything of it—even if Max does say something. Not unless he says my name aloud. Even then . . . would either of them pick up on my message?

She filled the hours with two things. working out and reading Shaw and Bessie's Bible. On Friday morning, she drank her coffee while rereading the

Gospel of Luke, followed by breakfast. After that, she sought out a good gym and joined it, using a debit to her new checking account instead of a credit card to pay the monthly membership. She threw herself into a training regimen exacting enough that she fell into bed exhausted that night.

Saturday was the same.

Coffee. Read. Eat. Work out. Eat. Read. Sleep.

Shopping helped for a while. The dropping temperatures warned that winter loomed near. She bought cold-weather clothes and a pair of waterproof boots. The apartment didn't come with linens, and her cupboards were bare. She shopped for sheets, blankets, a pillow, towels, and groceries. She hadn't performed a righteous clean on the HK since using the gun on the plane during the shootout on 9/11. It was filthy. She bought a cleaning kit and a box of .380 ACP ammo. She cleaned and oiled the little gun and refilled the HK's magazine.

Her combined activities could not keep her active mind busy more than a scant handful of hours. Too often she found herself thinking on the three weeks she spent with Roger, his abrupt decline, his passing. Those memories threatened to send her into a funk, so, Saturday evening, she called the Bradshaws and they talked for nearly an hour.

Laynie couldn't believe they would have enough of any topic to fill sixty minutes, but between the three of them, they did. For her part, Laynie told them about her new pastime, paintball. Shaw and Bessie were both amazed and drawn in by her descriptions of the game. She even confessed to taking their Bible—and reading it.

Bessie was thrilled. "Elaine, I can't think of a better home for our old Bible and all its memories than with you."

Shaw and Bessie talked about the fun they were having with their grandchildren, but neither of them mentioned Daisy. They had to understand that Daisy had served her purpose, and Laynie had been forced to leave her behind in order to cross over into the US.

After they spoke together, Laynie went to the gym and used her body hard, trying to exorcize the loneliness she felt, succeeding for a while. But the next day when she returned, Laynie found her gym unexpectedly closed—and not just closed Sunday. closed Sunday *and* Monday for the holiday!

Afraid she might pitch a rock through her own window out of boredom, she opted to run. She bundled up and jogged through her neighborhood, getting a feel for her neighbors, setting a demanding pace, logging five miles before calling it quits.

She took a long, hot shower, put on warm pajamas, and ate leftovers while she reread the Gospel of John.

Stared at the walls.

Called Tobin.

"Deputy Marshal Quincy Tobin," he answered.

"Tobin, er, Quince. It's . . ." She petered out at her name.

"Marta?"

"Yeah, it's me."

"Are you okay?"

"Sure. Never better."

"I see. What's new?"

Nothing. Laynie couldn't think of a single thing she wanted to tell him or a real reason for calling him.

Except what we shared on Flight 6177.

"Um, how's the shoulder."

"My shoulder? Perfect. Nothing better than a shot in the arm."

Was he yanking her chain? Really?

She snickered.

He did, too.

"I've thought about you a *lot*, since Moncton, Marta. Frankly, I've wished about ten times I could call you up and take you to dinner."

What? Laynie blushed like a teen. "Ummm. I . . ."

His twang reemerged. "This good ol' boy knows how t' show a woman a proper good time—an' you kin take thet t' the bank. So, what kinder cookin' turns yer crank?"

"Well, I . . ." Again, she stalled out.

"Ya like chitlins? Them's deep-fried pig innards, by-the-by. How 'bout fried okra? Fried grits? Fried chicken?"

Laynie snickered again. "I have never had chitlins. Or grits. And the one time my mama tried to make me eat okra? It wasn't fried. It was slimy. I threw up all over the dining room. She never served it again."

"Houston, we may have a problem."

"But I *do* like chicken!"

"Houston, hold the phone—what *kind* of chicken do you like?"

"Well, baked, broiled, or fried. Doesn't matter. I like chicken a lot."

"Saved by the bell! And what venue would constitute the setting of a satisfactory date?"

Laynie laughed and blushed at the same time. Tobin was flirting with her, flirting *hard*—and, truth be told, she was getting a big kick out of it.

Laynie had the perfect comeback, too. "Let's see. How about any venue that doesn't include getting shoved into an airplane lavatory or getting shot at by hijackers?"

"Owww! That stings, Fortier! And after I saved your bacon?"

"You saved *my* bacon? At last count, I took out three terrorists—how many did you handle?"

"Ouch again. Yer killin' me, Marta!"

They laughed together, and Laynie imagined Tobin's breadbox-sized hands and quirky grin. She didn't have to imagine his country schtick.

"Where do you live, Tobin?"

"I'm based outta D.C. but have an apartment in Arlington. You, Marta?"

"I . . . I've landed somewhere, for a while, anyway. And you know that my name's not really Marta Forestier, don't you?"

"Right. We covered that on the plane."

"It might be better though if, going forward, you keep thinking of me as Marta."

"Going forward? Does that mean we have a future? Be still my heart!" Though he said it all with glib humor, Laynie thought she heard a flicker of hope.

All she said in answer was, "You have my number now. I don't keep my phone on all the time, but . . . we can talk again."

CANADIANS DON'T celebrate Columbus Day, but they do celebrate their national Thanksgiving on the same date, the second Monday in October. Vyper, who held Thanksgiving and other traditional celebrations in derision, arrived at her office early Monday morning. Few administrative workers were in the office due to the holiday, although the full complement of RCMP officers were out on patrol.

Vyper had her own computer setup in her house—and its backup in her secret apartment, but from behind the RCMP's firewall, she had engineered a better and more anonymous Internet presence than what she could devise from home. Bottom line? She could do more from work with less risk.

Furthermore, over the weekend, she'd developed a niggling but persistent uneasiness regarding Zakhar's Odessa *mafiya* hacker. It had been too easy to stymie Syla's surveillance of Elaine Granger. In particular, the program she'd planted in Granger's phone service provider should have, at least once, alerted her to Syla's attempted intrusion—and should have sent him false data. Same with her credit card company. Her code inside the company's system should have sent Syla Granger's fake bus ticket purchase—and should have alerted Vyper to his intrusion. At *least* once.

It hadn't. Not even once.

Neither hacks had alerted her.

She'd wakened in the night, her nerves jangling with disquiet.

Now seated in front of her "other" workstation, she logged in, opened a command prompt, and keyed in the backdoor code she'd planted within Granger's phone service provider's system.

The window opened and . . . her monitor exploded in jumping, whirling, *Hopak* dancers in Kozak boots, peasant shirt, sash, and billowy red trousers. Ukrainian folk music and a harsh, repeating laugh blared out accompaniment to the cartoonish male dancers.

Vyper fell back in her chair, stunned. Chagrined. *Peeved.*

Syla! Syla had hacked *her* hack? Had booby-trapped *her* backdoor? *Grrr!*

As the first sting of affront washed through her, she turned the air blue with profanity. And no matter what she did, she could not end the high-kicking male dance characters or the music and hideous laugh. She had to force a shutdown, reboot her system, and run her own, customized virus software to rid herself of the laughing, taunting Ukrainian dancers.

Vyper shoved three sticks of Black Jack into her mouth at one time. Her jaws working like steam-powered pistons, she plotted her response.

If Syla thought he'd beaten her, he was about to receive a dose of reality! She could not—would not—allow Syla's disrespect to stand. She had her reputation to protect and, furthermore, she was better than him. No, he might think he'd won, but his attack on her was only the initial volley in all-out war . . . and *nothing* was off the table in love or war.

Vyper sneered at her rival. She had weapons up her sleeves neither Syla nor Zakhar knew of—and not every weapon need be a cyber one.

She logged on again and created a new entry point into Granger's phone provider's system. She located the code Syla had inserted to alert him of her intrusion, the code that had launched the attack of whirling Ukrainian devils. Vyper navigated around it and wormed her way deeper inside.

She saw that Granger had initiated two lengthy phone calls. One call Saturday evening was to the couple from whom she had bought the motor home. The second call, on Sunday, was of more significance. Vyper back-traced the number to the US Marshals Service, area code 202.

Washington, D.C.

Whoa! What have we here? Can I conjure a use for this? Turn it to my advantage? Why, yes, I believe I can.

Vyper spit out her gum and unwrapped a fresh stick. She added the phone number to the arsenal she was assembling. She executed the same painstaking drill into Zakhar's phone service provider. She avoided tripping Syla's alarms yet made no attempt to attack him.

I want you nice and relaxed when I hit you, Syla. Nice and relaxed.

She studied Zakhar's phone records and identified where it had pinged most recently. Syla must have warned Zakhar off the Detroit bus ticket and set him back on the right track. As of this morning, Zakhar was nearing Lincoln.

Elaine, Elaine. The Russians have your scent, my dear, and Zakhar is on his way. That checking account in your name? A mistake, I'm afraid, since your apartment is within a mile of the bank's branch.

But not to fear. Vyper is here.

Chewing slowly and methodically, she outlined and prepared her assault. When she was satisfied with her plan, she opened a plain-text document and typed a message, pounding away at it until its content was just right. tight, concise, and perfectly worded. The message was long, but it needed to be.

Vyper then pulled up a website that allowed users to send texts to mobile phones—anonymous and untraceable texts. Since each text message had a character limit, she "chunked" her lengthy plain-text document into short, pithy paragraphs to accommodate the character limitation.

Paragraph by paragraph, she copied and pasted the contents of her document into the program's message box, sending the entire document to her recipient in a long line of texts.

Vyper laughed. "Now for my next trick." She logged in to Yahoo and created a new email account, using false information and an IP anonymizer. When the account was ready, she composed an email.

She took her time with the message, including as much detail as possible, even screen shots to sweeten the bait.

She sat back, smiling, and treated herself to a fresh stick of gum. Vyper had done her research. She knew exactly which US FBI area office to send the email.

She couldn't care less about the Russian contract at this point, but her reputation would survive the encounter intact. Intact and quite possibly enhanced.

Oh, yes. Get ready, Syla. I'm about to burn you to the ground—you and Zakhar both.

CHAPTER 30

⚡ LP ⚡

AT 8:00 A.M., ZAKHAR'S phone vibrated. He picked it up. "*Da?*"

"I have pinpointed the woman's laptop."

Zakhar was impressed. "How were you able to do that?"

Syla laughed. "Actually, Vyper did it for me. She had already hacked the woman's laptop. I created chaos in Vyper's computer and, while she was distracted, I scoured her data and stole the woman's location."

"I will be sure to tell Baskin how inventive you were, Syla," Zakhar lied. "Rushailo will reward you handsomely, but he will also owe both you and the Odessa *mafiya* a debt of gratitude. Give me the woman's address, please."

Syla rattled it off. "It is an apartment complex. You will need to determine which unit she is in. Let me know when you have apprehended her so I can claim my fee."

"I will, indeed. I thank you again for your assistance."

Syla purred. "Ah, I nearly forgot. I have new treats for you—very special videos, just to your liking. I'll send the links to your laptop."

"*Spasibo*, Syla."

Smiling, Zakhar hung up. His victory was close, so close!

Naturally, Rushailo knew nothing of Zakhar's association with the Odessa mob—the Secretary of Russia's Security Council would never have agreed to place himself under obligation to the Ukrainians—but what did the facts matter, so long as Syla believed him? And if Rushailo were to fall under the Russian Federation's scrutiny for suspected association with the Odessa *mafiya*, would not Baskin fall from grace as well?

And would not both of those happy events favor Zakhar? The fewer Russians left standing with the authority to hunt him down, the safer he would be when he chose to disappear.

Two days ago, Syla had directed Zakhar from Winnipeg to the hick community of Lincoln, Nebraska. Lincoln was not large, as truly large cities go. Still, finding Olander among its 230,000 residents would have proven tedious and time-consuming without Syla's help. Syla had promised he would lead Zakhar directly to Linnéa Olander, and he had delivered.

IN ARLINGTON, VIRGINIA, Deputy US Marshal Quincy Tobin was enjoying his holiday—but not with any special holiday activity. On his day off he wasn't going to catch a parade or gather with fellow marshals for a barbeque. He was happy to get up at his regular early hour, take his time with his morning cup of joe, and further reflect on yesterday's conversation with Marta Forestier.

Not her real name, he corrected himself, *just the cover she adopted to board Flight 6177, London to JFK.*

Don't care. Like the sound of "Marta" just fine.

But he would like her by whatever name she adopted.

What a spunky woman, he mused. *Intelligent, courageous, and lethal wrapped up in one gorgeous package.*

When he found himself grinning like an idiot, he laughed aloud.

And she did say I could call her again.

That reminded him of the deputy director's business card tucked away in his wallet and the obligation he had to the Marshals Service. Until Marta had called him out of the blue, Tobin hadn't had reason or need to use that card.

He scowled. *Now I'm obliged to report contact with her?*

His phone vibrated an incoming text. Quincy picked it up, hoping it wasn't work. It wasn't—but he had no idea *who* it was. The text had no sender's phone number or name.

Text after text landed on his phone, five in all. He read them quickly—reread them, then read them a third time, slowly.

Elaine Granger? Who is that? And who is texting me?

He typed a reply. "Who is this? How did you get this number?"

The response was "A friend. Don't fail her."

Beneath the reply, a sixth text rolled in containing a series of ASCII characters. Tobin thought them gibberish or some kind of code—until he pulled his phone back and perceived the image the characters formed—that of a fanged snake's head.

"What the devil?"

He was reading the entire message again, text by text, when a single line pinged his phone.

"She called you last night."

Bam! The message slammed into him like a Mack truck, taking on urgent meaning.

"Oh, dear God!"

He fumbled for the card in his wallet. Regardless of how Tobin felt about turning Marta in, if he didn't rally help for her, she wasn't going to survive the next twenty-four hours.

He keyed in the number scrawled on the card's back and paced his apartment's living room. *I'm about to ruin someone's holiday, a* big *someone. This text had better not be bogus or my next paycheck sure will be.*

The call picked up. "Gordon Niles."

"Director Niles, this is Deputy US Marshal Quincy Tobin. I was the sky marshal on Flight 6177. We met in my hospital room?"

The man Tobin had called was immediately attentive. "I remember you, Marshal. What do you have for me?"

"Sir, I've just received a series of anonymous text messages—no phone number, so likely sent from the web. The messages reference one Elaine Granger, but I'm convinced the name is an alias for Marta Forestier. I think the best way to proceed is to forward the messages to you directly."

"Do it, Marshal. I'll hang up, read them, and get back to you."

Quincy forwarded the messages off to Niles, then checked the time and hurried to pack a bag. Regardless of Niles' response, Tobin needed the fastest possible transport to Lincoln, Nebraska. He had a friend who could arrange a private jet for him—and Tobin didn't care if the cost emptied his savings account as long as it got him there in time.

"TELL US AGAIN WHAT she said, Max."

Søren and Kari had sent Shannon and Rob to bed after managing to fake at playing several rounds of Uno that night. Later on, and several times over the next two days, whenever they could get Max aside without the younger children noticing, they asked him to repeat his encounter with Laynie.

Max was more than tired of it. He was irked. It was Monday, almost noon, and after helping Søren and Robbie with the chores, Max had friends he'd planned to hang out with before returning to school—that is, until Kari and Søren had sat him down yet again.

"Mom? Nothing has changed, okay? I've told you like a hundred times what she did, what she said—all of it."

Kari nodded. "I'm sorry, Max, so sorry for spoiling your weekend, but if we could have just five minutes more? I keep thinking Laynie must have given you a hint or a clue of some kind so that we could find her."

"Find her? Mom, if she wanted to see you, wouldn't she have just called? Or shown up here?"

Kari looked to Søren. They had discussed giving Max a tiny bit more information. Just enough for him to understand.

Søren mouthed an "okay" to Kari.

She took a deep breath. "You are a fine young man, Max. I know your heart and your character, so I'm going to entrust you with some . . . important information. I will need your promise first that you will never speak of it to anyone other than us—and I do mean *anyone*. Can I have that assurance?"

Max's eyes shifted from Kari to Søren and back. "You're kind of freakin' me out, Mom."

Søren said, "Do we have your promise, Max?"

"Yeah, okay—I mean, yessir. I promise."

Kari began. "All right. Here it is. A lot of what Aunt Laynie does is both dangerous and secret—even from me."

Max's face went slack. *Dangerous? Secret?* "What? You mean, secret as in CIA secret?"

"Not CIA, but close, yes. She . . . couldn't tell me which organization."

Max blinked. His mind was reeling. "You're kidding, right?" When he saw how serious his parents were, he mumbled, "You're not kidding? My aunt is a spy?"

"No, we're not kidding and, yes, she is . . . a spy. And the fact that she's hiding herself, not calling us, not just showing up for a visit? That tells us something."

"Like what?"

"Like she's afraid of leading some of those dangerous people to our door. Right now, they don't know we exist. She has worked hard to keep *us* a secret, because, if those bad people knew Laynie had a family she loved? They could use us against her."

"This is crazy, Mom."

"I know, sweetie. I know."

Søren cleared his throat. "I haven't met Laynie either. But according to your mom, she would not have approached you on purpose using the name Elaine Granger without good reason. That's why we want you to repeat what she said."

"Yeah. All right. Okay."

Max went through his telling of the game again, ending with Laynie's invitation to treat both teams to burgers. "Then she said, 'Well, I believe in being a gracious winner—and since I barged in on your game, what say I treat you all to burgers and fries?' and she said to me, 'You look like you could use a burger, Max,' and I said—"

Suddenly Max stopped. His jaw dropped. "Oh, wow."

"What? What is it?"

"She called me Max! I didn't realize it at the time, but she already knew my name. When we got to Mr. Lincoln's, everyone introduced themselves to her, but she had called me by name back when we were on the field—and we weren't on the same team."

Kari, as excited as he was, said, "That's what we meant, Max. Laynie didn't stumble on you by accident. She sought you out for a reason. So, think! Think, sweetie. What else did she say?"

Max scrunched up his face and tried to recall the loud and lively scene around the table while they devoured their food and everyone talked at once. "Well, I think she said, 'If you ever need another player, I'll be around.'"

"That's good, but you told us that already. What else?"

Max squinted in concentration. "Vince said that would be cool—I think he has a crush on her, but I'm thinking, 'Really, man? I mean, she's hot and all, but she's *old*, like in her forties' and—"

"Max!"

"Oops. Um, sorry. Yeah, I . . . I thought at the time that she looked familiar to me, but I couldn't figure it out." He stared at Kari. "I can now. She looks like *you*, Mom."

Kari smiled. "Yes, there's a strong family resemblance, especially the eyes—that and, you know. We're both *old*."

Max's face flamed. Kari and Søren laughed.

"What next? What did she say next?"

"Like I told you, she said, 'If you ever need another player, I'll be around.' And then . . . then she added, 'I'll be right here.'"

"Right here? As in 'right here' where? At the paintball course? Somewhere else on campus? *Where* in Lincoln?"

"No, she was—" Max grew agitated. "Mom, Dad, she was tapping on the table, like this." Max tapped on the dining table for emphasis. "She tapped on the table and said, 'I'll be right *here*.' And then she said, 'I'd like to play again, especially on upcoming Monday afternoons.'"

Kari grabbed Søren's hand. "That's it! The 'upcoming Monday' part. Today is Monday. We're supposed to meet her at the burger place. *Today*."

LAYNIE SLIPPED HER unlabeled CD-ROM into her laptop and installed the software for a subscription service called "Keyhole EarthViewer." Christor had supplied Linnéa with the program. Its developers had undertaken a new and ambitious objective to buy downward-facing satellite photos and stitch them together to create a larger and more complete overhead view. Their long-term goal was to map the entire face of the earth and make it searchable. The founders of Keyhole EarthViewer were just getting started, so the work was largely incomplete, but they had most US cities already mapped.

Laynie logged in under Christor's subscription ID and stared at the image of the "Big Blue Marble" as seen from orbit. She typed "Lincoln, NE" into the search field. Slowly, the earth rotated, and North America came into view. It grew in size as the program zoomed in on the United States, then

Nebraska, then the city of Lincoln. The area outside the city seemed blurry, out of focus, but the image of the city itself began to resolve. Using her laptop's mouse, Laynie dragged the image closer. Tighter.

She'd found the east campus—she recognized the elongated oval track of UNL's Tractor Test Laboratory. She sought the intersection of Holdrege St. and N. 48th, then zoomed in again.

There. That flat-roofed building had to be Mr. Lincoln's Burgers & Shakes. She pulled out, searching for a place to meet—not far away, somewhere with cover. Somewhere out of casual view. Across Holdrege she saw acreage owned and cultivated by UNL's agriculture college. Shrubs, bushes, and trees bounded the perimeter, but within the lot were beehives and a sizable orchard—columns and rows of trees.

She jumped onto the university's website and read about the variety of fruit and nut tree hybrids the ag college cultivated to test for insect and disease resistance. She jumped back to the Keyhole viewer and studied the orchard.

While it was now mid-October and cold, Lincoln had not yet experienced a killing frost. The trees would still have some foliage. Better still, the land around the orchard stretched to the north and west before meeting up with campus roads and school buildings on the west.

But how to securely convey the meeting place?

Laynie searched for an online Bible and found Bible Gateway's site. She did a number of keyword searches—and smiled to herself when she found a phrase. She read before and after the passage and picked up a useful phrase.

After she'd settled her thoughts, she grabbed up the Bradshaws' Bible and leafed through it, looking for something she'd seen earlier. She found it tucked inside the back cover. an unused picture postcard of Lake Louise, a souvenir from one of Shaw and Bessie's travels.

Laynie printed her message on the postcard. She reread it and nodded, pulled on her coat and gloves, patted the HK zipped into her coat's pocket, grabbed her wallet and phone, and left her apartment.

The lunch rush was ending when she entered Mr. Lincoln's Burgers & Shakes. She sat in a corner booth and waited for the place to clear out some before approaching the counter.

"Hey there. I was wondering if I could borrow one of your red markers for a sec? You know, the markers you use to write orders on the to-go bags?"

The kid shrugged. "Guess so, if you give it right back."

"I will." Laynie finished what she'd come to do, returned the marker, and started back to her apartment. Hours stretched before her until she'd leave again to ensure that the meeting place was safe.

"WHAT HAVE WE HERE? What fresh delusion is a *bleeping* Bible Gateway? Do these religious idiots believe the Bible of such importance that they had to create a 'gate' into it? The absurdity of ignorant people!"

Vyper tapped her latest pack of gum on the desk beside her keyboard while she scoffed. She took note of Elaine Granger's keystrokes as she ran a number of keyword searches.

She became slightly more interested when the woman settled on a specific Bible verse.

Pulling up the Bible Gateway website for herself, Vyper read the verse. "Odd."

Vyper observed as Granger closed the Bible website, loaded a CD into the laptop's drive, and installed the "Keyhole EarthViewer" program—a program Vyper often used herself. It was Vyper's opinion that the site would, at some point in the future, accomplish its grand goals—even exceed its visionaries' expectations.

"But not until their company is bought out by Yahoo or Microsoft. Or even Google." She pondered the possibilities for a moment. "Nah, not Google. Probably Microsoft or Apple."

Following Granger's keystrokes, she looked down at the same image Granger was exploring.

"That's interesting—and I think I get you, Elaine. Can I work with this?" She laughed and treated herself to another stick of gum. "Well, naturally I can. Who do you think you're talking to?"

Giggling at her own humor, Vyper typed in the IP address for an anonymous web-to-text messaging site—different than the last site she'd used—pounded out another set of texts, and sent them on their way to the mobile phone, area code 202, registered to the US Marshals Service.

She ended her texts with, "Don't screw this up" and added her ASCII character logo.

ZAKHAR PARKED HIS RENTAL car two blocks away and walked a circuitous route to the address Syla had given him, a small group of apartments. Acting with the confidence of one who belonged there, he sought out the complex's freestanding, sixteen-unit cluster mailbox.

Zakhar went around to the back of the box and withdrew a thin flat head screwdriver and a stiff piece of wire from inside his coat. He used the tools to jimmy open the postal worker's door.

He found that the apartment's manager kept the ever-changing mailbox up-to-date. He had dutifully printed the sixteen residents' last names on labels and affixed them to the appropriate mail slot.

A label reading "Granger" was glued to the slot for Apartment 11.

Five minutes later, Zakhar was inside Laynie's apartment, pawing through her meager belongings, certain he had found her. He was jittery and keyed-up with anticipation.

At last! You have teased, tormented, and denied me for years, Linnéa Olander, but I will have you at last! And when I have wrung every drop of pleasure from your body, I will strangle you until the light fades from your haughty blue eyes.

Then I will be quit of the obsession that has vexed me for years, the fixation that has almost driven me mad. When you die, I will be released from the evil curse you placed upon me.

Yes, when you die, I shall be free.

LAYNIE CROSSED 48th Street, headed back to her apartment, guarded, but marginally confident about the evening. As her foot reached the opposite curb, a sick feeling came over her, an intuition of danger and impending trouble—a heavy sense that she should not return to her apartment.

What? Am I being followed? Surveilled? Has Zakhar found me?

She knew better than to stop on the sidewalk or outwardly display dread. Instead, she kept her pace but turned left on 47th rather than proceeding straight down Holdrege.

She walked south on 47th, skirting Ecco Park, arriving at the bowling alley at the bottom of the block. She went inside and chose a table in the lounge where she had a clean line of sight to the door and easy access to the fire exit.

A waitress came and took her order for coffee and a sandwich.

It was crowded and warm in the alley, lots of families taking advantage of the holiday to bowl with their kids, but Laynie shivered. She hadn't noticed anything amiss, but when that scary-sick feeling overtook her, she had known not to continue on to her apartment.

It wasn't the first time she'd experienced such aid since leaving Russia.

Is that you? Helping me again? Answering Kari's prayers for me?

"All of God's promises are true, Laynie, because he is true. One way or another, he will work those promises into reality. He is God, and he will have his way."

Laynie stared into her coffee cup and acknowledged that she had choices before her. Decisions to make. Not today perhaps, but sometime soon.

She nodded in acquiescence.

As soon as I'm not running for my life.

SØREN AND KARI FOLLOWED Max's truck down the highway toward Lincoln. Søren's sister, Ilsa, was staying the night with Shannon and Rob. When Max finally pulled into Mr. Lincoln's Burgers & Shakes, Søren parked their car next to him.

Max got out of his truck and climbed into their back seat. "How do you want to do this?"

"We're just another family seeing their son back to school after the long weekend," Søren said. "Let's go in together and look around."

They saw nothing to concern them inside the fast-food restaurant. They also saw no sign of Laynie.

"We should get something to eat so we don't stick out like sore thumbs," Kari suggested.

They placed their order at the counter. Søren reached into his back pocket and stopped, his hand frozen on his wallet. "Max." He nudged his son. "Max. Look."

Off to the side was a corkboard papered with campus rentals and part-time work opportunities. A picture postcard was stuck to the board by a pushpin. Across its glossy face, in bold red letters, was printed, MAX.

"Cancel our order, please," Søren said.

Max grabbed the card off the board, and they left the restaurant, returning to the car.

"What does it say, Max?"

He had turned it over and was grimacing at the message on the back. It was short and cryptic. *I read The Preacher this morning—great book. The second chapter was the best out of the five. Sorry I missed Sammie's birthday. Hope to see you soon.*

"What does it mean?" Max demanded.

Kari took the postcard into her hand to study it. "It has to be from Laynie, right? She hopes to see us soon, so obviously she expects us to understand the rest." She chewed her lip. "The preacher. She read 'The preacher.' Anyone know that book?"

Søren snorted. "I think I do." He opened the glove box and fumbled inside it. Pulled out a Bible.

"The Preacher is King Solomon, the author of the book of Ecclesiastes."

"Second chapter!" Max shouted.

"The second chapter out of five?" Søren frowned fingering through the book. "That makes no sense. Ecclesiastes has twelve chapters, not five."

"What if . . . What if she meant the fifth verse?" Kari suggested. "Ecclesiastes 2:5?"

Søren found it and read aloud, "*I made me gardens and orchards, and I planted trees in them of all kind of fruits.*"

They were quiet, digesting the words. Søren shook his head. "Max? Anything?"

Søren snorted. "I think I do." He opened the glove box and fumbled inside it. Pulled out a Bible.

"The Preacher is King Solomon, the author of the book of Ecclesiastes."

"Second chapter!" Max shouted.

"The second chapter out of five?" Søren frowned fingering through the book. "That makes no sense. Ecclesiastes has twelve chapters, not five."

"What if . . . What if she meant the fifth verse?" Kari suggested. "Ecclesiastes 2:5?"

Søren found it and read aloud, "*I made me gardens and orchards, and I planted trees in them of all kind of fruits.*"

They were quiet, digesting the words. Søren shook his head. "Max? Anything?"

"Well, it could be anywhere. I mean, the ag college has orchards with all different varieties of trees, but—"

"But where? Where are the orchards, Max?"

He looked out the window. "I think . . . yeah. They are right over there, off that corner. Over that fence."

"That could be it, Søren," Kari said with hope. "I think she picked that place because we'll be hidden among the trees."

"Are we supposed to hop the fence, walk into the college's private orchard and just wait for her to show up?"

"No, silly," Kari laughed. "She told us when to meet her right there, on the postcard." She pointed. "See? 'Sorry I missed Sammie's birthday.'"

Her eyes were damp when she added, "Sammie's birthday was June 2. No one but Laynie and I would know his birthday off the top of our heads. June 2. That's 6:02."

Kari smiled through her tears, then laughed. "That's when we meet her. In that orchard over there at two minutes after six."

Max laughed with Kari. "Wow, Mom. Aunt Laynie is pretty smart."

His voice dropped to a whisper. "Guess she'd have to be, huh? Being she's a spy and all."

CHAPTER 31

LP

BY ORDERING AN early dinner that she did not touch, Laynie paid to keep her table. Her nerves would not allow her to eat anything more, so she sipped cup after cup of strong coffee. The caffeine kept her wits about her, but the acid did nothing for her uneasy stomach.

At half past five, Laynie paid her bill, left a tip on the table, and slipped away from the bowling alley. Dusk in October would fall sometime after seven, but the sky was already gloomy with the possibility of more rain. She walked casually down the streets until she was directly opposite the orchards.

She cut across the street and hopped the chest-height cyclone fence onto campus land, directly into the longest stretch of the UNL orchard. Within moments, she was hidden among the trees.

SØREN, KARI, AND Max left Mr. Lincoln's on foot, walking down the streets until they reached the campus. Max led them down winding paths around buildings until they reached the grassy area next to the orchard. In the waning light, they made out the long lines of trees and a row of beehives, their white paint shining out of the shadows.

Max gestured to his parents, and they huddled. "I don't know where to go from here, Mom and Dad. All those trees over there extend a couple blocks in that direction. That's a lot of orchard."

"Why don't we walk along the edge of the trees? Maybe she'll see us, Max," Kari whispered.

LAYNIE CREPT THROUGH the trees, using their even rows to keep her moving into the orchard. When she reached a break in their lines, she turned south until she approached an open, grassy space, and slipped silently along its edge.

Three figures were huddled across from the beehives. She heard their whispers through the lengthening gloom.

"Maybe she'll see us, Max," came a soft, feminine voice.

Kari!

Laynie raised her hand to catch their attention—but beyond them on the narrow maintenance road, a lone Suburban appeared, its lights off. The vehicle ground to a halt and two men jumped from it, shouting commands to Max, Kari, and Søren. Laynie ducked into the tree line and watched in dismay as the men commanded Max, Kari, and Søren to get on the ground. One of them patted them down, checking for weapons.

Not Zakhar!

Marstead? It must be!

Laynie covered her mouth with both hands and screamed noiselessly into them, *No, no, no! No one was to ever find them! You were going to keep them safe, God!*

She kept her eyes on the scene. The men, finding no weapons, holstered theirs, got Max, Kari, and Søren to their feet, and herded them together into one of the Suburban's rear seats.

Laynie unzipped her coat pocket and reached for her HK.

Only two of them.

Weapons holstered.

I will creep through the trees and come at them from the driver's side.

She squeezed the HK P7K3's cocking mechanism to chamber a round.

Behind her, a man said, "That won't be necessary, Miss Olander."

CHAPTER 32

LP

LAYNIE STOOD PERFECTLY STILL, waiting for a team of Marstead agents to rush her. Cuff and gag her. Throw her into the backseat of another vehicle.

Instead, the man behind her ordered, "Take your hand out of your pocket—slowly, Miss Olander, without the gun. That way, we won't have any misunderstandings or unfortunate mishaps."

Laynie withdrew her hand, splaying the fingers of her empty hand.

"Good. Now, please turn around."

He appeared to be in his fifties, medium height, prematurely gray hair artfully cut, a classic charcoal gray Burberry overcoat worn over a suit against the cold—the *de rigueur* complementary cashmere wool scarf about his neck, folded properly into the coat's front overlap.

"Who are you? Who are those men, and why have they taken . . . those people into custody?"

"They aren't in custody, and they are in no danger. We just didn't want any misunderstandings or un—"

"Or unfortunate mishaps. You said that already."

"Yes, and I was considerate enough not to have them wait in the cold while we spoke, Miss Olander."

He stepped closer. Laynie backed up.

"I'm not this Olander person you keep calling me."

"Ah, right. I understand your working profile is Elaine Granger? Well done, that. And to answer your first question, my name is Jack Wolfe. Director Wolfe."

Laynie stopped abruptly at the name. "Let me guess. You're Marstead senior management."

He nodded and smiled to himself, as though amused. "Actually, Marstead is but one organization that resides under my department's umbrella."

Laynie comprehended his deeper meaning. "You have more than one clandestine organization under you. You . . . you're something of a spy master."

"They told me you were insightful. I'm glad to see they weren't wrong."

Laynie kept her eyes on him, wondering when his goons would hustle her into a second waiting vehicle, where they would take her, and what kind interrogation they would subject her to—or if they would skip all that and make her death a quick one.

"What comes next, Mr. Wolfe?"

He raised his hand. From the trees, a man stepped forward.

Laynie scowled, both surprised and furious. *It's a freaking circus parade! Four men and two vehicles—and I had no idea we'd been burned? I have really lost my edge.*

The man handed Wolfe a portfolio. Wolfe opened it and extracted a single sheet of paper. Wolfe read it once through, then placed it on the outside of the portfolio and signaled the same man, who dutifully presented his back to Wolfe. Wolfe held the portfolio against the man's back and signed his name to the paper. Then he extended it—and the portfolio—to Laynie.

She kept her eyes on Wolfe, refusing to close the distance between them and take what he offered.

"It's your resignation, Ms. Granger. Accepted, signed, and backdated. However, given the unpleasant circumstances leading up to your 'retirement' from clandestine service, we've included . . . a retirement alternative for your consideration. You'll find the details in the folder."

"An alternative? What, a cushy job offer? Or compensation for Marstead trying to kill me?"

"Yes."

"Yes, what?"

"Yes, all three."

For a second time, Laynie noted the suggestion of an amused smile.

She failed to see the humor. "I'd be working for you?"

"Within my organization. A niche where your skills will be useful but well out of the public eye."

"And if I choose not to accept?"

He shrugged. "Please understand. We don't want you if you don't want us. On the other hand, Linnéa Olander is still the target of interested Russian and Ukrainian parties, and we can't have that. It would present an unacceptable security risk."

"I took care of Petroff. Unless I'm mistaken, Zakhar, Petroff's assassin, is my only threat. You could sweep him up you chose to. Who else would be looking for me?"

"You haven't heard, then?"

Laynie flushed. "All right. I'll bite. What haven't I heard?"

"Vassili Aleksandrovich Petroff was released from FSB custody two days ago, cleared of all charges. Secretary Rushailo has publicly stated his full confidence in Petroff—and appointed him Deputy Under Secretary to the Russian Federation's Security Council. That's quite a promotion, don't you think?"

"But . . . but I have insurance against Petroff!"

"Our sources tell us that Petroff had a recent private audience with Rushailo in which they discussed your letter and its accompanying CD-ROM. Petroff convinced Rushailo that the data you stole while you were his mistress would implicate the Secretary as much as himself.

"The FSB, as you know, is commanded by many of Petroff's former KGB colleagues and friends. Petroff had arranged with his friends to make the data public, which would have resulted in Rushailo's downfall if he didn't see things in the 'right light.' Sort of the Russkie version of 'If I go down, I'm taking you with me.'"

"But . . . how does that make Rushailo a threat to me? If I have insurance squirreled away against Petroff, then I have it against both of them—if what you're telling me is true."

"Ah, but you see, we have covert agents nicely placed inside Rushailo's administration and would rather not have you upsetting the Russian status quo at present, so . . . we leaked your CPA's address to them."

"You did *what?*"

"Oh, your CPA is fine. We moved him and let the Russians 'find' the insurance packages. Sadly, the unintended consequence was that Linnéa Olander is now in more danger from Rushailo than she was from Petroff. Apparently, too, a hacker within the US Odessa *mafiya* has been tracking you."

"What? The *Ukrainians* are looking for me?"

"Zakhar's doing, I'm afraid. We hope to 'sweep him up' soon, as you suggested, but there's no calling off the Ukrainians once they have your scent. You'd be quite the trophy for them to flaunt in the Russians' faces."

Laynie felt herself falling over a cliff . . . falling, falling, falling.

Wolfe stepped toward her and reached out a hand to catch her. He held her upright until she steadied, then he leaned in to whisper in her ear.

"Ms. Granger, *Elaine*, you have served this country with distinction for many years, going above and beyond what we should have expected of you. This man, Petroff, is a monster, and I am *personally* apologizing for the abuse and mistreatment you suffered under him. I don't want him to ever find you."

The relief washing over her was a tidal wave, sweeping her out to sea. Laynie couldn't catch her breath. Her legs lost their strength. Wolfe gestured for someone behind Laynie and a hand the size of a catcher's mitt grabbed her elbow and supported her, kept her from falling over.

"I gotcha, Marta. No worries, now, 'hear?"

The accent, that good ol' boy schtick, acted on Laynie like a whiff of ammonia. She gasped and caught her breath.

"Tobin?" She craned around to see him.

"Already tol' you. M' friends call me Quince." His mouth wasn't smiling but his eyes were—at least as much as he'd allow them to in front of Jack Wolfe.

"But . . . but what—"

Wolfe answered, "That's a long story, Miss Granger. You'll have plenty of time for that later. At this moment, we have bigger fish to fry, specifically, this Zakhar character."

"What about Zakhar? Are you going to let him keep pursuing me?"

Wolfe looked at his watch, as though late for an appointment. "Oh, we'll be dealing with him shortly, have no fear. However, it's *you* I'm asking right now. Come work for me, Elaine. With the emerging threat of radical Islam, our intelligence services are going to be slammed, but that doesn't mean we simply ignore Russia. You know Petroff better than anyone on the earth. With his ascent to power within the government, we can certainly use your expertise.

"You won't participate in covert operations. It will be more of a behind-the-scenes analysis job. You may find your work underwhelming, but you will be useful—and, more importantly, we'll keep you safe. Off the grid. Off Rushailo and Petroff's radar."

"And, uh, what about those people over there?"

"Yes, just who are those people, Elaine? Are they friends? Or something more?"

Laynie looked away, her jaw working. "It's complicated."

"It shouldn't be. As a Marstead covert operative, you swore to full disclosure. If you don't want 'those people' to someday be caught up by the Russians, it would be best to tell me."

Laynie chewed the inside of her cheek before admitting, "It's my sister . . . and her family."

Wolfe frowned. "You don't have a sister."

"Yeah, well, it turns out I do."

His frown deepened. "You hid this from us?"

Resentment heated in her. Her answer was sharp and barbed.

"Don't think for a minute that you have moral grounds to berate me, *Director* Wolfe. *Your* subordinates were the ones who gave the order to 'retire' me. I didn't know I had a sister when Marstead recruited me. If I hid my sister *after* she found me, it was because I didn't trust the Marstead bureaucracy—and the retirement order *you* are responsible for proved me right to do so."

Wolfe, clearly angered, didn't answer for a minute.

When he calmed, he said, "All right. I take your point. But you want your sister to remain unknown to our enemies, don't you? The Russians will never catch a whiff of your loved ones from us. I'll carry the knowledge of them strictly between us and the four trusted men I have on the ground here with me."

"But . . ."

"I'm afraid I must insist—for their sake, but also for ours. You'll be placed in a program similar to WITSEC. You already know Marshal Tobin here, and I can see that you trust him. I've obtained authorization to move him into our organization. We're forming a new team, something specialized. Compartmentalized. You, him, and select others. I'm certain Tobin would be willing to help you through the adjustment period."

Laynie watched Tobin's expression freeze.

"This is news to you? You didn't know?" she asked.

His eyes flicked once in her direction and away.

"We hadn't gotten around to asking him, but I don't think he's going to object, do you? What do you say?"

Laynie wasn't about to roll over that fast. "How? How did you find me, how did you discover this meeting place?"

Wolfe shook his head. "Naturally, we have to play our cards close to the vest—I'm sure you understand. Let me just say that, although we didn't have a time, we did obtain this location. We've been here waiting for you for the past two hours."

Laynie wasn't satisfied with Wolfe's vague answer, but the man gave her no chance to ask another question. He pressed her again.

"Accept my offer, Miss Granger. My plane is waiting. We're prepared to escort you to D.C. this evening and get you settled into your new role. You'll be safe. Reasonably free. Or you can decline and hope you don't lead the Russians or the Ukrainian mob straight to your family."

Laynie stared at the grass under her feet. Once again, what little choice she had over her life was really no choice at all. She gathered her wits about her, and strength returned to her legs. She pulled away from Tobin.

"I need to . . . my sister is here. She knows . . . a little, just that I've been undercover for a long time, nothing more. Not where or with whom. I want to see her. And my parents. They are both getting on in years, and my mother is ill. I want to see my family—my parents, my sister, her children. All of them. Those are my terms—and you owe me, you know."

Wolfe considered her request. "I suppose we do. Where do they live?"

"Not far. At my sister's farm, here in Nebraska."

"After which, you will accept my offer?"

Laynie nodded. "I suppose I will."

"This time only. We'll establish a secure communication line between you and them later, but no further visits for a while, not until they can be arranged securely."

"I understand."

He pulled a two-way radio from his coat pocket and keyed the mic. "Bring the woman. Just the woman."

Laynie watched as the agent opened the Suburban door and signaled Kari. She stepped from the car, confused. Laynie saw Max's worried face pressed against the glass. Heard a man's voice shouting in angry protest as Kari, with no word of explanation, was escorted away.

Laynie saw, through the twilight, the moment Kari spotted her. Kari shook off the agent's restrictive grasp and ran toward her sister.

"Laynie! Laynie!"

Laynie ran, too, and they collided, their arms pulling the other close. Tighter. Laynie's heart was near to bursting.

"Kari!"

"I'm here, Laynie. I'm here. Thank you, Jesus! Thank you for answering my prayers."

"Kari," Laynie sobbed. "I thought I would never see you again. I almost gave up hope so many times."

"Oh, Laynie, I almost did, too, but the Lord wouldn't let me give up. Our God truly is the God of miracles! Is *anything* impossible with him?"

Laynie laughed through her tears. "No, Kari. I . . . I guess I am beginning to see your point of view."

Kari put her mouth to Laynie's ear and whispered, "Are you safe now, Laynie? Will they let you come home with us?"

Laynie sighed. She began to draw back, shaking her head. "Evidently, I am the proverbial 'magnet for trouble' and trouble isn't ready to give up its hunt for me."

Pointing with her chin, she murmured, "That man over there is from my organization. He will let me go home with you for a short visit, just to see Mama and Dad, Shannon, and Robbie. After that, he has promised to hide me. He's also promised to establish secure communication between us. More importantly? He will ensure that you and your family remain unknown, undiscovered by my pursuers."

"By 'pursuers,' do you mean that man? The one you've been with?" Kari's next two words were nothing more than a breath of warm air against Laynie's ear. "The Russian?"

"Yes. I-I betrayed him, and he'll never forgive me for that. It's not his way. He's . . . powerful and, as I was just told, is growing more powerful.

Because he's an ongoing threat to me, he is, by extension, a threat to everyone I love."

Tobin materialized beside Laynie. "We need to get this done, Marta. You may ride with us to pick up your family's vehicles, then ride with them to their farm. Our vehicles will follow close behind."

He coughed to clear his throat. "I'll be hitching a ride in whichever vehicle you're in. Okay?"

"More than okay, Tobin. Thank you."

He steered Laynie and Kari toward the Suburban and opened a rear door. Kari, then Laynie, climbed into the second row of seats. Max and Søren, from the back row, silently observed.

Laynie turned in her seat. "Hello again, Max."

He was goggle-eyed. "Aunt Laynie?"

"One and the same. I'm sorry I couldn't be more forthcoming when I met you."

"I-I totally get it, honest. I, um—"

Laynie put a finger to her lips.

"Er, right. Sorry."

"You must be Søren."

Søren's wide smile greeted Laynie. "Finally. I was beginning to think Kari's sister was just a family legend."

"More myth than legend, I'm afraid."

Søren cut his eyes toward Kari. "What's the plan?"

"Home. As quickly as we can. To see Mama and Dad."

At the burger joint, Søren called and spoke to Ilsa, then Gene. Ilsa would keep the kids up past their bedtime. Gene, shocked and stuttering praises to God, said he would prepare Polly for Laynie's short visit.

Tobin and Laynie climbed into Kari and Søren's car with them for the less-than-two-hour drive to RiverBend. Max, not to be left out of high family drama, followed behind in his truck. It was fully dark now, but Laynie could see the headlights of the two Suburbans keeping pace behind them.

Laynie could finally ask Kari all the questions burning in her heart. "Kari, how are Mama and Dad?"

"Dad is well. He's eighty now, but quite healthy. Mama tires easily and is bedbound a lot. Dad, with help from the home health care aide, gets her up into her wheelchair several hours each day. But she is still the sweetest woman, Laynie. Still Mama."

"Oh, I miss her! And Dad! What time will it be when we arrive? Will they be awake? What about Shannon and Robbie? I can't wait to see all of them!"

Søren answered. "Don't worry, Laynie. They know you're coming. They are all there. Waiting for you."

Laynie sat back. *They are waiting for me.*

WHEN THEY ARRIVED, Søren parked in the driveway. The Suburbans parked near the house. Laynie saw two faces crowded together, peering from the window, staring into the dark. Her mouth dried up.

They will have questions, so many questions—and I will have no answers for them.

The door opened. The children stood there. Shannon held Rob's hand.

"Aunt Laynie?" It was Shannon. Robbie wouldn't remember her.

"Let's go inside, first, shall we?" Kari suggested.

Tobin withdrew to consult with the other agents. Kari led Laynie into the house. Søren and Max followed.

Laynie cast her eyes around the room, getting the lay of it, then focused on the serious-faced girl before her.

"Hello, Shannon."

Shannon studied her. "I remember you. You went away. You promised to come back, but you never did."

"I know. I was, um, unavoidably delayed, making me very late coming back . . . but I'm here now."

Shannon's expression told Laynie that her explanation wouldn't fly.

More like "crashed on takeoff."

Laynie changed her approach. "You have grown so much. Both of you."

Robbie, no sign of recognition on his face but sensing tension, edged a little closer to Shannon.

Laynie shifted her eyes to him. "You were just a little boy the last time I saw you, Robbie. Only a year old."

"He doesn't remember you. 'Cause you never came back."

Laynie sank to the floor, sat cross-legged on the carpet. "I'd like to explain."

Shannon didn't budge.

Laynie took a deep breath and dove in. "Shannon, the work I do is important, but it is also dangerous."

The girl's eyes narrowed. "Dangerous how?"

"Um, some people—bad people—don't like what I do. They would like to stop my work. If they knew about my family, they might try to hurt all of you. To get at me. Hurt me. Stop me. So, I have to keep my family a secret from them."

Shannon frowned and studied Laynie, weighing her words. "You never came back so that the bad people wouldn't find us?"

Laynie nodded. "That's why I haven't visited or called or written letters. I couldn't endanger the people I love most in the whole world. I hope you can understand and . . . forgive me?"

Shannon was more perceptive than Laynie expected. "Your job is a secret . . . because you fight bad people?"

Laynie moved her chin up and down just a fraction.

"Oh."

Shannon's eyes blinked rapidly . . . then she was in Laynie's arms. Sobbing.

"It's okay, Shannon. It's okay, honey," Laynie whispered.

"I'm sorry, Aunt Laynie. I've thought really horrid things about you. I'm s-s-so sorry!"

"How were you to know any differently, sweetheart? It's okay. Truly, it is. We just . . . you just can't ever say anything about me. To anyone. Ever."

"I won't! I promise, Aunt Laynie."

While she'd been absorbed with Shannon's questions and their subsequent reconciliation, someone else had entered the room. Laynie raised her head and froze.

"Daddy?"

Gene stood behind a wheelchair. He was much as she'd remembered, but stooped. Older.

Laynie's gaze shifted to Polly.

"Mama?"

"Laynie-girl. Come see me, sugar." Polly held out shaking arms, but her voice was unaltered by the MS.

Kari disentangled Laynie from Shannon's grasp, and Laynie stumbled to her parents, dropped before her mother's wheelchair.

"Oh, Mama!"

Every memory Laynie had of Polly rushed back upon her. the warmth of her arms, the scent of her embrace, her sweet voice, her enduring love.

"Laynie, baby. We been prayin' s' long t' see you again!"

"I'm sorry, Mama. Please forgive me!"

"Nothin' t' forgive, sugar. We're not that dense. We figgered out 'long time ago what you were about, why we couldn't call you 'cept in emergencies, why you couldn't come home more'n once a year. Figgered out why you were so closemouthed . . . so secretive."

"You did?"

"Well, first, we couldn't b'lieve it 'cause it was too much to swaller, but after you didn't come to Kari's wedding—Kari, your only sister? That's when we knew f'sure. And then when you stopped comin' home in the summer an' we didn't hear from you for years 'cept what Kari told us? Only confirmed what we'd come t' suspect."

Laynie laid her head in Polly's lap, and Polly placed her hand on Laynie's bowed head. "We just kept a-prayin' and a-prayin', Laynie-girl. Gave you into the Lord's hands, only thing we could do."

"I-I felt those prayers, Mama. If you only knew . . ." But Laynie could not share more with her family. She'd already transgressed lines that were never to be approached, let alone crossed.

"Say, can this old man get a hug?" Gene reached out his arms and Laynie went to him.

"Daddy . . ."

"Little Duck. Our Little Duck."

AN HOUR LATER, after many more embraces, after Robbie had outgrown his shyness and allowed Laynie to briefly hug him, after Laynie was certain Shannon had forgiven her because the girl had glued herself to Laynie's hip, and after she had assured her parents that, in the future, she would be able to call and write them again, Tobin knocked on the door.

Kari answered, but Laynie had been expecting the interruption. When Tobin signaled her with a tap on his watch, Laynie nodded. Then she turned to her family. "I promised my superior it would be a short visit. That was the only way I could convince him to let me come home to all of you."

She remained dry-eyed as she made the rounds, saying goodbye, hugging her parents, Shannon and Rob, Max, and Søren a last time. She was in control . . . until Kari walked out with her, until Laynie saw the Suburbans and the agents waiting, until Wolfe opened a rear door and made an impatient gesture.

Laynie turned to Kari and a sob broke from her. "I don't choose to go, Kari. I don't want to! I want to stay with you, with Mama and Dad. I want to watch Shannon and Robbie grow up—I want to, but I can't. Please understand. *Please*."

It was a moment before Kari could answer. "It hurts, I admit it. It hurts so much that you are *right here*, and yet you cannot stay with us, but suppose I do . . . understand."

She pulled Laynie to her heart again. "Until we meet again, little sister. Until then? I will continue to pray for you and trust the Lord to keep you safe."

"Thank you for not giving up on me. Thank you for continuing to pray for me, Kari. I need to tell you . . . I should be dead right now. My enemies were so close to catching me after I ran!

"But your prayers? I know that God has kept me hidden these past weeks because of them. I'm not . . . I'm not quite ready to, you know, take those steps to become a Christian, but it-it's not for lack of God's intervention in my life."

Kari smiled through her tears. "Acknowledging his hand on your life is a big step in the right direction. You'll get there. I know you will."

Laynie's laugh ended on a sob. "We're just two fellows . . ."

"Yes. Two fellows in a ship. Our hearts *belong* in the same ship, Laynie, they belong in Jesus. Please, Laynie. No one can count on tomorrow. Don't wait too long to give yourself to the Savior, to wholly surrender to the Lordship of Christ. He loves you so!"

A man's voice—Wolfe's—called to Laynie. "Let's go, Elaine."

"I'm sorry, Kari!" Laynie sobbed.

Kari breathed in Laynie's ear, "The Lord be with you, Laynie. We'll see each other again. Until then? Wherever you go, little sister, remember . . . our hearts will always be safest *in him*."

POSTSCRIPT
LP

ZAKHAR WAITED IN the Olander whore's apartment until midnight. By then his vexation was beyond his control. He slammed the apartment door behind him and stalked the few blocks to his rental car.

Thinking only of his frustration and how he would spring his next trap on the woman, he wasn't paying as close attention to his surroundings as he should have. But then he'd been trained as a soldier, a bodyguard, and the occasional assassin. Not a covert operator.

"FBI! Put your hands on the car roof! NOW!"

Five agents, their blue vests stamped with "FBI," descended on Zakhar. Within seconds, they had cuffed him and emptied his pockets.

"What is this for?" he demanded in heavily accented English. "I am American citizen. I have passport—you see? I have passport!"

"An American? Yeah, an' I'm from New Zealand." The female senior agent possessed the unmistakable inflections of the South Bronx—a far cry from a Kiwi accent. "You're under arrest for at least a hunnerd counts of possession of child pornography. I say a hunnerd, but we ain't finished countin' yet."

She held up his laptop. "Don't fret none, pal—we'll get the charges right. We got a lot more in the queue than just porn, 'cording to my boss."

"Lies! All lies!" Zakhar shouted.

The senior agent slanted her eyes toward him, and her sly smile widened. "Oh? Then, how 'bout this? Murder of two law enforcement officers, murder of a civilian, attempted murder, murder for hire, grand theft auto, impersonating an officer of the law,, and—topping the hit parade—*espionage*. Any of that ring a bell? Sure, ya did a lotta that in Canada, but not to worry. The US'll turn ya over to the Canuck feds—eventually. 'Course, we'll carve our pound of flesh outta ya first. It'll be years b'fore it's their turn."

She laughed. "Huh! B'lieve I hear the sound of a couple of back-t'-back life sentences, whatta ya think?"

To her subordinates she growled, "Do the world a solid and haul this trash outta here."

THE STROBING LIGHTS of Syla's security system warned him of the intrusion. He stared at the monitors—at the swarm of armed FBI agents lining up to breach his hiding place.

A raid. A federal one.

Syla was as stunned and surprised at what was unfolding as Zakhar had been at his arrest, but at least Syla wasn't going to be caught flat-footed! No, the location of his office high up in the mob warehouse would delay the feds long enough for Syla to implement his contingency plans.

Syla burst into a flurry of keystrokes, bringing up the window to a program that would wipe his hard drives, browser history, and online profiles multiple times. Nothing could stop it. Even if they shut down his machines, the program would resume upon reboot. But before he initiated the "wipe," he executed a specially prepared series of events, setting in motion the contingency plan that would be most personally gratifying.

Because Syla knew who had sent the feds. At least his payback would ensure that she never saw daylight again.

"Vyper, you're finished," Syla sneered. "Next time, don't play with the big boys."

He laughed. "Oh, wait! There won't *be* a 'next time!'"

With one eye on the monitors, half his attention focused on the FBI tactical team as they began their breach, Syla initiated his system-wide wipe. It started as he expected—but then . . .

Then things went very badly awry.

In the center of every single one of his eighteen monitors, a dot of light appeared. The dots flickered, grew larger, expanded, and unfurled into the red-and-white maple-leaf flag of Canada. Across all of Syla's twelve screens, the Canadian flag waved gently to a triumphant, full-blast, orchestral rendition of . . .

> *O Canada!*
> *Our home and native land*
> *True patriot love*
> *in all thy sons command!*

Syla hit Escape, then the enter and delete keys. He pressed Alt+Tab. He pounded Ctrl+Alt+Delete again and again. He tried in vain to "get behind" the anthem, to find his program window and execute the destruct sequence, but the "O Canada" bomb had locked him out. Even as the boots of federal agents pounded their way up four flights of stairs to the top of the warehouse, Syla fought to override the virus, but could not.

"FBI! Freeze! Get on the ground!"

Syla ignored their commands. He stared at his monitors—an entire wall of them—all flying the red-and-white flag of Canada. The anthem ended with a triumphant:

O Canada!
We stand on guard
FOR THEE!

"Yaroslav Bodnar, AKA, *Syla*, you are under arrest for violations under 18 U.S.C. section 2251, the Sexual Exploitation of Children act, the production of child pornography, 18 U.S.C. section 2251A, the Selling and Buying of Children, and 18 U.S.C. section 2252, activities relating to material involving the sexual exploitation of minors, the possession, distribution, and receipt of child pornography. Further charges are pending. You have the right to an attorney. If you cannot afford one . . ."

As the agents pushed him to the floor and the last echoes of the song faded, the maple leaf also faded. Syla cranked his neck to keep his eyes on his monitors. Out of the dissolving center of the flag, the fanged head of a venomous serpent emerged.

Grinning. Smirking. Winking.

The agents who cuffed Syla and dragged him from his lair were forced to endure his shrieks of outrage as they echoed far down the stairs and into the night.

"*Gaaahhh! Gaaahhhh!*"

TUESDAY MORNING, Vyper sauntered through the RCMP's front entrance doors as usual. She was still sniggering over the traps she'd set for Zakhar and Syla, giggling over the FBI reports she'd perused early this morning after hacking their system—the scintillating descriptions of their arrests and the lovely *vast* array of charges pending against them.

Well, I provided the American feds with sufficient evidence, didn't I?

She stepped into the RCMP lobby. That was as far as she got.

Armed RCMP security officers swarmed her from every direction, shouting instructions.

She dropped her backpack and sank to her knees as ordered. An officer pulled her wrists to her back and cuffed them. Then they got her on her feet and marched her into the commissioner's office. The commissioner was waiting for them, her outrage splashed in bright spots upon both cheeks.

Vyper had not met the woman personally—before today. She shrugged.

Probably not the best first impression.

"Would it surprise you, Miss Benoit, to know that we received credible intel late last night asserting that *you*, our very own cyber security specialist, were running your own little cyber enterprise from this RCMP facility? And would it surprise you to know that, in fact, we have found evidence to support such an accusation? An accusation of treason?"

Vyper swapped her wad of three chewed sticks of Black Jack from one side of her mouth to the other. "My wallet. Back pock—"

"*Don't you dare talk to me* with that foul, disgusting *gob* in your mouth!" the commissioner shouted.

An officer lifted a wastebasket and held it under Vyper's mouth. She rolled the sizable wad to the front of her mouth, spit the gum into the basket, and tried again.

"I beg your pardon. My wallet. Back pocket. There's a phone number."

They universally ignored her.

"You will be formally charged this morning under section 46 of the Criminal Code, high treason."

"You're making a mistake, Commissioner."

"Get her out of here."

About the time two officers took hold of Vyper's arms to "perp walk" her from the commissioner's office, the commissioner's secretary opened the office door.

"Excuse me, Commissioner?"

"This is not the time, Ms. Terry."

Someone behind the secretary edged her out of the way and pushed himself into the room.

The commissioner eyed the man. "And you are?"

"Bernard Dupont, Canadian Security Intelligence Service. My card."

"We were, of course, about to call and inform your offices of the security breach."

"Were you? Ah, me. Would that you had called us *before* you made such a spectacle of Miss Benoit's arrest."

The commissioner bristled. "How I run my organization is not your business, Mr. Dupont."

"I understand, but . . . if I may suggest that you excuse these officers from the room while we talk?"

Something in Dupont's manner made the commissioner reconsider. "Give us the room. And take that *person* with you."

"No. You will uncuff Miss Benoit and leave her with us."

"No! I must protest—"

Dupont gestured to the officers. "Get out."

As the commissioner's office door closed on the officers' departing backs, Dupont said, "You see, Commissioner, we placed Miss Benoit with you quite intentionally. She is one of ours."

"*What?*"

"Our agent. Embedded here. Within the walls of the RCMP. Doing what she does best. We allow her free rein to run her "little enterprises," and we don't care a whit if she amasses extra cash or even a fortune on the side, because she has proven herself more than loyal."

He pointed at Vyper. "Through her machinations and her rightfully earned hacker rep, she provides us access to those entities, both foreign and domestic, who plot against us and our allies."

The commissioner's mouth tightened as Dupont continued.

"Cyberattacks? Financial attacks? Terror-directed attacks? Any or all of them? We're an equal-opportunity Canadian security agency, Commissioner, meaning our only objective is to protect Canada. To ensure that end, *we don't care* how the job gets done as long as it gets done. Do you understand me? *We. Don't. Care.* We will *do* whatever we must and *use* whatever resources come to hand.

"As regards to Miss Benoit? In the ongoing cyberwar, she is our number-one huntress, a force to be reckoned with, utterly deadly to our enemies. Therefore, concerning her? I assure you. We most certainly *do* care."

The commissioner's eyes strayed to her employee. Vyper unwrapped a stick of gum. She fed it slowly—*leisurely*—into her mouth. Then, just as deliberately, she breathed on her nails and polished them on her shirt.

The commissioner pulled herself up straight. "But . . . but . . . be that as it may, I don't see how we can, given the circumstances, put her back into her position. So many of our people—"

"My point, precisely. Her cover is well and truly blown, *thank you very much.* The Prime Minister, I'm sorry to say, will find your actions *quite* regrettable."

The commissioner sank into her chair. "I-I'm—"

"Because of the mess you have created, we must now assign Miss Benoit elsewhere. Fortunately, the Americans have requested her services, and as it suits our purposes to remove her from the Canadian spotlight you have so inconsiderately placed her in, we shall grant their request."

He turned on his heel. "Come along, Thérèse. I hear the American's have big plans for you."

Vyper smirked as she rambled along after him.

America? Cool.

And Syla thought he was crashing my career? Ha!

Think again, loser.

THE END

―― ☙ ――

MY DEAR READERS,

Laynie, Quincy Tobin—and perhaps Vyper?—will return in *Laynie Portland, Renegade Spy*. As you might imagine, Laynie's adjustment to her new situation proves difficult.

Although Director Wolfe brings Laynie "in from the cold" to a place of relative safety, she will remain free only if she meets Wolfe's three conditions. She must accept the new identity he gives her, and she must meet with an agency "shrink" to address the emotional damage caused by her years undercover. This counselor, handpicked by Wolfe, will evaluate Laynie and determine if she is fit to participate in his secret task force. Moreover, Laynie must remain in Wolfe's witness protection program. The program will hide Laynie from those who are hunting her, but it will also greatly curtail her freedom.

But nothing goes as Laynie hopes. The rules grind and grate on her. They shackle her choices and constrict her movements. She feels controlled and manipulated. Her clashes with bureaucratic culture only serve to tighten the restrictions and send her spiraling downward, out of control.

Meanwhile, in the background, dark forces are at work, forces that compel Laynie to disobey directives in order to save a life. Rather than proving her value to Wolfe's satisfaction, Laynie's risky exploit marks her as a faithless renegade, a rebel whose insubordination may earn her harsh, ruinous consequences.

Laynie must fight to earn her place on the task force—even as unfolding events expose a looming danger. Wolfe's task force has a leak . . . *one that threatens them all.*

By the way, if you have not read the full, inspiring tale of the Thoresen family—a story that spans generations and concludes with Kari and Laynie finding each other—you will uncover all the answers to your questions in my series, *A Prairie Heritage*. Without cost to you, read the first three, full-length books of this series on Kindle, Nook, Apple Books, or Kobo in the single volume, *A Prairie Heritage, The Early Years*.

Thank you. I appreciate your readership and the fellowship we share in Christ Jesus, our Lord.

—Vikki

ABOUT THE AUTHOR

Vikki Kestell's passion for people and their stories is evident in her readers' affection for her characters and unusual plotlines. Two often-repeated sentiments are, "I feel like I know these people," and, "I'm right there, in the book, experiencing what the characters experience."

Vikki holds a PhD in Organizational Learning and Instructional Technologies. She left a career of twenty-plus years in government, academia, and corporate life to pursue writing full time. "Writing is the best job ever," she admits, "and the most demanding."

Also an accomplished speaker and teacher, Vikki and her husband, Conrad Smith, make their home in Albuquerque, New Mexico.

To keep abreast of new book releases, sign up for Vikki's newsletter on her website, http://www.vikkikestell.com, find her on Facebook at http://www.facebook.com/TheWritingOfVikkiKestell, or follow her on BookBub, https://www.bookbub.com/authors/vikki-kestell.

AUTHOR'S NOTES

THE SOVIET UNION officially dissolved on December 26, 1991. Its former Soviet republics became independent nations. Russia emerged as the Russian Federation.

In 1995, the FSK, Russia's Federal Counterintelligence Service and heir to the KGB, became the FSB, the Federal Security Service of the Russian Federation, by order of President Boris Yeltsin.

The referenced UNL dormitories, Burr and Fedde Hall, where Max and his friends played paintball, were in use when Laynie visited the agriculture college in *Retired Spy*. They were demolished in 2017.

www.faith-filledfiction.com | www.vikkikestell.com